FATAL INCIDENT

A NOVEL

JIM PROEBSTLE

EMERALD
BOOK CO.

Published by Emerald Book Company
Austin, TX
www.emeraldbookcompany.com

Distributed by Emerald Book Company

For ordering information or special discounts for bulk purchases, please contact Emerald Book Company at PO Box 91869, Austin, TX 78709, 512.891.6100.

Design and composition by Greenleaf Book Group LLC and Alex Head
Cover design by Greenleaf Book Group LLC

Publisher's Cataloging-In-Publication Data
(Prepared by The Donohue Group, Inc.)
Proebstle, Jim.
    Fatal incident : a novel / Jim Proebstle. — 1st ed.
    p. ; cm.
    ISBN: 978-1-934572-77-1
    1. Air pilots, Military—Alaska—20th century—Fiction. 2. Douglas DC-3 (Transport plane)—Fiction. 3. Aircraft accidents—Alaska—20th century—Fiction. 4. United States. Army Air Forces. Air Transport Command—20th century—Fiction. 5. World War, 1939-1945—Aerial operations, American—Fiction. 6. Alaska—Fiction. 7. War stories, American. 8. Historical fiction. 9. Mystery fiction. I. Title.
    PS3616.R64 F28 2011
    813/.6   2011923275

Part of the Tree Neutral® program, which offsets the number of trees consumed in the production and printing of this book by taking proactive steps, such as planting trees in direct proportion to the number of trees used: www.treeneutral.com

Printed in the United States of America on acid-free paper

11 12 13 14 15   10 9 8 7 6 5 4 3 2 1

First Edition

*For the crew and passengers of the Air Transport Command,
C-47 flight lost in the Mt. McKinley National Park of Alaska
on September 18, 1944.*

PROLOGUE

In 1941, the war in Europe was escalating, and the need for competent pilots to ferry airplanes for troop and equipment movement intensified. United States Army Brig. Gen. Robert Olds organized the Air Corps Ferrying Command in May of that year. The staff consisted of exactly two officers and one clerk. The new command's mission, however, was formidable: to move aircraft by air from factories to terminals designated by the chief of the Army Air Corps and to provide special air ferry services as required in order to meet specific situations. Pilots—many of them—were needed and in early 1942, civilian pilots were authorized to fly for the Air Transport Command (ATC), as it was then known. Each pilot was given a ninety-day trial period. Those found competent for transport flying were offered a commission as a service pilot, a rating with qualifications somewhat lower than that of combat pilots. By the end of 1942, more than 1,700 pilots had been recruited for the program, 1,372 of whom were commissioned as service pilots.

Its original role of primarily delivering planes and supplies to Britain changed dramatically as the United States officially joined the war against Hitler's Germany and declared war on Japan. Shipping lanes in the Atlantic and Pacific became far too dangerous, too slow, and ineffective. The airlift of supplies into China from bases in India, the delivery of the Flying Fortress to aid the army's striking power in the decisive battle of Midway, and the C-47 transports loaded with bombs and ammunition sent to the Aleutians at the time of the attack on Dutch Harbor were examples of how the ATC greatly influenced the course of the war.

The Alaska route went north out of Great Falls, Montana, across Alberta and the Yukon Territory of Canada, to Anchorage, over inhospitable terrain. Initially, the Alaska route was seen as a means of re-supplying American military installations in Alaska, Canadian pipeline locations in the Yukon and Northwest territories, and the Aleutian war zone. The mission also turned out to be one for ferrying airplanes from the United States for delivery to the Soviet Air Force at Ladd Field outside Fairbanks under the Lend-Lease Program. From there Soviet pilots would fly their planes to Russia for combat duty on the western front against Germany. More than eight thousand airplanes were delivered.

ATC personnel were based at Edmonton as well as other Canadian bases. A major mission for ATC pilots at the en route bases was search and rescue for Ferrying Command pilots and crews who were forced down in the remote wilderness. Much of the transport along the route was an airline responsibility, with Northwest Airlines and Western Airlines operating the routes under contract.

ATC began the war as an organization with heavy civilian influence. A large number of the staff officers were airline personnel who had been commissioned as army officers. Much of the command's strength came in the form of airline flight crews who were in military reserve status, while other pilots were civilian pilots who were commissioned on the basis of their civilian flight experience. When the war ended, the Air Transport Command employed more than two hundred thousand people in its service. It was the largest airline in the world, with routes that literally covered the globe.

CHAPTER 1

"Nick! Do you know what you're doing?" Martha screamed from her forward tandem seat. The noise from the sudden hailstorm was deafening.

"Hang on, Martha," was all that Nick said in reply. He needed all of his concentration to maneuver the 1936 E-2 Piper over the power lines and alongside the telephone poles for a shadowy forced landing on the two-lane dirt road just north of Mankato, Minnesota. The storm had come out of nowhere. Nothing on the forecast had given him even a hint of a drop in temperature that would cause hail—only a gentle rain shower and some clouds, but nothing more. One minute, he and Martha were enjoying a relaxing ride over the farmlands of southern Minnesota, and in the next minute the cloud cover thickened and a noticeable bitter chill filled the air. That's when the medium-size pellets began to relentlessly drum the surface of the plane.

Nick knew he needed to set the plane down quickly while he could still see the ground. He was concerned for Martha. It was their first trip together, and he had wanted to impress her, but now he had to stay focused on landing safely. With the E-2 it was strictly seat-of-the-pants flying. There were no flying-related instruments, only engine instruments for measuring things like rpm, oil pressure, and temperature.

Nick had to keep the ground and horizon in sight, while listening closely to the sound of the engine.

A final downdraft dropped the plane on the dirt road like a rock. Nick knew to keep his mouth closed, but Martha bit her lip badly, causing it to bleed and swell up. By the time the plane slowed to a stop, her handkerchief was thoroughly blood stained. "Wow!" Nick exclaimed in relief. "They don't teach that in pilot training. I guess that qualifies as my first emergency landing. Are you okay up there?" Nick asked with a blend of genuine concern and adrenaline-filled excitement.

"It definitely took my breath away. Does this happen often?" Martha twisted from her forward seat as best she could to be heard. Her question didn't undermine her excitement with flying, however. The whole day had been fabulous. It was just that this was her first trip with Nick, and in a plane. Expectations were ambiguous. Her friends thought she was crazy to go flying with Nick. None of them would begin to take this kind of risk, but this was classic Martha. She couldn't wait.

"No, this is a first for me, too. I'm glad we're in one piece." Nick was impressed with Martha's bravado considering she was new to flying. They had had a great day together and he didn't want it to end badly. "Looks as if we're grounded for a while, though." Nick was Visual Flight Rules rated; he could fly only during the day. They would have had plenty of time to get back to the Twin Cities, but the storm and the dark clouds had obscured his range of vision so quickly that his best judgment called for a landing.

"I hope that farm over there has a phone so you can call your mom and tell her you won't be home until tomorrow," he continued. "I need for the storm to clear before we can take off again, and we're likely to run out of daylight by the time it does."

"She won't handle that news very well."

"I'm only thinking of your safety, Martha. Besides, I like you too much to get on the wrong side of your mom. Sorry that I wasn't able to put a blue ribbon on the day, though, but I still had fun. I hope you did, too. If you're up to it, we can go again next weekend," he said as she turned to an odd-looking man with a camera dressed in a gray topcoat and felt hat running toward them on the wet, gravel road. Nick couldn't quite make sense of the man's actions until he began speaking very excitedly to both of them.

"That was the most fantastic landing I've ever witnessed. I work for the *Star Tribune* and I can tell you right off that my editor will love the picture I got. I was here for some weather photos, but this is much better. What are your names? I want the exact spelling. Have you flown long? Was this your first emergency landing?" The spontaneous interview went on for ten more minutes, making Nick feel self-conscious and Martha a little like a celebrity.

From that point on, Martha couldn't get enough of Nick. At twenty-three, he was very handsome and carried his trim six-foot-two, athletic physique well, just as he had when he was captain of the 1932 Staples, Minnesota high school football and basketball teams. It was his curly light-brown hair, however, that was his defining feature; all his childhood friends called him "Curly." What really attracted her though, was how smart he was about things. Take flying for instance—he got his pilot's license, Day VFR, single engine rating, in just a few months of after-hour training following his day job at Montgomery Ward's in merchandising sales. Didn't even tell her what he was up to. Just surprised her one day with an offer to go on a picnic. Maybe it was the picnic, or the warm summer day, or the freedom and excitement of being in the sky that got her keyed up, but from that day forward they were a pair.

As months passed, Nick and Martha spent a lot of time together. Nick even began teaching Martha how to fly. She picked it up quickly.

Good enough to put Nick's buddies in the flying club to shame. With both Nick and Martha's competency at the stick, their exuberance became addictive as they flew the cloud-filled, Minnesota summer skies.

"You and Bud are just alike," she teased, as she watched Nick work. "You're both so meticulous about your plane." Nick and his older brother were the first in their age group to own an E-2 Piper, and his pride showed. Because they were enterprising enough to do all their own maintenance work, it put the purchase of the used training plane from the flying club within their means. The brothers represented the best of the Depression: hardship that stimulated self-reliance and a craving for adventure. As teenagers in the late '20s and early '30s, they had known only the prosperity of their family's own hard work on a tenant farm outside Cass Lake, Minnesota—hardly a thriving center of commerce. Most of the land in the county was owned by the Leech Lake Band—an Ojibwe Indian Reservation. Stunning red and white pines were mixed with deciduous hardwoods, making for a spectacular wilderness surrounding the lake. For the family, however, the three-month growing season hardly allowed for much crop surplus that could be sold at the local market in Bemidji fifteen miles away. Paying for a hired hand was not an option. They worked six days a week farming and generally fixed broken equipment after church on Sundays.

"You're such a perfectionist." Martha jibed playfully as she watched him go through his pre-flight routine and adjusted her flight cap. "It's a perfect spring day. What could go wrong?" She knew that their trip that day would be anything but ordinary and, in reality, she respected Nick's attention to detail. His established procedure in the pre-flight engine run-up, taxi, and takeoff checks provided her a sense of safety, considering the risks they were about to take. Nonetheless, she loved to poke at his seriousness. "I'm your lucky charm."

"It's simple logic, Hot Shot. This baby's got to purr for me to be

comfortable with the stunts we're doing. No guesswork. No accidents."
Nick had begun calling Martha Hot Shot right after her first flight
with him where she took the stick and flew by herself. She liked the
nickname, but more importantly, she liked where their relationship
was headed. They dated in high school when she was a sophomore and
he was a senior. It was an on-again off-again relationship as Nick was
rather fun loving and carefree; it was hard for him to focus on one love
interest. After graduating they saw each other more steadily. It seemed
like the two were made for each other. She loved being a risk taker.
As the high school Minnesota State Champion in golf and tennis, she
knew she didn't fit the mold that polite society expected of fashionable
young women of the day. Flying offered the independence both Martha and Nick needed while being a catalyst for a partnership they both
agreed had promise.

"Are you going to trust me at the controls again?" Martha razzed.
While she was a "good stick," according to Nick, and one of the steadi-
est hands he'd seen—a natural—she was not a licensed pilot. After
many hours training together, Nick was convinced that her skills were
much better than those of most of his flying buddies at the club.

"Only if all the conditions are right," Nick agreed with a wink.

Martha was pretty and sassy with green eyes, short blond hair, and
a petite frame. To him, she was at her best when dressed in men's tan
flight slacks and at the controls of the E-2 while barnstorming small
towns around the Midwest. They would pick a sunny day and one of
the countless farming towns that interested them, like Owatonna, Sav-
age, or Granite Falls, and fly twenty feet over the buildings with Nick
walking the wing. It was a sight to behold. When they landed in a pasture or on a dirt road at the outskirts of town, people would line up for
one-dollar rides. Ten minutes each.

Today was going to be a repeat performance in Eau Claire, across the border in Wisconsin. The idea of flying was new and fascinating. Defying the laws of gravity provided a source of excitement unavailable elsewhere. The townspeople were mostly farmers, shopkeepers, and tradesmen. They ate it up.

"Do you think the airline brass will hire you if they know what you do on your weekends?" She raised her voice to be heard over the engine noise as she teased, knowing he had an interview with Northwest Airlines the following week.

"There's a lot Northwest might not approve of, Hot Shot, but I'm still gonna fly for them. What they don't know won't hurt 'em. Besides, this just makes me a better pilot. I know everything there is to know about this plane."

Martha had high hopes that they'd sell a lot of rides that day. The May sky was crystal clear with small puffy clouds creating a floating three-dimensional collage against blue matting. She felt she could almost touch the checkerboard farms below during the one-hour flight from the Twin Cities. After crossing the Mississippi River it was only another half hour before they approached Eau Claire. Nick prepared himself. They buzzed the town with him in a horizontal position on the wing, head first. On the second pass they readied themselves for their grand entry. Martha steadied the plane. Flying by the seat-of-the-pants, she used the sound of the wind, the tachometer, and the engine and propeller vibration to obtain the right speed. Nick slowly stood and maintained a firm grip on the safety straps, like waterskiing. Martha could hear the crowd's roar of approval over the engine noise. One pass was enough. They landed on a dirt road at the familiar Eau Claire County Park on the edge of town. A crowd had already begun to form.

"Nice job, Hot Shot."

"Not bad, yourself." Her radiating smile reflected her confidence and the importance of the part she played.

They flew most of the townsfolk around the area at least once. It was fun to watch the excitement on their faces, but it made for a long day.

"These long, early summer days are perfect for this. How much do you think we made?" Martha asked while gazing at the magnificent purples and oranges that filled the sky as the sun dropped below a distant tree line.

Preoccupied with preparation for an early-morning departure the next day, he asked, "What?"

"I'll bet we topped one hundred rides today, don't you think?"

"Haven't counted it yet." He knew that she really meant one hundred dollars. Her focus was primarily on the money that would give them the flexibility to go off on their own—like to Grand Marais in the morning. It was going to be a special day. Sunday breakfast flights were always her favorite—a few hardboiled eggs, two bear claws, and a quart of orange juice from the local grocery store would be their sole payload. The day was a blank slate—completely open to possibilities.

"Let's grab a bite to eat at the diner on the edge of town by the filling station, and we can count it," Nick said. "Shouldn't be much of a walk. Just give me a few minutes to tie her down first. Did you pack the bedrolls this morning?"

"In the back, Captain." They liked sleeping under the stars on clear nights. The Milky Way was always accented by continual streaks of shooting stars with vapor trails stretching brilliantly across the sky. In no more time than the passing of a moment, the stars would vanish without leaving a trace of their existence in the cosmos.

After a dinner of chili and grilled cheese sandwiches, Nick and Martha walked hand in hand back to the plane. She was looking forward to a lazy, morning flight up to Grand Marais in the Arrowhead section of Minnesota and was hoping the rest of the evening wouldn't be spoiled by Nick's advances. She had tried to stay chaste in their relationship, and for the most part had been successful, but she knew that nights together like this would test them both.

"Will we follow the St. Croix River tomorrow?"

"Would you like to?" Flying just above the hardwoods and pines along the path of a river gave them the chance to scare up a moose or a bear, which was always fun. After a short crossing over the southwest corner of Lake Superior, they would be there.

"You know I would."

Temperatures dropped unexpectedly that evening. By the time they had their bedding set up, it had become unseasonably cool—enough to discourage any extracurricular activities. Martha kissed Nick good night, and they snuggled into their separate bedrolls for warmth. Life was good, she thought. One day at a time. No real commitments until Monday when Nick would have his first interview for a Northwest Airlines pilot position.

The next day was as good as Martha had hoped. The breakfast was fine, the weather was great, and they even spotted a moose while flying along the river. However, reality set in quickly Sunday evening when they returned home. Martha's mother, Ida Copeland, confronted them on the porch of the Twin Cities rooming house she ran, where Nick and Bud were boarders. She never liked it when Nick took her daughter on overnight trips. This time was the last straw.

"I don't know how many times I've told you not to take my daughter on a weekend trip, Nick! This is the last time you'll defy me. Martha is not some tramp you can just drag through the trash. People talk, Nick, and a girl's reputation is easy to tarnish. Besides, I was worried sick. From here on out I want you to stay away. Do you hear me, Nick? Stay away!"

"That's not fair, Mom. Nick and I . . ."

"With all due respect, Mrs. Copeland, that's not going to happen," Nick interrupted. "Martha's agreed to marry me, and there's nothing you can do about it." The retort brought a quick slap to his face, catching Nick by surprise.

"Mom, you can't do that! I'm old enough to make my own decisions." Martha rarely raised her voice to her mom, but she needed to defend Nick if they were to make it as a couple. Ida frequently reminded Martha of the other, more stable men at their rooming house who had steady jobs on the Northern Pacific Railroad. To Martha, these men were always sweaty and dirty from their work. Regardless, these men suited her mom's pairing interests far better than Nick did. After all, this interest in her daughter's future was her prerogative, Ida often thought. Martha was too young to understand the reality of being a woman in a man's world. With Martha's father dead fifteen years from a farm accident and Ida's determination to make it as a single mom, raising Martha the right way left no room for compromise. The scars of the Depression ran deep for Ida. Her goal of security for herself and Martha was at the top of her list of priorities.

Nick's brown eyes grew dark with anger from the adrenaline generated by her slap. She had caught him good and the sting hurt, but his pride hurt more. He was also embarrassed because of the early Sunday evening hour and the neighbors who overheard their confrontation while out for a stroll in the perfect weather. The sidewalk was near the rooming house porch where they stood now—and where he and Martha had spent many hours holding hands on the swing.

"Marry this man! Not without my permission, you won't. Nick, you're going to get this girl killed with your wild notions of flying." Ida knotted her cotton-print apron in her hands as she talked, almost as if she were twisting it into a weapon. The angry comment about flying struck a chord, and Nick knew its source. That forced landing he made north of Mankato on Martha's first flight was hard to explain to a person who had never flown. Martha had done her best to minimize the risk, but the picture taken by an opportunistic reporter of the *Star Tribune* told the thousand words that Ida understood.

"We'll just see what happens after I get my pilot wings." He and Martha had talked of eloping while in Grand Marais, both of them anticipating her mother's negative reaction to their intentions to marry. Nick was ready for his life to move forward. While this wasn't his choice for a battleground, he wasn't going to give in. Not this time.

Nick and Bud paid up their rent and checked out of the Copeland rooming house for a new venue the next day. Nick returned only once. It was a warm July night in 1937, about midnight, on Martha's twenty-first birthday. She was packed. He wore his new Northwest Airlines pilot's uniform.

CHAPTER 2

1943

"So, is being a co-pilot all it's cracked up to be?" Bud asked while scanning the Hangar Grill lunch menu. The restaurant had become a familiar meeting place for the two, close to Bud's office at Honeywell in St. Paul and convenient for Nick making connections. The well-worn traffic patterns in the linoleum floor complemented the vintage décor of the family establishment. A light cigarette-smoke haze filled the air despite two ceiling fans circulating slowly. The counter where they sat had burgundy, vinyl-covered stools. It was for customers in a hurry, which generally fit their schedule perfectly.

Bud watched Nick earn his co-pilot wings after several years of hard work. He was as enthralled with aviation as Nick, but frustrated with being stuck in heating and air conditioning despite having an aeronautical engineering degree from the University of Minnesota, or the "U" as they called it. *Aviation is my future too*, he thought while checking his supply of cash. Bud routinely budgeted for each meal out. "It's where I want to be. It's the future," he said, ignoring Nick's attempt to answer his original question.

"Whoa! Slow down. What future are you talking about? Seems

like your lips haven't caught up with your brain," Nick blurted out. He knew that Bud sometimes thought faster than he spoke—a product of his introverted personality that caused him to switch topics mentally before he had expressed his current thought verbally.

"You know what I mean. Aviation . . . planes . . . flight! It's the future," Bud said, his face flush with frustration.

"Be patient, big brother. The jobs haven't caught up with that future just yet. And it's not going to amount to a hill of beans without geniuses like you." Nick used to call him the brains of the family because Bud was high school valedictorian, and Nick was merely salutatorian. He also gave Bud full marks for his 3.9 grade point average in engineering at the U while being a newlywed and working full time. No small feat. He was relentless, however, in kidding Bud about his athletic skills. He referenced unmercifully Bud's two sprained ankles on the first and only day of his football career as *the oxymoron of mind over matter.*

"As to your original question, if it wasn't for the weather and the passengers, commercial flying would actually be pretty routine. It is nice to see some of the sights, though," said Nick.

"Which cities are the best?" Bud loved geography and sometimes would spin the globe in his office while daydreaming about the countries of the world. There wasn't a state capital he didn't know or a latitude and longitude reading he couldn't find.

"Seattle and Portland—no question. The mountains are unbelievable, and the flying is more challenging. Chicago ranks third because the stewardesses really like the nightlife in the city." Nick winked. The turned-up corner of his smile told the rest of the story.

"I don't think Martha would like that part of the job," Bud said, reaching in his pocket to check on his money again before deciding what to order. "By the way, how's Martha doing with all of your time away? It's not like she's one to just sit around."

"It puts a strain on settling down in the marriage for sure," Nick explained after ordering a hamburger. "It seems like both of us have lost the old pattern of just being together and having fun. The big kibosh really came last week when Martha found a picture in my uniform coat pocket of me and one of the other pilots surrounded by a dozen pretty stewardesses. I'm not sure that fight is over yet." Nick leaned in closer and whispered, "Just between you and me, Bud, some of those ladies are real interested in showing their affection."

"My God, you're not involved with someone else, are you?" Bud liked Martha and the big brother tone of his voice revealed his dissatisfaction at even the hint of foul play on Nick's part.

"No . . . just the ever-present temptation," Nick replied, shaking his head in denial. "Nothing serious. It is hard to resist, though."

"Young women don't have it as good as we do, and that's a fact," Bud answered. "The influence from their mothers, straight out of the Depression, is undeniable. They're tired and poor and without many options for financial security. A good-looking guy like you, making good money, is a real attraction—wedding ring or not. Security is the name of the game—unfortunately for them, and us, I guess." They laughed self-consciously as Bud made his point. He hoped that Nick's premarital tendency to play the field wouldn't cause a problem. He knew how handsome his younger brother was in his navy blue pilot's uniform and why Martha might be concerned.

They ate their burgers quietly for a few minutes. The Hangar Grill was unusually active for Labor Day and Nick would need to leave for his flight soon.

"Did you see the headlines this morning?" Bud asked.

"You mean about the Allies bombing Rome?"

"Yeah, and the Brits are still trying to take credit for Sicily. I don't like what's happening. Mark my words," said Bud, "you and I are going to be in this mess soon. Once Eisenhower convinces FDR and Churchill that they can whip Germany in Italy, the stakes are going up. There's no way FDR and Churchill will back down to Hitler with Mussolini out of the picture."

"There's lots of talk among the pilots that the army will muster us for transport duty in the Air Transport Command. All the airlines will be called on for troop movements. Some of the guys, though, want front-line duty. It's probable that this war will be dominated by air power, and they want to be a part of it. When you think about it, though, transport duty wouldn't be too bad." Nick leaned forward and arched his eyebrows as he shifted to a more serious tone. "How about you? What are your plans?" he said, referring to the fact that Bud would likely be drafted.

"If I can't find a job in air defense, I'll probably enlist. I think I would be more help with my education, though. You know, use my mind instead of my nimble athletic skills." Both laughed. Bud was glad he beat Nick to the punch with the joke about his athleticism.

"Do you have something in mind?"

"Well, maybe. I've had some interest from a specialty aerospace unit of Goodyear Aircraft in Akron, Ohio, that I'm going to check out. This job in heating and ventilation sure isn't going to last long."

"Gee, you haven't said anything about moving. Do Mom and Dad know?"

"No, and I'm not going to tell them until it's a sure thing. You and I both know that neither of them will ever get on a plane to visit. And what are the chances of them taking a two-day driving trip for a visit?"

"I see what you mean," Nick said. Checking his watch he realized time was short. "Anyway, good luck! Unfortunately, I gotta run . . . flight's at 2:15. Thanks for lunch."

"Where are you going?"

"Chicago today. Winnipeg and home tomorrow."

"Are we still getting together with the family later this week at the lake?"

"Wouldn't miss it for anything. Martha and I will be there late Thursday afternoon. How about you and Helen?"

"Don't have the luxury of pilots' hours. We'll make it about seven o'clock Friday after work. Tell Mom to hold dinner."

Nick was focused on the pre-takeoff checklist that followed the start checklist in preparation for takeoff. He was flying with Ted Murphy, a pilot he'd flown second seat with before on the C-46, an earlier commercial version of the C-47. Ted was a stickler for procedures, and it wasn't Nick's nature to invite criticism as a co-pilot. Nick confirmed that the oil and cylinder-head temperatures were within limits, and that the fuel and oil pressure readings were in range at two thousand rpms.

"Mixture?"

"*AUTO RICH.*"

"Autopilot?"

"*OFF.*"

"Gyro-Compass and Horizon?"

"*ON.*"

"Fuel Booster Pumps?"

"*ON.*"

"Tail Wheel?"

"*LOCKED.*"

Nick paced Ted through each check—ending with the Elevator Tab response of *ZERO* and the Control Booster response of *ON*. "Bring the rpms to twenty-five hundred for takeoff," Nick said. It was like Nick was back in his E-2 with Martha. A solid routine led to a good flight. Nick was building a substantial reputation as a reliable co-pilot who was unwilling to take shortcuts.

Once safely off the ground it was Ted who initiated the conversation. "You seem preoccupied. What's on your mind?" He asked for two reasons. First, he liked Nick, and it wasn't like him to be so quiet. The fact was, Nick would always carry his end of a conversation. Second, a good pilot is always aware of a co-pilot who's not himself that day. Small details, but important in gauging the co-pilot's reaction if an emergency were to come up.

"My brother got me thinking about what's going on in Europe. He's a smart guy, worth listening to. Says we're all going to be in the thick of things real soon. That there's no way FDR will keep us out. What do you think?"

"I'm no world statesman, but I think your brother's only half right."

"How so?"

"The way I hear it, the Japanese are giving our boys fits in the Pacific. The Pacific Fleet is finally back on its feet, but they're going through hell to keep it there with the constant attacks. The Nips aren't going to give up. Those little bastards see our Achilles' heel as having to conduct a war on two fronts. They have a powerful navy and one more thing."

"What's that?"

"They have the most advanced air force in the world."

"Really? Ahead of us?"

"Everyone's ahead of us. We're the Johnny-come-lately in air power."

The altimeter needle began to move, as they climbed to look for smoother air. While the minutes passed and the slight vibration from the turbulence subsided, Nick thought. He realized that he'd been so focused on co-piloting for Northwest that he hadn't really been focusing on what was happening around the world. "So, what's the prognosis, doctor?"

"Get your rank up to captain pronto. You'll have more say in which part of the war you'll be involved in. Pilots will be at a premium. I know you're young, and it may be hard to accept, but men like you will become the backbone of the U.S. air response necessary to finish this war."

"You said finish?"

"Yes, I did."

Nick called Martha when he got to Chicago. The conversation didn't go well. He told Martha about his conversation with Ted and that he was going to take on more hours in order to make captain more quickly. Martha could handle the part about Nick possibly having to go to war and the extra hours, but it was the female voices and the noise of the bar in the background that rankled her. The telephone party line shared with the neighbors didn't provide the confidentiality that Martha needed to be candid, however.

"We need to talk when you get home. I don't like what my intuition is telling me," Martha said through clenched teeth.

"I didn't start the war. I'm just trying to get prepared," Nick said.

"It's not the war in Europe or Asia that bothers me right now. You better start paying attention to your home front, Mister." Martha resented Nick's freedom and was jealous of his ability to pursue his dream of flying. She felt cheated, having to work a part-time sales clerk job in the hardware department of Sears & Roebuck in downtown Minneapolis. She thought about Judy Garland, who was her age and from Grand Rapids, Minnesota no less, and Vivien Leigh, who was not much older, starring in *Gone with the Wind.* Martha wasn't a movie star and didn't want to be one, but she wasn't naïve either. She had experienced a taste of freedom with Nick while they were dating and now she was stuck. Things were happening in the world fast, and she wanted to be a part of it. She wasn't usually jealous of Nick, even when he strayed in high school. *But, that was then,* she thought. His freedom and the call from the bar represented a threat to the security of their marriage. This was more than she could handle. She hated the echo of her mom's voice saying, *He's no good for you. You'll see. Mark my words.*

She slammed down the phone frustrated and depressed.

CHAPTER 3

Everyone in the Morgan family felt lucky to have a summer cottage on Cass Lake. Henry and Rose raised Bud and Nick on Cass Lake. Henry had been stationed there for years, where he worked as a switchman for the Great Northern Railroad. They moved to Staples, Minnesota, when he was promoted to the larger rail yard. The three-hour drive north on back roads was just one of the sacrifices made to stay connected to the area they loved most. The cabin showed some wear and tear, but Henry was able to make ends meet. The women occasionally complained of a mouse in the kitchen, and the men had a long to-do list, which was usually just an excuse to spend a family weekend at the cottage. The lakeside hill was dotted with hardwood trees that filtered the beautiful sunsets and was covered with buffalo grass from the cottage down to the sandy shoreline. At the water's edge was an old, barnside boathouse with white vertical slats with green trim that needed repainting. It was storage to all sorts of summer items, including the twenty-five-horsepower Mercury engine and sixteen-foot wooden boat. The distinct smell of a two-cycle gas and oil mix for the engine permeated the inside. In front of the boathouse was a small hand-dug harbor the men had to dredge every year to keep the water's access from clogging with weeds and sediment. But the great fishing and family memories were the payoff.

"Thanks for holding off until Friday so we could fly together. I wasn't looking forward to the drive," Bud said over the engine noise. Bud and Nick were seated in tandem in the E-2 with Bud in the back at the stick. "I don't think Helen and Martha minded driving together on Thursday at all. It gave 'em plenty of time to gab." Bud knew the weekend would be special as he and Helen had an announcement to make, but he didn't want to say anything just yet.

"Chances to fly together don't come as often as they used to," Nick yelled with his head turned to the rear as much as he could. "This E-2's the best investment we ever made. I don't know what I was thinking the other day when I said Martha and I would fly up Thursday. Didn't make sense since we own this baby together."

"It crossed my mind, too," Bud said as he handled the controls. He loved flying as much as Nick, but he had few chances to log any hours. The two-hour flight was his alone, and he cherished every minute of it. The coup de grace was his textbook landing at the logging camp airstrip at Cass Lake.

"Too bad you're color-blind. The Northwest brass would love to get their hands on you.

"Maybe." Bud paused as he brought the plane to a spot where they could tie up. "But, I finally got that job offer from Goodyear Aircraft I've been talking about. I'm going to tell Mom and Dad this weekend."

"Then you're going to take it?" Nick sensed Bud's excitement.

"Well, I don't want to jump the gun, but it sure looks like a go."

"You're finally going to get to build planes. That's great! I sensed something was special about this weekend." Nick beamed with pride as he patted Bud on the back as they headed toward the makeshift tower. There was a noticeable difference between the brothers' movements as they walked across the airfield. Nick had an athletic gait while Bud's steps were marked by a lively awkwardness.

"It will be tough on Helen . . . not being around you guys and all. Akron's a long ways away, but it's a good career move and a really good offer. I'm looking forward to the challenge."

"I'm really happy for you."

"Just make sure that Mom and Dad hear it from us first is all I ask," Bud stressed.

"You got it."

As usual, the fresh walleye dinner with corn-on-the-cob was wonderful. Rose had even made her special marinated cucumber relish. The dining room table on the screened-in porch facing the lake allowed the mellow breeze to cast a spell over the early evening gathering.

"Rose and I feel pretty lucky to have everyone here at one time. Most of our friends' sons are off to war." Henry wasn't usually sentimental, but that night was different. "How long do you think it will stay this way?" He looked at Bud and Nick for a response.

Helen and Nick were quiet, knowing that this was Bud's chance to talk. "This seems like a perfect time for an announcement," Bud said. "You may remember my comment last week about my air conditioning job being converted to war supplies and, while I could stay there, I don't think it's the best use of my education. What I really want is to be in aviation. To make a long story short, I've accepted a position as a senior designer at Goodyear Aircraft. It's the job I've always wanted. It's not building planes, but it is designing long-distance, trajectory guidance systems. We badly need them in order to improve our rockets for the war. And, since the job is in a critical industry, it carries a draft exempt status. I should get my letter from the War Manpower Commission anytime now."

Bud waited for everyone's response, his mother's in particular.

Henry looked at her and said, "Well, Rose, what do you think about what our son said?"

She pulled a crumpled lace handkerchief from her apron to blot the tears forming in the corner of her eyes. "I just don't know what to say. We've been so afraid you would be drafted that I just can't tell you how happy I am."

"The job is in Akron, Mom. That's Ohio," Bud said, emphasizing the distance. "We won't be able to see you guys much."

"I don't care if the job's in Timbuktu. At least when we do see you, you'll be in one piece," Rose responded as she dabbed her tears with her handkerchief with one hand while squeezing Helen's hand with the other.

"Your mother and I are real proud of you. It's what you've always wanted."

"Martha and I were a little suspicious that something big was going to happen this weekend, so we brought a bottle of Morgan David Rose to celebrate," Nick said standing up. "Martha, wipe your tears and get some wine glasses while I open this bottle," he said lightheartedly. "This calls for a toast."

"We're going to miss you and Bud, but I am very happy," Martha said, throwing her arms around Helen's neck while on her way to the kitchen. Martha and Helen had become extremely close in the past few years and knew the separation would be difficult.

"I'll miss you, too," Helen said while using her apron to dab at the corners of her eyes.

Since there were no wine glasses in the cottage, Martha brought six juice glasses of various sizes. Nick poured the wine and gave a toast. "To my big brother, the future of aviation is secure with you in the game. I can only hope that sometime soon Hitler's boys will be runnin' scared from the rockets you and Goodyear make. And to Helen, we will miss your lovely presence and look forward to the day when all of us will be back at the cottage again. To family."

"To family," they all replied.

The next morning the men got up around six to go fishing. Mist rose off the lake as the sun came up, and waves lapped at the dock and shore. The drone of another boat heading out could be heard in the distance. In the corner of the bay, mallards began to fly, no doubt startled by a beaver or large muskie beginning its day foraging. Henry, Nick, and Bud busied themselves gathering rods and tackle boxes. All that could be heard was the sounds of them getting ready: the gas tank and equipment being placed in the boat, the creaking of the boat in the water as they shifted into their positions, and the oars pushing away from the dock. The three of them had said nothing at all, quietly acknowledging the shift about to take place in their lives. Two grown sons fishing peacefully with their dad on a summer morning in 1943 was not what war was about, and they knew it.

That evening after dinner, at Martha's urging, she and Nick excused themselves from the group and went down to the boathouse where they could talk privately.

"What's on your mind?" Nick asked as they stared out over the lake.

"I'm not comfortable with where things are headed for us." Her directness caught Nick by surprise.

"What do you mean?"

"Just let me talk. I haven't been comfortable for some time. You're gone a lot and around women who would gladly trade places with me. Honestly, I think I'm jealous. And I don't know how to make myself trust you."

"What are you trying to say, Hot Shot, that I've done something for you not to trust me?" Nick was a little defensive because there were a few times he'd strayed before they were married. It wasn't a behavior he was proud of—but he had been faithful since the wedding. "You know there's nothing to worry about. It's just the way the job is set up. I can't control that."

"I saw the picture, Nick. They're pretty, and you were smiling, maybe even happy. I can't help but think that life back home isn't very exciting for you. We don't even do any of the fun things we used to do."

Nick had been holding back on an announcement of his own. He was waiting for the right time. The talk among the men at Northwest about the need for pilots had stirred his patriotism to contribute more directly to the war. As much as he didn't want to spring his intentions on Martha, it had suddenly become the right time. "Martha, you know how I've talked about the Air Transport Command. Well, it's happened. I wanted to tell you sooner, but I knew that Bud had a big announcement this weekend. I wanted to give him his moment. I was planning on telling you when we got back, but, now will have to do. I'm shipping out for training in Edmonton in three weeks. My primary duty will cover Alaska and the Northwest territories. I think I can get my grade up to captain soon with my training, and then I can call my own shots."

"Oh, Nick. Why didn't you say something?"

"I wanted the time to be right, and I just signed up last Thursday. It means that I'll be away for long stretches, and I know it may be hard on you . . . being alone and all."

"Is this what you want?"

"It's either this or combat. If I were single, I'd choose combat. But I'm not. We've got a future to think of. And there's one more thing you will be happy about."

"What?"

"The army doesn't employ stewardesses." She put her arms around his waist, silently accepting that this was Nick's admission that she had a right to be concerned.

"I guess the ATC is better than combat, but it's still going to be hard," Martha said, acknowledging that neither of the choices was her first pick. She wondered if they would ever get back to the blissful days of flying the skies together over Minnesota and Wisconsin. She held the embrace in a futile attempt for reassurance.

Before leaving the next day, Nick announced his ATC decision to the family. Henry and Rose decided to stay on at the cottage for another week. It was a time for change, Henry thought, and he wanted to reflect. They had raised their boys to be independent, but he didn't know what to think about planes and flying—his world was on the ground with railroads. But what he did understand was the excitement in his boys' eyes. It was the same excitement that he had had with the railroad thirty years earlier. They were hooked.

CHAPTER 4

Edmonton, Alberta
August 5, 1943

My Dear Martha,

Well, here I am about to embark on a new and different route.
Tonight I fly to Fairbanks, tomorrow to Anchorage, and then
immediately I start out along that long chain of barren, mountainous, volcanic islands that make up the Aleutians, stretching westward
toward Siberia and Paramushiru Island, which is occupied by Japan.
The fall is when the heavy mist, fog, rain, and winds come. I've
heard of fog unbroken for 1,500 miles, which just seems to make me
more anxious to see it. Truthfully, I believe most of these stories of
tough weather up on "the top of the world" should be discounted some.
Within the next two weeks I shall know. Maybe, I, too, (then being
one of the few pilots actually flying the so-called toughest weather
in the world) will come back with fantastic tales of daring and of
marvelous exploits.

Yours,
Nick

Nick was glad that the privilege of using the army officer's club on base came along with his rank as an ATC co-pilot. The steel-frame building was nothing to look at from the outside, but inside it had everything a young military officer could want. The pool tables nestled in a bay room off the horseshoe bar area were always active. The walls were wood paneled in aged cedar, which added its rich caramel tone to the club's ambience. Oversized photographs of Alaskan wilderness scenes, well-known bush pilots (such as Noel Wein, Ed Boffa, Al Palmeter and James "Andy" Anderson), and various aircraft decorated the walls. Among the photographs were impressive Alaskan game-hunting trophies: mounted heads of moose, elk, bear, and deer. The most appreciated wall, however, held the gorgeous collection of Alberto Vargas pinups. Vargas was a hero among military personnel for his poster art of scantily-clad females. The club was the place to meet some of the fellas and enjoy downtime. Up until now, however, Nick's use of the club had been spotty. His rotating flights involving numerous locations and with captains whom he wouldn't always see again had not allowed the contact to build any enduring friendships.

"You want another one, Captain?" the bartender asked. Nick was going to fly in the morning and wondered whether a second beer would hurt. Tomorrow would be his first trip over the Valley of 10,000 Smokes out toward the Aleutian Islands. It was awful terrain. If the weather was good the flying would be "on top" from six to ten thousand feet. If it was bad, it would be really bad. The fog could become a nightmare, forcing the pilots to fly just above the surface of Bristol Bay and the Pacific Ocean. But it was the sudden unexpectedness of the weather conditions that made flying difficult for the pilots.

"Probably not a good idea. I've got to work tomorrow morning," he replied with a resigned tone. "It's co-captain by the way." He was just finishing a postcard to Martha bragging about the 98 he got in his pre-liminary test in navigation. *Combined with the 96 and 98 in CAR and Radio, I think I've got a good chance to make captain soon.*

Just then a man about ten years his senior with captain stripes stepped toward the table and said, "I'm relieved to know that I won't have to do all the flying myself tomorrow." He extended his hand. "I'm Captain Marshall Smith. We're going to be working together on the 'Chain' over the next few trips."

Nick was surprised that the captain knew who he was as they'd never met. Nick thought he would meet Captain Smith for the first time in the briefing room the next day. "Nice to meet you, Captain. How did you know who I was?"

"I make it a habit of getting to know my co-pilots, particularly the young ones. Glad to see you turned down that second beer. Can I call you Nick?"

"Sure. Would you like to sit down? Do I really look that young?"

"Doesn't make any difference since I know you were born in 1914. Makes you twenty-eight, I believe. Or is it twenty-nine? Either way, it's still pretty young for a co-pilot nearing the rank of captain."

"I am impressed," Nick responded as he stood to shake Marshall's hand. "It is twenty-nine, by the way." The captain's grip exuded confidence, and his smile was friendly. "Where are you from anyway, Captain?"

"A small town in southern Minnesota—Mankato."

"What a coincidence," Nick said as his lips curled slowly. "But I have a strong suspicion that my being from the Gopher State as well is no surprise to you."

"It's not that I don't trust you, Nick. It's just that I've seen young pilots pushed beyond their experience by the war. It makes me a little skittish, and I like to know who I'm about to saddle up with, that's all. Tell me a little about yourself . . . you know, the stuff that's not in your file."

They both laughed out loud.

"Cass Lake is my original home. Not much of a place most of the year. It's on the Leech Lake Indian Reservation; just a crossroad between Routes 371 and 2. It's pretty much a railroad town good for shipping white pine to the mills. In July and August, the fancy people from the Twin Cities favor us with their presence while they vacation on Star Island."

"How'd you get hooked on flying in a place like that?" Marshall asked with genuine curiosity.

"When I was in grade school, my dad would take my brother and me over to the dirt landing strip used by the logging company. The whole idea of people flying was pretty thrilling to me. As luck would have it a plane was coming in one Sunday afternoon while we were there. I'll never forget it. This guy named Ed Boffa stopped to refuel on his way to Alaska. As you probably know, a lot of the early Alaskan bush pilots flew over Minnesota on their way to and from the wilderness. Our logging camp was a favorite stopping place because of the good fishing on Cass Lake."

"Was this Ed Boffa the same guy who became famous as one of Alaska's pioneer bush pilots?" Marshall asked pointing to the photograph on the wall.

"One and the same," Nick replied. "And on that day, he gave me and my brother a ride. We saw the forests and lakes from 'up on top,' as he called it. I can't quite explain it, but being in the clouds and seeing the bald eagles soaring below us . . . well, quite frankly, neither of us have been the same since."

The captain smiled, knowing exactly what he was talking about. It wasn't just because it was the newest thing going, although that added to the excitement. The complete sense of freedom up on top, charting your own course, was unparalleled. "I know the feeling, Nick. It happens to all of us. So, what happened to your brother?"

"He's an aeronautical engineer for Goodyear Aircraft in Ohio," Nick responded with a great sense of pride even though he knew Bud would give his right arm to trade places with him. He knew he was flying for both of them.

"That's great! It must run in the family. By the way, 0600 comes pretty early. I'm going to call it a night."

"Good idea, Captain. See you bright and early in the briefing room."

Nick was up early the next morning in anticipation of their flight from Fairbanks to Elmendorf Field in Anchorage. Then it would be off to the U.S. military installation at Dutch Harbor the next day. Their first leg of the flight was uneventful, giving Nick a chance to settle in with Captain Smith's method of sharing the workload with co-captains. He learned quickly that he would be given much wider latitude in flying responsibilities than most captains would give him. Most held the co-captain role in the same category as an administrative assistant. While they wanted their co-captains to be experienced, they didn't relish doing the teaching themselves. Not with Marshall. Nick handled their first landing together at Elmendorf.

The trip over the Aleutians on Tuesday would take them through almost all of the Alaskan time zones and take several hours, so they needed an early start in order to make their pick-up time commitment of 0930. About fifteen army enlistees would be very anxious to leave for their first furlough back home.

After a thirty-minute weather delay early that Tuesday morning, Nick and Captain Smith had liftoff and were headed southwest toward Kodiak Island. From there, they would change course due west for Dutch Harbor, halfway out the Aleutian chain. With the rising sun behind them, the day was clear and they were up on top at eight thou-

sand feet with unrestricted visibility. It gave Nick time to write another
postcard to Martha.

En route to Dutch Harbor
August 7, 1943

My Dear Martha,

Suppose you heard that Warren Porter was found on a mountain side
up North a few weeks ago today—or hadn't the information that he'd
been lost been released there? You remember him from the Northwest
Christmas party. Probably not since it is under ATC control. Don't
know any details. Don't worry about me though; I'm not taking any
more chances than I would anywhere. Too much to look forward to.

By the way, someone stole the insignia and stuff off my summer uniform that I left in the MacDonald Hotel at Edmonton last
week. Hard to make sense of it. Probably a souvenir hunter.

Just did a fly-by over Kodiak Island and saw several large brown
bear and moose. When we buzzed them they ran like crazy. May have
been the first plane they've seen.

Say hi to Bud!

Yours,
Nick

"I just told my wife about Warren Porter's crash. I try not to worry
her, but if she finds out on her own, which she will, it just makes matters worse. Any words of wisdom, Captain?"

"It's not the information that worries them," he said while changing course slightly. "It's the lack of communication. Put yourself in
her shoes. We're practically halfway around the world, taking risks
they'll never understand. It's the not knowing anything that causes

most women to become stressful and overreact. They just want regular updates. Hell, you'd probably overreact too if you didn't know what your wife was up to for long stretches of time. My advice is to keep the postcards coming.

"What bothers me are the crashes that are never recovered because of this god-forsaken wilderness. We never learn a damn thing about what went wrong. No chance to make it better for the next pilot in the same straights."

An hour later Marshall gave the controls to Nick and said, "It's a clear day; let's do a training exercise while we're near the Valley of 10,000 Smokes. We've made good time and another half hour won't hurt the schedule."

"What do you have in mind, Captain?"

"Take the ship west toward the Shisho Volcano on the horizon, but before you do, tell me the elevation of the volcano's rim." The captain's reference to the plane as a "ship" was new to Nick, although common among ATC pilots. It evolved from early navy terminology with the C-47 being roughly the equivalent in purpose to a freighter. It would find a permanent home in Nick's vocabulary, as well.

Nick thought for a minute. He knew these volcanoes were dangerous because they rose so abruptly on the chain. Worse, however, the fog could close a pilot's visibility in just a few minutes. Low stratus clouds sometimes moved in from the sea or down from the mountains. He had talked to one pilot who had seen it go from a blue hole in the sky to nearly zero visibility in six or seven minutes. "It's my first trip, Captain, but I would bet my life on sixty-five hundred feet."

"You just did. Set your altimeter for 6,550 feet and put it on 'the pilot' with a heading directly for the volcano. You can change your mind any time, but if you do you owe me a steak dinner back in Anchorage. If you don't, I owe you one, that is, if we're around to eat it."

"The pilot" was the autopilot for the C-47, and Nick knew he'd only need a few seconds to disengage it. The volcano was about fifty miles away and grew bigger every minute. As they approached, the smoke and steam rose from the countless fissures from surrounding volcanoes. Jagged rock formations from previous lava flows and meager vegetation dotted the harsh landscape. It shocked Nick as to how quickly his visibility was impaired by the steam clouds and how turbulent the air became from updrafts. He looked to Captain Smith for reassurance. He got none. *I've always been right on this stuff in the past,* Nick thought. *But what about now?* In an instant, the C-47 emerged from the cloud, and the volcano was front and center, bigger than life. Nick instinctively pulled back on the controls and put the plane into a climb.

"Medium-rare porterhouse," Marshall said with a smile. "Your desire for safety over being right is admirable."

Nick wiped the perspiration with his shirtsleeve, shook his head like he had water in his ear, and said, "Your bet would have got us killed if I hadn't pulled out!"

"Are you ready for lesson number two?" Marshall replied.

"What? I mean, sure, I guess."

"Level off at 6,550 feet and make your approach again."

Nick was beginning to think this guy was crazy, but he was the captain. After making a big loop over the Bering Sea he put the plane on the pilot for the target just as Captain Smith ordered. He could hardly control himself as they approached. The air was sucked out of Nick's lungs as the C-47 roared just over the leading edge of the rim of the volcano and then over the immediate drop-off into the crater on the backside. Within seconds they crossed the opposite rim with equal drama.

"So, what do you make of it, Nick?"

"That I was right in the first place," Nick said confidently.

"I would disagree with your conclusion. It proves that you didn't know you were right, which can be just as dangerous as being wrong. Here, let me show you something." Captain Smith took the controls and made one more pass, pointing out the remains of a Japanese Zero on the leading edge of the western slope. "When I was assigned to troop evacuation during the attack on Dutch Harbor, that Zero was hot on my tail, flying just below me trying to get a good shot of my belly. The visibility was terrible. I knew that he was vulnerable, but only because I was absolutely sure the volcano was sixty-five-hundred-feet. That's what I want you to learn while we're working together. It's the decisions under pressure when you're not able to check the flight maps that count."

Nick was used to being the best among peers and not familiar with being successfully challenged. He vowed to make the most of his time with Captain Smith and to learn the elevation of every critical peak and volcano on the chain. Two weeks later, however, Captain Smith was transferred to a training command for new captains in Edmonton, Alberta.

CHAPTER 5

A minor mechanical issue with the right-main landing gear delayed their return departure for Anchorage until 1015. Nonetheless, the soldiers they picked up were not discouraged by the delay; they were just glad they had a way home. It had been exceptionally hard duty for the fifteen men of the 7th Infantry Division, who were part of the assault against the Japanese on Attu Island.

The short mechanical delay gave Nick and Marshall a moment to relax and an opportunity for Marshall to prepare Nick for his first exposure to soldiers fresh from combat. "Once we're in the air, Nick, I want you to spend some time with the men. Sit with them and just listen. That's all I want you to do," Marshall said.

"They seem okay, pretty lighthearted actually," Nick replied.

"Mark my words, Nick, you'll understand my meaning for the request after you've had time with the men."

Once the flight leveled out, Nick left the cockpit and started to walk through the main cabin when a young man with exceptionally dark and wavy hair asked, "Where you from, Captain?"

"I'm just the co-captain on this ship, soldier. Maybe someday I'll get my rank up. I'm originally from a small town in Minnesota—Cass Lake—and now the Twin Cities area. How about you?"

"Canton, Ohio. That's the home of football you know," the soldier said with pride.

"What's your name, soldier?"

"Private Anthony Palumbo, sir, but you can call me Tony."

"Big family?"

"Five brothers and two sisters, sir. Lookin' forward to getting home, too, but two brothers and one sister won't be there. One's in Pearl, one's in Italy, and sis is in the Army Nurse Corp stationed in Queensland. That's in Australia, you know!"

"Sounds like you're proud of her. What's she doing there?"

"Teaching medics how to administer anesthetics. Pretty important, don't you think?"

"You probably saw how important her work is first hand . . . on Attu, that is." Instantly, Nick felt he had crossed a barrier as the light seemed to switch off in the soldier's eyes. "Sorry, I should have left that alone," Nick said.

"No, that's okay," Tony said with obvious hesitation. "It's probably better to talk about it now with someone who wasn't there, before I get home, I mean. But there's no way anyone would understand by just listening to me talk."

"How did it go down?"

"The brass thought there were five hundred Japs. We had about eleven thousand men. The landing was unopposed—just cold as a well-digger's ass in the Klondike, you might say, and foggy, like pea soup. I damn near got frostbite on my toes. We didn't have enough wool uniforms and a lot of men suffered badly. As we advanced through the jagged hills, enemy fire came from everywhere. We lost a lot of men. As it turned out there were close to three thousand enemy troops. After two weeks of hard fighting, much of which was in shitty weather, it came down to the final skirmish you might say."

"How many of the enemy was left?"

"The brass says it was about eight hundred. But, Captain, it might as well have been eight thousand. They came at our line with everything they had that night—except ammunition. Any other troops would have surrendered.

"By the morning of May 30 there were twenty-eight left who gave up. The rest were killed. It was so dark and the fighting was so fierce that I don't know how many I killed . . . don't know that I want to know either."

"Do you think it's true that they were left there to die?"

"Hard to imagine a government that would sell out their troops like that, but yes, I do. I'll tell you this though: I don't ever want to experience anything like it again. The blood, the bodies, the sounds of people dying—I don't think it'll ever get it out of my mind."

Nick knew the Japanese were noted for their legend of *Yamato damashii,* or "spirit warrior." They believed that this spirit made Japan invincible in war and became obsessed, almost possessed, in war. They also believed their Emperor Hirohito was a supreme deity, which conferred a *sons of God* mentality to each soldier. They gladly gave their lives for the emperor. What Tony experienced was not unusual for soldiers in battle with the Japanese. The relentless brutality was beyond the typical American understanding of war. The Chinese had known it, however, in their defeat at the hands of the Japanese, but it's difficult to prepare a soldier for this kind of hostility. Nick had read an article by Robert Sherrod, *Time's* war correspondent, that described the situation at Attu best. "The results of the Jap *banzai* fanaticism stagger the imagination. The very violence of the scene is incomprehensible to the Western mind. Here groups of men . . . met their self-imposed obligation to die rather than accept capture, by blowing themselves to bits. The ordinary, unreasoning Jap is ignorant. Perhaps he is human. Nothing on Attu indicates it."

Nick rested a hand on Tony's shoulder and said, "Enjoy your time with family, soldier," and left him to his own thoughts. Nick could see the effects that the surprise attack on Dutch Harbor and the Battle of Attu had on these soldiers. Their nerves were raw because it easily could happen again. Already rumors circulated that the Japanese had a garrison of five thousand on Kiska, an island only seven hundred miles away. It was understandable that the men were very worried of having to endure a repeat massacre.

Nick was quiet when he returned to the cockpit. The captain could see the look of incredulity on his face. "Now you know why you're here," he said.

CHAPTER 6

Fairbanks, Alaska
September 1, 1943

My Dear Martha,

Rain again today. I've played more pool up here in three weeks than I've played all my life. Went to Bahama Passage last night. The shows are the one real connection with civilization. Outside papers here are always a month old. Getting tired of eating frozen meat, crackers, bread, soup, and canned milk. Going to Anchorage now if the pass is open sufficiently. Then up the north coast of Bristol Bay to Bethel and then further north across the Norton Sound to Nome.

Yours,
Nick

Nick was a confident enough athlete to think he could win at most anything. And the boys he was playing pool with were good enough at pool to "let him believe it." His losses weren't enough to quit, however, and besides, he enjoyed the company. With his routes taking him to Edmonton, Fairbanks, Anchorage, Juneau, Seattle, Dutch Harbor, Nome, Billings, Whitehorse, and multiple stops on the CANOL (Canadian Oil, a development of Imperial Oil west and north of Great Bear Lake), Fairbanks had been as much like home as anywhere lately.

Tonight would be a special break in routine as he and Anne Walsh were going to the Bob Hope, Jerry Calonna, and Frances Langford show. Their troupe arrived in the afternoon by an army Lockheed 14. The show would go on from a flatbed truck and the boys were sure to enjoy it. Weather was perfect.

Anne was an army nurse stationed in Fairbanks. Nick had met her while visiting a pool hall buddy at the hospital who had broken a leg hiking in the White Mountains north of town. She was friendly with dark brown eyes and pretty with short brunette hair, but kind of a tomboy, so she fit in with the various activities the men were doing. Nick was comfortable around her and was glad for a break from the constant companionship of men.

"This isn't a date, is it?" Anne asked, teasing Nick about their upcoming evening together. They had been spending a lot of time together. Their friendship had grown, but they were careful to remain just friends. In fact, Nick was one of the few pilots not making advances.

"I feel uncomfortable enough as it is without your kidding. The guys are going to make me pay for this plenty when they see me tomorrow. We're friends. Let's keep it that way."

"Relax. I'll make sure they know you're not my type."

Nick was serious. He had examined his life and was ready to make a change from his Northwest days. He wanted a full life with Martha, and the idea of a family seemed perfect.

The weather was changing, and they felt a chill in the air while casually walking toward the mess hall. Nick commented, "On the flight in from Bethel yesterday I saw another squadron of P-38s pass on their way to Russia. It's hard for me to get used to how close Japan, Russia, and the U.S. are at the top of the world. From what I've seen, most of their pilots are pretty green. I hope the planes last long enough to cause problems on the Russian front with Hitler's boys." He made an upper-cut gesture to make his point. They tucked their heads down to avoid the swirling dust from a small devil wind on the street.

"It frightens me to think of all the countries at war," Anne added. "It's really hard for me to believe that with Japan between China and the Allies and Germany between Russia and the Allies that Hitler and Hirohito can actually believe in their strategy. Am I missing something, Nick?"

"All their chips are on the table. Neither country seems to have a fall-back position. They're in it for supremacy. They're in it for the long haul, and more lives will be lost . . . many of them American." Both were quiet with this thought as they approached the performance area. It was quite a gathering of GIs, officers, and contract workers. They all stood in a big semicircle around several flatbed trucks that were backed in front of the wood frame mess hall. Someone was testing the speakers as the show was about to start. Shows like these made a difference and were a welcomed break from the routine on base. You could see it in the men's animated expressions and light-hearted interaction.

"A change in plans came in this afternoon, so I can only stay for half the show. Let's stand near the back," Nick said.

"That's too bad. Is there a problem? Is Martha okay?"

"No, it's nothing like that. We have to pull out for Anchorage and Bethel at 2100. Duty calls, another pilot got sick. I just hope I get to hear Frances Langford sing 'I'm in the Mood for Love.'"

"You and about five hundred others."

Anne had three brothers and no sisters. She knew how to work side by side with these love-sick men without letting herself get involved.

It was her feeling that if she began a relationship with a coworker it would be hard to live normally as friends with the other men while doing her job. This night would be like all the other nights after performances. She would have to fend off the advances of love-sick GIs with emotions stirred up by the music. For the most part, their intentions were not completely misguided—they were lonely, just like she was, and missed someone special.

"Is there an important person waiting for you to return to Cleveland?" Nick asked as if reading her thoughts.

"I hope so. His name is Tom. We went to high school together and dated pretty steady until he enlisted. Considering all that could happen, we chose to hold off on the big commitment until after the war."

"Was that the right decision?"

"That's a good question. I just don't know. But I think about him every day and pray he's safe. He's in the 36th Division, stationed in North Africa."

When Nick arrived at Bethel the next day, the communications officer tracked him down in the briefing room with an important telegram. "I think you're going to want to read this one right away, sir."

SEPTEMBER 2, 1943

NICK. WE FINALLY DID IT. THE DOCTOR IS SURE THAT I'M ABOUT FOUR WEEKS PREGNANT. I LOVE YOU.

MARTHA

Nick was excited, but not totally shocked. After the weekend at the cabin the tension between them escalated. Martha couldn't shake the thought of him with other women. She was jealous and wouldn't drop it. The nagging wore on Nick, and in classic Nick fashion, he came right out during one of their disagreements and said, "Let's get serious then and have a baby." The idea of starting a family broke the emotional logjam for them. The timing was right, and they put their hearts into it during the rest of his stay.

Enroute to McGrath from Bethel
September 3, 1943

My Dear Martha,

I hope the baby is a boy. What do you think? We're going to have a swell family.

Been shuttling for two days straight working like dogs. We didn't get into our sleeping bags until four this morning and got up again at nine and back on our horses. There was a wonderful show of the Aurora Borealis–Northern Lights last night directly above us. It is amazing that they're 50 miles above our altitude. They're similar to the ones we see in Minn., but much grander above the Arctic Circle. Wished you could seen them. The upper atmosphere literally shimmered with colored ribbons of phosphorescence. The crew couldn't control their oohs and aahs. Had a few of my own, though I am getting used to them on most night flights. Too bad that most people never experience these celestial oddities.

Thought of you tucked away in that nice soft bed, cozy and warm all night while we were up here above the cold moonlit peaks and tundra.

Yours,
Nick

CHAPTER 7

"Captain Nick Morgan—that's the flyboy I'm lookin' for, dad," Robert "Red" Johnson announced while showing a smile that could charm a snake. Red had a habit of calling everyone "dad" when he wanted their attention, the same way people from Minnesota called a man fella. It was his thick Oklahoma accent, however, that turned every head in the flight operations room that morning in Anchorage.

"Captain Nick Morgan you say," said Warrant Officer Martin Mason in a harsh, nasally voice with a thick New Jersey accent. He sat behind a long, paper-laden operations counter. It was his job to schedule the ATC flights of all the pilots and co-pilots based in Alaska, which might seem routine if it were not for the unusual complications. There was no counterpart in the operations of an airline. It required a deep appreciation for human nature, monumental patience, powerful insight, and the discretion and tact of a seasoned divorce lawyer. All pilots and co-pilots benefited from shared flying time, which gave each captain an opportunity to pass on his version of the truth regarding the C-47 and, simultaneously, gain exposure to co-pilots seemingly barely out of high school. Martin had to know the disposition and mood swings of every pilot, while instantly matching their names, faces, and reputations in order to balance the experience and skill of every crew. Hence, he shared the most hidden details and frailties of many and a cleverness to make it all work. Attesting to the complication of the task was the interrupting chatter of four dedicated Teletype machines receiving and sending requests for flights, manpower switches, new schedules, and changes to schedules.

"This is flight operations, cowboy, not a corral," Martin said loud enough to grab the attention already generated by this big sodbuster. "You sure you're in the right place?"

"That's a good one, dad. Nope, I got the right place, alright. You boys got me saddled up with him on the next bus to Fairbanks." Red Johnson was about as out of place as a person could be. His big hands and leathered skin told the story of growing up on a ranch in hard country. Experience with oceans, snow, mountains, and glaciers was as foreign to him in Perry, Oklahoma, as roping cows and Saturday night rodeos were to the Inuits.

"God save the Union," Martin whispered sarcastically to one of the captains who was in the process of filing a flight log nearby. "I think I've seen it all."

"Excuse me, pard? If you think I'm goin' to stand here and put up with some lip from a paper pusher, ya got another thing comin'. Now, I got a plane to fly, and if you don't know where Captain Morgan is, maybe you can point me in the direction of someone who does." Red tended toward settling things with his fists when someone else's mouth infringed on his rights. It always started off with spittle flying in every direction when he got excited.

Martin's ego was damaged by the abrupt verbal retaliation. Most pilots deferred to his position of expertise and authority, since it was Martin who made up the flight teams and adjusted the schedules to meet individual demands that involved fishing, hunting, gambling, and women for many of these men. As a staff officer, Martin could pile on additional misery to a pilot's life with undesirable schedules, flying partners, paperwork, and bureaucracy.

"I'll be with you in a minute after I take care of this *captain's* flight schedule," he replied coldly, emphasizing the rank of the man in front of him. "Sit down over there and cool your heels, Tex."

Red's ears turned red with anger, but he realized he was off to a bad start for his first day. He was a big man who was accustomed to a rough life. If push came to shove, he'd generally get the best of it. *Not now*, he thought. "You might as well go ahead and put a brand on me, too, while I'm sittin' over here," Red said with a lightheartedness that diffused the situation. The men in the room rested easy knowing that the tension had passed.

At that moment, Nick walked through the door. A blast of damp, cold October arctic air rushed in before he could shut the door. "Anyone seen an Okie with wings from Camp Gruber?" he asked with his back towards Red.

Martin's head-nod provided the answer.

"One and the same." Red lifted his body enthusiastically off the bench and covered the distance between the men in two strides in order to shake hands. "My friends call me Red. I hope you do, too. But, this little cricket over here, however, can call me Mr. Johnson." Red's smile packaged the comment meant for Martin, and the men in the room laughed out loud. Even Martin lightened up.

"What'd I miss?" Nick questioned, looking to others with his palms up.

"Sometimes you don't need to know how the well was dug to know there's water at the bottom," Red answered, reaching across the operations table and shaking Martin's hand. "I'm right sorry for stepin' on your toes, Little Cricket. It won't happen again." From that day on, everyone in flight ops called Martin "Cricket."

———————

Nick and Red's flight to Fairbanks had been delayed until late evening. Although their ship had been upgraded to the C-47D "Skytrain," it was still a tight squeeze for the big men. The cockpit was filled with instruments and dials, and the dashboard rose to just about eye level for most pilots. Red's and Nick's heights were an advantage in this respect, but quickly gave ground when leg space was considered. All in all, with the center console, peddles, and steering column factored in, they were real cozy.

Since becoming a captain thirty days earlier, Nick had adopted Captain Marshall Smith's habit of checking out his co-pilots. He didn't have much of a track record to run on yet, but he remembered the first impression Smith had on him. "I missed you in the officer's club last night. Thought it might give us a chance to get to know each other beyond what's in your file," Nick said after leveling off at a comfortable nine thousand feet. The brilliance of the winter moon was like a backlight to the curvature of the earth to the west. In the distance, however, the sky appeared to be shaped like a wedge, dividing their view into layers—a growing blackness below with a plateau of vapor, almost exactly at their altitude, and the clear night sky above.

"Woulda liked some time in the club, Captain, but I had a bunch of postcards to get out. Alaska's about the strangest country I've ever seen, dad. My friends would call me a liar without the pictures. Just had to get 'em done before I got sidetracked." Nick liked the way Red called him dad; it reminded him of Martha and the baby.

Just at that moment, they hit some turbulence. Nick called for a weather update from Elmendorf. No major changes, just an unusual extension of the mild front that would be with them the remainder of the 350-mile flight to Fairbanks.

"It's holding at zero degrees," Red said in his first official communication outside of normal procedure. He continued to focus on the outside air temperature (OAT) gauge, knowing they would lose seven degrees for every one thousand feet of elevation.

"What are the options?" This was a good time for Nick to find out more about his new co-pilot's training background.

"Out on the panhandle this might be the beginning of what my Uncle Jeb would call a *Norther*, but hell, we can't get too much further north than this."

"What then?"

"Maybe it's just a fall storm or at worst just a bunch of clouds with no tit to drain the water." He paused while thoughtfully scratching the two-day old shadow on his cheek. "We don't want that."

"Why not?"

"Well, any cloud at this temperature has the potential for ice. It's a crapshoot, though."

Bingo, Nick thought. *Maybe Pecos Bill here does know something about flying.* "See if you can tune in Ladd for their version of the weather." Luckily, the cargo was only ten pallets of dry-good supplies and no passengers, eliminating the need for seatbelt announcement formalities. Red did a passable job of operating the direction finder on the radio, which was controlled by a tuning dial and small crank for turning the receiving loop. After a few fingernail-on-slate screeches, the base responded with a vagueness that indicated they were equally in the dark.

"What now, Red?" Nick had registered that in thirty minutes they would be at the halfway point in the flight—not a concern for fuel, simply a symmetry in logic all pilots seemed to possess when considering whether to return to base or to continue on to their destination.

"Your guess is as good as mine, pard." They waited and watched the OAT gauge for changes. None came.

"There are two things I've learned about you in the last forty-five minutes that weren't in your file."

"Am I busted?"

"On the contrary. First, your priorities of choosing people over beer after a long flight are solid. I like that. Second, you don't bullshit your captain with superfluous information. I can work with both. Welcome aboard."

Suddenly, the windshield became opaque. Almost instantly, the world of the cockpit ended with a gray panel-covered window—there was no visibility. It was already too late for the pilot heat, prop, and windshield anti-ice systems to have an impact. "Start the de-icers!" Nick commanded as his attention shifted immediately to the certainty of icing on the wings. Red flipped the switch to activate the expansion and contraction of the rubber "boots" on the edge of the wing that could be inflated and deflated with air. "Get the landing lights on, so we can see." From the side window Nick could see that a sheet of ice had formed on the starboard wing; it looked like a big piecrust. The rubber boots, swelling and collapsing like elongated hearts, shattered the crust of ice into large flakes. About a half inch of ice had also formed on the rim of the engine cowling and propeller hub.

Suddenly there was an erratic banging from behind the cockpit. It sounded like someone hitting the outside of the plane with a sledgehammer. "Get some alcohol on the props, now!" Nick commanded. "The propeller blades are icing up." In this condition the centrifugal force of the propellers' rotation whirled the ice chunks against the aluminum. Since the accumulation on each blade was inconsistent, the balance of the three-hundred-and-eighty-pound propellers was greatly disturbed. This caused a severe vibration, which seized the entire ship. Red labored at the hand pump to send alcohol to the propeller blades to free them from ice.

"God dammit!" Nick yelled over the ominous racket. "Try Ladd Field again!" At that point he noticed the air speed had dropped to 122 miles per hour.

Both men knew that with a load of ice the ship was a completely different aircraft with unknown flight parameters. At some point the ship's airspeed would no longer support flight, but they couldn't know exactly what that speed was. It would likely come sooner than later considering the cargo load.

"Altimeter's dropping fast," Red said rhetorically as both men looked at the dial on the dashboard. They had lost three thousand feet in just minutes. At their current altitude of six thousand feet, they would have to negotiate a gap in the terrain by hugging some relatively low mountains to the east while staying clear of several unnamed treacherous peaks in the McKinley range to the west.

"Can you see what's wrong with the de-icers?"

Red looked out the window, but he already knew. "The ice is accumulating too fast for the de-icer boots to work. Had this problem on a flight to Kansas City. It wasn't pretty, but I can walk you through it, if you want."

"I'll tell Ladd to give us clearance for an emergency landing." Nick knew they'd never make it to a runway the way things were going. They were at forty-eight hundred feet and Fairbanks was still two hundred miles away. Dropping at two hundred feet per minute would put them right into the Wood River in about twenty-five minutes.

"This is where you earn your stripes, cowboy. Tell me what to do."

"Well, the problem, dad, is that the boots are pulsating beneath the ice shield that's formed on the leading edge of the wing—kinda the way a chicken heart still pumps after its head been lopped off. Goin' nowhere fast. We got to shake that bar of ice loose."

"Okay. But the manifold pressure gauge shows a steady loss of power. Can you feel it?" Nick asked, indicating the feeble response from both engines and mentally recording another drop of two hundred feet. "That doesn't have anything to do with the ice."

"I think the air scoops to the carburetor are icing over," Red said, remembering the ice storm over Kansas. The carburetor air scoop is an oval-shaped metal mouth on top of the engine. Air is as important as fuel and must pass through the scoop or the plane will die like a drowning person.

Nick knew exactly what to do. He concluded the training exercise and yanked open the side window to get a better look at the port engine. He could see the ice forming around the lip of the scoop's mouth. "Hang on!" he said as he cut off the fuel mixture to the engine. His intuitive actions no longer required the advice of his co-pilot. Starved for fuel, the engine backfired viciously, spitting a flame from the air scoop and sending more vibrations throughout the ship, which knocked the ice off the scoop. Immediately, he pulled the fuel level to reengage the proper fuel mixture; the response was glorious. The engine produced full power. After repeating the process with the starboard engine the plane was able to climb. "The engines are suffocating. Cut the mixture until they backfire. Then slam them on again."

"That's what I was going to explain. I'll watch my side for build up," Red assured. The backfire spits a tongue of flame from the air scoop, but, it's the force of air that breaks the ice free. The procedure was brutal on the engines, but it beat an attempted landing in a river in the middle of nowhere.

They were able to hold a course at forty-five hundred feet while exercising the procedure every three or four minutes. Every time the plane shook they held their breath until the ship regained stability. Nick reflected on Red's skill and composure during the ordeal and mentally placed two plus signs next to his name as a future flying partner. "So, where did you get your flying experience?"

"Crop dustin' on the panhandle, until the drought kilt just about everything in sight. It's the only gal darn job I ever liked, but the dust bowl plumb wore me out. Uncle Jeb used to say we had two-year-old catfish that didn't know how to swim."

At that moment, they emerged from the clouds into a clear night under a full moon. "I'll be damned," Nick said, almost anticipating a refrain from the Halleluiah Chorus. The vibration of the plane quickly disappeared as the last of the ice was thrown from the wings. It's customary for captains to restrain themselves from showing uneasiness in a situation with co-pilots when confronted with "escapes," particularly new co-pilots like Red. So, in this case, a simple bump with the heal of his hand on the leather-padded cockpit dash acknowledged their achievement while simultaneously preserving Nick's dignity.

"Tell me more about Uncle Jeb and those catfish."

CHAPTER 8

"I'm pretty new at this," Red said, "but it looks to me like we're plumb locked in for awhile." Red and Nick were eating a late breakfast in the officer's club at Ladd Field. It was situated near the northeast runway with a clear view of takeoff and landing activity. Nick always preferred this club for its closeness to the airfield. The Elmendorf officer's club in Anchorage was near the barracks. It might as well have been in a warehouse district.

"I'm not sure of the exact translation of *plumb*," Nick said, enjoying a little fun with Red's drawled expressions.

"You're not, huh. Well, let me tell ya. It's pretty much like when I put a hammerlock on my younger brother. It's a sure thing. You might say being 'locked in' leaves a margin for escape. Being 'plumb locked in' is like solitary confinement. Ya know what I mean, dad?"

"Yeah, I guess I do," Nick said with a wry smile. "It seems to me though, that I'm going to have to learn another language if we're going to work together much.

"I went over to flight ops for a weather check and it seems this pea soup is here to stay. At least for the next eight hours, so it does seem like we're *plumb locked in*. Any idea what you want to do for the day?" Nick knew that down time like this could bore a man to death.

"What are my options?" asked Red.

"Well, since we can't go outside in this weather, there really are only three options: writing home, playing poker, or playing pool," Nick explained to his new friend.

"Maybe you could tell me a little about this place first while I consider the choices?"

"Fair enough," Nick said as he considered the short life span of the airfield. "Ladd started in Fairbanks as a small cold-weather test station in '39, mostly to test clothing and equipment under extreme elements."

"What do you mean?"

"Well . . . let me think about it. You know how a plane is held together by rivets?"

"Yeah."

"These guys would determine if all the rivets on a plane would pop out if it was brought into a warm hangar from a temperature of forty below. There was also a guy named Washburn who was contracted by the Quartermaster Corps to test new cold-weather footwear. Something developed by an outdoorsman named Leon Leonwood Bean."

"That's a handle a man won't forget."

"You're right. Anyway, Washburn's a mountain explorer—pretty good one. He spends a lot of time in Alaska."

"It's about time they develop some good equipment," Red said. "Everybody knows the troops need better. Hell, we need better." His comment demonstrated to Nick that Red had done his homework on cold weather war conditions. For all of time, armies had lost more men and battles to cold weather than to the enemy. The standard issue provided to the troops in this war wasn't any better. Frostbite was a problem for everyone, including the pilots.

"Things changed around here in late '41 with Pearl Harbor. Why don't we head on over to the pool hall while we're talking though, and

I'll fill you in on the way." Just outside the officer's club, they passed three Russian pilots outfitted in Russian beaver-trapper's hats and sturdy wool shirts.

"Good morning," Nick said and added a friendly gesture of the hand.

They responded enthusiastically in Russian.

"Everybody's got the day off," Nick offered in explanation after seeing the bewildered look on Red's face.

"I've been meaning to ask you about this, pard," Red said while doing a 360-degree pirouette as they walked away and at the same time emphasizing with his hands the unexplainable existence of Russians on a U.S. military base, "but I'm not sure I can find the right question."

"Do you know anything about the Lend-Lease Program?"

"Can't say as I do."

"Well, that's what changed this place in '41. Ladd is a critical link in the Alaska-Siberia Lend-Lease highway. It's a program for Russians to pick up P-38s and B-25s purchased from Uncle Sam. They fly them to Siberia via Galena and Nome, where they will be eventually used to fight Hitler. We train their pilots in Billings, Montana, and they pick their planes up here."

"I thought they were the bad guys," Red said with genuine confusion in his voice.

Nick shrugged.

They arrived at the pool hall and were lucky to find one of the eight tables open, considering how the day was shaping up.

"You any good?" Nick asked.

"I can nab a fly off a cow's butt with my hand faster than a chicken can jump a June Bug." He paused and gave Nick a look of confidence as he waggled the pool cue indicating his readiness to play. "But only if I need to."

Nick privately considered any circumstance requiring him to nab a fly off anything, let alone a cow's butt. Maybe Red meant that his hands were fast and steady—a good quality in a pool player, but he wasn't going to ask. Instead they just started playing—Nick racked and Red broke. Red talked almost nonstop while they played, revealing more of his background—a dead brother from the war, a father who had turned to alcohol, and a mother who just plain gave up from the hard living in the Oklahoma dust bowl.

"People are real poor where I come from. You ever been in a drought, Nick?"

"No. In Minnesota we got as much water as we need. But, I do understand poor."

"Ain't that always the way. Some have and some don't, but everyone's poor. That's what got me into crop dusting in Kansas. I had to find a way to live."

"Some have it worse than others, though. You see the young man at the table by the window writing postcards?" Nick motioned with a nod of his head over his shoulder in the direction of the table. "There's a guy with a right to beef. You'll meet him tomorrow on our flight. Name's Robert Endo. He's a nice enough guy I guess—a little moody at times. He's a flight service PFC and an adopted son of Japanese-American parents, and lived in San Francisco when he enlisted."

"What's his nationality?"

"Formosan mother and American father, I think. In any case, eight months after enlisting, both parents were sent to the Japanese internment camp in Manzanar, just west of Death Valley in California. The best he understands is that they're living in a tar paper barracks under confinement."

"That's downright crazy!" exclaimed Red. "How's he supposed to keep his head into flying for the army?"

"You're right. It's good he isn't flying ships. He's very private about the matter, so it won't do well to ask him about it. He'll open up as he gets comfortable with you, but in the meantime, you need to know he's not always 100 percent focused."

After a few hours of trading money, Nick and Red called it quits and headed off toward the mess hall for lunch. Coincidentally, the three Russians they passed earlier were headed in the same direction. Nick knew the crew leader, Vladimir. "How was the movie?" he asked, knowing their path brought them from the theater.

Vladimir's translation to the other men generated broad grins. "Lana Turner," Vladimir said. "Movie named *Slightly Dangerous*."

Red interjected with a low cat whistle. His hands accompanied the sound by outlining the legendary breasts of the star on his own body. All of them shared boisterous comments in Russian and English—which a person of any language could interpret—followed by a hearty laugh.

"How long will your men be here, Vladimir?" Nick asked.

"Tonight only. Back to motherland tomorrow for these two. P-38 pilots," he responded in choppy English.

"Give 'em hell when you get to the front line," Red said, punctuating his comment by punching his fist into the air.

"German pricks," one of the men uttered in a heavy Russian accent. "We kick butt," he continued in broken English.

The men parted once in the mess hall, seating themselves at separate tables. A few minutes into their lunch, Nick noticed that Robert Endo had joined the Russian men and seemed to be having a passable discussion with them.

Red and Nick parted company after lunch for some down time and to write home.

Fairbanks, Alaska
October 9, 1943

My Dear Martha,

How many number 18 stamps do you have? Don't let them waste as I may need one in case we can't get a special issue for my bowling shoes out here. That boiled ham and cabbage dinner sure sounded good. No, I don't know "Paper Doll" and haven't heard Sinatra. However, his publicity doesn't give me any desire to. Going down to the mess hall soon for my normal hamburger dinner.

Yours,
Nick

Not wanting to share personal feelings or specific flight instructions in advance through postcards became standard protocol when Nick wrote Martha. It seemed pointless to even try since he knew every communication was scrutinized by security personnel. At times like tonight, he tired of the trivia their communication was reduced to. He couldn't say that his duty in Edmonton for more captain training would keep him there awhile, hence the bowling shoe request. Every now and then he would slip and Martha would receive a postcard with a sentence clinically cut out of the physical card itself. Unfortunately, this kept his emotions bottled up.

At dinner he ran into Anne Walsh. They ate together and afterwards, rousted out Red to take in the movie. Maybe later he'd write another letter to Martha if he had time, Nick thought.

CHAPTER 9

It was hard for Martha to stay motivated at home and, at the same time, share the excitement of the baby with Nick. This had been a long stretch with him being gone for more than two months. Their limited communication heightened her feeling of isolation. They wouldn't be together again until Thanksgiving. She wanted to move back in with her mom, but Nick would not hear of it. "See her as much as you like while I'm gone, but when I'm home I want it to be just you and me, in our own place," he had said. Her morning sickness had become increasingly acute, as well, and seemed more severe than most of her women friends had experienced by a wide margin. She felt guilty complaining, though. The war was hard on everyone. In reality, she was lucky to have her part-time sales clerk job for the little money it brought in and for the small amount of social stimulation it provided.

"Thanks for meeting me to do a little shopping for the baby," said Martha. Alice was a friend of hers from church who was also pregnant. She offered to meet Martha for lunch and to do a little shopping with her before she had to go to work at Sears.

"Have you decided on a name yet?" asked Alice.

"It would help to know the sex, of course, but maybe George if it's a boy and Constance or Molly if it's a girl."

"When's the due date?"

"The doctor thinks April 16."

"That's great. Mine's in June. Our kids will be friends, won't they?"

"Maybe for life."

"Are you planning to convert that small bedroom to the nursery? I mean, if you are, we could look at some of the things that aren't boy or girl specific."

"Good idea. I haven't been to see what Penney's has. Maybe we should go there first." Martha liked the diversion that being with Alice provided. Alice's husband was in the navy, and she understood the loneliness that letters never really eliminated. However, Martha thought that Nick could be a little more forthcoming in his writing and resented his limited communication in postcards. "It's not like our marriage and my being pregnant requires top-secret clearance by the army," she had written in one of her recent letters. She just wanted him to be a little more loving and little less exacting. That's all.

"Do you really think we need a baby crib and a bassinet?" Martha asked as they approached the baby department. "If Nick were home, I'll bet he could make a bassinet and save the money."

"Good luck! If I know Nick, your baby will be in the first grade before that will happen."

They both laughed enthusiastically. It felt good to Martha to stop ruminating on things she couldn't control. And, Alice was right. While Nick could do anything he set his mind to, it wasn't likely that a bassinet would be one of those things. They enjoyed their hour together—new mothers visualizing and preparing for what was to come. Their conversation while shopping and anticipation of a life neither fully understood was a nice retreat from the anxiety they both felt about the future.

Martha only worked until five o'clock that day and returned home while it was still light. The fall day was unusually pleasant, and reading the card she found in the mailbox from Nick made for an enjoyable moment. "How many 18-cent stamps to ship his bowling shoes and his hamburger dinner" however, wasn't what she necessarily wanted to hear. Nonetheless, just to hear from him was good. She knew he had been training in Edmonton for the last several weeks, which kept him in one place for awhile. It sounded more like a resort assignment to her, with all the hiking, fishing, and related outdoor activities. She knew he loved training under Captain Smith and, in reality, this duty would be one of Nick's few with relative stability during his service. Now that he was a captain, his seniority among other captains was at the bottom, which meant his schedule would incorporate lousy destinations and flight plans, which would once again fling their cards and letters out of synch for some time.

She also opened a letter from Helen. Her description of Bud's excitement in finally having a job related to flying made Martha smile. They missed everyone and couldn't wait for Thanksgiving, although it meant a lot of driving to and from Akron. "Ohio is very different from Minnesota," Helen related. "Much more industrial, but still pretty with more defined hills and the gorgeous fall color in the landscape." The big news exploded on page two with large block letters in burgundy and yellow crayons exclaiming, "I'm finally pregnant!" Martha and Helen were more like sisters than sisters-in-law. They shared everything, albeit via letters. As Martha folded the letter and put it back into the envelope so she could save it for Nick, she thought how nice it would be to have someone to whom she could talk and confide in person. Even though the front page constantly proclaimed Hitler's blitzkriegs and the escalation or the war in Europe, Martha felt somewhat secure in her little corner of the universe. She was content knowing her baby was healthy, her husband was relatively safe with his Alaska assignment, and there were people with whom to share her life.

CHAPTER 10

Robert Endo had always gone by Robert rather than the Americanized Bob, because his adoptive mother felt it generated a sense of formality and respect. Discrimination was a normal experience growing up in San Francisco with Japanese-American parents, even though his adoptive father had a steady job with the Southern Pacific Railroad. Using "Robert" was a small antidote. He learned to appreciate the culture given him by his parents, but also knew that his America was not the same America afforded his Caucasian high school classmates. He carried most of his mother's physical characteristics; small build, jet black hair, and dark almond eyes, so it wasn't uncommon for people to assume he was Japanese. This was an additional source of frustration, since, if anything, he should have been confused with being Chinese from his biological mother's Formosan descent.

His biological father was an American from Seattle, who died in 1918 during the WWI battle of the Argonne Forest, just after Robert was born. His mother worked twelve-hour days in a laundry to sustain their lives. The manual work left her as lifeless at the end of each day as the clothes she washed. In spite of the many financial and living hardships they endured, she was a good mother to Robert. Almost two years to the day of his father's death, however, she died from pneumonia. Her sickness was provoked by the hot and sweaty laundry conditions coupled with a rundown physical plant unequipped to ward off an unusually damp and cold San Francisco winter. Robert's soon-to-be adoptive parents, Hikaru and Joy Endo, adopted him from a shelter much the way you might pick out a pet dog. Adoption of mixed-race babies received little oversight. Joy had been the one who cared for him during the time his mother worked at the laundry. In respect for his stepfather, Robert always referred to him as Endo-san in traditional Japanese style. Growing up, Robert accepted the reality that his adoptive parents were the single reason for his existence. They provided everything within their means while raising him, and while they tried their best to help him be a part of the American way of life, he remained somewhat invisible. His introversion as a teenager and lack of social skills limited his ability to make friends. He never really fit in.

The U.S. Government's judgment to intern all Japanese adults at the beginning of the war with Japan crushed Robert's patriotism. Hikaru and Joy Endo were shipped off to Manzanar in March 1942, four months after Pearl Harbor. Poor timing under any circumstances, but the situation was emotionally complicated by the fact that he had just enlisted and been accepted in the army's air force (USAAF), and he was furious at what his government had done to his parents.

It had been a year and a half since their internment. During this time it had been impossible for Robert to conduct any direct communication with his parents at the Death Valley camp other than official status updates. And these communications were meager, coming only from a liaison officer who filtered the words in every postcard sentence like a reduction sauce—to its barest of comments, such as "Hi," "How are you?" and "I'm fine."

Robert and Vladimir lingered over lunch after the other two Russians had left. "You are in separate place, not here," Vladimir commented in his vastly improving English. Vladimir's native tongue was *Chaplino,* the written language base for the Asian Eskimo dialect spoken throughout the arctic regions. Vladimir grew up until age ten on the Chukotka Peninsula in the easternmost part of Russia. His seemingly natural talent for language was discovered after his family moved to the Vladivostok Russian military base, headquarters to the Russian Pacific Fleet, directly across the Sea of Japan from Hokkaido, the north island of Japan. His father, an officer, had access to the best education available for his family on base, and he pressed Vladimir to develop his talent early. By seventeen Vladimir could speak functional English and Japanese and several Russian dialects.

"Forgive me. My situation sometimes gets the better of me," Robert replied, acknowledging his lack of attention to Vladimir with a slight shrug of the shoulders. He took a pack of Lucky's from his shirt pocket, struck the pack on the table to settle the tobacco, removed a cigarette, and lit it. The deep inhale had its anticipated calming effect. The smoke from the exhale trailed from his nostrils and lips simultaneously as he talked.

"Some days are more better than others? You agree?"

"Yeah, something like that."

Vladimir knew he should change the subject. "I have noticed much activity over last two days with the small group of civilian visitors. Is it special delegation?" Vladimir's comments always indicated an unusually perceptive understanding of military protocol and base politics. As a boy, his father was host to many delegations at Vladivostok. Whispered conversations and heightened security kept people on the ready. "Everyone is on best behavior for sure," he said.

Robert enjoyed Vladimir. Their conversations somehow took him away from his anger at his country over his parents' situation, and his wartime responsibilities. Maybe it was because they generally talked about the base as if it were a movie or play. He enjoyed discussing their observations about the day-to-day base operations. Their different perspectives helped pass the time.

"I heard Cricket tell Captain Morgan in flight ops in Anchorage that these men were here from New Mexico . . . being taken on a flyover of the Yukon Flats area north of here." Robert knew that Vladimir was familiar with Cricket since his pilots' activities were controlled out of the very same flight ops group. "Pretty hush, hush from what I've heard."

"Hush, hush? What das mean?" Vladimir asked, taking the last drag from his cigarette before stubbing it out.

"You know. Like no one is supposed to know anything."

"What is located at Yukon Flats area?"

"Not much. Just some played-out gold mines and a few trappers and Eskimos. Fort Yukon is the only town. An end-of-the-earth kind of place. There are about sixty people, and it gets extremely cold. You might have some relatives there since it came with the Alaska Purchase." Robert smiled.

"Eighteen sixty-seven," Vladimir replied in an even tone while squaring his shoulders to meet Robert's smile.

"What's 1867?" Robert asked, completely missing the connection in history.

"That is when we sold Alaska to America. Some of the old men still think it to be a huge mistake, like history-changing mistake."

"Let's just hope you don't have any relatives living there if we go to war with Russia. They'll all be put into camps, just like my parents. It pisses me off every time I think of their situation!"

"We have Siberia, you have intern camps. Small people always get hurt during wars."

Vladimir shared Robert's pain, but given his assignment, he knew it was unwise to connect on a human level. Vladimir's father had been a loyalist to the Russian imperial family of Nicholas II. Along with his wife and children, Nicholas had been moved as a political prisoner in August 1917 to the Siberian capital of Tobolsk and in the spring of 1918 to Yekaterinburg. They were executed in the cellar of their prison house. Vladimir's family was also among the early victims of the political fallout and the many subsequent executions during the civil war. He survived the atrocities through a coincidence of names. His father pleaded on Vladimir's behalf, declaring in tears that his namesake, Vladimir Lenin, would find excellent use of his language skills. The boy was spared and at nineteen became one of the young-est comrades of the newly formed Cheka organization—birthplace to the KGB. The Cheka became a devastating weapon against the ene-mies of Lenin, inside and outside of the Russian Federation. Working undercover assignments over the years for the very organization that executed his family was a personal hell, but it was his only way out. Despite the many assassinations and corrupt entanglements of the Cheka, Vladimir survived the various political reorganizations. The Cheka became the NKVD in 1922 to address both internal security and state security. It endured one of its significant challenges in July of 1941, when Stalin was surprised by Germany's attack on June 22, 1941. The Special Section of Counterintelligence was formed. Code and cipher systems were changed, and Vladimir was named one of its agents. While NKVD mostly focused on internal affairs of state and the Glavnoye Razvedyvatel'noye Upravleniye, GRU, on external affairs involving international espionage, Vladimir remained assigned to the NKVD overseeing the Russian pilot program in Alaska.

Robert and Vladimir each momentarily reflected on their private storehouses of hidden pain and sheltered emotions buried deep behind the stoic expressions they shared. Their mutual silence testified to a burden so heavy that it prevented a complete disclosure of their innermost thoughts.

Shifting back into the moment and breaking the silence, Robert said, "I'm on Captain Morgan's flight tomorrow after the weather lifts. I'll give you an 'official' report of Yukon Flats when I'm back."

As Robert walked away, Vladimir poured another cup of coffee and considered his own situation. As a NKVD Agent, he had much to lose if his identity were uncovered.

It was in 1925, after three years as an apprentice cryptographer and four more years as a backup translator that he got his first real assignment. He was stationed as a "listening agent" attached to the Russian Consulate in Shimoda, Japan, on the Izo Peninsula south of Tokyo. His official objective was to translate sensitive Japanese documents that fell into the hands of operatives working undercover in the growing international trade activities of Japan. Under the direction of his superior in Moscow, Commander Boris Sidorov, however, his role was to secretly report on any suspicious matters of Bolshevik interest, thereby continuing the honorable Chekist profession of isolating individuals through spying, and thus making it impossible for anybody to trust anybody else. After a long year in obscurity, he discovered a series of documents completely discrediting the consulate general as nothing more than a traitor to the Federation. Large amounts of gold were being smuggled through a well-developed channel of Japanese and Russian operatives. Lenin himself had been advised of the discovery and the invaluable services of Vladimir Dubisskiy.

At the end of his second year in Shimoda Vladimir met Okimi Nakamura. She spoke no Russian, of course, and worked in her father's flower store by the river. She was eighteen and delicate with a tiny waist, small shoulders, and an indirect way of making eye contact. They met briefly while he was on one of his many walks by the river, where his unhurried pace that day was measured by the flow of the river's current. She was leaving her father's store when two rickshaws collided, blocking their progress. She was on her way to deliver some fresh-cut jasmine, and he was on his way to a routine meeting involving a translation for an NKVD operative. Their spontaneous eye contact temporarily suspended the confusion of the moment while they maneuvered around the accident. The exchanged gaze ended as quickly as it began when her almond-shaped eyes dropped immediately. In years to come he would hardly believe that this vision was anything other than a dream. He followed her without notice until she made her delivery and returned to her father's shop.

The next day he entered the shop nervously. "Good morning," he said quietly to her as she approached to help. His throat felt as if it were about to seize shut with anticipation.

The morning sun reflected off her eyes and her gentle smile seemed no less brilliant than the many bouquets of flowers filling the water pots throughout the store. "May I help you," she replied with her eyes averted.

He carefully considered his thoughts in Russian and made sure of the correct translation before he said in Japanese, "I saw a lady on the street the other day carrying the most beautiful bouquet of flowers. I was hoping to find out what they were and if they had special meaning."

"I will try. What did they look like?"

"They were white with perfectly formed petals, similar in shape to a water lily, but much smaller, and with an irregular stem."

"Let me show you." She led him across the dirt floor of the store to a wooden cutting bench. She pointed to bunches of jasmine and asked, "Are these what you saw?"

"Yes," he said, reaching out to touch one of the petals.

Her hand intercepted his as she said, "You must not. It will leave a stain."

His heart raced with the electricity produced by her fingers touching the back of his hand. It was as if his senses had been immediately filled to their limit and were about to burst. Struggling for composure he said, "I've never seen them before. They are extraordinary. There's nothing like them where I come from in Russia."

He was unsure of his next steps. He wondered if he should buy them or tell her that she was the lady he saw on the street with the flowers. Instead, he decided to ask, "Can you tell me about their meaning?"

"Do you know of *hana kotoba*?" she asked.

"No, I do not."

"It is our Japanese flower language. In Japan, a samurai considers himself a person highly sensitive to art and beauty. They use the language to express their desires in their kimonos, as women do. He treasures flowers and takes them as a part of life as a warrior."

"The jasmine, what does it mean?"

"It is offered as a gesture to express gracefulness in the person receiving the flowers. His intention is to express friendship. Is there someone you would like to present a bouquet to?"

"Yes. Yes, there definitely is."

He left nervously after paying for the flowers. After two hours of pacing the streets of Shimoda rehearsing what to say, he returned to the shop to present the bouquet to Okimi, although at that time he had yet to know her name.

In the months that followed, Vladimir returned to shop regularly. He paid special attention to Okimi's father and mother, presenting them with gifts when visiting the shop. He knew that Japanese culture frowned on mixed relationships and Okimi's father and mother could be shunned in their community if the relationship wasn't approved of. Initially, Vladimir barely acknowledged Okimi in favor of small talk with her father. Her parents were impressed with his Japanese and the thoughtfulness of his various gifts. Despite his lack of interaction with Okimi, their infatuation grew. His intelligence, patience, and quiet demeanor helped him bridge the chasm between his world of Lenin and Stalin and her world of the deity emperor Shōwa. Chaperoned walks gave way to the privilege of Vladimir being allowed to take her on walks alone along the river after her work was done. His hardened emotions from his years as a NKVD agent slowly relaxed with each encounter. Why he had allowed this to happen, he couldn't answer, as he knew that his world would eventually destroy their relationship.

"You're not happy tonight, Vladimir-san. Am I doing something wrong?"

"No, no, no. It is not you." Their relationship had not progressed beyond holding hands, but at that moment his need to kiss her was beyond control. He cupped her chin with his hands and looked deeply into her brown eyes. He said, "You are the most perfect flower in the field." With that their lips met, softly at first, yet with an unsure familiarity. They broke and smiled, allowing their bodies to reposition as close as possible on the bench. Their next kiss was complete with the passion of an unfulfilled love and a commitment to be one.

"I love you, Okimi, very much," he said while holding her hands. "But I'm afraid it isn't enough."

"What do you mean?"

He wasn't quite sure what he meant. He only knew the pain of having just received the crushing news that day of his reassignment. The war was changing everything. He had become greatly valued by the NKVD hierarchy as he had become recognized as a trusted comrade with important talents necessary to the Federation's future international security.

"I have been ordered back to the Vladivostok military base to begin training as a pilot in the NKVD. I must leave for Russia tomorrow. I don't know when we will be together again."

The sorrow in her eyes broke his heart. She desperately reached for another kiss as if that would make what she just heard go away.

Vladimir returned to Shimoda only once, briefly. He and Okimi pledged their lives together, and he promised to return one day. The intensity of the war eliminated all possibility of that reunion occurring any time soon. Years of flying security missions for the war effort, coupled with extensive language training, prepared him for his current assignment coordinating the movements of Russian pilots and aircraft under the Lend-Lease Program at Ladd. More importantly, Russian counter-espionage intelligence had identified the United States' activities in Alaska as critical to the Federation's national security. An agent of Vladimir's skill, with access to critical procedures and knowledge of flight operations, would be an important investment.

By now, Vladimir had drunk more coffee than he wanted. He rarely allowed himself the luxury of reflecting on what life might be like if he and Okimi ever saw that day they dreamt of so fervently years ago. Generally he was secure with his role with the NKVD, but at times like this his resolve weakened. Sitting in an empty mess hall in a foreign country, hoping for an outcome that was not likely to be, weakened the soul. He stood, inhaled deeply from his cigarette, and mentally packaged his dream, carefully so not to tarnish it, where he could retrieve it again as he had so many times in the past.

CHAPTER 11

"What's up with Robert?" Red asked Nick once they found smooth air after takeoff.

"What do you mean?"

"He's got a burr under his saddle, right sure. I know I'm not the main hoss on this plane, but a little respect should come with the second seat. I might as well have been the hombre hired to shovel shit in the barn the way he responded to my simple good morning."

"I'll talk to him. We don't need an attitude on board with the luminaries we're carting around today. Take over for a few minutes."

Their early-morning flight had taken them to the southeast of the Yukon Flats area, north of Fairbanks. They were to escort some ranking army brass and important civilians on a sightseeing tour of the Yukon Valley. They flew for about forty-five minutes northeast. They would turn around and make their approach with the sun rising at their back. The Yukon River was their marker as they flew at five thousand feet—lower than normal, since Nick's instructions were to give these men a visual understanding of the terrain below. The early cloud cover was clearing and the river's extraordinary positioning in the valley was a striking centerpiece, even for these experienced pilots, with the morning sun's rays reflecting off the White Mountains to the west. The Yukon River was very important to the development of Alaska because it traversed the entire state from the Yukon Territory in the east to the Bering Sea in the west. Being the longest river in the region, it was the principal means of transportation during the Klondike Gold Rush. Nick spotted a paddle-wheel riverboat out the starboard windows and used it to engage his guests. "My name's Nick Morgan. I'm your captain for this little excursion."

"Good morning, Captain," several of the men responded in unison. "We're a little informal on these trips, so if you don't mind I'd like to introduce my crew." Pointing to Robert, Nick said, "This is Flight Service PFC Robert Endo. He's got about a year and a half with the USAAF and will take care of pretty much anything you need while on board." Robert's sullen expression went unnoticed. "I'm Captain Nick Morgan, as I said before, on loan from Northwest Airlines and serving in the Air Transport Command. The co-pilot keeping us on course is Red Johnson. I'm going to let him do a lot of the flying today since he got his wings as a crop duster in Oklahoma, and I was told you wanted an up-close view of the area. If he had his way, you'd be shaking hands with some of the locals we'll pass along the way." The men laughed. While Nick's friendly nature put people at ease, his unmistakable sense of control gave them confidence.

The major with the gold-leaf cluster spoke first. "I'm Major James Gordon and these men are my guests on this project," he said, indicating the other man in uniform and two other men in civvies. "As you know from your briefing papers, we're not at liberty to discuss our objective, Captain. We do acknowledge your help, though." His unwillingness to introduce the others made the point that they weren't interested in striking up any kind of a friendship.

"Well, before I leave you, I want you to know that flying conditions are near perfect today, so we'll be at our best and still get you back home in one piece. Something I wanted to point out to you gentlemen, before we miss it, is the paddle-wheel riverboat traffic still in use. The Yukon River is the only highway down there. It's been busy since the gold-rush days. And, it's a pretty handy guide for us pilots, also." The men showed interest in seeing the river. With their safety belts unfastened in the exceptionally smooth air, the two men on the port side got up and leaned over the seats to get a good look.

"How busy is the river today with the mining pretty much played out?" The gentleman asking the question was the one dressed in civilian clothing—khaki slacks and a plaid flannel shirt—and was probably in his early forties.

"You're right about the gold being played out, but the mining isn't completely dead. Nickel and copper are still being pulled out pretty regularly. The locals also rely on the river as a supply line for most of what they need to survive on over the winter. Right now, there's still a fair amount of activity. But, by mid-November when the river starts to freeze, transportation shuts down fast. From then on, dog sleds and bush planes are the only way in or out until about May."

"Who lives down there?"

"Mostly Eskimos of Russian descent, a few contractors, and some hard-core wilderness types. I also understand that the native village of Venetie is still active. Some talk of protecting the land and encouraging additional families to settle in the village. That's about the extent of my knowledge."

"Thanks for the introductions and information, Captain. We'll let you know of our specific interests." The major turned his shoulder away from Nick, leaving no ambiguity about the conversation being over.

Nick indicated to Robert as they moved forward in the cabin that he wanted to talk. "You seem a bit uncomfortable, Private. What's up?"

Nick only used rank in his discussion with his crew when he wanted absolute attention.

Robert's demeanor was defensive, shifting on both feet and barely maintaining eye contact with his senior officer. "It's personal, sir."

"When you are on my ship, nothing is personal. Both your co-captain and captain can see it in your face."

He shifted some more, hands in his pocket, clearly allowing himself to become upset. "Permission to speak freely, sir?"

"Granted."

"I'm not sure I can handle another mail call, sir."

"Meaning?"

"Yesterday, sir. I received a letter from my parents and everything other than 'hello' and 'we love you' was cut out. It's not fair what's happening to them!" Robert exclaimed. "And now, I see the way these men look at me . . . like I'm some sort of traitor."

"Take it easy, soldier. I'll see if I can help you get better information when we get back, but you can't let it affect your responsibilities on this flight. We clear?" Nick disliked being so direct, but he knew he needed to be firm as Robert had become darker and more isolated recently, both on and off the job.

Robert's lack of a response raised Nick's need for an answer. "Private?"

"Yes, sir. I'll keep it in check."

"Now, why don't you offer to get those men some coffee . . . with a smile?"

When Robert returned, he saw that the four men had fashioned a map table out of several collapsed seats. He served each a cup of coffee. It was easy to see the area of the men's focus was the vast wilderness section northeast of Fort Yukon. All conversation stopped until the coffee was served, a second trip for more sugar was accomplished, and he left.

After several hours flying over relatively uncharted portions of the Yukon Flats and northwest to Chandler just south of the Brooks Range, the major walked to the cockpit and addressed Nick directly.

"Captain, I'd like a course adjustment to the northeast toward an unnamed range of mountains about one hundred miles south of the Artic Ocean. Can you find them?"

"Yes, sir."

"Strange sight-seeing tour, don't you think, Captain?" Red said after the major left. Red had been particularly quiet about the trip until now.

"My orders didn't disclose anything that would tip off their objective. Leave with a full tank of gas, take them where they want, and bring them back in one piece. That's pretty much it. It is hard to imagine what the major's up to."

"Where'd they come from?"

"Some place in New Mexico. Alamogordo, I think their flight plan said."

"I know that area. It's the desert's version of what we're flying over right now. It made the dust bowl, where I grew up in Perry, look like some life-after-death, celestial oasis for camel jockeys." His broad smile, combined with the sun's ray catching the corner of his eyes, softened the Okie tone to his voice. "Did you notice anything else?"

"Just that one of their bags is marked, CLASSIFIED: J. ROBERT OPPENHEIMER—PHYSICIST. Obviously, above our pay grade."

The remainder of the flight went without incident. Only a few questions were asked by the group from New Mexico, and they were specifically directed at Captain Morgan while separate from the others. In all cases Robert and Red were not included. They were questions about accessibility, weather conditions during the fall, wildlife populations, and activities of the locals, if there were any, of specific locations they passed over. Nick answered as best he could, but much of the area they were flying over hadn't officially been mapped. Any knowledge of the outposts came from anecdotal tidbits from the few trappers that bush pilots encountered when making supply deliveries and hide-cartage trips to Fairbanks. Pilots, like Nick, were a practical source of information, as well, for their occasional flights and related observations while serving the army in Alaska.

———

Enroute to Fairbanks from Yukon Flats
October 14, 1943

My Dear Martha,

We had an interesting trip today. Can't tell you much other than it was over uncharted country. We passed over old gold mining areas near the eastern border of Alaska. Just about every creek bed in the area has been dredged. They are inoperative now on account of the war. There are trails, roads, and sluices all over the hills there. It certainly must have changed a lot from the virgin country it once was back before the '90 gold rush. From there we flew to the Brooks Range and then up to the Artic Ocean. Very desolate. We get good radio reception in the air. I sure use it a lot, and I'm glad you bought it for me. Playing "Begin the Beguine" now. Heating the batteries after they're dead increases the chemical activity, and they last for a while longer then. War news has still been discouraging.

Yours,
Nick

CHAPTER 12

"Doesn't make a lot of sense to me," Robert explained to Vladimir while they continued their lunch in the mess hall. "It's hard to imagine why we flew over so much useless landscape yesterday. I mean, we're fighting a war and the army is wasting time on a sight-seeing tour . . . with a major no less."

After lunch Vladimir opened his second pack of cigarettes. He lit up as Robert told him about the flight. His questions were subtle and gently maneuvered Robert through a recollection of the entire flight—even the part about being chastised by the Captain because of his attitude. He had to be careful not to show too much interest, though. "Big waste of time, yes? Maybe Japan will launch full-scale attack on Fort Yukon. Just like Dutch Harbor." Both men laughed. Robert lightened up a bit while they lingered over coffee.

"My father would have same kind of visits at Vladivostok. Many staff people from Kremlin would always waste his time. Difficult to tell their purpose, but always a waste of time. Like your Major Gordon, what could he know from New Mexico that would benefit war effort here?"

"Maybe Fort Yukon is classified and Mr. Oppenheimer is some famous geologist who will discover a new gold vein to fund the war effort?" Robert's question was filled with sarcasm, yet only outlandish ideas seemed to make sense.

Vladimir's weekly report back to Moscow included a summary of their discussion. It was his job to submit an encrypted message of everything that went on, regardless of its apparent importance. He knew from his experience as a listening agent that a team of people at NKVD headquarters under the command of Agent Andrey Sirak meticulously pieced together bits of information from hundreds of listening posts in at least eight countries. To his knowledge, he was one of only a dozen agents positioned in the United States. The relationship with the United States was simply one crafted out of practical need. There could be no basis of political friendship with their vastly differing ideologies. Lenin's pre-WWI Bolshevik revolution had seen to that. Now, Stalin and Roosevelt shared only one common interest in what the Russian's called the Great Patriotic War and that was to defeat the Third Reich. Beyond that, each government's self-interest took over.

Vladimir's efforts had a direct affect on the war with Germany. He trained the Russian P-38 pilots in Fairbanks who then dealt strategic blows against the German First Panzer Division, Fourth Panzer Division, and a reconstituted Sixth Army. Vladimir's information on the performance of each of the Russian pilots in P-38 training also supported their successful deployment. Generally, his weekly reports were consumed with this kind of tactical information, but occasionally he combined this information with his general observations covering the occurrences taking place at Ladd and Elmendorf Airfields. The mention of the Fort Yukon tour led by Major Gordon and J. Robert Oppenheimer's classified bag and civilian involvement would be detailed in the "other items of interest category" in his next report. Sending the reports was easy for Vladimir because he had a ready-made shuttle service provided by the constant deliveries of P-38s from Alaska to Russia.

Only he and Agent Sirak knew the combination to the lock securing the ammo box used to carry the report. Once received, NKVD headquarters would direct their efforts in an encrypted reply communication, if need be, based on Agent Sirak's priorities.

Three days after sending his report Vladimir received the following message.

```
RETURN IMMEDIATELY TO MOSCOW FOR FURTHER
INTERROGATION REGARDING LAST REPORT. REPORT TO
ME DIRECTLY UPON ARRIVAL.

AGENT ANDREY SIRAK
```

To be recalled abruptly came as a shock to Vladimir considering the priority of his involvement in the P-38 program. And, he couldn't ever remember Agent Sirak sending his orders directly.

Two days later Vladimir arrived at the Balashikha army base outside Moscow at 4:00 p.m. A driver met him on the tarmac and chauffeured him directly to Lubyanka Square, which was just past Red Square. His post in rural Alaska did not prepare him for the formality and imposing design of this immense, yellow-masonry building that covered an entire city block. Noticeable also was Stalin's destruction of many old churches that once decorated the area around the square, which he had heard about from other agents. The combination of this destruction and the onerous presence of the remaining NKVD headquarters' building, known for its torture cells, reaffirmed a sense of fear experienced by many during the Chetkan period of internal spying and policing.

He had very little sleep during his series of flights covering more than four thousand miles and the international dateline, but he knew that it would have to come later. Right now, his mental framework, influenced by past experiences with Chetkan brutality and coupled with the intimidation of twenty-four–hour security surveillance over present NKVD operations, left Vladimir a little wobbly in the knees. He couldn't shake the feeling that he had made a horrific mistake in his last report. He'd gone over it multiple times during his flights, however, and found nothing unusual. He was escorted into the building and through a series of poorly lit hallways to the third floor. His escort gestured toward a simple wood-frame chair where he was expected to wait. No one talked.

After ten minutes of waiting a harsh voice called out from beyond the door: "show him in!" The military admin on duty snapped to attention with a look of uncertainty on his face. The man behind the door was clearly someone to be feared.

"Agent Sirak is ready for you," the admin stated as if Vladimir was not cleared to hear the original request.

Vladimir Dubisskiy stood at attention upon entering the corner office. His gaze encompassed a large, elegantly furnished room with mahogany-paneled walls and many matching tables, which he assumed were for briefings or closer observation of maps. There were two large windows adorned with elegant blue drapery with red piping and red sashes, matching the colors of the Russian flag. These windows overlooked the Red Square.

The entire atmosphere was in contrast to the starkness he witnessed elsewhere in the building, indicating that Agent Sirak held an important position in counterintelligence. More commanding than anything, however, was an exceptionally large map of the United States hanging on a sidewall. Otherwise, the office was very efficient and reflected a man well in control of the events surrounding him.

"Please be seated," Agent Sirak said, motioning to a table near the large map. At about fifty, six feet two, and in excellent physical condition, the man commanded a formidable presence. "We have not met, no?" He extended the wooden cigarette box after removing one for himself.

"Thank you." Both men paused to light up. Vladimir exhaled a lungful of smoke and continued. "No, sir. I don't believe we have met, at least not to my knowledge."

"Your reputation precedes you," said Sirak. "I have admired the attention to detail in your work for many years." Vladimir noticeably relaxed as the tension from the anticipation of an unknown wrongdoing on his part drained from his neck and shoulders. "I even remember Shimoda. It was your first real assignment, I believe . . . barely into your twenties. Am I right?"

"Yes, sir."

Agent Dubisskiy was shocked to hear Agent Sirak describe his involvement with remarkable detail. Agent Sirak's description of the consulate general's greed and the intricate network of operatives covering up the gold-smuggling operation was as if he had read Agent Dubisskiy's report yesterday. "It was the details of your report then that struck me as commendable," Agent Sirak concluded. What riveted Vladimir's attention was the lack of waste in anything he said. Each word was chosen for a point and well coordinated with body language and gestures that marked him as a strong leader. What Vladimir didn't know was that Agent Sirak was the originator of the Special Section of Counterintelligence of the NKVD, which he conceived of from first-hand discussions with Stalin immediately following the invasion of Germany. Agent Sirak's place in Stalin's inner circle of advisors, where state secrets were regularly discussed, was a closely guarded relationship, which left no room for mistakes.

"Have you ever reconnected with that lovely young Japanese girl— what was her name? Okimi Nakamura, I believe."

Vladimir's shock at this intimate level of knowledge was obvious, and he could barely reply. "Only once, regrettably. Several years ago."

"Come now, Agent Dubisskiy. You are not surprised that we knew your situation, are you?"

"That was many years ago, sir, and I am surprised that it came up in this discussion when, in fact, I have never discussed her with anyone."

"She still works in her father's flower shop. She's fine and still single. Considering the magnitude and direction of the war, however, that may not be important. I thought you'd like to know. You see, Agent, I too am preoccupied with the details."

"Thank you for the information." He swallowed as if to provide a delay in order to protect the many thoughts flooding his mind. Okimi still working in that little shop, the sweet smell of the flowers, their beautiful colors and arrangements, and, most of all, the perfection of the white jasmine all struggled for attention in his emotions, none of which could be released.

"On to the matters at hand," the senior agent said, moving his attention to the large map of the United States. "I'm sure you are tired from your trip, so I will make this discussion brief. We can follow up tomorrow with additional questions you may have. Do you know what has our interest, Agent Dubisskiy?"

"Sir, I've read that report a dozen times and I cannot find it."

"Let me enlighten you to one of the significant developments in America. I'm sure you're familiar with U.S. geography, but I'll refresh you with the whereabouts of a small mountain town in New Mexico called Los Alamos here." He pointed to a dot on a map, which placed the town about thirty miles northwest of Santa Fe.

Classified, Vladimir instantly recalled as he remembered his discussion with Robert and the seeming irrelevance of the New Mexico connection took center stage.

"Let me fill in the pieces for you, Agent Dubisskiy. Since 1942, General Leslie Groves and physicist J. Robert Oppenheimer have been leading the U.S. project to design and build the first atomic bomb. Apparently, Mr. Oppenheimer had some boyhood connection to the geology of the Southwest and a school he briefly attended. As it turned out, this very school has facilities that suit the United States government purpose perfectly for this very secret project. If you don't already know, this project has enormous implications for the outcome of the war, and probably the political climate of our world for years to come. Before I go further however, tell me more about this Robert Endo."

As Agent Sirak listened to Vladimir's response, he mentally categorized the thorough description of Robert's upbringing, schooling, current responsibilities in the army, and psychological pressures stemming from his parents being interned. Vladimir smiled and relaxed during his description of their almost daily routine of eating together and discussing the happenings of the base.

"This Robert has become a friend, no?"

"In some ways he has, sir. Our discussions help me improve my English and keep me in tune with American culture in addition to base activities. We maintain sarcasm throughout our discussion as an amusement. It helps him talk."

"You haven't asked as yet, Agent Dubisskiy, but for your information I believe that "classified" may also refer to Yukon Flats." Vladimir's eyebrows raised in notable interest.

"You understand of course, that if it is, finding out why that team of people was flying around Yukon Flats has become the most important element of your assignment. Information related to activities in the area and how it is connected to Los Alamos has the highest importance to the national security of the Federation."

Vladimir had a peripheral knowledge about the race to develop such a bomb through his counterintelligence briefings, but he was never considered close enough to the politics of the project to be informed or involved first-hand. He basically knew that Germany, America, Japan, and Russia all wanted to have the weapon first as a tool to assert military supremacy. Beyond that he knew little. "I'll need to be more informed in order to understand what to look for, what questions to ask . . . what questions not to ask."

"Precisely. Over the next three days you will be exposed to everything you need to know. Pay attention. There aren't any textbooks. Once back in the United States you will report your findings directly to me, no one else. In code, of course. There can be no compromise involving this assignment. Are we clear?"

"Yes, sir."

"I'm sure you are exhausted at this point. Arrangements have been made for you to stay on premise. We will meet tomorrow for breakfast at 0630. Have a good rest, Agent Dubisskiy."

The door to the office opened in perfect timing with the end of Agent Sirak's sentence. The uniformed admin gestured in a way that clearly indicated the end of the meeting and offered to lead him from Agent Sirak's office back through the massive complex again, but this time to a room where he could rest. As he followed, crossing many corridors and up several flights of stairs, it wasn't the excitement of classified U.S. locations that fired the neurons in his brain—it was the fragrant smell of Okimi's hair, fresh from a rainwater bath, that renewed the bond held for so many years.

CHAPTER 13

Vladimir lay on the flat, hard mattress trying to wake from his night's rest. He barely remembered going to sleep. Despite the discomfort endured he had slept straight through the night, courtesy of the events over the last few days. His shoulder hurt from being in the same position too long; it almost felt dislocated. *Must have slept on it wrong*, he thought, as he rotated it back to life while sitting on the edge of the bed. In the morning light he could see that his eight-foot-by-eight-foot room was more of a cell. The lack of window coverings, other than vertical steel bars preventing an exit, enhanced the austere accommodations. No toilet or basin. No closet. Just the bed and a small desk. The only light in the room was activated by a wall switch and came from a bare bulb hanging on a drop cord from the ceiling. He reflected on the comparatively soft duty he had enjoyed while in Alaska when contrasted with the meagerness of homeland hospitality.

Outside his door he heard shuffling and then an abrupt knock. After pulling on his pants, he opened the door. Sirak's admin saluted and offered directions down the hall to a communal bathroom. "Agent Sirak will be ready to see you in twenty minutes." There was none of the social dialogue he had come accustomed to while working with the

Americans, no acknowledgement that he had traveled a great distance and that his body clock thought it was still the middle of the night; there was just the hard stare of a comrade not wishing to disappoint his superior.

"Tell Agent Sirak I'll meet him for breakfast at six thirty, as agreed. Come back here in fifteen minutes, and I'll be ready," Vladimir replied with an authoritative tone, still wiping the sleep from his eyes. As the admin quickly departed another soldier stepped from around the corner and remained on duty outside Vladimir's room. It came as no surprise to him that he had most likely been under guard all night.

"Good morning, Agent Dubisskiy. I trust you rested well?" Agent Sirak said upon Vladimir's arrival at the table set for breakfast in a private dining area. "Please be seated. Our sleeping accommodations aren't much I'm afraid, but I doubt you noticed after such a long trip."

"Thank you. All I needed was something flat." Despite the immense power this man had garnered with his direct connection to Stalin, Vladimir felt relatively at ease with him. Maybe it was the agent's comfortable directness or his willingness to communicate man to man without the shield of the office. Maybe it was just the fact they both shared a common role in their agent experiences. Regardless, Vladimir was beginning to feel a sense of importance with his new, although not totally comprehended, responsibility. After all, very few agents could claim they shared a private breakfast with the head of Russian Counterintelligence. Yet, he also knew that he was being drawn in, the way a cobra dances with its victims until within striking range. There were no friendships here—no false pretenses.

Vladimir was very hungry and was happy for the generous breakfast.

He couldn't remember the last time he had had good *bliny*. The traditional egg and flour crepe-like dish was perfectly done and accompanied by caviar and lox. A second course of *oladyi* pancakes served with sugar and jam and sausages was more than he could handle. Over tea, both men smoked and enjoyed the brief break from their tension-filled world.

"I hope our food makes up for our lack of accommodations."

"It's beyond excellent," Vladimir replied. "It has been a long time since I've had such a meal." He knew the gesture of providing a variety of well-prepared foods imparted importance to what was expected of him.

"We have several people that you will meet in training for your new assignment. First will be Igor Kurchatov, the scientific director developing a working design for an atomic bomb. Do you know what I mean, Agent Dubisskiy, by an 'atomic bomb'?"

"I know it's immense in its destructive capabilities, but I only know about it in general terms."

"In simple scientific terms the destruction is caused by an isotope of uranium-235 reaching an explosive critical-mass reaction. It's not only its ability to eliminate a city as large as Berlin that matters, though. We know the German, American, and Japanese scientific communities are all being challenged to build one. Stalin, however, has been more consumed with the western front and the war with Hitler and still must be convinced of the future for such a weapon. But believe me: the first country to develop the atom bomb will have control over the world. Right now, the Americans and British are our allies, but that will end with the defeat of Germany.

"Anyway, Comrade Kurchatov will give you the necessary background to recognize the intelligence we need to observe the American progress."

Vladimir knew all too well through his years as an agent that the paranoia of Stalin politics was always a factor in the progress of any significant undertaking. The standard of proof in any discussion with Stalin was not related to the question of whether the event was factually true, but whether Stalin believed you were lying about it. This always added unnecessary delay to the development of strategic events. Every person that Agent Dubisskiy met would need to vet him to make sure he wasn't a possible political adversary. "How do you suggest I gain their trust for this assignment in the short time available?" Agent Dubisskiy asked, knowing that developing a trusting enough relationship to work with a new agent usually took months.

"Your involvement comes with the support of my office. They will not set traps of deceit or they will answer to me."

It was all Vladimir could ask for, although the endorsement from Sirak would not eliminate the paranoia. It would only heighten the consequence. A betrayal against Vladimir would also involve Sirak, but a betrayal by Sirak would put Vladimir in the middle.

"The other man you'll see today is Lavrenti Beria. He will coordinate the resources necessary to make such a project successful—elements like the supply of uranium, electric power, and ore. I think if you become familiar with our challenges, you will be more skilled in knowing what to look for in America. These men have been given instructions to make their staff available to ensure your knowledge is complete."

"Thank you. Who are the other comrades involved?"

"They will contact you as your progress requires knowledge of them. Remember one thing!" Sirak slammed an open hand on the surface of his desk. "Alert me immediately of any individual who references the project code name, 'First Lightning.' That will be your trigger to bring them into your circle, as they will already know who you are."

"First Lightning," Vladimir said in confirmation.

"Yes, but under no circumstances are you to use this name without my authority. In the meantime, I suggest you take advantage of your training in languages by offering your services to teach Russian at Ladd and Elmendorf. Our intelligence suggests that interest will be high among some of the officers, and your services will be favorably received if kept on an informal basis. It seems that the Americans talk loosely when together. Blend in and you might overhear something of importance."

Vladimir returned to his post in Fairbanks the third week of November, less than a week after his meeting with Agent Sirak. He needed time to think through the implications of his added assignment. Robert's understanding of base activities would help, but Vladimir found out that Robert had left on furlough and would not return until the end of the month.

CHAPTER 14

Annette Island, Canada
November 21, 1943

My Dear Martha,
Couldn't get past Sitka or Juneau yesterday as it was closed down
tight. Had to come back to this muskeg island. Everything here
is built on muskeg and shakes like jelly when the trucks run over
it. We're all lying in bed now. The wind is blowing outside and the
heavy drizzle that started last night still persists. I'm going to sleep
now—will mail it at the next Pan Am stop.

Yours,
Nick

The port of Prince Rupert was deemed to be especially important as an American sub-embarkation port and ammunition dump, but Canada's ability to defend it against attack was very limited. The airfield constructed on Annette Island, Canada in '42 was only sixty miles to the north of the port and started as an "on-loan" Civilian Conservation Corps (CCC) project, a leftover work program sponsored by Franklin Roosevelt during the late '30s as a substitute military build-up strategy to please a congress that wouldn't approve legitimate military troops. Flight activity on the island increased dramatically following the June 3, 1943, Japanese attack on Dutch Harbor, just before Nick arrived in Alaska. War zone escalations wreaked havoc on the facilities. Permanent housing was completely inadequate. Everyone slept in tents. Nick hated the tents because the oil burners froze up when it got too cold. The good news was this CCC camp broke protocol and had a mess hall where a fellow could get a beer.

Nick was breaking in a new co-pilot, Fred Dollimer from Weirton, Pennsylvania, who was very inexperienced and abnormally introverted. Conversation, even in the shared tent, was sparse.

"Hey, Fred," Nick said. "What do you think about our navy's efforts in Truk?" The war news was about all they shared outside of flight duties. In this case, Truk, the forward headquarters of the Japanese Combined Fleet in the Caroline Islands, about six hundred miles southeast of Guam, was the one bright spot for discussion. On November 11, the navy's attack on the base crippled the Japanese fleet.

"Half their cruisers and half their fighter planes were lost, as I understand it," Fred replied. "With Admiral Koga's flagship and operations headquarters on the battleship *Musashi* in the bay at the time, it was great news." Fred prided himself on having his facts straight. Since Koga was Yamamoto's replacement as commander in chief of the Combined Fleet this strike by the navy was significant. Saying nothing more, Fred turned out the light on his side of the tent and rolled over to get some shut-eye, which gave Nick time to himself. Talking with Fred was like having a conversation with a good parts manual—a minimalist use of words to convey a thought with no expression or desire for interaction based on unfounded opinion. With any luck they would get out of Annette and on to Seattle tomorrow, Nick hoped.

Seattle, Washington
November 23, 1943

My Dear Martha,

Saw the ferry when we came in last evening. It is camouflaged now. Ceiling out of Juneau yesterday morning was pretty tight, but we skimmed out over the water through the fiords and channels and made it to the States. Seattle is full of air-raid shelters and traffic lights only have a narrow slit of light showing. All signs are turned out in the evening, of course.

Yours,
Nick

Nick loved his trips to Seattle, despite the occasional stopover on Annette Island. Living conditions at the base were good, and off-base activities were interesting. Once Nick checked in he decided to "mosey" over to the officer's club. He would have never "moseyed" anywhere before, but since he'd been flying with Red all kinds of new words—"mosey," "June bug," "chicken neck," and "sodbuster"—were creeping into his vocabulary. He laughed to himself at the thought that Red could probably use them all in one sentence and still communicate a coherent thought. It was around eight o'clock by the time Nick ordered a beer.

"Are you still nursing that same beer, Captain?" the somewhat familiar voice asked from behind. "And I can see that it is captain." Nick swiveled to see none other than Captain Marshall Smith, his first captain, flashing a big smile and extended hand.

"I'll be tarred 'n' feathered. It is a small war. How are you, Captain?" The men shook hands, enthusiastically expressing the genuine gratitude that only men at war could understand through a chance encounter. Seeing a familiar face reassured both parties that there was hope for a favorable outcome to the war. Upon catching a glimpse of the gold-leaf cluster, Nick quickly interjected, "Sorry, Major. Didn't notice the promotion. I hope you'll say 'yes' to a cold one on me to celebrate?"

"You're damned right I will, soldier. By the way, have you ever been back to the Shisho Volcano?"

"As a matter of fact, I won my steak dinner back off a co-pilot from Oklahoma." Their laughter exposed just about every wrinkle on their faces. Major Smith sat down with ease at the table.

"I thought you were in Edmonton training new pilots?"

"I was. And believe me, they were new. But, the army's got me on a new assignment here. Not sure what to make of it yet."

"How so?"

"You're familiar with the big Boeing plant, right?"

"You mean the one under disguise?"

"Yeah, that one." Most of the pilots had flown near enough to Boeing's largest production plant to see one of the most unique camouflage efforts of the war. Seattle was the home to the Bremerton Ship Yards and Boeing's aircraft plants, which were producing twelve B-19s a day in one plant alone. People were afraid that they were a primary target for a major Japanese attack. The plant had been covered with an elaborate mesh of wood, chickenwire, canvas, and natural materials to make it look like a normal Seattle neighborhood, sitting as peaceful as you can be on a hillside—at least from an enemy pilot's point of view. "Ingenious, by the way," said Major Smith, "designed by some guy named William Bain. Just like a movie set.

"Well, it seems that we just plain run out of pilots to test these planes and shuttle them into use, so some brigadier general has it in his mind to train women to do the job. The program's called WASP—Women Air Force Service Pilots."

"You may not believe me when I say this, Major, but that's one hell of an idea!" Nick responded. The major was unaccustomed to an enthusiastic response when discussing the program.

"You're the first person I've heard say that. And, I hope you're right because they got me running the show for these ladies to get airworthy right quick."

"My excitement is because of one Martha Morgan, my wife. I never saw anyone, including myself, handle the E-2 we flew the way she could. No reason she couldn't fly anything you threw at her." Nick knew that Martha was struggling with the pregnancy, the need for security and family, and the opportunities she was missing out on. This WASP program would make Martha ache even more for the freedom she craved.

"I'm glad to hear you say that, as this program has a lot of the regulars upset. Ego, I would say, is at the heart of matters. It could be people are jealous of this Jackie Cochran, who will be coming on board to help in the training, too. She is one hell of a pilot, but it will still take more than one pilot for the program to work if we're going to get these planes where they can do the most good.

"Hell, it doesn't stop there, Nick. Why, there are women all over Seattle who have taken over critical war jobs, including working for

Boeing on the assembly line for the B-29 Superfortress. 'Rosie the Riveter' is what they are being called."

Nick raised a glass to the major and said, "I'll bet you a steak dinner that you'll get a silver cluster for how well these ladies perform in flight."

"That's a bet I'd like to win." While Major Smith wasn't the kind to bet on a career promotion, the idea of becoming Lieutenant Colonel Smith did sound good.

Nick thought of how excited Martha would be to be part of this program. With the baby coming, however, it was just out of the question. *Martha would have been perfect*, he thought, *someone who Jackie Cochran would be impressed with.*

"What's next for you, Nick?"

"Just a long-overdue leave for the holidays, I hope. I've got to ship some boys out to Bethel tomorrow. And from there, I'll likely be on to Nome and then back to Anchorage. After that, timing should be just about right to do a Thanksgiving furlough shuttle to Fairbanks and on to Minneapolis."

Once up on top the next day and with a three-quarter empty plane on their flight to Bethel, Nick thought it a perfect time for a little flying experience for Fred. It also would give Nick time to re-read his letter from Martha that he had received at the Pan Am mail stop in Seattle. It was his habit to save these letters and enjoy them over and over.

November 12, 1943

My Dearest Nick,

It seems like this stretch of absence from you has been the hardest of all. I try to stay busy with my work at Sears, but explaining the use of tools to women who have never used them is frustrating. I know they are trying to do their best with their husbands away, but it gets pretty boring.

My mom came over to talk today, but we don't seem to be able to communicate very well. She knows that you're the most important thing for me, and, well, she can't seem to get past our eloping. Don't get me wrong, Nick, you're the best thing that's ever happened to me, but I don't want to lose my mom either. We need to figure something out when you get home.

Our baby's doing a pretty good job of keeping me sick. Every morning it's the same thing! You'd think with all the vomiting that I'd be able to hold my weight steady. Oh, no! I've gained five and one-half pounds already and my clothes are beginning to not fit. I can't wait for you to come home, but by then I'll be as big as a balloon. You'll still love me, won't you? Things will be better next April when the baby arrives. Do you think it will be a boy or a girl? I hope it's a boy for you. I like the name "George." Or, maybe "Henry," after your dad? No, "Henry Morgan" sounds like a maker of brandy. Maybe "Nick, Jr."? That's a good name, too.

I really liked the pictures you sent of the new Alaskan Highway, if that's what they're going to call it after the military gets done with it. Thanks for telling me that the pictures in Life Magazine were from Adak. My girlfriends at work think that Alaska is wonderful and that the pictures are all so beautiful. They imagine us together and believe I'm lucky being married to someone who does exciting things like you. It's hard for them to understand how lonely it gets at home and how much I'd like to be there doing things with you. If it wasn't for the baby, I'd do anything to be there.

Thanksgiving is going to be so special for us and I can't wait until you're home. Tell me as soon as you get your assignment. Let's not fight over anything. I wonder if Bud will be able to get time off so they can be here, too. That would make it even more special.

I love you very much and I can't wait for this stupid war to get over so our life can really begin!

Love & Kisses,
Martha

"Do you have someone back home, Fred?" Nick asked as he pulled himself out of thought about Martha and the baby.

"Do you mean a girlfriend or someone like that?"

"Yes, I guess I did."

"Naw, I spend most of my time hunting. Deer, mostly. Never was very good with the girls. Had one once for about two weeks, but we never talked or did anything."

"Maybe you'll meet someone out here?"

"Not really looking, but it could happen I suppose. I think I'll stay on after the war, though. Maybe I can find a girl that likes to hunt and camp."

"This would be the place for that," Nick said privately questioning the thought of whether it was better to be in the war single or attached. Both had their advantages, he considered, but his choice was that it was better to be attached. From the sounds of Martha's letter, she would agree, although the circumstances involving a pregnant wife are completely different from those of a girlfriend. He smiled, reflecting on the image of her plump body and pretty face.

They refueled in Anchorage and were back in the air within the hour with a full load of relief troops for the supply depot in Bethel. Other than the harsh weather, the duty was pretty good. Bethel was one of the closest points in the military supply chain to the Aleutian Islands in what had become known as the Thousand-Mile War, triggered by the Japanese attack on Dutch Harbor. For most of these boys, it would be like working in a cross-dock shipping facility, loading and reloading planes and ships for various destinations. The airfield had grown rapidly to support its strategic location.

With their quick stop in Anchorage, Nick and Fred assumed the natural master and apprentice relationship as captain and co-captain, with Fred finalizing the flight plan, a task taking about fifteen or so minutes, depending on the route, destination, and weather. After that, the co-captain was expected to inspect the readiness of the plane for flight, which involved checking up on any and all mechanical matters that a master mechanic, who probably would already hold a captain's opinion in contempt let alone that of a co-captain, had already signed his name and reputation to in a log book. In reality, the co-captain added value by checking the radio gear for a few minutes, normally spending the remainder of the hour helping with the loading of baggage and mail.

Nick was never one to hold the formality of his rank over a co-pilot when it came to flying the plane. With the full load of troops now on board, however, and Fred's limited flying credentials, it was prudent to hold with tradition in this case. They flew south from Anchorage to the base of the Alaska Peninsula and then west out over the Bristol Bay to a point just south of Bethel, where they turned north. They approached the Kilbuck Mountains in a full moon. There was so much snow on the ground and so few brush and trees to absorb the light that a landing could easily be made without any lights at all. The sky above was wonderfully clear, and the stars and moon were brilliant. It was then that the thought about Martha and being his co-pilot in the old days struck. *We'd have a grand time together out here*, he imagined. Nick put the plane on "the pilot" and read Martha's letter one more time. He sent Fred back to the cabin in order to talk with the soldiers returning from furlough and begin to learn first-hand why this job was so important. Nick never forgot his time with Tony on that early flight with Captain Smith. *It's lonely on my end of this war too*, Nick reflected after reading the letter once more. He was anxious for the time off at home.

"The beacon at Bethel is straight ahead," he announced. "Buckle up, and we'll be on flat ground in less than thirty minutes." Fred returned and prepared for the landing.

CHAPTER 15

Bethel, Alaska
November 25, 1943

My Dear Martha,

Looks like I'm going to be stuck here for a week or so while we get the engines overhauled. The ship was squawking quite a bit coming in last night, and we used ten gallons of oil in the right engine and five in the left—per hour! Good time to get caught up on paperwork. Sorry I'll miss Thanksgiving with you. Give Bud and Helen my best.

One of our boys, an Alaska pilot who was with us for a while—now with Wien Alaska Airlines—just brought an army boy out of the bush who had been lost for 84 days! Hard to imagine, but he'll make it just fine. I heard a re-broadcast of the "Duffy Tavern" show last night in which Fred Allen plays the clarinet. It was quite funny. By the way, I'll look around for a birthday present for Bud. I saw some seal-hair slippers he might like.

Yours,
Nick

It wasn't so bad to get stuck in Edmonton or Seattle or Juneau, for that matter, but Bethel. "Goddamn!" Nick muttered to himself, purposely extending the second syllable for emphasis when he heard the news. He was hoping the mechanics would give him a quick fix and a green light to take the plane back to Fairbanks for the overhaul, where he could get another flight to Minneapolis-St. Paul. He wasn't at all sure that they just didn't want to show their muscle a bit. Even though the relationship between the pilots and mechanics is fairly harmonious, it still can be delicate. It's easy for too many pilots to parade around in lamb's wool–lined flight jackets and Ray-Ban sunglasses while the *fixers* find it difficult to wear the tinsel. Most grease monkeys have overalls splotched with varnish dope and hands black with grease. The good ones know that if they plan to survive the increasing technological demands of each new aircraft, then they need to make learning a constant and keep their nose in a manual. Their glory is in the back room counting the flights that unglamorously made their destinations. And, upon rare occasion, retching in a toilet in prelude to digging through the manuals to figure out why a flight didn't make it. The power to ground a ship for an overhaul gave small outward satisfaction to the importance of the work they did.

The head mechanic approaching Nick was Becherer, but people called him Beck. "Did it seem a little unusual to you, Captain, that your engines were drinking oil like my dog drinks apple cider?"

Nick had never heard of a dog drinking apple cider before, but he knew that it was a trap to go there. He could barely stay up with Red's peculiar sayings, and he wasn't going to add Beck's to his list. "It's our job to make these tin buckets fly, Beck, not complain about a minor inconvenience like a few missing quarts of oil. Besides, did I have a choice?"

"Not at nine thousand feet you didn't, but I do see in the service records that this isn't the first of these leaks you've encountered."

The fact that this leak was just discovered in Fairbanks would make no difference, Nick thought. Despite the fact that oil leaks were notorious in the C-47, Nick knew the chance of coming out on top in a debate over oil leaks with the head mechanic was about as possible as surviving a polar bear attack. "This ship reminds me of an old outboard motor I used to have. It lasted just about forever until I took it in to see why it used so much oil. The mechanic at Northstar Marine back in Cass Lake told me all the reasons why I didn't deserve to have the motor because of my abuse, and said that if I didn't let him fix it, he wouldn't sell me a new one when it did give out."

"Sounds like you were getting good advice, Captain."

"Maybe, but two days later, after I gave him thirty bucks to fix it, somebody stole the damn thing."

"What's your point, Captain?"

"Well, it seems like it's just when you get things working to your satisfaction that someone else wants to make it better. I'd still have that motor today if he hadn't fancied it up so much as to be a covetous temptation for someone else."

"You'd be better off flying just cargo routes, Captain, and let the people take another bus, if you know what I mean."

"Why?"

"Not so many will get hurt when you run out of oil at nine thousand feet." Beck waived his hand wearily toward a young man who had followed him to the flight deck and addressed him directly. "Rebuild 'em both, Junior. Have the job finished next week for the captain."

"There goes my Thanksgiving with the misses and the family," Nick said, kicking his feet into the gravel scattered on the tarmac.

"I think I did 'em a favor by making sure they'd have you home for Christmas," Beck retorted.

The conversations between the mechanics, like Beck, and the experienced pilots tended to be a little dramatic. Pilots generally played the character attributed by mechanics, who were convinced of their lack of general knowledge about the planes they flew.

"Does your dog really drink apple cider?"

Beck just winked as he and Junior walked away.

One week to the day after Beck's order to rebuild both engines, the army commandeered Nick's plane for dedicated service to the Aleutian chain. This bothered Nick for the obvious reasons but mostly because replacement planes were like someone else's used car—you never quite knew what you were getting. As far as he was concerned, the ATC always got short shrift when it came to priority over well-serviced planes, which generally went to the USAAF.

He sent a Teletype off to Cricket in flight ops to get a status on his new ship and wasn't happy with the news of a three-to-five-day additional wait.

"I guess that mechanic who fixed my boat engine works for you guys now?" Nick said upon seeing Beck at the mess hall.

"The problem is, our reputation with the brass is too good," he replied with a straight face, holding his mess tray out for a serving of hash.

"How do you figure?"

"Easy. They need a plane; they order us to bring one in for a major overhaul. When it's done, it's perfect." Beck shrugged. "What can I do?"

"Let's shoot some pool tonight," Nick offered. "You buy the beer since it's your reputation causing me to stay an extra week."

"You're on for the beer. But, there's a poker club in camp with a game tonight at 1900 you might be more interested in."

"Okay, as long as the stakes aren't too serious."

"There's no obligation, Captain. If you want out at any time, just say so."

"I'm a little rusty, but count me in."

CHAPTER 16

Martha's hopes for a Thanksgiving reunion were dashed with Nick's plane being grounded in Bethel. Everyone had been disappointed. Bud and Helen left on the Saturday afterward for the long drive back to Ohio. Sunday was a waste. Christmas shopping had been light the past week, people being very selective with what money they were able to spend. The job was still better than sitting around, however, particularly since it provided the break in monotony with Nick being away so much.

She had been on her feet a lot though and wondered how much the day's morning sickness, extended nausea, and light fever would make work more difficult. Leaning over the toilet bowl for the third time convinced her to call in sick. It wasn't like her to let her co-workers down, but some days were a lot worse than others and the doctor had warned her to be cautious.

At 10:00 a.m. she was still in her flannel nightgown and bathrobe, nursing a cup of coffee at the kitchen table. She stared at the trail of steam swirling from the cup, fixated in her thoughts about what Nick might be doing. Of course, it was about 7:00 a.m. in his part of Alaska, or 0700 as he would say, so he was probably just getting up. She hadn't received any cards in the last few days and that always put her on edge. The story in the newspaper about Warren Porter being found dead and partially consumed by animals after his prop plane crash was hard to dismiss. Her reality provided a thin veneer of emotional protection when hard news was received.

By noon she was dressed and found herself sitting in the living room looking out the bay window waiting for the mailman. *Maybe I'll get a card from Nick today*, she thought. *That would be nice.* It was cold and wet outside with gray, overcast skies laying a blanket of gloom on the world. It didn't seem very Christmassy. But she remembered Nick's description of Bethel—some god-forsaken place out by the Bering Sea with only tundra and snow, and not a tree in sight. She could only feel worse for him as she viewed the small print of the town's name on the map she used to trace Nick's trips. *By the size of the type, this is a tiny place*, she thought, *just enough to service the airbase.*

To her delight, when the mailman finally came there was an envelope from Nick, which always meant several cards, as sending multiple postcards separately was more costly. Their likelihood of being written over several days due to weather-prompted flight delays added to her optimism. She always preferred Nick's thoughts when he took more time. She poured another coffee and curled up on the couch before treating herself to her prize. She could almost feel his presence on each card—his smell definitely. Touching the cards immediately bridged the thousands of miles between them and stirred a longing in her heart. She would read and reread each one with care. Knowing that he would interrupt each day to privately "talk" with her was special. Probably every army wife felt the same way. Martha hung on to these moments as if they were her only reality with Nick.

Bethel, Alaska
December 1, 1943

My Dear Martha,
Was initiated into the Casino Club in room 110 down the hall. It cost $100, but I'm already $15 ahead.

Yours,
Nick

Bethel, Alaska
December 3, 1943

My Dear Martha,
I'm beginning to worry about what I'll amount to. I'll probably become a gambler. We've been sitting here for almost two days gambling from the time we get up in mid-afternoon until we quit at five or six in the morning. It's getting so I don't have enough time to write. My whole day is shifted around. Some of the poker, blackjack, and craps get pretty rough, but I'm still not down.

Yours,
Nick

Bethel, Alaska
December 4, 1943

My Dear Martha,

Had a big smoker on Saturday night. Won a ring from a fellow
in a poker game and tried to get him to throw in an automatic .22
target pistol, but he wanted too much. My poker hasn't been too
good. Think I'll give it up. They want me in a game again tonight,
but I think I'll go to a couple of old shows.

Yours,
Nick

Emptiness filled her and tightness gripped her insides. "He doesn't
miss me at all," she said under her breath. "This is just a big adventure."
Tears came easily as the cards fell from her hands onto the floor. The
insensitivity of his words spoke to a complete lack of his understanding
as to how important she hoped Thanksgiving would be for them. Their
relationship was replaced by a poker game in a backroom parlor filled
with cigar smoke and the smell of cheap whiskey.

December 8, 1943

My Dearest Nick,

I know that I can't expect you to understand how lonely I am when
you're away, but I have always felt some comfort thinking that you
felt the same way. Your three cards today detailing the vacation
you seem to be enjoying with the boys playing poker makes it difficult

for me to share any compassion for your situation. It doesn't seem to me that the lost Thanksgiving for us was much of a disappointment to you when compared to the excitement of your gambling escapades. Maybe Mother was right. You'll always put yourself first. Your baby and I will need a father and husband when you return—will you be there?

The family had so many plans that involved you and when you couldn't make it all of us genuinely felt sad for your hardship. I can safely inform them that you survived quite well. It concerns me, Nick, that I don't seem to know who you are at times. This makes me feel very alone and sad. What's happening to you? Your baby and I don't have much of a choice but to wait and hope that your carelessness for how we feel and your insensitivity over our situation will pass.

Maybe I should wait until tomorrow to see if I feel the same way about your cards before sending this letter.

Love Always,
Martha

Now, Martha wished she had gone to work and never read the mail. There wasn't anyone she could call. Certainly not her mother, as this would surely reinforce Ida's opinion of Nick as insensitive and self-focused, nor Helen, as it was an expensive long-distance call away, and not Rose either—her German stubbornness intimidated Martha. *And this is bound to make his Christmas trip home a big mess as well. How do I get past this?* she asked herself. Knowing that her feelings wouldn't just disappear and would certainly lead to a big fight when he got home, she just wished Christmas would go away. She couldn't find the logic, however, that could put things back the way they were when the day started.

Her coffee had turned cold, and by the end of the day Martha decided that sending the letter would not solve anything. It was likely not to catch up with Nick until just before he returned home anyway. She refolded it and slid it into the addressed envelope, carefully placing it on the mantel as a visual reminder of something important to be done.

CHAPTER 17

Robert discovered that using his Thanksgiving furlough time to visit his parents at the Manzanar Relocation Center was more on the order of a pilgrimage—certainly not like the weekend homestay he used to experience during college. Two full days of travel, so far, and if weather cooperated he still wouldn't be there until after dark, about ten o'clock. Captain Morgan had pulled some strings to make the trip happen, for which Robert was grateful. *Captain didn't have to do that*, he thought, while waiting for his final shuttle leg from Camp Irwin in Barstow, California. Still, his feelings remained mixed, as Captain Morgan had been riding his ass quite a bit for having an attitude. Said it was "unbecoming." *Let the president of the United States put your parents in a prison for no reason and see how your attitude changes*, he reflected defensively.

Camp Irwin was a military reservation of approximately one thousand square miles and previously known as the Mojave Anti-Aircraft Range. The desert setting made it a logical training site for many who were shipped off to the conflict with the Germans in North Africa. From here, Robert would take a Piper shuttle north of the Mojave Desert just skirting Death Valley toward the east, to a makeshift airstrip near Independence.

The thermals from the desert and the nearby Sierra Nevada Mountains made for a very bumpy ride. At one point, Robert hit his head on the ceiling of the cockpit from a sudden air pocket drop. Despite his experience in the air, however, the nighttime flight added additional stress. The airstrip was an unmanned facility in the middle of nowhere with tumbleweeds blowing across the runway and one area-light on a pole for visibility. Robert could see a second set of lights flick on from a car parked alongside the runway as they made a trial pass over the strip before circling and coming in on a final approach. A driver from the Relocation Center had been scheduled to pick him up for the short thirty-mile trip south.

"You okay with this landing, Captain?" Robert asked, his first words to the pilot in the last hour.

"Yeah. You see that flat shadow to the right of the headlights?"

"I guess."

"That's the airstrip. You've got to have a little faith for this landing to work. Don't worry. It's not my first."

Later, the pilot and Robert shook hands as he gathered up his bag from the back of the plane.

"Good luck," the pilot said quietly. "I hope you find what you came for."

Robert nodded soberly.

"You must be PFC Endo," the driver said as Robert walked up to the car with his duffle bag slung over his shoulder.

"Yeah, that's me."

"Not many people take that ride if they don't have to."

"I'm in the army's air force, assigned to the Air Transport Command in Alaska," Robert said. "I can say with experience that this strip here ranks as the loneliest I've ever seen." Other than the initial polite exchange, the forty-minute ride to the center was quiet. Robert concluded the driver was probably familiar with his situation and reason for the visit. *Why make the guy uncomfortable*, he thought, *by talking about the obvious*. By the time they reached Manzanar, snow was being driven across the narrow road out of the mountains to the west. On a good day, the weather was quite pleasant, but, unfortunately, the intense desert heat during the summer and vicious mountain storms during the winter made a "good day" hard to come by. The security guards were in heavy wool coats with collars pulled up and scarves wrapped tightly around their necks, all-in-all not happy to leave their warm posts.

"These early winter blizzards can be a son of a bitch," the driver commented as he pulled up to a bleak barrack with tarpaper siding that was to be Robert's home until he left the following afternoon.

"The sarge will meet you here for mess at 0600. Anything you need, you tell him."

"This sure ain't the Top of the Mark," Robert said rhetorically, referring to the nineteenth-floor, glass-walled cocktail lounge of the Mark Hopkins Hotel in San Francisco. Inside, the floorboards creaked with each step and allowed a bone-chilling draft into the room. A cot with a sleeping bag, a stained porcelain sink and toilet, and a naked bulb for light in a wall fixture above the cot was all the room had to offer. He fell into bed exhausted from traveling and the stress, knowing that this trip would be hard on everybody.

The next morning, Robert was shocked when he saw how desolate and foreboding Manzanar truly was. His reaction came primarily as a byproduct of defeated expectations, for he had read glowing reports in the *Manzanar Free Press* about "a successful adaptation to the cultural conditions achieved through a community of involvement in this fast-growing town." He could see the newspaper pictures and headlines— "Beautiful Communal Gardens," "Comfortable Living with Good

Medical Care," "Safe Environment." *Propaganda!* he screamed silently. *The rest of the country may be okay with Roosevelt's little executive order, but they're not standing here freezing their butts off in this hellhole.*

"I'd like to see where my parents are living," Robert stated to the sergeant over breakfast.

"Not going to be able to do that, soldier, as the barracks are off limits. Doesn't make any difference, anyway. Your mother's been quite sick. She's in the hospital, so I'll take you there."

As they drove across the center's square mile of wooden barracks in the blowing snow, Robert grew heartsick as he reflected on his parents' beautifully landscaped little home on San Francisco's west side and what pride both took in its presentation of flowers and perfectly manicured little garden.

Robert bowed upon seeing Endo-san standing in the ten-foot-square waiting area of the hospital. It had been almost a year and a half since his parents were sent there, and longer since Robert had seen his father, whose demeanor was that of a beaten man—emotionally, not physically. The spark that used to be in his eye when he played with Robert as a boy was gone. There was no smile at all, only hidden desperation he hoped his son wouldn't see.

"You don't look well, Father."

"They treat us well, but our age makes it hard for us to adapt," Endo-san replied while gesturing to the winter gale outside. "Your mother has had it harder than most." He lowered his eyes, and his shoulders shrugged as if to say "it doesn't matter anymore."

"What's wrong with mother?"

The sergeant intervened with his reply: "Some have had the bad fortune of contracting a difficult strain of pneumonia."

"I was talking with my father!" Robert glared at the sergeant, akin to the way a hostile inmate would look at a corrupt prison guard. In truth, the sergeant wasn't at fault, just trying to be helpful. He clammed up out of respect while returning the stare.

"It's nobody's fault," Endo-san said. "She's been coughing sputum for months. Also, a constant fever offset with teeth-chattering chills. We're most concerned, though, about the chest pains and shortness of breath. She's not well, my son, and I don't want you to be shocked when you see her."

The men walked onto a ward of twelve women, all suffering from various maladies. When they stopped at the foot of the third bed, Robert was indeed shocked, as he doubted that he would have recognized his mother on his own. The woman in the bed barely dented the white sheets and obviously had been experiencing nausea and vomiting from the stains and smells. She was hooked up to an IV for fluids, and upon questions about her chart's notations, Robert understood that frequent bouts of diarrhea with rapid heartbeats were also a problem.

"Mother. Mother . . . it's me, Robert." He leaned over and grasped her hand while rubbing her forearm in a soothing manner. He heard the desperation in her fast breathing. It was like the very act of staying alive exhausted her.

"Can you hear me, Mother?" He asked firmly to attract her attention.

Her almond eyes barely opened, and the vagueness in her expression told Robert that she was confused. "How long has she been like this?"

"For about one week now," Endo-san replied. "She is the flower of my life, and I don't believe she has the strength to make it through another bout of this pneumonia. This is her third one."

Robert spent the rest of the day at bedside with his mother and father. In actuality, he felt that she improved as the day progressed, so much so that their conversations reminded him of being at home. She smiled and rubbed his hand and gestured to give him a kiss on his right temple. The encouragement helped Robert, as he knew his time was drawing to a close. He would have to leave after dinner, as his orders called for his return to Ladd in a week. The farewells for all three of them were extremely hard because they were all certain that this time together would be their last.

"Here's a list of the places where I'm staying until I get back to Fairbanks, Father, if you need anything." Robert's focus on the logistical aspect of the departure helped him hold his emotions inside. He kissed his mother and embraced his father before leaving.

The winter storm had subsided late that afternoon when he departed Independence, which made for an easier flight to Camp Irwin. The Santa Ana winds in Barstow, however, delayed his connection on a troop plane to San Francisco until the next day. His thoughts were filled with emptiness for his parents' future, despite the flicker of hope based on his mother's improvement that afternoon. It was all he could do to contain himself with the anger he felt for a country that could do this—his country, their country!

He found a quiet, relaxing corner of the bar at the Mark Hopkins Hotel that would keep him clear of the soldiers, primarily new recruits, who celebrated and carried on much to be expected. With the dimout order lifted the first of November, he ignored the others and stared out at a city that was desperate to show off its lights. The sensational lounge in the sky with 360-degree views of San Francisco had become famous overnight. Servicemen would buy and leave a bottle in the care of the bartender so that the next soldier from their squadron could enjoy a free drink; whoever had the last sip would buy the next bottle. The soldiers gathered before shipping out for one last toast to the Golden Gate Bridge, believing that the bridge was good luck and would bring them home. Story had it that as the soldiers sailed off under the Golden Gate during the day, wives and sweethearts would draw together in the lounge's northwest corner, where they would tearfully gaze out the windows to watch them go. It had become known as the Weepers' Corner.

"Hey! Look what we got here!" an Irish recruit slurred drunkenly out of nowhere. "It's a real live Nip. What the fuck's he doin' here?" he said, motioning to his comrades in the direction of Robert. "Shouldn't you be in a prison for people like you?" the drunken soldier said in a mock tone while directing his glass toward Robert, bringing him to the attention of his cronies.

Robert's hot button was hard-pressed. He leapt off his stool and head-butted the soldier completely by surprise. The soldier's draft-beer glass was launched vertically, covering his friends with its contents. Within seconds, blood spewed from the man's nose. The three others with the man erupted in retaliation against Robert, descending on him from all sides. "That's what they did to us at Pearl . . . you sneaky bastard," one of the men said as they kicked and beat Robert senselessly. Luckily, the MPs in the bar were quick to stop the assault, but not before Robert sustained a broken nose, two cracked ribs, and bruises everywhere.

As the first to throw a blow, Robert was put into cuffs and hauled outside for his own protection and to shut down any thoughts of a brawl from erupting further. In the hall of the hotel, the bartender joined the MPs and Robert as they had him spread-eagled against the wall. "Listen, officer," the bartender interjected. "This guy didn't do anything that any one of us wouldn't have done. It pissed me off, too, when I heard that jackass make the comment." Once the bartender explained the comment, the MPs began to realize that Robert was a bit of a fall guy here and took the cuffs off.

"I'm not so sure I agree with how you handled this situation, soldier, but it's not fair for it to go on your record either," the MP in charge said. "Get that nose fixed and cool off. Walk away next time!"

"I've fixed a few noses over the years," the bartender offered with a friendly smile. "It'll save you a trip to the hospital, if you want."

"Sure, why not," Robert replied. After waiting a few minutes, the man returned with two twelve-inch wooden dowels, each about a quarter of an inch in diameter.

"Hold on," he said, holding both dowels in his right hand after inserting one a few inches into each nostril. With a quick snap of his wrist the bones were back in place.

"Damn. That was worse than the boot!" He rubbed his nose on both sides, checking to feel if everything was aligned. "Thanks for helping, I think."

"The hospital would have been worse."

"I'll be on my way then." The two men shook hands, and Robert left for an inexpensive, out-of-the-way hotel he had planned to stay at not far from the wharf.

Early that next morning Robert heard a knock on his door. It was a Western Union agent. "Telegram, soldier," the agent said as Robert opened the door. "Holy shit. You don't look so good. You alright?"

"Thanks. Yeah, the worst is over."

The door closed and Robert opened the telegram, wondering how anyone knew where he was. Once he saw Endo-san's name he remembered the list of places he left a few days earlier.

November 30, 1943

Robert: Your Mother died quietly in her sleep the night you left. The doctors say it was heart failure. Your visit meant so much to both of us. Help to end this awful war.

Your Loving Father

Robert had never been good at relationships. He was jealous of the soldiers leaving girlfriends and wives that would miss them—jealous of people who fit in and didn't have to fight racism, which made him feel less significant and unimportant. He was jealous of people whose mothers didn't have to die in some god-forsaken desert. But more than the jealousy, he was angry! Angry that his adoptive mother, the only woman who loved him, was taken from him.

CHAPTER 18

After the San Francisco incident, Robert decided to spend the last two days of his leave in Anchorage with his only real friend, Cricket. Surprise visits, however, were not high on Cricket's list, and he was cautious of spending too much one-on-one time with Robert.

"You could've called," Cricket said as they walked into the mess hall for lunch.

"Yeah, but all this stuff is just too much to handle," Robert said after explaining his visit to his parents, his mother's death, and the fight at the Mark Hopkins. "It wasn't until I was on the flight here that the thought of spending the next two days with you made sense. Besides, it's been a few months."

"I understand, and I'm very sorry, but . . . well, you know, everything's so visible here."

Robert always felt that his lack of interest in girls while growing up was a byproduct of his introversion and shyness. He couldn't put two words together when talking to a girl, and, quite frankly, would rather walk on the other side of the street than make eye contact with a creature of the opposite sex. It was later, however, as the equipment manager for the boys' junior varsity basketball team while a sophomore, when he noticed an interest he couldn't explain. He was privately embarrassed and horrified. He had heard the older boys talk about "queers and homos," but had no real-world attachment that put their comments into a context that made sense. Yet, he couldn't explain these locker room feelings he would experience, particularly around a kid named David. He didn't know David. He hadn't even met David until he became the manager. In addition to his physical reactions, Robert developed an emotional yearning around David, an aching that left him wistful and vulnerable. Convinced that his reaction was a deep-seated sickness and one that would not do well being discovered by others, Robert quit the manager's job, desperate to protect himself from ridicule. He climbed further inside an emotional barricade that lasted throughout high school.

"But you're the only one I can count on. I just don't want to be alone. Not right now."

"Where are you staying?"

"A little out-of-the-way place on the edge of town—the Vista Motel. It has housekeeping cabins with separate entrances. Mine's number 21."

"I've got a full load of work this afternoon. I'll try to be there by 1800, but only if we eat in."

"No problem. I'll pick up some stuff. Thanks, Cricket, this means a lot to me."

Vladimir had planned this trip to Anchorage at the last minute. And, since he had three new pilots leaving with P-38s soon, he thought he would get clearance for a final check-out with his men and make a visit to Cricket to review their compliance with procedures. An open communication line with Cricket, he thought, would be good. Cricket's knowledge of the movement of every plane, pilot, and military passenger in Alaska would be invaluable intelligence if Vladimir could access it. On his way to the flight operations center, he saw Cricket across the street in the mess hall parking area talking with Robert. He was surprised to see Robert and was about to approach when the men parted company—Robert giving Cricket a very brief and different sort of pat on his backside.

Vladimir instinctively turned away to avoid being noticed. He waited for ten minutes or more before entering flight operations.

"Officer Mason, how's life?" Vladimir asked Cricket in his heavy accent while exhaling a billow of cigarette smoke. The two men interacted regularly because of the frequent traffic of Russian pilots, and while Vladimir always called him Cricket when having a beer, it was always Officer Mason at flight ops. They had a decent working relationship, as Vladimir made every effort to be a good guest.

"In a minute, Vladimir, after I finish these flight schedules," Cricket responded distractedly, holding the palm of his hand out to forestall any further comments.

Vladimir looked around the ops room while waiting—not much but a sparse office area with a bench for no more than two or three people and a counter separating all visitors from Cricket's work area. The chatter from the Teletype with incoming instructions and requests for flight plans echoed off the linoleum floor. For the most part, pilots simply got their flight plans and maybe engaged in some social interchange before leaving, so this arrangement was adequate. The windows were single pane and sure to frost up in the winter, making the potbelly stove in the corner a real necessity when the temperature dropped—commonly below zero. A cord of hardwood had been stacked neatly outside, suggesting that a weather forecast had already been posted.

"What can I do for you my Russian comrade?" Cricket asked in a welcoming tone after a few minutes. "Didn't expect your visit."

"Three of our newest recruits will be coming through from Edmonton this week. Their English is not so good. I thought some comments about procedures from you, which I could pass on to our pilots, could avoid problems."

"Good thinking. A little polish on protocol couldn't hurt."

Vladimir was aware that Cricket knew that he and Robert were acquaintances. He thought it was odd that Cricket didn't inquire about Robert, considering the general nature of passing on information from person to person, particularly when there was a connection.

"The Lana Turner movie is still on, right?" Vladimir loved Lana Turner. "Are you going tonight?"

"No, I've got too much paperwork to catch up on. Maybe another time."

They chatted a bit more before parting.

Vladimir had years of experience in three languages and cultures looking for things out of the ordinary. What he witnessed that day was definitely out of the ordinary, so he decided he would keep an eye on Cricket that night, particularly if he left the base. Vladimir had seen Russian men pat each other on the butt before, but it was always in a businesslike way that was to foster camaraderie not in an affectionate way to show endearment. There was a subtle difference, but Vladimir was trained to detect subtleties.

What had been promised to be a busy night "catching up" turned out to be not so busy after all. Vladimir observed Cricket leaving flight ops around 5:45 p.m.

The sun had set a couple hours earlier, so with the cover of darkness, Vladimir decided to follow Cricket. He kept his distance, staying in the shadows of the various buildings they passed as they made their way to the entrance gate. The final fifty yards were completely exposed. Vladimir figured that Cricket intended to leave the base in one of the Pioneer taxicabs that were always waiting to cart GIs into town. It was too early for the usual crowd of GIs so it was just the two of them approaching the gate. Vladimir stopped to tie his shoe, stalling for the right moment to follow without being noticed but staying close enough not to lose sight of Cricket's cab. Vladimir jumped in a second waiting cab and pointed to the taillights up ahead. "Follow that car," he said.

His driver was an older man who had emigrated to the United States in 1910 from Moscow. Lucky for Vladimir that Russians weren't all that uncommon in Anchorage, or Fairbanks for that matter, as many generations were still intact. It kept his identity less memorable, should someone ask later. Vladimir limited their inevitable exchange of the Old Country and the harsh politics of Stalin to a minimum. He avoided eye contact in the rear-view mirror completely. He did not want to be remembered. They followed for about three miles, keeping a safe distance. Cricket's taxicab was in easy view as it pulled away from a cabin at a motel called the Vista. The vacancy sign flashed off as the two cars passed on the highway. Vladimir's only option to stop without being obvious was a general store a quarter mile down the road. It would have to do.

"Keep the change," Vladimir said, thanking the Russian driver with a good tip. Vladimir went inside and purchased a candy bar and a soda, all the while keeping his eyes on the dimming taillights of his departing taxi. Otherwise, the road was quiet.

Within twenty minutes, Vladimir had positioned himself outside the window of the cabin where Cricket's taxicab was seen. He was easily concealed by his dark clothes and by a large cedar shrub off the two-lane service road winding through the private cabins and trailer court.

The cotton curtains in the window would shield him from anyone inside. The cold air stimulated his already heightened senses. He could see his breath as he moved quietly. He was happy he had gloves. By cupping his hand on the window pane and tucking in his ear real close, he could actually hear some of what was being said.

"It's probably not smart to stay," he heard one of the voices say, sounding like Cricket's.

"But I can't just ignore the facts of what's going on either," came the reply. "Maybe if we try to not overreact and just enjoy the evening, things will be better. I got a couple of steaks we can broil. Along with the potato salad and beer, it shouldn't be too bad. What do you say?"

"Okay, Robert. You win, but not overnight. We can't be too careful."

Vladimir could hear movement by the men and got a glimpse of Robert embracing Cricket with a familiarity that could only come from a genuine feeling of shared desire. Then, there were no sounds for several minutes as the men held their position and kissed and embraced passionately. "Easy, Robert. Not so fast. Why don't we enjoy those steaks first?"

Vladimir felt like a pervert as he watched. *How can this be natural?* he asked himself. In disgust he turned away.

Recognizing that his focus for this "listening" objective was lost, he departed the motel area and began the walk back to the base. Nearer to town he found a taxicab. During the ride he mentally constructed his next message to Agent Sirak, including what he had learned about these two men.

CHAPTER 19

"Captain, can I talk to you in private for a few minutes?" Cricket said to Nick as he approached the counter in flight operations. He motioned like a hotel doorman to an open door where there was a private meeting space, suggesting it as a place to talk.

"What's up?" Nick replied matter-of-factly.

Once inside the room, Cricket closed the door, shutting out the ever-present clatter of the Teletype machines, and sat down on one of the chairs at the small table. The room was void of any decoration except for the required picture of President Roosevelt in a cheap wooden frame and a bright blue ashtray on the table. "I've had a unique request, not one I've actually had before," he said as he lit a Camel.

Nick settled in his chair, but said nothing—waiting for Cricket to continue.

"It seems you and your crew must have impressed Major Gordon from New Mexico during your flight in October."

"How so?"

"I just received orders from the brass at the 11th Air Force that your services have been requested for a curtain-call flight back to Yukon

Flats. Since you and that Okie co-captain are certified on the C-45A, they'd like you two and PFC Endo to handle the flight."

"I've only seen one of those planes at Ladd. Why not have the regular pilot and crew handle the flight? Besides, it only needs a crew of two."

"I've been able to keep my job in flight ops by not pissing off the brass with questions that imply that their logic may not be sound. Besides, that pilot is on furlough until the third week of December, and they want this flight to go in three days. As far as PFC Endo is concerned, I think it will become clear when you hear me out."

"I can't speak for Red, but I haven't flown that plane in months."

"Well then, I'll get you two shuttled to Ladd later today. Sounds like a few practice hours are in order. I'll process the paperwork."

"Any idea as to what this is all about?"

"Nothing concrete. May be connected to their last trip, although the flight plan for this one is classified. It's likely they don't want any new crew involved in their activities."

"I'll round up Red. Let me know when the paperwork is done."

"1530. Be prepared for some ground time as well, which is where PFC Endo comes in. You're going to be the guests of Grant Pearson, acting superintendent of the national park. He's there with a guy the army is going to have test cold-weather gear. Camp's already set up, and they'll need additional help with the camp duties—more suited to a PFC. They'll be expecting you Thursday. PFC Endo will meet you in Fairbanks.

"By the way, it's a winter camp."

———

After alerting Red, Nick got his own gear packed. A "winter camp" meant tents, so preparing to be in the cold twenty-four hours a day definitely changed Nick's packing plans. With the time left, he put his mind to getting a postcard off to Martha. After missing Thanksgiving, he thought, surprises on the home front involving potential Christmas delays would not be good. A heads-up postcard to Martha was definitely in order.

Anchorage, Alaska
December 9, 1943

My Dear Martha,

Red and I are heading out today on a trip to the Yukon Flats. Sounds like a boondoggle by some brass from New Mexico. Pretty hush-hush. The good news is that I can get my time in a little faster on this assignment. I definitely want to make it home for the holidays, for a hike in the woods and the snow like we did last year—remember? Bad news is that we don't control the itinerary on this trip. Sounds like we'll have some ground time for sure while they snoop about.

Glad you found a meat locker. That should save money and help a little by reducing trips to the butcher stores.

Yours,
Nick

With the days getting shorter, the afternoon sun was fading fast by the time Nick and Red met at flight ops for their departure. Each had a full duffel in preparation for a stay of several days in cold weather combined with various outdoor activities. Other than the discussion with Cricket, there were no orders.

"Strange, don't ya think?" Red asked as they walked to the ship that would take them to Ladd. "I mean, I sorta feel like a coon up a tree with the dogs howling. I know how I got here, I just don't know why. And do people really sleep in tents in the winter?"

"Wish I could help you, partner."

The flight to Ladd followed the Susitna River just north of Anchorage and continued past Mt. McKinley, which stood to the west at 20,320 feet. The framing effect of the sun's last light behind the great mountain left a halo-like, glowing outline that suggested an accessible, more friendly world beyond its rim. Immediately below them, in contrast, was the Matanuska-Susitna valley, completely obscured into the depths of darkness with the great mountain as its shield. Nick and Red rarely enjoyed this flight as passengers. The intense view from the plane overtook their normal discussion involving checking and rechecking the elevation movements of the plane as a result of drafts, winds, and thermals. Tonight was relatively easy, however, with excellent visibility and passive weather. But they knew that could change quickly with the potential for wind shear from lenticular clouds around mountain peaks and snow buffeting a plane up to eighty miles per hour. The final pass between the Alaska Range to the east and the McKinley Range to the west was only about ten miles wide with peaks from twelve to fifteen thousand feet on both sides. It marked the beginning of their descent into Fairbanks and Ladd Field.

"Let's get an early start," Nick said.

"You're the boss. Give me a time and I'm there."

"0715 in flight ops. That'll give us time for breakfast."

"Are you concerned about this trip, Captain?"

"No. I just don't like surprises. Whatever this trip involves is above our pay grade, and I'm not comfortable with our lack of seat time in the C-45A. Cricket has made the ship available to us all day. We need to make the most of it."

"Aye, aye, Captain."

The two men walked casually across the tarmac toward the hangar that housed the C-45A for a visual inspection before heading off to the mess hall for dinner. Beechcraft made this plane and nicknamed it the Expediter. It was excellent for utility transport or photo surveys because of its size and performance. It was designed for a small payload of no more than eight passengers and two crew, considerably smaller than what Nick and Red were used to with the C-47 and about half its physical size. It had excellent climb rate, which made it useful in mountainous terrain. Both men sat for several minutes in their respective cockpit seats visually checking the instrument panel for differences. Basically, all the same gauges and dials were there, as with the C-47, just in different locations. Easy to figure out in normal flight, but could account for critical, split-second variations in response time during an emergency.

"This has always been one of my favorites," Red said.

"Mine, too. Flew it on several charter flights for Northwest where the airport runways wouldn't accommodate the larger ships. Always reliable."

"My experience, exactly."

Their confidence soared. The C-45A performed beautifully, adding to their enthusiasm with the upcoming assignment. Each looked forward to the morning and the break from their routine.

CHAPTER 20

Since his return from Moscow, Vladimir's routine of ensuring that his new pilots were scheduled and adapting to their P-38 training had taken over most of his attention. His offer to teach Russian to some of the officers was considered, but it was ultimately refused by the base brass. They said an army officer fluent in Russian would be on base soon to do the honors. Vladimir was insulted to think that this person could even begin to match his skills with the two languages. *Goddamn Americans always think they have the answer*, he thought. It bothered him that he would have to mention this in his next report to Agent Sirak.

The war on the eastern front was brutal and the demand for planes and pilots grew constantly. It was Wednesday morning, December 10, and Vladimir was attending to the mountain of paperwork required by the U.S. Army for each pilot entering the States. The Russian officer responsible for shuttling the new pilots to Fairbanks and for delivering his communications from Sirak entered the small office the army provided Vladimir. "Hello," Vladimir said, welcoming the man but wanting to keep his discussion brief. Years of being an agent taught him that a minimalist approach with other Russians was best. Stalin had taken the Lenin approach to eavesdropping and spying on each other to a new level. One could never be safe. After their exchange of new pilot dossiers and the locked ammo box, the officer and Vladimir continued briefly in his smoke-filled office with routine news of the war and his flight to Alaska.

"Good-bye," the officer said, making no eye contact or other gesture of familiarity when parting even though the men had made numerous similar exchanges for almost two years.

"Have a good flight home, comrade," Vladimir said, acknowledging his departure to Moscow in the morning.

Vladimir thought about how only he and Agent Sirak knew the combination to the ammo box, which led Vladimir to feel that his responsibility in this matter continued to be of the highest importance. He cleared his desk before spinning the dial to each of the combination locks. He was anxious. Even with his expertise in encryption, it took him a few minutes to perform the translation into Russian. He wrote it down to ensure absolute understanding and then burned both documents.

AGENT DUBISSKIY,

IT IS OF EXTREME IMPORTANCE TO FOCUS YOUR
PLANNING ON THE RUSSIAN ESKIMO VILLAGE OF
VENETIE FOR ADVERSE ACTIVITIES AFFECTING
DESCENDANTS OF RUSSIA. ALL MOVEMENT SHOULD BE
MONITORED FOR THOROUGHNESS. VISITORS ON 11.12.43
NEED CATALOGUED. POSSIBLE MOVEMENTS MUST BE
DOCUMENTED. KEEP ME APPRISED OF ACTIVITIES
BETWEEN PFC ROBERT ENDO AND WARRANT OFFICER
MARTIN MASON, THE ONE THEY CALL CRICKET.

AGENT ANDREY SIRAK

Vladimir reflected for several minutes on the extent of Sirak's knowledge. *Clearly there is another Russian operative providing intelligence to Sirak, otherwise how could he know of activities taking place tomorrow?* he thought. And the reference to Cricket—Vladimir was certain he had never mentioned Cricket to Sirak. It concerned Vladimir that another operative might be watching his movements. Be that as it may, Vladimir also knew that Sirak had no concerns about Russian descendants. It was his coded way of focusing attention on the Yukon Flats location. With December 11 being tomorrow, what visitors is he referring to? Vladimir easily recognized that the other operative or operatives had better intelligence than he did, and direct access to Sirak! He lit another cigarette and ignited the papers in a waste can with the same match. He noticed an involuntary increase in his own anxiety level as he did, typical when the target of a NKVD listening initiative was so close to home.

Fresh air would do some good, Vladimir thought as he donned his parka and opened the outside door. He needed to think. The sun was down, and he found the walk refreshing in the comfortable twenty-degree weather. Winter hadn't really set in as expected and the respite was welcome. Just then, around the corner from the commissary, came two pilots he recognized immediately, Captain Morgan and Co-pilot Johnson.

"Good morning," Vladimir said as he walked past the men. "How's Robert Endo? Haven't seen him in weeks." He knew better than to try to engage in an extended conversation, but he also knew that Robert may provide the answers he needed. *If these men are on base*, he thought, *maybe Robert is here also*. He hadn't seen Robert since his rendezvous with Cricket.

"He's been on furlough. You can ask him yourself if you want, though. He's expected on base here tomorrow," Nick replied. He always marveled at just how good Vladimir's English was and meant to ask about it when he had the time.

"Thank you," Vladimir said and moved on.

The next day, Vladimir cleared his work responsibilities early and went to find Robert. His instinct from years of eavesdropping assignments told him that something was about to happen and that Robert was his key. The mess hall was always the best place to connect without attracting attention, and besides, his clearance wouldn't allow him to just roam the base in search of someone. He arrived early, sat at a corner table, and busied himself by reviewing dossiers of his new pilots. He saw Robert enter the chow line about 1215 and quickly positioned himself in a parallel line in order to exit at the same time.

Robert took a table by himself at the window without noticing Vladimir. Vladimir approached within minutes, before the seat could be taken, asking, "You've been away, yes?" He sat down, placing his food tray across from Robert's. "Is everything alright? Vladimir expected to feel awkward around Robert now that he knew his sexual proclivity, but he didn't. He certainly didn't condone homosexuality, and he certainly would use it to manipulate Robert's involvement if leverage was needed, but for now he was just another man trying to get through the war.

"As good as can be expected." Robert realized how much he had come to enjoy his companionship with Vladimir. They had no obligations to each other, just a common bond as outsiders to the system—in some respects to the war itself. Robert felt a unique level of acceptance by Vladimir. "Yes, I have been gone. It wasn't an easy trip. My mother died in Manzanar a day after my visit."

"My deepest regrets, comrade," Vladimir replied, shifting to a genuine use of his word for "friend."

He listened to Robert's saga over the last several weeks, including a reference to his trip to Anchorage where he met with Cricket. There was no mention of the liaison, of course, but the timeline validated the truth of his movements. They talked more of Robert's visit to the camp, and Robert revealed his disgust with the conditions and treatment his parents had to endure. At one point he said, "If I could do something to end this war I would, and right now I'm not sure whose side I would take."

"On my trip back to Moscow while you were gone, I had the same feeling. All my boyhood friends are dead, lying in a ditch somewhere on the western front. And for what? I just want it to end."

"So, what brings you back to Fairbanks?" Vladimir steered their conversation toward present activities.

Robert looked around before responding. "It seems that our dignitaries from New Mexico want another look-see of the Yukon Flats area. This time it's for a few days. I'm to be their gopher for the trip."

"Gopher? That is little ground animal, no?"

"Sorry, it's just an expression. It means that I'm the one who will *go for* things whenever the brass has a request," Robert said slowly, enunciating "go for."

"That's a good one," Vladimir laughed. "I know of this job, too. What do you think they will ask you to go for?"

"Don't have the foggiest idea. Cricket just said they wanted the same crew. We're taking the C-45A, so we're definitely planning on landing."

"When are you leaving?"

"Tomorrow is what I was told, but I've not seen our 'cargo' yet. They're expected to arrive sometime today."

Vladimir turned his face toward the window and watched a transport takeoff on one of the runways. He needed to press Robert for more, but was reluctant. If he was going to bring Robert into his confidence, he would have to choose his words very carefully. "I need to inform you of something important," Vladimir said, following his instinct that this was the right time.

"You sound serious."

"It is. Serious enough to get both of us killed."

"Go on," Robert said, cautiously leaning closer while on the edge of his chair, resting his elbows on the cafeteria table.

Vladimir lit another Camel, took a long drag, and exhaled slowly while looking around the mess area to ensure that they wouldn't be overheard. "You and I share a common threat. For me the threat is losing someone I love who lives in Shimoda."

Robert cocked his head without losing eye contact as if to say, *now you have my attention.*

"For me the threat is losing Okimi. For you, it's bigger. Your parents have many relatives in Japan, no? They will be at risk of attack by the U.S. that will be beyond what the world has seen. The reaction by the Japanese government to such an attack will likely keep your father in prison for years to come. But if I tell you more about this threat, I add to my own risk of being jailed as a spy in your country."

"What are you saying?" Robert wasn't alarmed or threatened. He was intrigued and wanted to know more.

Vladimir had to be careful. His career would be over if the conversation went badly. He was within a minute of making a move that could cause him to spend the rest of his life in a military prison. In his entire career as an agent, it was this moment that held the greatest risk. It was this moment that his judgment would either spell success or failure. Up until now he had always been right. He never quite knew the formula for bringing in a new operative—developing trust, compelling circumstances, timing, good judgment on both sides—but it always came in a moment of spontaneity. It was never planned. *Had his estimation of Robert's deepening discontent been correct?*

"Can I trust you to let me explain what I know? Before you answer, let me say that if you share my concern, we can work together. If not, nothing can ever be said between us again." Vladimir meticulously observed Robert's body language for clues. His interest was high. He was positioned on the edge of his chair; his arms were open, not closed and defensive.

"It's okay, go ahead," Robert responded with an expression of curiosity.

Vladimir paused for a full minute, taking in Robert's expressions during the silence. He was convinced that he could trust him. "My government is certain that the United States is close to the successful development of an atom bomb—close enough to begin planning the testing process. It's referred to as the Manhattan Project. Are you familiar with this effort?

"Not by that name, but there's been scuttlebutt about a bomb of enormous destructive power. Details are very hush-hush."

"Germany, Japan, and Russia are also working on such a bomb, but my superiors think that the United States will be first. What does that mean? Such a bomb with the power to destroy a city the size of Manhattan will mean that key cities in Japan and Germany will be targeted. As I said, for me I may lose Okimi. For you, the peaceful existence of the Japanese people in the United States is at risk. You can see that this bomb would be very bad for many people. I have been instructed to pay attention to progress of this Manhattan Project."

Robert rubbed his lower lip with his thumb and index fingers while he thought. He then spoke deliberately to Vladimir, maintaining fixed eye contact. "My peaceful existence in the U.S. ended when they put my parents in prison. What they've done to my parents and others is inexcusable. If I could help to save innocent victims from a bomb planned for Japan, I would. But I'm not aware of anything about the Manhattan Project."

"I would never put you in jeopardy, Robert. At this time, anything involving the men from Los Alamos over the next few days would help me very much." Vladimir paused to inhale. "Can I count on you and leave my request at that?"

"Okay." Robert was energized for the first time since his parents' detention. He finally felt like his life had a purpose and that he would be able to do something to help his father. His pact with Vladimir felt very freeing.

CHAPTER 21

Major Gordon handled the brief introductions while they were standing next to the C-45A. "Since we're going to be together for a few days, we might as well get to know each other. We know who you are and you know who I am, but I believe we neglected to introduce my companions on the last trip. This is Dr. Robert Oppenheimer," he said, pointing to a willowy man with sharp facial features who stood about six feet tall. Dr. Oppenheimer's stare off into the distance and compliant handshake clearly let everyone know that he didn't expect to be communicated with unless instructed. He seemed more interested in finishing his cigarette before boarding. "This is Lieutenant Max O'Reilly," the major said.

Lieutenant O'Reilly was more sociable. He greeted each crew member with a hearty handshake and a smile. "Glad to be aboard," he said in a thick Irish brogue. His sturdy physique pegged him as an athlete, probably football or baseball player or maybe both, and his clear eye contact and confident stance marked him as a man of single-mindedness.

Last to be introduced was Ronald Reisdorf, a young man in civilian clothes. He was hard to read during the introductions, as he was preoccupied with adjusting his steel-rimmed glasses that were constantly sliding down his long nose. He didn't have much to say and appeared to be more a thinker and doer than a talker. Nonetheless, he greeted everyone pleasantly. The major gave no indication to the men's responsibilities, or the purpose for their trip.

Everyone boarded the plane. Nick and Red climbed into the cockpit. The guests took seats near the rear of the craft, leaving room for Robert up front. With only eight seats there wasn't much privacy.

There was a thick layer of fog covering the airfield. It extended over the river valley and didn't stand much of a chance of burning off for several hours. The tower informed Nick that they would not reach clear skies until three thousand feet.

"Major," Nick said, standing in the aisle. "We can wait a few hours for this pea soup to clear or charge ahead on schedule. Your call."

"Are you suggesting there's risk in making the takeoff now?"

"No, just uneasiness for those not familiar with the turbulence of blind takeoffs in mountainous terrain."

"Captain, I can assure you that you don't need to treat us like some of the skittish Northwest passengers your airline caters to. Move on."

"As you wish."

The C-45A followed the taillights of an army Jeep for their runway approach and tuned the plane until the magnetic compass matched the precise direction of the assigned runway. Once the gyrocompass was set, Red took special care to concentrate on it to hold course within a degree or two. After completing their cockpit checklist of instruments, engines, and flight controls, they were ready. The landing lights were off to eliminate their reflective glare off the fog.

"Ready for takeoff," Nick said.

As they gathered speed into the fuzzy void and then felt the ship's lift-off, each man prayed silently that they would avoid the sinister, lurking disaster manufactured by their imagination. Despite the perfection of the takeoff, Nick couldn't shake the feeling that he had been punished like a schoolboy in the principal's office in his reaction to the major's brusque remark about "catering to passengers." Within minutes they broke through the fog and into a perfectly blue sky. With the winter sun low on the eastern horizon, they could just make out the peaks of the White Mountains, poking their majestic crowns of snow heavenward.

Within the hour Nick was circling a runway cut into the forest just to the north of Yukon Flats. During the winter the gravel runway wouldn't present any challenges as long as it was clear of any snowdrifts or chunks of ice from the snow plow. Nick made a first pass of the runway at tree level to confirm the runway was clear, and in minutes they were on the ground. Nick was happy it was a daylight landing, as communications with ground personnel was non-existent. Two vehicles met them, though, as they taxied into position to tie the plane down.

Grant Pearson, acting superintendent of the Mt. McKinley National Park, and Bradford Washburn, mountaineer, scientist, and explorer on contract with the U.S. Army to test the effectiveness of cold-weather gear, met the entourage with two drivers as they disembarked from the plane. "Good afternoon, gentlemen," the major said with familiarity once on the ground. "Lieutenant, help the crew with the dispatch of our gear while Mr. Oppenheimer and Mr. Reisdorf join these men to begin our planning for tomorrow's activities. We don't have a lot of time." The major's tone was full of self-importance as he motioned with his hand for the others to get into the lead Jeep. "Brief these men as to what's expected," he added.

Lieutenant Max O'Reilly buttoned his coat and rubbed his hands for warmth as the vehicle drove away. "Looks like your job is to babysit the help, Lieutenant," Red said, not concealing the irritation in his voice.

"Seems as if the army hasn't informed you much about the nature of this junket," the Lieutenant said with an apologetic tone.

"No, I'd say not," replied Nick, "but I have a feeling you're about to." The crew stood there on the frozen airstrip waiting for an explanation.

"First, let me apologize to you, Captain, for you not receiving this information first, but hopefully you'll understand when I tell you that this mission is top secret. You will not know what that mission is, but I can say that your selection as a crew was based on your previous familiarity with the project team. Everything about this mission is on a need-to-know basis."

"So, what's our role to be," Nick said, emphasizing an acceptance of what he had no control over. He made a mental note to tell Cricket what he thought about this assignment. Outwardly he controlled his dissatisfaction.

"You and the co-captain won't be needed until our flight back. PFC Endo will be assigned to me, with your permission, of course, for camp details and mess duty."

"Robert, I don't believe the lieutenant is really asking for my permission, but are you okay with this arrangement?"

"The C-45A only requires a crew of two, so I'm not surprised. And, with you being an ATC contract pilot, not regular army, the lieutenant outranks you on the ground," Robert stated flatly.

"What's the length of our stay?" Nick asked, moving on.

"Not definite, but the plan is for two days. You're free to take in the sights . . . just be ready for a departure when the major orders. Mr. Washburn has arranged for us to stay at his winter camp not far from here. The others will stay there, too. Any other questions?"

Nick conjured the meaning of the word "sights" as he looked around at the frozen landscape filled with a mix of barren hills, forested glens, and open pastures. *Two days here could be interesting*, he thought. *Maybe I can try to find that mountaineer couple John and Peg Cable I met last year.*

"Captain, permission to speak?" Red asked.

"Permission granted."

"Lieutenant, it's not my purview to know everything, but the presence of Mr. Pearson has me a little confused. He's quite a bit off the ranch as the acting Mt. McKinley Park superintendent, don't you think?" Red's study of Alaska was showing with the implication in his question of the great distance between their current location and the park.

"Can't comment, co-captain, other than to say that Mr. Pearson's knowledge of Yukon Flats area has special relevance to the mission."

"Sounds like I'm going to have to satisfy my curiosity another time." Red's tone of dissatisfaction was anything but subtle.

"If there are no other questions, let's get the gear off the plane and loaded up," the lieutenant said, ending the short query.

CHAPTER 22

The flight from Ladd with the team from Los Alamos was on time. Grant Pearson and Brad Washburn waited in their vehicle and chatted with the few minutes available. Grant had arrived shortly before noon direct from the U.S. Army Recreation Camp at Mt. McKinley. He flew the Piper J5-A himself.

"Uncle Sam has asked us to do some strange things, but I think this little project takes the cake. I just don't get the purpose of showing these folks around. So, what do you know about this mission, Brad?"

"Not much. Didn't they give you an explanation?" Brad asked, knowing that as a contract worker his own ignorance in military matters was par for the course. He first met Grant about a year earlier when testing cold-weather equipment at Mt. McKinley Army Recreation Camp, where Grant had assisted with various expeditions.

"No. And I don't think we're going to get one either. Sometimes these army bastards can be a pain in the ass."

"That's strange . . . the lack of an explanation, I mean," Brad said, knowing that Grant hated being in the dark. Grant had an arrogant streak in him and generally thought he was right. On the rare occasion when he didn't have an answer, he would stand there with his hands jammed in his pockets, jaw extended, and get a sullen look on his face, trying to blame someone else for his ignorance. He hated the title "acting superintendent," because as far as he was concerned the current National Park Service superintendent didn't measure up, and crowded his freedom. He carried himself with the swagger of the superintendent title and assumed that the job would soon be his once his boss retired. Both Brad and Grant were of the same height, but Brad was wiry, whereas Grant was more muscled. Both were young men in their early thirties, but Brad's accomplishments as a mountaineer and cartographer overshadowed Grant's self-aggrandized reputation as an Alaskan pioneer. Grant would have you believe that there was nothing he hadn't accomplished in the Alaskan wilderness. Truth was—Brad felt he was overrated.

"Maybe they are waiting until we're all together to give us a briefing," Brad continued with his standard sense of practicality.

"Maybe."

Brad knew that what really galled Grant was being ordered around. The politics of being an errand-boy didn't suit Grant's self-image. Luckily the flight was on time, as even waiting a short time in the vehicle at the beck and command of the major put Grant in a sour mood.

"Who's the pilot?" Brad asked, noticing the textbook landing.

"Nick Morgan, on loan from Northwest. That's about all I do know other than we're to be the tour directors for this soirée."

"Seems to know his business," Brad commented, ignoring Grant's sarcasm.

"Good afternoon, gentlemen," Major Gordon said, shaking their hands vigorously. After dispatching the flight crew and his lieutenant, Major

Gordon motioned Brad and Grant to their Jeep. He could see by their blank expressions as he approached that a little public relations work was in order. Introductions were made and they climbed inside the Jeep. "We appreciate your help. I apologize for the lack of information surrounding this little project. And I'm afraid it's not going to get any better either since the purpose of the trip is classified. I did ask for the two best men available, however. Both of you came highly recommended in your knowledge and abilities. I'll try not to make you feel like Girl Scouts in how we work together over the next few days, but in reality, I will be getting information from you, but won't be able to give anything in return about the mission."

"Can you give us an overview of what you'd like to accomplish?" Grant asked.

"I'll do that as soon as we get to camp and lay out the maps. I assume that our camp will be secure, Mr. Washburn?"

"No problem, Major. It's all been arranged."

"Good."

The camp was a short distance from the airstrip over an extremely rough logging road. The two miles took them about a half hour. The five men were quiet during the crowded ride out of necessity, as the grind of the Jeep's gears, shifting back and forth between granny and low, coupled with the bouncing load in the back, made conversation difficult. No other vehicle or people were seen.

Once out of the Jeep at camp, Brad explained the sleeping situation as the responsible authority for the test camp. "We've got you set up in the tents over there," he said, pointing to four tents removed from the main group of five additional sleeping tents and one large community tent for the on-site test team. All the tents were constructed of heavy canvas and set up for winter, elevated on six-inch wooden platforms and insulated on all sides with bails of straw. "You decide the sleeping arrangements, and my men will finish up with the right number of cots," Brad concluded.

"Put me in the far tent on the right by myself, with some kind of table we can use for maps," said the major. "We'll convene in fifteen minutes. The rest of you can divvy up as you want."

"Include Ronald in my tent, let the lieutenant bunk with Mr. Pearson, and the flight crew can stay together. I assume that you're already situated, Mr. Washburn?" Dr. Oppenheimer dismissed any further discussion of the sleeping arrangements with a wave of his cigarette.

Grant kicked the frozen ground in disgust to the notice of no one.

The meeting in the tent was a brief discussion focusing on the logistics of getting the team into the area called Chalkyitsik, about fifty miles east of Fort Yukon. Neither Brad nor Grant could think of anything important about the fishing village. There were only four cabins and a wooden, one-room schoolhouse. As far as they were concerned, it had never been anything but a fishing and hunting camp for Black River Gwich'in Natives.

"We'll be traveling by dogsleds. The forecast for tomorrow is five below, so dress warm. Breakfast is at 0600 and departure time will need to be no later than 0700 to make it in time to explore the area. Most of the trip will be in semidarkness, but the dogs are good. By the way, you're welcome to any of the gear we're testing. Independent feedback is always good," said Brad with a smile.

"We'll need to stay the night there in order to cover the territory you're interested in," Grant added. "We can use one of the cabins."

"Okay, our plan is set," said Major Gordon. "I'd like to spend the rest of the afternoon with Dr. Oppenheimer and Ronald, so if you men will excuse us . . ."

"No problem," Brad replied. "Grub will be ready in the mess tent at 1715."

———————————

"Join us if you'd like," Captain Morgan said, addressing the major and his team from New Mexico as they came into the mess tent.

"We'll do that," the major replied. It was clear that he spoke for the team.

Robert Endo had been assigned by the lieutenant to serve their table to help the mess staff with the additional nine people. He seemed to be handling the task well. "Pretty limited menu tonight, gentlemen, but I think you'll like it. Mashed potatoes with hamburger gravy for the main course, salad and sheet cake to round things out."

"Any coffee, soldier?" the major asked.

"Comin' right up."

"What's with Robert," Red whispered to Nick, twisting his body away from the group. "My dog's not that happy, and he's never been neutered and has the run of the farm."

Nick just shrugged as if to say, "don't argue with success."

"Did I hear you say, Captain, that you had to drain the oil out of the plane," the lieutenant chimed in.

"You're probably not used to the temperature extremes we get here. It's been my experience that keeping the oil inside on very cold nights makes for a much easier start the next day, particularly if there's an emergency where you absolutely have to have the plane fly."

"Is there a point when the oil won't work?"

"My rule of thumb is around negative fifteen. Otherwise, the engine, starter, and battery take a beating."

"We don't have to think about things like that back home."

"All you need is to let your major down once on takeoff, and I can assure you that you'll think about it from then on." Nick nodded toward the major in an effort to warm up the relationship a bit. "We took the liberty of draining your oil in the J5-A, also, Mr. Pearson."

"Thanks. Saves me a trip after dinner," replied Grant.

To Nick the reply demonstrated a level of inexperience and poor planning on the part of the acting superintendent. Why would he make the additional round trip back to the plane unless he just plain forgot, or worse yet, didn't know any better?

Robert Endo stayed and helped the mess staff clean up after everyone was gone. It was only then that he ate dinner—alone. He wasn't sure exactly how to approach the next two days or what events would bring, but his thoughts strayed toward excitement. One thing he knew for sure, he did not like Major Gordon's superior attitude. *He can go fuck himself,* he thought.

CHAPTER 23

Fort Yukon, Alaska
December 10, 1943

My Dear Martha,

Red and I spent the day with John and Peg Cable. You remember—I told you they're the couple from Ohio that just picked up sticks and moved to Fort Yukon. Wanted some peace and quiet. Sure got their share of that along the Porcupine River. They had us out snowshoeing most of the day. Beautiful wilderness—great experience. Tested some thermal long johns intended for cold weather duty. Pretty good results. Boy, I'm woofed! I'll sign off for now.

Yours,
Nick

<hr>

"You done writing, Captain?" Red asked, creating a cloud of vapor with his breath in the near-freezing temperature in the tent he, Nick, and Robert were assigned to. The small wood tent stove barely made a dent in the below-zero temperatures that crept in from the outside. They were all were huddled up in their sleeping bags—there were eight cots, but with only the three of them they had the run of the accommodations. It was about 2100 and Robert was sound asleep on the corner cot and Nick and Red were soon to follow.

"Just finished," Nick said.

"I know it's above my pay grade, pard, but what do you think of all this?"

"You mean our little vacation?"

"Yeah."

"Hard to tell. My guess, though, is that it has something to do with a possible mineral find or something along that order with Oppenheimer being a scientist. It's just a guess. How about you?"

"They've had a lot of questions about people living in the area . . . numbers, and so forth. Kinda like they might be in the way of whatever they're thinkin'."

"Interesting point."

"So, it's my guess it's got something to do with a power dam on the Yukon River. Just can't figure out why these are the folks investigating . . . and why it's so damn secret."

"Your theory is better than mine, but I'm all tuckered out. It was a good day with John and Peg. I admire their spirit. Wish I had some of it right now though, so I could continue our conversation. See you in the morning."

Red had a bit more staying power than Nick, so he continued to think about the possibilities. Within minutes, however, he found himself nodding off. As a result, he turned off the kerosene lamp to avoid wasting fuel. There was a wind buffeting against the flaps of the tent that reassured Red that the warm, down sleeping bag was the place to be.

Robert absorbed the conversation between the captain and co-captain as he feigned sleep. If he was going to be of any use to Vladimir, he knew he had to get into either the major's tent or Oppenheimer's tent—or both—while they were gone. Normal camp activity during the day eliminated that possibility. It would have to be at night, but the need to be careful was an understatement. The location of his corner cot in the tent diagonally across from the other two men would help. He had given it thought during the day and had come up with a plan.

With a razor blade he was able to pick the nylon thread from a seam holding the canvas tent material together at the corner. This would be his exit. He reworked the seam in a drawstring fashion that would allow him to come and go without the noise of undoing the main zipper and front flaps. The drawstring made it easy to open and close the corner while avoiding drafts that might wake the others.

He successfully slipped out after carefully plumping up his sleeping bag with clothing to simulate his presence. The small slit would not allow him passage while wearing his big parka, so he layered as best he could. *God, is it cold*, he thought, anxious to get the coat back on. The wind had died down a little, but not much. His Russian fur hat, called an *ushankas*, was definitely an asset. First, he moved slowly toward the major's tent under the light of a full moon. He could hear his beating heart over the crunch of the dry snow under his feet. Robert was well aware of the remaining sled dogs in camp bedded down on the south side of the mess tent. Luckily, the wind was blowing north and would cover what little noise he did stir, but regardless, he needed to be extra careful. With the men at Chalkyitsik, this was his chance. Shadows from the trees played with Robert's nerves as he crossed the camp compound. He meticulously walked in the remaining imprints of the major's tracks from the morning. He had to hope that the wind and drifting snow would eliminate his tracks, but he couldn't be too careful. A dead tree limb dislodged from a nearby pine by a gust of wind and dropped to the ground. He was so surprised that his legs felt weak. He wasn't used to this. *What would Vladimir do?* he wondered as he unzipped the front flap of the major's tent and crawled inside, carefully leaving his boots at the entrance in order not to track in snow.

Inside the tent Robert had to be extra careful. He figured the major to be an anal son of a bitch, checking and rechecking everything. Alterations would be noticed. The table used for maps was empty. Robert wondered if the maps had been a ruse to get a private tent. The bed was minus a sleeping bag, and the extra wool army blankets were neatly stacked near the foot of the bed. The desk reminded him of a Civil War general's field desk, where lieutenants would line up for debriefings and orders. In truth, he could find nothing remarkable on the desk or about its contents. With the help of his penlight, he did notice a bound report on the nightstand detailing the history of the Yukon Flats area. *Hardly unusual, considering the nature of the trip*, he thought. It was closed, but one of the pages was dog-eared. The heading on that page was *Fall Weather Conditions. He must mean next fall*, Robert thought, *since Christmas is just around the corner*. He spent another ten minutes carefully rummaging through things but found nothing noteworthy before leaving the major's tent. *I could get good at this*, he thought.

Somehow Oppenheimer's tent was less intimidating, perhaps because he wasn't a major. His confidence was bolstered by the successful entry into the second tent. Two cots, one left and one right, occupied most of the space. A rough-hewn wooden nightstand separated the cots at the head and contained nothing other than light reading material, he observed. A trunk with a lock was at the foot of each bed. The one on the left was unlocked and contained a carton of cigarettes, a few personal writing items, and some civilian clothes. By their small size he estimated they were Ronald's. The trunk on the right was locked—not a complicated lock but effective. Robert had anticipated as much and reached for a small screwdriver and a paper clip from his pocket. Sure enough, the mechanism responded. There was more material here, enough to warrant a chair for a more comfortable position.

The official reports were telling. Some were marked CONFIDENTIAL. The first detailed the beginning of a "hidden city" called Hanford located east of Seattle. It explained its purpose as a major supply source of plutonium. Robert had no idea what plutonium was used for, but if large-quantity production was under way in Hanford as indicated, the supply had to be somehow connected to the Flats area. The other document of interest was a map of the Yukon Flats area itself with concentric circles around a point sixty miles east of the village of Chalkyitsik and two to three miles north of the Black River. Penciled in the margin were the words, "hot zone." *They must be considering the location as some sort of test site, but why Chalkyitsik?* he thought. It was difficult for him to form any real conclusions.

A quick check of his watch indicated 0400. Camp would be stirring soon with the cooks preparing breakfast for 0600. He locked the trunk and closed the tent carefully, ensuring that everything was as he found it.

The sub-zero temperatures had finally taken a toll, but he hadn't really noticed because he was so intensely focused with his findings. When he returned to his tent he found that his hands had become numb, which caused him to struggle with the drawstring opening to the tent. He felt clumsy. But patience had always been his ally and soon enough he was safely back into his sleeping bag.

Robert's eyes were stuck together and the inside of his head hammered in unison with the ringing alarm clock that rudely interrupted his short night's sleep. He fought the urge to ignore the disruption with the reality that he had to make it through the day as if nothing had happened.

"Come on, Robert," Red called out while pulling his pants up. "There are things to do."

"Can't we just surrender to the Nips and go back to bed," he replied, taking on the persona that this was just another morning. "God, I just slept awful . . . the wind never stopped."

"That may be, but your Captain and I have a special treat for you this morning before our guests return. Besides, the wind wasn't just blowing on your side of the tent. Hell, I woke up once last night and noticed that you were so sound asleep you were like a pile of rocks."

Robert went deep inside of his recollection of the previous night to replay anything that may have tipped the co-captain off that he had gone AWOL. The stark simplicity of Red's comment coupled with his own actions reminded him of his proximity to a court-marshal.

"You're probably right. So what's the big surprise?"

It was Nick that responded, "I remember a conversation on one of our flights where you mentioned that you'd never been on a dog sled. We're going to fix that this morning. Made arrangements with John Cable yesterday . . . and one of the crew here. It's gonna be Red's first go at it, as well."

Not a bad idea, Robert thought, *as it might be the one way to stay awake.* "Okay, I'm in. When do we leave?"

"Right after breakfast, if you ever manage to get your ass out of that sleeping bag," Red said.

John arrived early, and by 0900 everyone was ready to harness up the dogs. John's sled was set up with six Siberian Huskies, which would allow him to carry a passenger. One more sled was set up as a double with six Alaskan Huskies. The army had all Alaskans, as they were bigger and more powerful, ideally suited for distance and endurance. Though not considered a breed, their genetic mix from gold-rush days allowed for perfect adaptation to sledding. John preferred the

Siberians, which were smaller, built for short-distance speed, and distinguished by unique markings and almond-shaped eyes. One additional army sled was harnessed with just four dogs, making it easier to maneuver. With his past experience with Minnesota mushing, Nick would drive that one by himself.

"I'm amazed at how disciplined the dogs are, and how well they listen to the drivers," Robert commented to Red amid the clatter of playful barking and driver commands.

Alan, a sergeant from the crew, would act as lead. "Let me give you a little heads-up on our run. We're going to keep it on the gentle side today, just enough to give the dogs a workout. I'll lead. Captain, you'll follow me. And John will be in cleanup. Once we're out on the trail everyone will get a chance to drive. Any questions?"

With no responses other than eager faces, Alan commanded, "Mush, mush," followed by the "mushes" of Nick and John. The power, agility, and grace of the dogs working together was immediately impressive. Equally impressive was the physical strength required by the musher to handle the dogs and maneuver the sled. The responsiveness of the dogs transferred a confidence in the musher and a stability to the ride.

The day off turned out to be the perfect break for everyone. The polar twilight through most of the day gave a soft light from the sun's refraction. Riding behind the dogs on the snowy trails in a forest of tall pines with their snow-covered boughs was amazing. It was eerily silent except for the dogs' panting and the soft sound of their paws hitting the ground. Every so often one of the mushers would call out, "Gee" or "Haw," which Red and Robert soon figured out was the command for right or left respectively. They covered about twenty-five miles of scenic trails between frozen lakes, mountains, and rivers with open spots of moving water. As Alan promised, each person went solo on the single sled, giving them time on the runners and the opportunity to experience a unique sensation of teamwork with the dogs. It was a great day.

By the time they returned to camp it was almost 1630, barely enough time to tend to the animals and sleds and get ready for chow. John decided not to return home until the morning. "Peg will be happy with me being gone. She's got three straight months coming up without a break from me. Too much of a good thing, she told me the other day," he said.

Dinner came and went with no sign of the major's team. Robert was already in bed at 1915.

"Our PFC isn't much for the outdoors," Nick said to Red over a cup of coffee.

"Can't say I much blame 'em. I'm about ready to turn in, too." The constant jostling on the sleds and the work needed to keep them on track was tiring, particularly for the two greenhorns.

At about 1945 a large commotion of dogs could be heard heading into camp from the northeast. "I would have guessed they wouldn't return until tomorrow," Nick commented while stubbing out a cigarette. "I think I'll check things out."

"Captain," the major called out as he recognized Nick approaching the group. "Let's have that plane ready for takeoff by 2045."

Nick resented being ordered around by this overstuffed officer, but swallowed his pride. "Are you sure your people are up to it?" It only took a few glances at the others to see they were dog tired. "A night's rest might make the flight a little more palatable."

The major walked over in the crunchy snow to Nick and stopped with his face eye-to-eye with Nick's. "I'm not sure you'd make it in the regular army, Captain. Seems like comfort is more important to you than getting things done. Now, if there are reasons why we can't lift off in an hour, I'd like to hear them. If there aren't, then I'd suggest we get to work."

"Twenty forty-five it is, Major!" Nick saluted, subverting his immediate negative reaction to the major's air of superiority. He turned and walked away toward the tent where Robert, and by now Red, were sound asleep.

"Up and at 'em, boys," Nick said as he shook the bottom of both cots. "Major's got his tit in a wringer about something, and he wants liftoff in fifty-five minutes." Seeing just a little movement from Red and none from Robert, he shook the beds harder. "Let's go!"

Robert and Red stumbled around the tent scrambling to get dressed, get their gear, and get their brains out of a sleep fog. Nick prepared a flight plan. In twenty minutes all three were walking toward a Jeep in the cold night air. The vehicle hadn't been started all day, and the inside was like an icebox. It took several grinding turns of the engine to get a response. Once started, Nick let it idle, almost as an act of mercy, while they packed their gear and positioned the plane's engine oil in a box to keep the container from falling on its side. *It was exactly for situations like this, and for assholes like Major Gordon, that made draining the oil the right call,* he thought. His plan was to get to the C-45A with enough time to call in his flight plan, have Red put the oil back in the crankcase, and have Robert stow their gear. He had no intention of allowing the major even the slightest excuse to agitate his crew any more than they already were.

"Red, Robert, let's just get this flight over with. Any comments from our passengers that cause your blood to boil, bring 'em to me. As you would say, Red, the major's got a burr under his saddle, and I don't intend to make it our problem. We clear on this?"

"Completely," replied Robert, respecting the captain's approach to head off a problem.

"In the desert, the Mescalero Apache strip their enemy naked, stake 'em out on top of an ant hill, pour honey on their gonads, and . . ."

"Enough, Red," Nick interrupted. "Besides being a court-marshalling offense, we don't have any ant hills or honey." The tension eased and the men went to work.

The trip back to Anchorage went as well as could be expected. Other than Nick and Red everyone slept the whole flight.

It was almost midnight when Robert, completely exhausted, returned to his quarters and quickly got ready for bed. He decided to stow his gear before hitting the sack. He unzipped the daypack after dealing with his duffel bag and noticed a folded slip of paper on top. *What's this?*, he thought, because he had no recall of putting it there. He unfolded the paper, revealing a handwritten note that said:

ROBERT,

TAKE THIS NOTE TO VLADIMIR AND MENTION, FIRST LIGHTNING.

A FRIEND

CHAPTER 24

Nick was awakened early the next morning by one of the non-coms from flight operations rapping at his door. "Captain, Captain," he said half out of breath. "Cricket said it would be okay to wake you. Sorry, sir."

"Oh, he did, did he? What's so damned important?" he said, wiping sleep from his eyes.

"We got a troop ship coming through in about an hour from Bethel. The captain radioed that he's coming down with the flu and can't continue on. These boys on board are long overdue for furlough, and Cricket wants to know if you'd take the rest of the flight."

"Where's it headed?" Nick was a little defensive, afraid it might get in the way of his own long-awaited furlough.

"Minneapolis-St. Paul and then to Chicago. Cricket said we have another pilot that can bring the ship back if you'd like to start your Christmas holidays early, sir."

"Tell Cricket I owe him one. I'll be ready in half an hour." This was the first good scheduling news Nick had had in months. After a quick shower he packed his duffel bag, being careful to protect the various presents he'd purchased. He took a minute and stopped to wish Red a Merry Christmas before leaving.

By 1000, Nick was in the air with perfect skies. He smiled at the thought of how excited Martha would be with the surprise. They had to make a quick stop in Norman Wells on the CANOL to deliver some Caterpillar parts and then refuel in Edmonton. There was no reason why they couldn't be in Minneapolis by 1930. No reason they couldn't make Chicago by 2130. He'd be home the next day by noon—almost a full week ahead of schedule.

December 12, 1943
Enroute Norman Wells

My Dear Martha,

I'll hand this card to you when I'm home—sure looking forward to time with you and 'family'. I saw a distinctive, unnamed mountain today, about six thousand feet, in a conspicuous position where the Mackenzie and Liard Rivers come together. I named it Mt. Martha on the map. Further on, at the confluence of the Mackenzie and Keele Rivers lies a beautiful, uncharted lake with high cliffs on either side about seventy miles north of Mt. Martha that splits the range from east to west. I have put it on the map as Lake Martha.

See you tomorrow on my surprise arrival.

Yours,
Nick

Nick was in the air again, on schedule out of Edmonton, when his flight engineer knocked on the cabin door.

"Captain, don't mean to interrupt, but we've got a passenger out here who says she knows you. Wants to say hello, if it's alright."

"She? Not a lot of those in the army."

"She told me her name is Anne Walsh."

"Oh hell," Nick exclaimed. "Anne's not a she; she's a sister."

"I heard that," came the voice on the other side of the door.

"The ship's yours." Nick was happy to give the co-pilot a turn at the stick.

"Anne, you old son-of-a-gun. How long have you been on the plane?"

"Just boarded. Heading home for the holidays."

"Cleveland, if I remember right. Is the lucky boyfriend going to be home from North Africa?"

"You do have a good memory, Captain."

"Just keeping track of the competition," he said lightheartedly. "This flight only goes as far as Chicago. You do know that?"

"A bus will take me the rest of the way."

"You didn't say good-bye before leaving. I figured you had been relocated."

"Yeah, right after we had that date together. Remember?" They laughed. "I'm really sorry about not leaving a note," Anne went on. "You were on your way to Bethel, and I needed to catch a plane for Billings the next day. A pretty lame excuse, I know. Billings has a great hospital, and I'm in the ER. It seems that the duty here for flight training isn't hard enough. Most of these guys have a lot of free time and get hurt fishing, backpacking, climbing, hunting, you name it. It's like summer camp for most of these boys.

"How's Martha?"

"Bigger than a blimp."

"Wow, I hadn't heard."

"Found out after arriving in Bethel. She's pretty excited, but the morning sickness isn't any fun."

"*She's* pretty excited? What about you, mister?"

"That's what I meant, we're pretty excited. It's just harder to be tuned in when you're gone the whole time."

"I'll bet you plan to make it up over Christmas."

"Going to surprise her tomorrow night. She's not expecting me until next week. What about you? Do you hear from Tom?"

"The postcards are usually a month late, but he's put in for leave over Christmas. Sure hope he gets it."

"His duty is a lot different than ours."

"From what I can tell, they're moving on to Italy. His communications duty puts him in some tough situations."

"You must worry about him a lot."

"I just keep moving forward each day, thinking that it'll be over soon. I try to help the boys in my ER the way I would want Tom helped if he were hurt."

"Well, we're about ready to begin preparations for landing in Minneapolis-St. Paul, so I need to get back to work. I'll buy you a cup of coffee on the way to Chicago."

"You're going to Chicago?" The enthusiasm in Anne's voice hinted that she hoped they could spend more time together.

"Yes, but it will be late, and my early turnaround the next day means I have to get my beauty sleep. I'll take a rain check for the next time we run into each other."

The next day Nick arrived in Minneapolis on time. He let himself into their place in Minneapolis and made a peanut butter and jelly sandwich while waiting the two hours for Martha to get home from work. He was a little disappointed that the house hadn't been decorated for Christmas yet, but thought that it would be fun for them to do together. They could do it that night. It felt good to just sit on the couch and do nothing. It wasn't long before he was sound asleep. The lack of sleep from the Yukon Flats trip must have caught up with him, as he didn't awake until he heard the key in the front door. Martha had stopped after work to visit with her friend Alice and by now the house was completely dark.

He instinctively got up and sprang toward Martha from the other room exclaiming, "Surprise, Honey! I'm home!"

"Aaaaaah!" Martha screamed in complete shock and dropped her groceries. She slipped on the rag-braided, circular entry rug, caught a heel, and lost her balance with a buckled knee. She hit her head on the brass handle of the entry door and dropped to the floor with a hard thud. Blood came quickly.

Nick could see the entire event in his mind's eye, as if it were replayed in slow motion—him awakened from a deep sleep, calling out Martha's name enthusiastically, her shock that someone was in the house, causing her to slip on the rug and fall. "Oh my God, what have I done!?" He turned on a hall light and quickly retrieved a towel from the kitchen to act as a compress for the wound. He placed a small pillow from the couch under her head as he made attempts to revive her. The blood was making quite a mess.

Martha's head began to turn slowly. She groaned in pain as she tried to open her eyes. "Don't hurt me," she pleaded. "I don't have any money."

"It's me, Honey. It's me. I'm so sorry. It was an accident."

Recognizing Nick for the first time, she said, "What are you doing here? You're not due home for another week."

"It's a long story, but I think we need to get you to a hospital first. Are you okay to stand up?"

"I think so. Why did you scare me that way? I hope the baby's okay," she said with an added level of alarm.

"Your face took a pretty good whack on the fall, but I think you'll be fine. What's Doc McNally's number?"

Fortunately, the Doc was in and said he'd meet them there.

"Just keep her quiet and still," he told Nick before hanging up.

Nick quickly grabbed a few things Martha needed and made it to the hospital in twenty minutes. The next couple hours were occupied with waiting and filling out forms. Luckily it was a Monday, and Doc McNally was still on call. He showed up shortly after they arrived. After a brief examination, he diagnosed a broken nose and administered some pain medication. He packed her nose with sterile gauze. "The important part is that the baby will be okay," he said as he secured the dressing with tape across the nostrils.

"What were you thinking, Nick?" Martha said after the doctor left.

Nick tried to explain, but in retrospect none of it made sense to him either.

"I know you meant well, Nick, but you weren't considering me in this little surprise of yours. I'm glad you're home early, but couldn't you have just called? God, my nose hurts!"

"Sorry for trying to add a little fun into things. Let's just drop it," he said defensively. "It was an accident." Nick walked away frustrated, trying to make sense of two broken noses in his life within the last thirty days.

The next morning things weren't any better. He heard Martha exclaim from the bathroom, "This is awful. I look like a prizefighter, Nick. Come here!"

He groaned under his breath, knowing that his penance was far from over. He walked across the hardwood bedroom floor and down the hall in his cotton pajamas toward the bathroom.

"I can't believe it," he heard her say.

He was shocked when he first saw Martha. She faced the medicine cabinet mirror poking at a mass of greenish-yellow bruises across the bridge of her nose and cheeks. The bruises were much worse than those of Robert's. *Must be the effects of the solid brass door handle. It couldn't have been worse if I'd sucker punched her with brass knuckles myself,* he thought. *Would people think I hit my wife? Why am I even thinking that?* The anticipation of a perfect Christmas vanished as dread filled the pit of Nick's stomach.

"It's not too bad," he lied.

"Not too bad! It's a disaster. There's no way I can even cover it up, Nick. And the throbbing just won't stop."

Nick knew the whole mess could have been avoided if he hadn't been so stupid. It didn't seem fair. He had been looking forward to coming home for so long and went to such an effort to make his arrival exciting and fun. "Is there anything I can do?" he asked feebly.

Martha started to cry. "Nothing's right anymore. You'd rather be off with your army buddies gambling than be home anyway. And now this! You'll have to call me in sick," she said with a defeated tone, knowing they needed the money. He reached to console her, but she eluded his grasp and was gone before his hand could reach her shoulder. She stormed out of the bathroom and down the hall, and then slammed the bedroom door behind her.

He stared into the bathroom mirror only to see a blank expression staring back at him. He put both hands on the edge of the porcelain sink to prop himself up while he considered his predicament. *The de-icing challenge with Red was much easier than this,* he thought. *At least we could predict events.* This situation had gone completely out of control—well beyond the turmoil of the broken nose.

She spent the rest of the morning alone in the bedroom while Nick aimlessly wandered the rest of the house. No matter how he reviewed the facts and circumstances leading up to the broken nose, he couldn't make the logic work that would claim his innocence. He read for a while, but struggled to hold onto the words. He switched from magazine to book with no improvement. Music from a local radio station settled some of the hostility generated by the silence. He moved around their small living room, refreshing himself with the pictures of Martha and him, family and friends, and the few art pieces they had collected. The envelope on the mantel caught his attention, as it seemed out of place. He was surprised to see that it was addressed to him, but there was no stamp. Nick wrestled with the ethics of opening a letter that was never sent. The envelope had been sealed, so he felt it was probably similar to the postcard he wrote on the flight home—why mail it when you can hand it to the person? He opened the letter.

December 8, 1943

My Dearest Nick,

I know that I can't expect you to understand how lonely I am when you're away, but I have always felt some comfort thinking that you felt the same way. Your three cards today detailing the vacation you seem to be enjoying with the boys playing poker makes it difficult for me to share any compassion for your situation. It doesn't seem to me that the lost Thanksgiving for us was much of a disappointment to you when compared to the excitement of your gambling escapades. Maybe Mother was right. You'll always put yourself first. Your baby and I will need a father and husband when you return—will you be there?

The family had so many plans that involved you and when you couldn't make it all of us genuinely felt sad for your hardship. I can safely inform them that you survived quite well. It concerns me,

Nick, that I don't seem to know who you are at times. This makes me feel very alone and sad. What's happening to you? Your baby and I don't have much of a choice but to wait and hope that your carelessness for how we feel and your insensitivity over our situation will pass.

Maybe I should wait until tomorrow to see if I feel the same way about your cards before sending this letter.

Love Always,
Martha

The three postcards detailing his "gambling escapades" were inserted into the envelope along with the letter.

Doesn't she see that these postcards are my attempt to keep her from worrying? I didn't tell her about the consequences of losing an engine at nine thousand feet. I didn't burden her with the monotony involved in waiting four days for a new engine and then adding the frustration of having the ship commandeered by the army. Does she really think that gambling is my new mistress? All I can do is deal with the reality presented. Why does she have to get so emotional about everything? Nick's thoughts bore a hole in his stomach. *And the last straw was the comment referencing her mother. Maybe it is easier to be single while at war,* he thought, reflecting back on his conversation with that new co-pilot he flew with about a month back. Nick's shoulders were tight with tension. He needed some understanding, too, he thought. But today, however, was not the day to engage a pregnant, hundred and twenty–pound adversary with a broken nose, bruises, and hurt feelings. He smiled a bit at the image.

"Can I get anything for you, Hotshot? I'm going out for a few minutes and thought maybe some pistachio ice cream might help." It was her favorite and Nick wasn't above bribing her at this point.

"Don't you care how I look at all?" came her reply. "I suppose you want me to look fatter than I already am with this baby!" The bedroom door slammed.

He left the house without another word, seriously questioning whether or not Martha had lost her senses.

CHAPTER 25

The last few days had taken all of Robert's energy. It was late when he finally drifted off Saturday night, and it was all he could do to crawl out of bed Sunday morning. Since he had no assignment for the day, he just sat on the edge of his cot, head in hands, struggling with the reality of how to approach his new challenge. Finally, he picked up the note and stared at it as if it would magically explain itself.

ROBERT,

TAKE THIS NOTE TO VLADIMIR AND MENTION, FIRST LIGHTNING.

A FRIEND

He had made a bargain with Vladimir that he felt honor-bound to keep, but his inner voice told him to check with Captain Morgan first. A clear resolution was not apparent to Robert. He played it over in his mind as he got dressed. Not coming to a conclusion, he decided to grab a late breakfast before the kitchen closed at 0930. Red was exiting the mess hall as Robert arrived.

"Good morning, sunshine."

"Good morning," Robert mumbled. "Did you see the captain this morning?"

"I did, but you won't, pard. It seems the captain drew a lucky straw and is on his way to Minneapolis-St. Paul as we speak." Red motioned to a C-47A on the runway being readied for takeoff. "If you ask me, he earned an early furlough with all the fuss and babysittin' he did. Anything I can do?"

"It'll wait. Nothing important anyway," Robert said. "I better move along if I expect to get any breakfast at all."

The men parted.

Robert found a quiet corner, as usual, and dug into his scrambled eggs, pancakes, and sausage. He was starting to recover from so little sleep over the last few days. He continued thinking about the note, wondering what "First Lightning" could mean and which one of the party put it into his pack. Just then the mess hall door opened and Vladimir walked in and looked around the room. Robert decided to hold out a bit before telling Vladimir about the note until he had a sense of where this little development would take him. Vladimir approached without getting any chow, as if he had been looking for Robert.

"Good morning."

Robert ignored the acknowledgement and didn't invite his friend to take a seat.

"Is it okay if I sit down?" Vladimir persisted.

"I suppose, but I can't stay long."

"It's not good time to talk about your trip?"

Robert was uncharacteristically quiet, focusing more on his plate of food than the question. The turn of his upper body away from Vladimir was enough to let Vladimir know that he didn't want to talk.

"We need to talk sometime today . . . maybe at lunch?"

Robert realized that Vladimir wasn't going to go away, so he said,

"Now is probably as good as any time. It's just that I was hoping to get the captain's advice. And now, he is gone on Christmas furlough."

"We have come to trust each other, Robert. Am I right?"

"Yes."

"Then let us use that trust to say what we know. My superiors are very anxious to learn of your experiences. Why don't you give me, how do you say, the *gist* of what occurred." Vladimir lit a cigarette, exhaled, and leaned back in his chair as if to say he had all the time in the world.

Robert sketched out the weekend, highlighting his search of the tents and the fact that the men were off on their own virtually the entire time and that he had learned very little.

"What is it that you're not telling me?" Vladimir was experienced at interpreting nervous behavior in operatives, especially the new ones. "Something happened."

"Nothing I'm ready to talk about, yet."

Vladimir leaned forward, making eye contact. With a stern face he said, "This is important, Robert. I don't have time to fuck around. Does it have something to do with you and one of the other men?"

"What do you mean?"

"I know about you and Cricket. Are you involved with another man also?"

Robert was caught completely off guard. "That's none of your business! And what does it have to do with us?"

"Nothing, my friend . . . except that I never bring a comrade into my world without knowing everything possible about him."

Robert was clearly alarmed at what Vladimir knew about him.

"Relax, comrade. I am not here to judge you, although I trust that you would like to keep your personal life a secret. No?"

Robert nodded.

"Share with me what you have not said, and let's talk no more of Cricket."

"Do I have your promise?" Robert knew that by asking the question he was also making a bargain.

"Yes, you do."

Robert reached in his coat pocket as Vladimir lit another cigarette. He produced the note without preamble and said, "It was in my day-pack when I returned last night. I thought that the captain would give me good advice."

"You were fortunate that the captain was on his plane to Minnesota. Having this note in your possession would have gotten you some time in the stockade. The captain would have had no choice but to expose the note and you. Do you have any idea as to who put it into you pack?"

"Not really. I am assuming it was one of the men from New Mexico, but it could have been the captain or Red Johnson or any of the crew at the camp for that matter. What does it mean?"

"I'm not sure. All I know is that a very important communication channel has been opened."

"Could it be a trap?"

"I don't think so. My superiors told me about the code name 'First Lightning.' Only a very small group of people know of it. Don't do anything right now. That includes communicating with your captain! We must be in agreement on this. Agreed?"

"Agreed." Robert's voice held a sense of resignation.

"You performed well on your first assignment, Robert. Trust me and we will work well together. Now, I must report back to my superiors for instructions. I will know something by the end of the week. Let me have the note." His extended hand elicited the involuntary return of the note by Robert.

Robert was surprised with the relief he felt in releasing it, but not without the private acknowledgement that his life had just changed.

That afternoon, Vladimir drafted his cipher to Agent Sirak and placed it into the locked ammo container. There would be no more flights for another week after tomorrow and it was his rationale that the faster this note left the country, the better.

Now it was time to wait.

CHAPTER 26

The only good that came from Martha's unsightly bruises from the broken nose was that her supervisor immediately recognized that her injuries didn't make her appearance very customer-friendly. He gave her the holidays off as paid sick leave. She was just as happy, as the added discomfort of the regularly occurring morning sickness was taking its toll.

Later Wednesday afternoon Nick brought up the letter. He tried to bury it, but he couldn't let Martha continue believing in its contents without more information.

"Oh, Nick. I knew you wanted to be home on Thanksgiving, but I wished you would have said something. I just hate those postcards. They never say what I hope you really feel."

"Sometimes I just have to bury all of those thoughts about us. The poker games are nothing but a diversion to keep me from going nuts. Regardless, your letter helped me see it from your side as well. I'm glad you didn't send it, and I will try to do better," Nick said, putting both arms around Martha. He held her there for a long while, exhausted and feeling that the family Christmas was just not meant to be.

Martha snuggled in response to Nick's embrace, feeling that the events over the last few days were now past them. She stood up, took Nick's hand, and led him to the bedroom.

Once in bed Nick felt the tension dissolve, all the while rubbing Martha's back. He knew she loved to have her back scratched and it helped her concede to his affections. Nick's desire for lovemaking was understandable, as they had not been together in months. Nonetheless, he sensed her discomfort in feeling like a "Goodyear blimp," as she had said earlier in the day. *It's hard for Martha not to feel inadequate*, Nick thought, so he took extra care not to rush into things. They talked and touched and kissed for some time before actually making love. Afterwards they shared their excitement with Bud and Helen arriving at the end of the week—the holiday could begin.

On Thursday, Martha suggested to Nick that he go over to the Northwest Airlines flight operations center to catch up with a few of his buddies that might still be there. *Why didn't he stay home to fly commercial, like these men?* she asked herself as he walked out the door. *After all, the country always needs pilots at home, too.* Looking back, she wasn't quite sure how he got caught up in the emotion of flying for the army. On top of everything, getting pregnant happened a lot faster than either had expected. "Can't cry over spilt milk now," she said to herself while doing the lunch dishes and ruminating over the lack of control she had over her life.

Nick returned home about three o'clock. He walked up the front stoop and across the porch to the front door only to find Martha crying and holding a crumpled letter from Bud and Helen in her hand when he walked in. "What's the matter?" Nick said, surprised with her emotional setback.

"They're not coming. Nothing's right." Tears and sobs choked her words.

"Who's not coming?"

"Helen and Bud." She thrust the tear-stained letter at Nick as if it were his fault. "He's your brother, can't you do something?"

She saw the genuine dissatisfaction on Nick's face as he scanned the letter. "This is too bad. Says here that he's up to his eyeballs in work, and the War Department is putting pressure on his group to meet their deadlines. He wouldn't do this, Martha, if it wasn't important."

"But I was really looking forward to them coming. First Thanksgiving and now Christmas." She threw her arms around Nick and broke down. This wasn't like Martha, but she couldn't hold everything in any longer.

"Ah, Hotshot, it'll be alright. We can still have fun with our friends, and we'll still see Mom and Dad."

"It won't be the same without them."

That evening Nick and Martha had a quiet supper together, which allowed Martha to share the many disappointments of being by herself so much and not having any real outlet for life other than work.

"But what about the baby?" Nick said.

"It's not the same. It's there, and I know that I will love it when it's born, but there are times when I wish I wasn't pregnant."

Nick was shocked with her comment, but remained quiet. Maybe he didn't understand what was really going on with Martha. "What do you mean?" he asked.

"Oh, I don't know. Sometimes I'm so excited that I can't wait, and sometimes I wish it had never happened. I feel trapped, Nick." She sobered at her own words and realized the selfishness they contained. Everyone had told her how wonderful it would be to be a mother and what a miracle it was to have a child, but it all went so fast. It was just yesterday that she and Nick were flying around without a care in the world. Everything was in front of them—no commitments and no real worries about the future. "I feel helpless," she confessed.

"You'll get over it," he replied without actually registering the depth of her feelings.

"But when you're gone, my only connection is through postcards. The baby is on its own course with no help of mine, the holidays are ruined, and we can't change that, I feel like a fat cow even though I eat sensibly, and my face is a mess. And now, at least until after the holidays, I don't even have a job to go to!"

Nick was starting to get it. Even though he couldn't totally understand, he knew she was right from her perspective. She felt helpless and clung on hard to the only things she had. But that wasn't working. He knew right then and there that he would have to put his interests aside for the holidays if he was ever going to help her get back on track before his return to Alaska. He also suspected that the pregnancy probably launched a quiver full of unknown emotions that added fuel to her despondency. In reality, he was just as out of sorts as she was. Ultimately, he recognized that she didn't want his pity; she wanted his understanding.

They talked until eleven o'clock that night.

Over the next week the bruises healed remarkably well and those that weren't gone could be camouflaged with makeup. Nick had made a special effort to treat her like a woman instead of some fragile object. Dinners with old friends were often interrupted, however, with stories of those that weren't going to come back from the war—people they all knew, people whose very loss forced each of them to become older and more closed with their emotions. But all in all the week before Christmas was far better than Martha expected. She felt her confidence return, along with some of the sassy edge she had always had. He had even bestowed her with a remarkable bequest—spending an entire evening at her mom's boarding house. Martha actually thought it was funny watching her mom and Nick prepare dinner together. It was her kitchen and she was definitely in charge. In fact, Nick "yes ma'amed" her all through the setting of the table, and as well as the rest of the evening for that matter. Still, with Christmas on Saturday, the holiday weekend wasn't going to be the same without Helen and Bud. *I'll just have to get over that*, she thought while finishing up some last minute shopping on Thursday.

"Don't forget that Major Marshall Smith will be coming over tonight," Nick said. Martha knew that Marshall was Nick's favorite mentor and thought it would be fun to have him stay at their house overnight until his flight the next day back to Seattle. She was also looking forward to hearing about the Women Air Force Service Pilots program Nick told her about and especially about Jackie Cochran.

"It's a shame he doesn't have any more time off for Christmas," Martha said. The major had to return to duty on Christmas Eve. She was grateful that Nick got an extra week of furlough.

"As long as Boeing keeps churning out the planes, he'll be doing double duty," Nick replied.

Before they left for the airport to meet the major's plane, Martha made sure their small home was perfect. The tree was a perfect eight-foot Frazier decorated with bubble lights, homemade Christmas ornaments, popcorn strings, and tinsel. A messenger angel topped the tree, announcing Christ's arrival. A modest number of wrapped packages lay under the tree waiting for Christmas Day. Martha always liked candles, so she had carefully placed several in the windows and on the mantel to light after they came home. The frost in the corners of the windowpanes perfectly framed the view of the snowy outdoors from the cozy living room. Nick had strung several strings of multi-colored lights across the eaves of the house and on the bushes in front of the porch.

"Do you think the major will like our house?" she asked, knowing he would.

"He'll love it, Hotshot. But right now we need to leave for the airport. The flight gets in at 2100, and I don't want him to be waiting for us," Nick said, looking at his watch.

"I'm coming."

The airport was crowded, and Nick was glad he allowed extra time for parking. They arrived at the gate with fifteen minutes to spare, just a few minutes before the announcement that the flight from Cleveland had landed and was taxiing up to the gate. Everyone coming off the plane was met by relatives or friends. There were screams of delight and hugs and smiles all around. It filled Martha with joy to watch all the expressions of happiness. But there was no major.

"What could be the problem? I hope he made it," she said with a hint of disappointment.

"He's probably talking to the captain about something. I'll go on board to see. Wait here while I check."

The gate area was clearing out and still no major. It had been several minutes.

Finally, she heard one of the stewardesses say, "Are you Martha?"

"Yes, I am."

"If you don't mind, I'd like you to come with me. Captain Morgan thought you might like a picture with the major and himself while the plane is empty. We have a few minutes. It's just a short walk outside to your left."

Martha actually hadn't been on a passenger plane before and was very excited as she climb the stairs to enter the main cabin.

"To your right," the pilot pointed.

"Surprise, surprise! Merry Christmas!" came the sounds of what seemed like ten people. Martha nearly dropped to her knees with joy, exhilaration, and pure shock when she saw Helen and Bud wrapped in Christmas paper and bows tied around their head—Bud's was green and Helen's was red.

"Oh, my God! I can't believe it!" Tears of happiness poured from Martha eyes. Helen joined the crying fest instantly. Hugs and frivolity continued until the captain, one of Nick's flying buddies, indicated they needed to ready the plane for the next flight.

Before they exited, Martha threw her arms around Nick and just beamed. "I love you for doing this. You've made everything perfect."

"Merry Christmas, Hotshot."

The four of them spent the entire Saturday talking and catching up. Martha couldn't believe it. It was perfect. How Nick had pulled off the weekend flight was amazing. The rouse of an overnight guest to ensure the house was ready for company was genius. Martha and Helen baked and made preparations for dinner while Nick and Bud exchanged stories.

Nick was fascinated with Bud's knowledge of designing and building tracking devices with measurements so fine-tuned that rocket flights would be accurate through winds, clouds, and various weather conditions over long distances. Nick was sharing his story with Bud and Helen about the strange events in his Yukon Flats experience when Martha said, "Oh, Nick, that reminds me, I wanted to show you one of your last postcards. I was so upset about everything else, I just forgot." She went to the bedroom and retrieved a shoebox full of postcards. She sorted through them, found the right one, and showed it to everyone. "Can you believe this? Might as well not even send it."

———

Anchorage, Alaska

██████████████████████

My Dear Martha,

Red and I are heading out today on a trip ████████████████
██
The good news is that I can get my time in a little faster on this assignment. I definitely want to make it home for the holidays for a hike in the woods and the snow like we did last year—remember?

██
██

Glad you found a meat locker. That should save money and help a little by reducing trips to the butcher stores.

Yours,
Nick

———

"Does this happen often?" Bud asked Martha.

"Not like this one."

"Everything sent is censored," Nick added, "but this is very unusual." He went through Martha's file and showed Helen and Bud other postcards where the various flight locations and happenings along the way had not been blackened out.

"Someone had a hair up their butt on this one," Nick said, not wanting to raise a red flag. He knew it was the Yukon Flats postcard, after all, he wrote it, but he didn't want to concern Martha about the "classified" nature of the mission. "Thank goodness they're not all like this, or Martha would get a new boyfriend."

They all laughed.

Bud proposed a toast. "To a special Christmas we'll all remember."

CHAPTER 27

Within the week of Agent Sirak's receipt of Vladimir's report, Vladimir was back in the air headed toward the Russian Naval Base at Vladivostok. His mission would not become clear until his meeting with Agent Sirak at the base. Vladimir was glad for the shorter flight but wasn't sure if the location was one of convenience or strategy. He landed at 2200 and was taken directly to quarters, where he was kept under secure guard. He was told his meeting was scheduled at 0600, immediately upon Agent Sirak's arrival, which was odd, because a flight from Moscow meant the agent would arrive via a long red-eye crossing over many time zones.

Vladimir waited in the sparse military office the next morning only fifteen minutes. None of the hospitality of a solid breakfast was offered, as before in Moscow.

"I am glad you are here, comrade," Sirak said upon entering the room.

Vladimir snapped to attention. "Good morning, sir." It was obvious to Vladimir that Agent Sirak had come directly from his flight. He was unshaven, and he looked exhausted. *Something is really important*, Vladimir thought.

"Our need to understand the progress of the bomb by our allies in the United States, as well as that of our enemies in Japan, has reached critical proportions. Your note obtained by PFC Endo was very valuable, more so than I'm sure you realize. I'll fill you in on its meaning before we're done. In the meantime, the reported acceleration by the Japanese of a similar project has reached our attention. Needless to say, General Secretary Stalin is rapidly realizing that Germany, the United States, and now Japan are outstripping our advancements on the development of this bomb. This has caused considerable repercussions. First Lightening has become a strategic priority that the general is ready to act on."

"It would help if I knew more about the note," Vladimir said. "Can you give me some clue, sir?"

"Just a little, enough to answer only the important questions. The note you received came from a deeply entrenched agent. It tells us the United States is nearing a testing phase in their development of an atom bomb. No other country is that far along."

"What's the significance of Yukon Flats?"

"We've always believed that the United States would choose an area in the Southwest as a test site, but the efforts by these men indicate that an alternate site in Alaska is being considered. Ultimately, this puts the bomb within easy striking distance of our Pacific Fleet here in Vladivostok."

Vladimir nodded with raised eyebrows as if to say, *holy shit*. "What do you want from me, sir?"

"Japan also surprised us with their advancements. As you know, the consequences there would be much more severe. Our intelligence needs to be confirmed. I have you scheduled to go there tomorrow. You will meet up with a Japanese mole we trust and make an exchange. The documents he claims to have will tell us what we need to know. Your language skills continue to serve you well, Agent Dubisskiy."

"And for those documents I am exchanging . . ."

"Money, enough for him to disappear and lead a very happy life."

"But that's not the end of it, is it?" Vladimir asked, recognizing an old NKVD pattern of negotiation.

"Correct. Once you have confirmed the documents are as promised . . . eliminate him."

"And if they are not?"

"Eliminate him, just the same, and bring the money back. Our country cannot be connected with these documents now or in the future. The Emperor would not tolerate such a transgression, and Russia is not ready for another military action."

For Agent Sirak to be directly ordering the death of a valued operative indicated a very high-value mission. *Not one I can afford to mess up either*, Vladimir thought.

"You'll get your instructions at sea. You're leaving in two hours. Get a good breakfast. It will be a hard trip."

The men stood and shook hands in preparation to depart. Vladimir turned to leave when Agent Sirak stopped him and said almost as a question, "You've not asked your destination."

"I am confident that it will be disclosed on board."

"You have learned well. I will do you the favor of telling you now that it is Shimoda." The agent saw a subtle flush across Vladimir's face. "I have come to trust your judgment, Agent Dubisskiy, and I know that agents do not live by serving their country alone. You'll have very little extra time, but enough, I suspect, for your purposes. Just remember that Japan is at war and security is very tight."

"Thank you. Thank you very much, sir."

"Don't thank me, Agent Dubisskiy," he said with a complete lack of expression. "I also wanted you to know that we have access to Okimi, and her family, if something should go wrong. Good luck, comrade."

The first leg of his trip was by air. By noon Vladimir's pilot was on landing approach to a carrier southeast of the Kuril Islands in the North Pacific, two hundred kilometers off the coast of Hokkaido, the northernmost island of Japan. Seas were rough, and if it weren't for the safety cable, their landing would have terminated in the ocean. Within an hour Vladimir was transferred onto the C-54 submarine, and for the next three days they headed south while traveling deep in the ocean trenches along the Kuril Islands and Japan.

His briefing was short. It was a simple plan. On their third day Vladimir was to meet his contact at 2350 on the east side of the peninsula protecting Shimoda's fishing harbor. The contact and his wife both worked as operatives. *They must be well trusted*, thought Vladimir, *and indicated the rare need for backup should the plan fail*. Vladimir was familiar with the coastline. There was a small beach nestled between the rocks, which was perfect cover for his landing. He would be escorted by his contact to a safe house outside Shimoda and would be permitted to use that house the following day and night. The following day he would travel north under cover to Yoshida, a small farming town just off the coast. There he would meet the new operative, make the exchange, and eliminate the loose end. He would be picked up by the same sub at 0400 on the third day, at a predetermined spot on a beach near Yoshida. Timing was of the essence, and there would be no radio contact. His small pack contained his work papers indicating his status as a sailor from a ship currently in Shimoda's harbor, a map, a change of clothes, money, a knife, a high-beam flashlight, and a Nagant 7.62 mm caliber double-action military revolver with a dozen rounds.

CHAPTER 28

At 2300 on the third day of traveling, the C-54 sub rose to periscope depth while eight hundred meters offshore in order to establish a surveillance position. The good news for Vladimir was that the weather was relatively mild at two degrees centigrade with winds at just five knots. The new moon provided the perfect cover for the short boat ride to shore. They waited.

At exactly 2330 the contact coordinator reported seeing three bursts of light coming from the shore. In just a few minutes the sub surfaced, responded with three bursts from its own spotlight on deck, and launched the rubber skiff carrying Vladimir and his handler. The sub was back under the water in fifteen minutes. The plan and execution were flawless, and by 2355 Vladimir was on the beach, shoving the skiff back into the water for his handler's return trip.

His contact approached immediately.

"Jasmine, comrade." Vladimir said the code word in a muffled tone more out of habit than the need to be quiet. The beach was deserted and the ocean sounds drowned out any noises the men made. Regardless, his hand was on his revolver until he received the necessary confirmation.

"New moon, comrade," the man replied.

Both men eased a bit, having followed through with the protocol of coded recognition.

"Follow me quickly." The man pointed to a narrow path between the rocks, leading away from the beach. Despite the darkness, their heightened senses allowed them to move with confidence. Vladimir assumed that this operative was being well compensated for taking such a risk, and was relieved that he would not be connected with the documents. Vladimir was always straightforward in following orders, but killing another man never came easy.

They circumvented Shimoda, which was about a mile away, and made it to the safe house—a barn on the south edge of town situated next to the operative's home. Bedding was available in a rear tack room of the barn and soon Vladimir was sound asleep, confident that all was in order.

The mooing of a small herd of cows waiting to be milked awakened him early. The night sky had given way to a sunrise that revealed a small farm with a house, the barn he was in, and a few corrals for animals. He groaned as he stretched, trying to loosen up from a night of sleeping on the hard, clay ground. The land was adjacent to a high bluff overlooking the ocean. Pine and deciduous trees lined the bluff, breaking the harsh winds off the Pacific. The pasture abutted the bluffs, and off to the right, separate from the pasture, was a small vineyard with barren grapevines. Beyond the bluff was an expansive view of ocean and sun. As Vladimir gazed at the vista, for the first time ever he had a feeling of insignificance. He watched the first sliver of sun breach the horizon, painting the night sky various shades of deep purple, and within minutes the morning sky burst forth with bright orange exploding just above the horizon in the east. *The land of the rising sun,* he thought, *unbelievable.* A woman approached indicating with hand gestures that he was to head for the house. "How long have you lived here?" Vladimir asked as they walked toward the house.

Surprised by his facility with the language, she answered, "Thirty years."

By the time they reached the farmhouse, the man was exiting the barn. He waived to them, indicating that he would join them momentarily.

As they stood waiting for the man, Vladimir reflected on the required impersonal aspects of their meeting, particularly that of not exchanging names. It's what was expected between operatives, however, as neither wanted an informality that could hinder the execution of responsibilities. In this case, a man's wife was involved, as well. *They must be trusted, indeed*, he thought, as this case was very rare. Only necessary pleasantries were exchanged during the morning meal, with Vladimir returning to the tack room afterwards.

Around 1100, he could stand it no longer. He informed his host that he would be gone for a while and began what turned out to be a short walk to town. He followed a worn trail through a series of pastures that led him to the harbor. A foreigner would usually stand out, but since it was winter he was able to hide under his authentic clothes. His adept understanding of body language and movement, coupled with his understanding of the language, allowed him to blend in among the dockhands, appearing to be a common sailor temporarily in port.

The winter day was agreeable, and the normal, mid-day activities of the small fishing village provided a lively pace. He positioned himself out of view across the street from the Nakamura Flower Shop of Okimi's father. He had not remembered that a greenhouse was situated behind the store. Not unusual, however, as without it the business of a florist would have surely died out during the winter.

It wasn't long before his wait was rewarded. He felt his heart skip and involuntarily held his breath as Okimi emerged from the front door. It had been sixteen years since he last saw her. Then, she was eighteen, and her face was like a palate of naturally arranged colors on a canvas of perfectly proportioned features. From this distance, however, he could see that she had matured, yet the years had protected her beauty. Her gray smock and matching, loose-fitting pants obscured the exquisiteness of the body he remembered from so long ago. She remained only a moment, until a horse-drawn cart arrived and was loaded. She gave the driver some brief instructions and returned to the store.

Vladimir retreated casually, blending in with the noonday traffic of tradesmen and vendors heading toward the harbor. He did not want to attract attention and wanted to avoid contact with the local Tokkō on duty. Often referred to as the "thought police," the Tokkō were like the NKVD in his country. Vladimir had become an expert at blending in while in plain view.

Once back at the farm he sought out his host. "I'd like to get this message to a young woman," he said.

"That can be very dangerous if it is discovered."

"It cannot wait," Vladimir replied, handing the man the note. "Do you know Okimi at the Nakamura Flower Shop?"

"Yes."

"Wait for a reply and return immediately."

The man looked at the note to confirm he understood its purpose.

Prepare a very special arrangement of jasmine for an honored warrior. Will pick up at appointed time and place. VD

"Are you sure this will be understood?"

"Yes, absolutely."

Okimi's eyes glistened when she read the note given her by the farmer she recognized. It had been years since she had had contact with Vladimir, but the promise he made was finally to be fulfilled. She struggled to remain calm as she turned her back to the farmer and composed her reply. She placed the folded note at the bottom of a clay pot so the man could see. She then potted a small geranium from the greenhouse as if everything was normal. "I hope your wife will enjoy this," she said.

"She will nurture it as her own child." The farmer knew that her response was only meant for one person. "Thank you," he said, departing the shop.

It was mid-afternoon when Vladimir's host presented him with the plant. When Vladimir had removed the note, the man went to the house to give the plant to his wife before retreating to the barn to attend to chores.

Vladimir's breath was short with expectation as he unfolded the paper and shook off the dirt. His life had been in the service of Russia, doing things he did not always agree with and, at times, hurting others. He knew deep down that he would have been a different person if the obligations of state did not govern his every act. He knew of only a handful of agents who had wives. Much like his host, they were a team. Horror stories existed, however, over the circumstances of torture inflicted when their cover was exposed. The outcome was never good. Most agents avoided this compromise and were content with the temporary relationships developed along the way. Maybe Vladimir was more traditional or more sentimental, but he longed for a loving relationship of substance. He hadn't thought any further than meeting with Okimi, but he knew she was that perfect person for him when he read the note:

The friendship of a warrior would be welcome at 2100. Please enter quietly at the open door of the greenhouse behind the shop.

The note was signed off with a simple drawing of a jasmine flower with five petals.

Vladimir pondered the possibilities of that evening with both anxiety and great expectation. Finally, he could stand his anticipations no more. He needed something to do. "Do you need help with anything?" he asked his host.

"What do you mean?"

"Anything," he said. "I'm just not accustomed to sitting all day like this. Doing some physical work would be nice."

"Are you a farmer?" his host asked.

"Not for many years."

"Then all I have is dirt labor."

"All the better," Vladimir responded, not knowing that he was about to spend the remainder of the afternoon mucking the barn and feeding the livestock. The hours in the barn helped him overcome the knot in his stomach.

After dinner the woman pulled her husband aside and whispered something to him, just out of Vladimir's hearing. He would leave soon and hoped that nothing had gone wrong—it was 1900.

"Your help was appreciated today. You grew up on a farm?" his host asked.

"Yes, but only until I was eight."

"It is hard work. Makes a man sweat hard—the purification of a warrior."

"It is true to one's spirit," Vladimir added.

"My wife thinks that the spirit of a warrior causes the warrior to smell." His wife was avoiding eye contact at this point and the man chose his words carefully. "Maybe the warrior would like a bath before his appointment?"

"Oh, now I understand," Vladimir said, smiling. With a quick smell under his arms and a wave of his hand in front of his nose he confirmed what the thoughtful woman was trying to say. Too many days in the sub combined with sleeping and working in the barn had left its mark. The man had obviously mentioned to his wife the nature of his appointment, and she was kind enough to do her part to ensure its success.

"Yes. Thank you," he said, bowing. "Very excellent suggestion."

After heating the water for thirty minutes, the bath was ready. "Ah," Vladimir groaned with pleasure. *The woman's a genius*, he thought. She had also volunteered to wash the clothes he wore, and he would wear the extra set in his pack. By 2030 he was ready for the walk into town.

"What is my best approach to town and the flower shop?" he asked the man.

"You are wise to take my advice. This is an exceptionally dangerous time to be out. The Tokkō will be extremely suspicious of a foreigner on his own at night."

The thought of implicating Okimi made Vladimir shudder.

"This route will take longer, but it will be safer," the man said, pulling out a piece of paper. "Let me show you."

"How much longer?"

"Thirty minutes," the man said, noticing a frown on Vladimir's face. "She will wait, comrade, don't worry."

The man's directions were easy to follow. They sent Vladimir around the town to approach the flower shop from the north instead of the south. He observed that coming through town between the buildings would have been treacherous, as several Tokkō soldiers were on watch. For what, he wasn't sure. *I'm just glad it's not me*, he thought. The moon was just a sliver, so finding the greenhouse was difficult. But finally, there it was, a low, cheap, glass-paneled building, barely visible in the night shadows. There was a kerosene lamp dimly burning at one end.

He slipped inside through the open pedestrian door and stood motion-less, gaining his orientation. Except for the slight hissing sounds from the steam heat, the greenhouse was silent.

Okimi approached as quietly as a praying mantis on the limb of a leafy, spring bush.

Once she was convinced she recognized him in the shadows she announced herself by tapping on one of the opaque window panels. Vladimir quickly turned toward the sound and saw his beautiful flower wearing a plain kimono robe with little embroidery; it was elegant in its understated design. He was finally able to reach out to her. Their embrace made Vladimir weak. Okimi cried quietly on his shoulder as her dream had finally come true. Neither said a word. The feeling of well-being was enough.

"Are we safe here?" he asked, thinking of her first.

"Yes. This will be our home for the night." She walked him down an aisle with larger plants blocking the view from either side. Okimi had prepared a place for them to sit and lie down on the clay floor. She gestured that he rest on the blanket first and said, "My parents have grown old and are fast asleep. There's nothing for us to fear." She could feel the tightness in the back of his neck, his body rigid and ready to strike out at an enemy at any moment.

"It has been a long time," she whispered.

"Yes, too long."

"I knew you would come back. My mother tried to persuade me to forget. I suppose I would have done the same for my child, but I never stopped believing in you."

Vladimir held her hands and felt the calluses earned from the years of work in the flower shop. "You work hard for your father. Is it enjoyable?"

"It is my life. The beauty of the flowers is enough to make me content.

And every now and then someone will order a bouquet of white jasmine. Thinking of you makes me happy."

They kissed their first kiss of the night. A soft and tender kiss, searching for the perfection they desired. Regardless of their lost years, they kissed confidently in complete acceptance of each other. Their eyes remained open and in the dim light from the kerosene lamp their gaze confirmed a trust beyond words. Neither of them was in a rush.

"Your hands are so hard, and your lips are so soft. I hope that it is because they have not seen much work," he said, smiling in jest, but honest in his intent.

"There is only you."

"It makes me happy to hear that, but it is also unfair. Everything is so different now . . . with the war."

She put her fingers to his lips. "I understand. It is no one's fault."

They repositioned themselves lying next to each other on the blanket. Vladimir stroked Okimi's cheek to reassure himself of her very presence. They talked for a long time, sharing events over sixteen years from entirely different worlds that were now entangled in the same war. She told him that most of the men were gone from Shimoda, fighting the Americans. Her brother was on the Marshall Islands, and she hoped he would return home safely. Vladimir's stories of the Americans reflected an image of reasonableness and helpfulness to the Russians in their war with Germany. He explained that he lived with the Americans and found them to be intelligent and fair.

"None of this war makes sense to me, but the Emperor commands it."

He heard the futility in her voice and could feel her rejection of the war in her body's tension. "Let us talk of other things," Vladimir said. "But before we leave this discussion of war, you must promise me one thing."

"What is that?"

"Stay away from large cities . . . remain in Shimoda. It is perfect. Do not move or travel. Do not ask why or you may be afraid. Just trust me in this." Vladimir's belief in the bomb's existence motivated his comments, of course, but he didn't want to frighten her. "Will you promise?"

"Yes. I don't know where I would go anyway."

"Good."

Vladimir wrapped his arms around her as though to protect her from what he knew. And soon they were kissing and comforting each other with gentle touches and embraces that allowed each to express their desire.

She could feel him push up against her and wished he would continue. Even though she had never been with a man, she wasn't worried, just sensitive to her inexperience.

Vladimir had concerns as to where this night would go. He came prepared with condoms, but wasn't sure if having sex was the right thing to do. He knew that this may be the last time he would ever see Okimi, and, while he didn't consider himself overly modest or proper, he did respect her to his core and didn't want to create a false expectation through his actions. All of that went out the window when she placed her hand on his inner thigh and rubbed gently. He slid his hand into the top of her kimono and discovered a soft breast with a nipple that was hard with anticipation. He wedged his leg between hers. It was met with a drive from Okimi that left no doubt as to her commitment. They kissed and explored each other's body as they slowly removed their already loosened clothes. Vladimir's condoms were as much of an indication of his intentions as the extra blankets that seemed to appear out of nowhere.

Okimi wanted the experience to be perfect. She was no longer a young girl and in her mind, her satisfaction would depend on whether Vladimir's relationship with her would be strengthened. In his eagerness, however, it was more painful than anticipated, and she let out a muffled cry during penetration. It wasn't what she had expected. Vladimir removed himself.

"I'm sorry," she said. "You may not understand, but it is my first time. I wasn't sure what to expect. Maybe if we go a little slower."

They relaxed and spent more time sharing the magic of being naked together under the blankets. By early dawn they had made love twice. Vladimir would be forever indebted to Agent Sirak for arranging for him to go to Shimoda. They began to see the subtle shift in the darkness of the night sky through the greenhouse panels and knew their time was coming to an end. It would be hard, as they both knew a time like this may not come again.

"I will think of you always," Vladimir said as he held her tight. "You will be my single thought of my existence on the day that I die."

"I will always hope for more but will be happy for what we have had," she responded. She reached to the inside pocket of her kimono and produced a photograph they had taken sixteen years previous. "It has been precious to me, and I want you to have it to remember who we were when you are old."

Vladimir cried softly as they embraced, knowing that she spoke the truth. He left the greenhouse before the morning daylight would betray him.

CHAPTER 29

Short on sleep, Vladimir was happy when he saw the arrangement his host had prepared in order to make the trip from Shimoda to the farming community of Yoshida. It was basically a straw-covered quilt. The man was to deliver forty bales of hay that day to a buyer. Vladimir could easily disguise himself between the bales and sleep most of the way. The horse-drawn wagon, however, would make for a long and bumpy ride.

"Have you done this before?" Vladimir asked the man.

"Once every two weeks I make this delivery."

"What can we expect along the way?"

"Just the normal checkpoints as we enter each new town."

"Checkpoints?"

"Routine stops. Nothing to worry about. I know every one of them. Just stay quiet until I make this noise." At that point he rapped twice on the frame of the wagon with a pole he used to prod and guide the horses. "Two strikes means all clear." He rapped once. "One strike means someone is approaching." He rapped three times. "Three strikes means big trouble."

"In that case I'll keep this loaded and in a ready position." He flashed his Nagant revolver to impress upon his host that he meant business.

"I'd like to thank your wife for her help before I leave."

"You're welcome to, but I don't have a wife. She died four years ago of torture by the Tokkō. She was a nice woman who never hurt anyone."

"Who was the lady here?"

"My visiting sister. She was very close to my wife and became an operative right after my wife died. She was here as it was suggested that we have backup if needed. It was easier for us to say she was my wife. She left right after you left last night."

Agent Sirak's attention to detail constantly amazed Vladimir. He usually could spot the players. *She was good*, he thought. *I never saw it coming.*

"We need to leave. It will be a long day."

By noon they had passed only a few travelers, mostly locals going about their daily routines. At about 1300 two Tokkō officers approached the wagon, and Vladimir was awakened with a single, sharp rap of the stick on the wagon. The wagon came to a stop and the farmer engaged the officer in charge in a conversation about the weather and the nature of his trip.

In time, the officer said, "Why do you drive so far to deliver hay?"

"It is for my dead wife's brother. Here, let me show you the delivery receipts." At that, the farmer produced a clipboard of receipts over the last six months. "I get a good price from a wholesaler in Shimoda and pass it on to my brother-in-law. He is poor, and he needs it for his livestock."

The officer walked slowly around the wagon poking a stick into the load between the bales. Vladimir was ready if he needed to act. "Your brother-in-law is lucky to have such a good relative. This is good hay, no rot at all."

"He will repay me in the summer with a new calf."

The men said good-bye and the wagon started to move. Within minutes Vladimir heard two sharp raps, indicating all was clear. He fell back to sleep.

By mid-afternoon, Vladimir was starting to get restless cooped up between the hay bales. "I need to stop to relieve myself and stretch my legs," he called out.

"There's a perfect spot just up the road. I'll let you know."

After conducting his business, Vladimir walked around for a few minutes. They were in the countryside about five miles west of the ocean and ten miles or so south of Yoshida. They were on track to arrive around 1900.

"Will there be an opportunity for food?" Vladimir asked.

"Just south of town is a roadhouse where I usually stop. Here's some food my sister made for you before she left. I'll let you know when we're about forty-five minutes from the roadhouse. There won't be any opportunities to get out after that."

"You've done a good job. It will be in my report when I get back."

"Here is the map giving you the coordinates and passwords for your meeting. Study it now while you have light and give it back for me to destroy before entering the town."

———

It was dark when the men shook hands and Vladimir left the protection of his host. In a short time he would be at his brother-in-law's farm unloading hay.

"Thank you and good luck, comrade," Vladimir said.

"You are different," the man said. "You care for people and are loyal to those you love. Those are admirable traits, just not very common for an agent. Good-bye." The men parted company.

The meeting location was an abandoned travel shelter on the old ocean bluff road and was about an hour's walk away. He wanted to be in place well in advance of the other operative. Their meeting was scheduled for midnight. In his mind there was no time to waste.

The location was wide open, giving anyone in the shelter a good view of the surrounding area, if it were daytime. But, at night it was vulnerable. Any light in the shelter could be seen for quite a ways off. And with very little moon, it would be hard to detect if someone was approaching. Vladimir surveyed the area for an alternative place to wait. He wanted to have the advantage. He found a pile of rocks on the bluff about twenty-five meters away that would work, but the sound of the ocean would make it difficult to hear someone approaching.

At 2300 he saw the glow of two lit cigarettes near the shelter that indicated two men were present. The precise planning of this mission did not allow for an extra man. Something was wrong. The men seemed more concerned about staying warm in the shelter than going about their duties. They were definitely Tokkō officers on assignment. Vladimir watched intently for thirty minutes to determine if there were others. When he determined they were alone, he slowly positioned himself within listening range. They were irritated, pissed they drew this assignment. "What are we looking for anyway?" one soldier asked.

"I think the general is crazy with the idea of spies," the other one said. "Someone found a blanket made up to look like straw, and now we have to spend the night out here."

They both lit second cigarettes with a disregard for being seen. Vladimir concluded from their inexperience that the shelter wasn't a prime target of the Tokkō. He waited until 2345 to act. One of the soldiers indicated that he needed to take a piss. The soldier walked a short distance from the shelter and unbuttoned his trousers. With his focus, and his hands, on other things, Vladimir was easily able to sneak up and quickly slit his throat with such meticulous precision that no alarm or noise was registered by the slain soldier. Being close to the officer's size, Vladimir donned his coat and hat and picked up his rifle with the bayonet fixed.

In a few minutes the other soldier came outside, curious about the delay. Seeing his partner at some distance from the shelter he said, "What's taking so long, you old man?" He stood staring off toward the ocean finishing his cigarette, chuckling to himself. Vladimir started walking in the soldier's direction with his head down fiddling with the buttons on his fly. In a flash, Vladimir impaled the other soldier on the bayonet. He quickly disposed of the bodies in some tall weeds out of the way. He was back in the rocks by 2355.

Midnight came and went. Something was wrong. He had some latitude in time, as his pickup was not until 0400, but he needed to complete his mission. He decided to wait. Time was of the essence, but nothing happened. At about 0100 he saw the quick flicker of a penlight, the sign he was to receive from the mole. Vladimir approached from behind without the man's knowledge and said, "The ocean is calm, comrade."

Startled, the man whirled around to face Vladimir, calmed himself, and said, "It won't always stay that way, comrade." The men shook hands and went into the shelter out of the cold.

"Why the delay?" Vladimir asked.

"Yoshida is a small town and word travels. This evening there was a disturbance when a local man turned in what people say was a relative for concealing a traveler in his wagon. Apparently, the relative goes there regularly to deliver hay, but today a blanket of some sort had been made up to blend in with the load. They think he was transporting a person. It was the first time the blanket was seen and the local man didn't want the Tokkō to think he was involved. When they found out, more soldiers were called out to search the area for a possible spy."

"And the wagon driver, what happened to him?"

"Took away to be interrogated."

Vladimir reflected on the oversight of the quilt and the harsh consequences it would have. *It's an unforgiving business*, he thought.

The documents promised were in a binder presented by the operative, making them easy to review. Vladimir went to work without wasting time. Most of what he was able to understand described an atomic bomb project centered around Japan's Riken Scientific Institute and other university physics laboratories. The chief figure was Yoshio Nishina, a leading scientist and physicist of international stature. Pages from a diary of Masa Takeuchi, a worker in his laboratory assigned to the thermal diffusion project, and copies of a journal kept by Bunsabe Arakatsu, a physicist from Kyoto, were also included.

Several pages were devoted to the Japanese efforts to keep pace with the developments of physics in the 1930s, including both theory in Europe and techniques in the United States. The Japanese scientists had built a small cyclotron in Nishina's lab at the Riken Institute in Tokyo. Nishina's assistant, Ryokichi Sagane, was sent to Berkeley to work under E. O. Lawrence, the American physicist who arranged for a two-hundred-ton magnet in order to build a second, much larger, cyclotron. The Japanese army sponsored the development of the atomic bomb in September 1940—large-scale research began at Riken in December. The navy became involved in late 1942, which led to the "Physics Colloquium," a galaxy of leading Japanese scientists to achieve such a weapon. Last, a section was included describing a secret manufacturing site in Konan, Korea, because of its vast uranium resources.

After about fifteen minutes of review, Vladimir said, "The documents appear in order. Let me complete our end of the bargain." He handed the man the bundled money for his inspection.

"All bills are unmarked?"

"Yes."

Using the few seconds of distraction needed by the operative to count the money, Vladimir reached into his pack for the Nagant revolver. The silencer was already in place. One shot to the heart and one to the head finished his end of the business. He pondered his own detachment during the cleanup of the blood spatters on the wall and the money from the ground. An out-of-body experience oriented him through an efficient routine, which culminated in vomiting, but only after the realization that the mission was complete. It was always that way with Vladimir.

With the remaining time and some additional effort, he was able to muscle the dead man's body to the beach where the pickup was scheduled. He hid in a clump of shrubs at the base of the bluff for two hours before delivering the three short bursts on his flashlight at 0400. The body came with them to the sub, as he knew its discovery in Yoshida would initiate an investigation that would compromise other Soviet comrades.

CHAPTER 30

Most of the discussion in Elmendorf flight ops that morning among the men centered on the hard-fought battles in Italy. It was January 1944, and the euphoria over the successes in North Africa and Sicily had vanished with the realization that defeating Hitler and the fascists under Mussolini was coming at a tremendous cost of American lives. It was all the army could do to hold its ground against violent assaults. In the Pacific theater, the Marines had exerted dominance in amphibious warfare tactics on Tarawa. Thankfully, a shift took place from a heavy loss of life on both sides with the Marine movement in the Battle of Cape Gloucester on the island of New Britain in New Guinea. Reports of swamps and mosquitoes worse than Guadalcanal received as much headlines as the capture of the Japanese airfield in New Gloucester.

"We haven't seen the worst of it yet, in my opinion," Cricket said. Most of the men agreed.

When Nick entered, it was his first contact with operations since his return from Christmas. He had the luxury of being a passenger on the flight back. "Happy New Year," he called to everyone on both sides of the counter. The familiar clackity-clack of the Teletype machines blending with the banter of the men and the clouds of cigarette smoke felt like home.

"Hey, Nick." The general chorus of welcomes and "Happy New Years" was enthusiastic. "We thought maybe you went AWOL," one of the men said.

"I've got Cricket to thank for that," he replied, tipping his hat in genuine appreciation.

"I'd like to take full credit, but timing is everything. Besides, the army owed you one after that stunt they pulled in Bethel, leaving you high and dry without a plane." While the decision on Cricket's part was motivated as much out of practicality as it was out of retribution, it reflected his skill at balancing the needs and emotions of his pilots with the ridiculous schedules they were often asked to fly.

"Maybe. But I still appreciate it." Nick went on to describe what had become a hilarious story about his surprise announcement at home with Martha that ended with him explaining, "took me my entire furlough to get my ass out of the doghouse."

The men rolled with laughter at the absurdity of the circumstances.

"Maybe I need to issue an instruction kit with these little favors," Cricket said, smiling. "All you pilots seem to know about is flying planes. Between your wives, your girlfriends, and the mechanics, I could become a full-time advice columnist."

Nick got down to business checking the duty roster for pilots and was surprised to learn that he was scheduled for training in Billings. Unfortunately, pilots can't rest on their laurels. Nick knew that, but the drudgery of studying new devices and methods, in addition to the instrument-training sessions with the Link Trainer, could become tense, depending on the disposition of the master instructor. To the uninitiated, the Link Trainer could rival Chinese water torture. It is a box set on a pedestal and is designed to resemble a real plane. In the simulated cockpit the deception is quite complete. All of the controls and instruments are duplicated, and once under way the sensation of actual flight becomes quite genuine, even down to the sound of the slipstream and engines. The device is governed by a godlike instructor who can create headwinds, tailwinds, crosswinds, fire, engine and radio failure, and ultimately, all manners of deception. If he's having a bad day, he can combine the curses for an ugly rendition of pilot hell in fiendish proportions. Every pilot accepts the reality that almost half their time is spent in training, both for the safety of the crew and passengers and the knowledge necessary to maintain pace with the changes in technology. All would agree, however, they would rather be flying.

Cricket caught Nick's attention before his departure for a word in private. This was not like Cricket.

"Have you run into PFC Endo yet?"

"No," Nick replied. "Why?"

"Not entirely sure, except he's been pretty withdrawn over the holidays."

"You're aware that his mother died recently? Maybe it's connected with the holidays and his dad in Manzanar."

"Maybe, but he and I usually grab a beer every now and then. No contact at all lately. It's not so much that he's moody, more like he's secretive."

"I'll keep an eye on him and let you know. It's odd, though, because Red and I were commenting just the opposite on the last trip out to the Flats."

"Maybe it's my imagination. Say hello to Billings for me. Oh, by the way, we've had reports of new activity in encrypted RF traffic to the motherland. The politics of Russia's ally status is confusing to everyone. Anyway, the source can't be pinpointed, but they appear to be reporting air movements. Read these new security briefs from senior command on procedures and information clearances."

"You got it."

It was at lunch about an hour later while Nick was attending to paperwork in preparation for his Billings trip that he ran into Robert. "Why don't you join me while we eat and fill me in on the holidays?"

"They were depressing. Stayed pretty much to myself, actually, after receiving the bad news."

"I'm truly sorry to hear about your mother. Cricket told me. Any word from your father?"

"Just a card telling me not to worry about him and that mom is in a better place. That part I agreed with."

"What about him?"

"It's tough not to think that he'll never leave that place."

"If it's any consolation, there are a lot of people, important people, who believe that what we're doing with Americans like your parents is wrong. Unfortunately, it's one of those overreactions that will take some time to undo."

"Do you really believe that?" Robert said, pulling his head back from his food, curling his lip to reveal his resentment.

"Yes, I do." Nick recognized the isolation Cricket saw in Robert as he struggled to make conversation. *Maybe depression is an acceptable reaction considering his state of affairs,* he thought, reflecting on how he might deal with similar circumstances. While certainly not to the same degree, he saw comparable bouts with depression in Martha as she struggled with the reality of being pregnant and alone. Nick related the broken-nose story to Robert hoping to make him laugh and to pick up his spirits.

"At least your wife has someone," Robert said, neglecting to even acknowledge the coincidence of broken noses.

"You have friends. What about Cricket?"

"What do you mean?" he responded sharply. "Who told you about him?"

"Relax, Robert. I don't mean anything other than I thought he was a friend. Nobody told me anything."

He didn't respond. After a few moments Robert lit a cigarette and said, "What do you think that trip to Yukon Flats was all about?" He wanted to stay clear from any more conversation about Cricket.

"Hard to say. We're not on the 'need to know' list."

"But what could they be doing so far away from civilization?"

"Red and I talked about the same thing on the flight back and concluded that our speculation wasn't going to get us any closer to the truth." He could tell that Robert wanted to pursue the discussion further, but Nick felt that such a discussion would go against protocol, as a captain second-guessing the nature of a top-secret mission. "Let sleeping dogs lie."

Robert desperately wanted to tell the captain about the note, but the warnings from Vladimir rang like a gong in his head. Instead, he went back into his shell, making up an obligation that required him to leave.

Nick wasn't convinced he learned anything new as to why Robert was depressed, or for that matter, anything that might raise his spirits.

Conversely, Robert was more convinced than ever that the system he belonged to no longer held his trust. The captain was his only hope in the system for an answer, and Robert truthfully felt that Vladimir offered a more honest assessment of the facts. *Probably best to just stick to myself and my job from here on out*, he thought.

En Route to Billings, Montana
January 22, 1944

My Dear Martha,

On my way to Billings for Captain check-up training. The studying and training becomes monotonous, but the duty is easy, with extra time for activities. I'd like to do some more dogsledding. I really enjoyed that day with John.

The army is giving this ship to Inland Airways when we arrive at Billings, so we decided to take the scenic route in. We went down along the Beartooth Mountains to Red Lodge, then over to Yellowstone to the Geyser Basins, which were steaming and spouting. On to Shoshone Lake and dam to Cody, the Jap concentration camp at Heart Mountain, and finally into Billings. The Crow Indians live out in the hilly plateau region southeast of Billings in a really primitive manner.

Give George a pat on the belly for me.

Yours,
Nick

Nick and Martha had started referring to the new baby as George. It wasn't a name they had decided on yet, but an endearment they used to show their preference for a baby boy.

"Holy shit," Nick said under his breath while having coffee the next afternoon in the mess hall. He couldn't believe it. The front page of the Sunday *Billings Gazette* held a quarter-page picture showing the devastation of the town of Cassino, Italy. It featured the concrete skeletons of the town, its buildings completely destroyed and shrouded in smoke from cannon fire and bombs. Nick wasn't used to having access to current events like this and was stunned to read that the 36th Infantry Division was decimated after sunset on January 20. The article went on to describe the scene:

THE LACK OF TIME TO PREPARE THEIR RETREAT MEANT
THE SOLDIERS HAD TO MAKE AN APPROACH TO THE RIVER
THROUGH HAZARDOUS UNCLEARED MINES AND BOOBY
TRAPS IN THEIR PATH. THEY LACKED THE NECESSARY
TRAINING TO CROSS AN OPPOSED RIVER. MANY MEN WERE
ISOLATED AND VULNERABLE TO THE COUNTERATTACKING
15TH PANZER DIVISION TANKS. THERE WAS NO ALLIED
ARMOR SUPPORT. BY THE EVENING OF JANUARY 22 THE
141ST REGIMENT HAD VIRTUALLY CEASED TO EXIST,
WITH ONLY FORTY MEN MAKING IT BACK TO THE ALLIED
LINES. THE ASSAULT HAD BEEN A COSTLY FAILURE,
WITH THE 36TH INFANTRY DIVISION LOSING 2,100 MEN
KILLED, WOUNDED, AND MISSING DURING THE 48-HOUR
CONFLICT.

The story was like a surprise punch to the stomach, as the curse of Nick's unfailing memory recalled that Tom, Anne's fiancé, was with the 36th Division. He left immediately after Link Training the next day to find her at the base hospital.

CHAPTER 31

Several months had passed since her reassignment to the hospital in Billings and Anne thoroughly enjoyed her duty. Rather than dealing with the immediate stress and pressure of battlefield casualties, as she did in the Aleutians, the day-to-day routine involved recovery and treatment planning to get the wounded back home. Montana was about as far away from the war as one could get. The doctors and other nurses were great to work with, and the eight-hour schedule was fair to everyone since they all pulled duty during the various shifts.

Pilot training was at an all-time high, so living quarters on the small base were at a premium, which caused some nurses like Anne to be temporarily housed at the MacDonald Hotel. It was elegant compared to the barracks on the base, so Anne wasn't about to complain. Plus, having her own room afforded her a level of privacy that provided a pleasant break from constantly being surrounded by other nurses.

The extra pilots at the training center, coupled with the traffic from the Northern Pacific Railroad, injected vitality to the normally quiet cowboy town in the Yellowstone River Valley. The airstrip was in the shadow of the Beartooth Mountains, and the constant drone of the planes landing and taking off was like having audio-Christmas wrapping around the town. One got used to it, though.

Outdoor activities were the mainstay during the summer and fall, with mountain hiking, trout fishing on the river, and elk hunting on the range; but the winter cold and snow kept things pretty shut down. Anne stayed busy at the hospital, for the most part, and generally took in a movie with her nurse friends once a week. The single nurses were happy to entertain the soldiers, but most of Anne's friends were married or engaged. They wanted to keep their social lives separate from the men stationed temporarily at the base and supported each other through the disturbing news reports received via mail, radio, or newspaper.

One of the doctors heard of the 36th Division's decimation on the radio the night of January 23 and approached Anne at the end of her shift with the news. "I don't want to alarm you, but the word on the 36th isn't very good," he said quietly. Anne had talked frequently of Tom, just as all hospital personnel did of loved ones in the war. It was a way to keep them safe. The more she talked about Tom, the more real his existence remained, giving her a sense of control.

"I hope it didn't affect the 141st Regiment," she said, stunned but reluctant to connect the bad news with Tom without all the facts. It would be easy to spend the majority of your time worrying if you just focused on the bad news. Anne had learned that the reality of war yielded more survivors then dead. She held to this tenet not only for Tom but also for all the injured she had nursed. She hated partial news like this and struggled sleeping that night. She went about her duties the next day on target with her responsibilities, but she was noticeably removed from the interaction among the staff.

The afternoon *Gazette* on January 24th identified the 141st as being the hardest hit.

Nick found her early that evening holed up in her room desperately hanging onto hope but fearing the worse. He knocked quietly.

No answer.

"Anne. I know you're in there. It's Nick."

"Please go away. I just want to be by myself."

"C'mon, Anne. You need a friend. Let's talk."

He heard some movement and then the shuffling of footsteps from inside the room. The handle rattled as she unlocked and opened the door. Her puffy, red eyes peered around the edge of the door. She looked like a child banished to her room for disobeying.

"I wanted to see how you're doing, Anne. It's not good for you to be alone right now."

"I know that Tom was one of the ones that made it out. I can just feel it," she said, clinging onto a wish she had no jurisdiction over. "Everything will be okay." There were no lights, which gave the room a depressed effect in contradiction to the thin veil of hope presented in her words. In truth, she knew the darkness was a cover to a potential reality she desperately hoped would not find her.

"I hope to God you're right, Anne. Have his parents sent any information?" Nick knew that not enough time had elapsed in order to communicate specific casualties in any other way than a telegraph, but he wanted to get Anne to talk.

"No . . . nothing."

"I'm sure you'll hear from them when they have something." Nick walked into her room as she relaxed her grip on the door.

She threw her arms around him and just sobbed. "I miss him so much. I just can't bear never seeing him again," she said between gasps for air. The strength of his body comforted her—his arms helped her feel safe.

"It's been almost a day since the radio broadcast. Shouldn't they have word to people by now?" Anne knew better than to expect the unrealistic and understood that many days, sometimes weeks could go by before next-of-kin were notified. The longer the wait, in fact, was sometimes better, as the ones who made it through had to rely on their own letters to communicate with loved ones back home.

"You know the military. Everything has to be confirmed. Even if he's okay, he may show up on the missing-in-action list for a few days."

"That just means he's dead, and his body hasn't been found," she said in anguish. The tears flowed all the more as she clung to Nick for support. He was the only source of strength she had accepted since receiving the news. Despite the number of times she lent her shoulder to other nurses receiving bad news, she had shut herself off.

"Let's get out of the room for a while. Some fresh air and a meal would do you good."

"I don't feel like going out; besides, I look a mess."

"I'm the captain here," Nick replied. "Just splash some cold water on your face and you'll be fine. Staying holed up is the worst thing for you. You know that."

She knew he was right and began to push back the tears from the corner of her brown eyes. "Okay, but I don't want to see people. They'll just ask questions that will make me cry all over again." She departed for the bathroom to get presentable. When she returned, her brunette hair had been brushed and some rouge had been applied to add color. A flicker of a smile was offered as a sign to Nick that she cherished his encouragement.

"Chinese?" he asked.

"How about Wong's on Fourth Street?" she replied.

The influence of the Chinese migrant workers in the construction of the transcontinental railroad decades earlier had left a wide swath of communities with a wonderful selection of restaurants run by first and second generation Chinese. Wong's was new and somewhat undiscovered, about a fifteen minute walk away.

They strolled quietly, not so much with a purpose, but more with a sense of controlling time and events. A gentle snow was falling, adding a glisten to the town. The sounds of their boots on the boardwalk broke the muffled quiet. People were inside for the most part. The few they passed seemed to be preoccupied with not being late for an arrival of some importance. Anne was stung with the fear that she would never make such a walk with Tom, regardless of how badly she wanted it. She had always held her duty as a nurse, helping others, as a source of hope. "I never thought it would happen to me," she said.

Nick put his arm around her, sensing a new wave of desperation. "C'mon! Hang in there. We don't know anything for sure. You're just going to worry yourself sick." *What a stupid thing to say*, he thought. *Of course she's worried sick.* "What I mean to say is that I understand that you're worried, and I hope you get good news about Tom soon."

She interlocked her arm around Nick's waist and gave a gentle squeeze of thanks. "There's a little Catholic church around the corner. Do you mind if we stop in for a few minutes?"

"Not at all." He wasn't Catholic, but he knew that that had little relevance.

St. Matthew's was empty. The inside reflected the sparse economic conditions of the last twenty years of war and depression. It was a basic sanctuary with a simple wooden pulpit off to the left and worn pews for about two hundred parishioners. On the right, next to the statue of St. Matthew, was a bank of candles. Most were lit in the hope of a divine intercession for a loved one or for forgiveness for some unbearable transgression. Anne walked directly to the candles to add her prayer for Tom's safety.

All she had was a quarter to put in the donation box. She cried softly, realizing the futility of saving a man's life in exchange for a quarter and some well-intentioned words. *Whatever was done is already over,* she thought. *If he's gone, I pray that he went without pain. If he's injured, I hope that he's being cared for and will come home soon, and if he's okay, I give You thanks for looking over him. Dear God, please end this war soon,* she prayed.

She remained kneeling at the altar for several minutes, generating whatever strength possible from the visit.

"It's hard to make sense of things," she said while walking away from the church with Nick.

There wasn't anything he could say. She seemed to respond better to a gentle hug from his arm around her and his hand on her shoulder. The collapse of her head on the side of his chest said everything. His instinct to try and fix things seemed useless. Nick wanted desperately to help Anne, but couldn't. It was her need for his comfort that triggered an emotional intimacy—a new level of closeness.

Supper provided a brief diversion as they talked of their holidays and lighter experiences over the last six months. The food gave Anne a feeling of contentment, reminding her of the frequent, similar connections she had with other nurses over the past few months in their time of grief. She looked at Nick with genuine warmth as she recalled significant moments filling their friendship and his compassion for her plight. *Martha is very lucky,* she thought.

"Thanks for rescuing me tonight." An uncontrollable desire emerged within Anne along with the comment. She knew instinctively that it surfaced from her respect for Nick and the closeness of the situation. "Let's go back, Nick," she said, feeling immediate guilt and attempting to establish a roadblock.

Outside the restaurant in the cold air, Anne slid her hand into Nick's coat pocket as they walked with the same lack of purpose back to the hotel. The line between the love she felt for Tom and the security and affection she was experiencing with Nick was starting to blur. They arrived at the MacDonald in twenty minutes, but Anne was reluctant to part ways. "Do you mind if we walk some more?"

"Of course not." The role of a supporting friend was beginning to change in Nick's mind, as well, as the tingle of their hands nestled together in his pocket played on his imagination. "Where do you want to go?"

"I just don't want to be alone, I guess. Anywhere's fine." She turned to face Nick and the urge to embrace him was overwhelming. She knew she shouldn't, but she couldn't stop. Her mouth reached up to his, expecting him to interpret the move as a friendly gesture. It was not to be, as the intimacy of emotions shared sparked a kiss well beyond one of mere friendship. The rule of twenty seconds stimulated a desire surprising both of them.

"I'm sorry, Anne. I shouldn't have," Nick said in an automatic, but unconvincing apology.

"It's my fault," Anne pleaded. "I just don't know if I can be alone. You've been just perfect tonight, and I think my feelings for Tom are coming out on you. Is that wrong?"

"I'm flattered, but are you sure you want to?" He remembered the excitement in making love with Martha before she was pregnant. The intensity, the passion. He knew that this would be the same—still wrong, but somehow justified, however, by what Anne was experiencing.

"Let's only do what we feel right about tonight," she said, gesturing with a step toward the front door of the hotel.

Nick was conflicted, overcome by the moment, which overshadowed an obligation so many miles away.

The room was small with only a chair and a single bed. Inside the door each had barely removed their parkas before Anne initiated an embrace of such intensity that she could clearly feel Nick's immediate erection. She imagined its warmth and stiffness underneath his trousers and underwear. Her thoughts of Tom were relegated to a protective corner of her brain, allowing her the freedom to substitute Nick for Tom in a moment of passion that would never be. *It has to be right*, she thought as she unbuckled his pants and reached in.

Their satisfaction was reached quickly in a desperate frenzy that could only be described as a train wreck of emotions between two people locked in circumstances way beyond their control. Neither could have possibly imagined the passion that took place, which left them somewhat bewildered lying next to each other on the sweaty sheets.

Anne started to cry. "This is all my fault." She sobbed and curled up in denial, her back to Nick and still naked under the sheets. "Please don't think less of me. I've never been unfaithful to Tom. I just miss him so much, and I'm afraid I'll never see him again."

"I'm as much a part of this as you," Nick said, lighting a cigarette. "We obviously have some deep need for each other—different reasons maybe, but powerful. Maybe we're trying to fill a void that we aren't strong enough to handle on our own." He put his arms around her reassuringly. His eyes had long adjusted to the night shadows of the room as he stared up at the opaque milk-glass ceiling lamp.

"Are you happy with Martha?"

"Yes, definitely. But maybe I'm not handling the time away and the pregnancy as well as I should. I don't know."

"Have there been others?"

"No, none." Even if there had, the answer would have been the same. There's no way that Nick would have cheapened this experience in Anne's fragile state by answering yes. "I can say that you have been a very good friend and maybe we're using that friendship to hang on while the war takes its course through our lives."

"Can you stay with me for a while? The room is so empty, and I just don't think I can handle being alone."

"For a while, but not the night. Someone may see me in the morning."

"Thanks." Anne could feel his body curled around hers and knew the night wasn't over. *This can't be wrong, and I hope to God that Tom will understand*, she thought. Nick's arms were wrapped around her, brushing the underside of her breasts. She could feel her nipples hardening and an electric feeling deep inside as she rolled over, stroked the hair on Nick's chest, kissed his forehead, and pulled him on top of her.

CHAPTER 32

Billings, Montana
January 25, 1944

My Dear Martha,

Just got in from two periods in the Link. Had a swell session in celestial night—identification of the stars. Liked it a lot, and really feel I know my way around the heavenly bodies now.

Bad news for Anne Walsh. Her fiancée, Tom, was in the battle at Cassino, Italy. No word yet, but it doesn't look good. She's been a real friend to others in the same position—not sure she's going to handle the news well herself, though, if it's bad. You would like her a lot—great gal.

Yours,
Nick

Nick struggled with his disassociation from the night before and his postcard to Martha. He knew he was forcing a routine that no longer fit. Fortunately, he was paired back up with Red in his routing through Billings and had been scheduled for an early departure for Edmonton the next day to deliver some troups and bring back some wounded men for extended recovery. He hoped the flight would provide the distraction to get his head back on right. Still, Nick was hoping to see Anne to say good-bye and get an update before departing. He wanted to be there for support if the news was bad. They also needed to talk, but the assignment to Edmonton prevented that from happening.

"Where are you right now?" Red said after stepping Nick through the takeoff procedures.

"What do you mean?"

"Well, you sure as hell aren't here. Seems like you're a million miles away. I remember once you told me to always be on top of the moods of the crew as it might affect their ability to fly. Seems like that advice applies double to the captain, since we do have twenty enlisted men in the back that are sorta hoping the guy in charge is paying attention."

"Yeah, you're right. Let's get this ship off the ground, and I'll fill you in." Nick knew Red was right, and with 475 miles of clear air in front of them the time would be perfect to talk. *Maybe it was better this way. Having a chance to say things out loud with Red before getting into a discussion with Anne that he wasn't prepared to handle was a good idea,* he thought.

They leveled out at eight thousand feet. "You take the stick today; I'll talk," Nick said. He lit a cigarette, inhaling deep, as if steadying himself for some unknown encounter. And, in many respects, it would be just that. Twin smoke trails joined the men in the cockpit from the exhale. He'd never felt the way he felt about Anne with anyone other than Martha. What happened had knocked him off his feet—not just the intensity of the sex, but the deep emotions that were conjured up between the two of them. The line between friend and lover proved to be extremely short. In truth, he was shocked at Anne's willingness to share herself so completely. He'd always considered her a good friend. And, while he recognized a certain appeal to her good looks and close comfort in the openness of their connection, it never occurred to him that any circumstance would bring them together like the other night. In minutes, he found himself stubbing out the butt of the cigarette he'd just lit and lighting a second as he continued to replay events.

"If I didn't know better, pard, whatever's got you all tangled up might just have a female name attached to it," Red said, realizing that he'd never seen Nick chain-smoke before. "When you said 'talk' did that mean out loud?"

Nick sighed before beginning. "Okay. I think I'm ready. You learn a thing or two about people along the way; that's exactly what's got me vexed." Nick went on to explain what happened with Anne. It felt right to discuss the relevant details without betraying her, since Red knew of their friendship more than anyone. Other than for a few weather-related radio communications with Edmonton flight ops, Red listened and Nick talked for almost an hour.

"I must admit that I'm a little jealous. I kinda had my eye on Anne ever since we met," Red said. "She's the kind you take home to meet the parents."

"That's what I'm struggling with."

"What do you mean? You're already married with a little one on the way!" Red's negative judgment was not concealed. He had never met Martha, but he knew she was the one for Nick.

"I don't know what I mean. But this is different . . . a real connection. It makes you think that if she were there first, there wouldn't be a Martha."

"I don't know if you're lookin' for my opinion or not, but a dose of cold water may be in order. Can't you see that Anne needed you, someone she trusted. Being with you was like being with Tom. Sorry to break the news, but more 'an likely her feelings for you were really her feelings for Tom. I'm not saying they weren't real that night, but it might have been her way to hide from the reality of losing Tom."

"Really. Well it sure ripped a hole in the side of my ship," Nick said with a true feeling of loss. He was quiet for several minutes while processing Red's comments. One side of him didn't want Red's assessment to be true as he considered the excitement shared between he and Anne. He regretted what happened with Anne, yet he couldn't deny the startling feeling that something significant happened. However things turned out, he knew he and Anne would have to sort things out together when he returned to base. Images of their encounter raced through his mind, stirring the very emotions of desire he was fighting. *The sooner the better*, he thought.

Their return flight to Billings that day was delayed until the next morning by the addition of three severely wounded men being sent to Anne's hospital for more extended care. All were missing a limb of one sort, compliments of the Japanese, and required the physical therapy available in Billings.

The flight was uneventful except for the barrier Nick had created to block the door for any conversation about him and Anne. Red didn't pursue it either, knowing that Nick held the only key.

"Good luck, pard," Red said as they left flight ops in Billings. He gave his captain a gentle pat of reinforcement on the back. "Let me know what an Okie friend can do to help."

"Thanks," was all Nick said as he walked away in the direction of the hospital.

"She left this morning for Cleveland," the nurse on duty told Nick. "Tom's parents wired yesterday with the bad news."

He walked aimlessly from the hospital back to his quarters not knowing what to do. The emotions inside were like the contents of a shaken pop bottle ready to explode. He realized that he was only thinking about Anne and that any thoughts of Martha had been blotted out. Not knowing what to do, Nick went to the officer's club for a few beers and a sandwich. He tried to figure out what his next step should be, but his emotions for Anne were on a perfect collision course with his commitment to Martha. He was living a dream without an exit. Even his own normally good common sense abandoned him. Somehow he needed to find a way to talk with Anne. *It is the only way*, he thought.

He swung by the MacDonald Hotel, if for nothing else but to find a way to be as close as possible to her. He thought he might find some direction as to what he should do next. Standing on the wooden boardwalk at the front door of the hotel, he could feel the experience of that first embrace. He went into the lobby as if actually expecting she would be there.

"Are you Captain Morgan?" a voice intruded as if from a different reality.

Nick turned to see it was the desk clerk from across the room trying to get his attention. He approached the man, circling the large hand-carved wooden table and cushioned leather chairs in the center of the hotel's lobby. "Yes, I'm Captain Morgan."

"I have a letter for you. Anne Walsh thought you might show up looking for her, and she wanted me to make sure you got it."

"Thanks." Nick took the letter eager with anticipation. "Was there anything else?"

"No. She was in a rush to make a flight—back home, I guess. Someone close to her was killed in Italy is all that I know."

Nick walked toward town in the gray shadows of the winter afternoon while trying to envision the feelings he thought Anne would express in the letter and wondering how he might react. He knew that whatever it said would impact his future. He wasn't sure he was ready. He pictured Anne with a look of closure, as if the letter were being delivered personally to tell him how she felt. He could feel Anne's hand slip inside his as she talked of their future. Nick was reinforced by the image and held onto it as he walked. After some time, he found himself in front of St. Matthew's, the little Catholic church they had visited a few nights earlier. The serendipity made sense. He entered and found the same pew from before and opened the letter with anticipation and care.

January 26, 1944

Dear Nick,

As you have no doubt heard, I just received news from Tom's parents that he was killed in action at Cassino. It's hard to put into words how empty and sad I feel knowing that all of our dreams of being together are just that—dreams. You remember that we once talked about whether it was better to stay single during the war or to be married. I believe now that the answer is that I would have preferred to be married. Being single hasn't lessened the pain I feel, nor the anger in me that this war has taken the one I love. Being married would have afforded Tom and me at least some time together and a few nights like the one you and I experienced. We would have been able to lock each other's memory into our souls as we shared whatever life, however short, we had. As it is, only the anticipation of that memory was real. You helped me find the fleeting experience Tom and I had foregone in an effort to protect each other, for what reason I now do not know. I will hold on to my feelings for you, Nick, as a remembrance of something that could have been—something that in other circumstances could actually become real. For now, I will just close my eyes and forever remember our time together and the closeness we enjoyed. I think Tom would have understood.

Before leaving Billings I filled out my transfer request for the army hospital in Bethesda, Maryland. I understand that it is a first-rate hospital and, unfortunately, growing quickly. I can be useful there and fulfill my hopes of helping out men who have been broken by this terrible war. For you and me, it means an end. I could see something in your eyes that night that made me feel bad, and in truth, guilty. If I caused you in any way to waver in your love for Martha, I will forever be sorry. I would never forgive myself. Accept what we had as special and beautiful, but, nonetheless, as a substitute for what we both dearly missed. Embrace Martha and be joyful in the prospect of your life together with your family. If you think of me occasionally, as I will you, do so as two friends caught in circumstances beyond their control, willing to share their need for someone else with each other.

I hope this war is over soon and that God holds you safely in His hands. I wish you a long and loving life with Martha. Say hello to Red and the others. I'll miss them and all the fun experiences together.

Good-bye.

Love,

Anne

It was completely dark when Nick was able to summon the strength to leave the church. The words in the letter were unrelenting in their power. She had left no door open, and he knew that she was right in what she had done. Her strength was simply greater than his. He mulled over whether it was his weakness or his genuine feelings for Anne at the source of his ambivalence. "I love you, too, Anne," he said under his breath.

CHAPTER 33

The chilly but sunny day in the upper Sonoran area of New Mexico was for Dr. Oppenheimer and Major Gordon a pleasant alternative to Yukon Flats, Alaska. They had come to the remote part of the Southwest to evaluate a second site for the Los Alamos project. The ever-present cigarette clinging to Dr. Oppenheimer's lips provided no obstacle as he conversed with the major. "It's more goddamn tolerable than the Flats, but it still has disadvantages." The vegetation—sagebrush, pinion, and juniper—coupled with far more acceptable temperatures were obvious advantages as the two men surveyed this remote area of New Mexico forty miles northwest of Carrizozo.

"I agree," the major replied. "It's pleasant now, but with a test scheduled in late summer, the heat will be a son of a bitch. It won't be a pleasant exchange for the early fall temperatures of the Flats."

"Point taken, Major, but the site preparation will go smoother. You damn well know the military will start their efforts a year in advance, which means we'll be working on it all twelve months." He sucked the cigarette with such intensity that it actually bent before removing it from his mouth to light another. "What I don't like, though, is the volcanic history of the area."

"Are you talking about that lava flow to the east of here?"

"Exactly. Ronald's done some research, and the activity's not that old in seismic terms. If this test goes as planned, we're going to give this area a hell of a jolt." Ronald Reisdorf had continued to be a trusted confidant to Dr. Oppenheimer throughout the project. Dr. Oppenheimer had handpicked his protégé. Some argued that Ronald was too involved for a civilian contractor. Smart as hell, though, as a Harvard physics prodigy—nobody disagreed on that point.

"What are we talking about?" The major had been gazing at the vista, but he turned back to make direct eye contact for emphasis as he asked about the jolt.

"My best guess is the equivalent of twenty kilotons of TNT."

The major issued a low whistle. "Jesus Christ!"

"That's why both site alternatives need to be absolutely remote. The army will have to get the people living here out on some pretense and build a perimeter of security."

The major removed his visor cap, which was in complete contrast to the wrinkled canvas fishing hat worn by Dr. Oppenheimer, and wiped the perspiration from his brow with a handkerchief. "The army's going to have their hands full accomplishing that with the sheer size of either site. The military police will want to know our decision months ahead of any activity."

"We'll give them that. Our team has been requested to provide a complete Manhattan Project dog and pony show to no less than the 509th Composite Group and his holiness, Brigadier General Leslie Groves, on the twenty-first of March in Colorado Springs. I'm not at liberty to give you the details yet, Major, but every aspect of our plan will be scrutinized. In the meantime, my vote for the test site is to pinpoint a location in this area of New Mexico as the first choice and Yukon Flats as the second. Physically, they both meet our standards, so we'll need to be prepared to argue the value of both. In the end, though, I think it's the proximity to our scientists at Los Alamos and the ability to mobilize the brass in and out that I think will make the difference."

"Are you sure you understand the full merits of Yukon Flats? Just a month ago that was your first pick."

"I think so. Ronald and I are going to review all the data tomorrow to be sure. It's likely we'll need one more trip for final validation." As if to make a point, Dr. Oppenheimer stomped out his cigarette in the rocky dirt in one of the rare times that he didn't light another.

Ronald was a rare breed. As an American-born citizen his cover as a Russian spy was authentic. While communist infiltration in the United States was not uncommon—even FDR's brain trust had been invaded by card-carrying communists from both countries—most were foreign born. At Harvard, Ronald's true genius as a physicist was unparalleled. It was his study and firm conviction in socialism and collectivization, however, that motivated his misplaced idealism. The Lenin "experiment" made sense to him as a one-world order. He believed Stalin's leadership was perfectly timed. On the contrary, he thought that the United States was too yielding in its commitment to world leadership, and he believed capitalism to be the soft underbelly of U.S. credibility. It was the Nazis, though, that confirmed the one thing he believed all of his life—there are very few ideologies destined to lead on the world stage. And within each ideology there are just a handful of people with the intellect capable of envisioning and planning a one-world order. Ronald was of the staunch belief that the United States and Germany would be pushed aside as a result of having to maintain costly wars on two fronts. He knew for a fact that the "super bomb" would be a reality soon, and the island nations of Britain and Japan were vulnerable to a bomb capable of destroying an entire city the size of London or Tokyo. Russia and its commitment to social order made sense to Ronald. In the process, Russia's current alliance with Uncle Sam only made her stronger.

Yet, as a Russian GRU military intelligence spy, he had never met his handler. All communications took place via a BP3, the most sophisticated undercover encryption communications system in existence. Built by Polish telecommunication refugees hired by the British Secret Service, the BP3 was constructed as a vastly improved miniaturized suitcase version of the outdated and bulky Mark XV, which was housed in two wooden cases.

The BP3's enormous power enabled intercontinental communications, although he was quite sure his handler, code named Mighty Mouse, was American. The namesake from the recent Marvel comic book release combined with too many encrypted colloquial word choices and unique sentence structure tipped off his handler's likely U.S. upbringing—probably the northeast portion of the United States if he were to guess.

The GRU spy network secretly got their hands on a shipment of BP3 prototypes after staging what all believed to be their complete destruction. Ronald considered it an important honor to have access to his own personal BP3 system, proving the importance of his work and his intellectual capacity to change the world order. Every other method of communication was second-rate compared to the BP3. His message tonight would have to be carefully crafted.

JANUARY 26, 1944
COMRADE MIGHTY MOUSE,

MANHATTAN PROJECT SUMMIT MEETING IS PLANNED
FOR MARCH 21, 1944, IN COLORADO SPRINGS WITH
BRIGADIER GENERAL LESLIE GROVES AND TOP STAFF.
ALL TIMETABLES AND PLANS—INCLUDING BOMB DESIGN,
TESTING LOCATIONS, NUCLEAR FORMULATION, BUILDING
SPECS, AND SECURITY—WILL BE REVIEWED IN DETAIL.

PRELIMINARY ITINERARY FOR LOS ALAMOS TEAM
INCLUDES STOPS AT ANCHORAGE, FAIRBANKS, AND
YUKON FLATS EN ROUTE TO COLORADO SPRINGS
PRIOR TO MEETING. DEPARTURE FROM LOS ALAMOS TO
ANCHORAGE ON MARCH 15. EXACT DETAILS NOT FINAL.
ALL PROJECT DOCUMENTS WILL BE ON BOARD.

TECUMSEH

Ronald had chosen his operative code name, Tecumseh, from his belief that, if it had not been for the bad luck resulting from the actions of a drunken brother at the Battle of Fallen Timbers, Chief Tecumseh and the Indian Nations would have successfully defeated the U.S. Army. This action would have radically changed the shape of the United States political landscape. It was no coincidence that Ronald considered Tecumseh a genius for all ages.

CHAPTER 34

Mighty Mouse knew the circumstances surrounding the Colorado Springs meeting of top army brass would not come again. Its importance was beyond anything he had ever handled. He planned to encrypt the message from Tecumseh with a different code to ensure absolute security before sending it that night to Agent Sirak through the scrutiny of his GRU handler. It was the end of January, just forty-five days from the Los Alamos team's arrival. Because of his unique position in the U.S. military to have access to sensitive flight information and routes, he knew that he would be relied upon to craft a strategy. He also knew that those responsible for this rare collaboration between the NKVD and the GRU would demand a plan to successfully secure the Manhattan Project documents at all costs. For all he knew, Stalin himself would have direct involvement in the plan. On the line was an international power shift in the race for the super bomb and a fallout between the United States and Russia, if the plan failed. The pressure for a plan of absolute certainty and precise implementation was immense.

Mighty Mouse was pulled out of his deep thoughts about the complexity of such a plan when a new co-pilot came through the flight ops door, letting in a cold blast of air. "Goddamn," the man said, reacting to the extreme cold and stiff winds. "I don't know what I did wrong to end up here, but this sure isn't Cincinnati, Ohio."

"You'll get used to it, soldier," Cricket responded with his usual "lend a hand" attitude. "What can I do for you?"

"I'm new at the base, and I thought I'd stop over to get the lay of things . . . maybe some tips on how things run and how I can fit in."

This is how things are supposed to work, Cricket thought as the ever-present clatter of the Teletype machines filled the background. Any opportunity to properly break in a new pilot was time well spent. "We can take some time right now, if you'd like. My name is Martin Mason, but people call me Cricket. It's my job as warrant officer to look after you pilots as you come and go from the base here in Anchorage. I can walk you through the routine of schedules, assignments, flight plans, and, in general, how to keep on my good side."

"Just what I need," the man said, extending his hand in introduction. "My name is Bob Parker. I hail from Cincinnati, Ohio." As the men got down to business, Cricket put his thoughts about the communication he would send that night on hold.

Nobody would ever have suspected Cricket's involvement with the Russians. His Jersey Catholic upbringing was no match for his education on the streets in the slums of Newark. His dad died in a railcar accident—crushed between two cars in the yard. The railroad company didn't pay a dime; they claimed he had liquor on his breath. Cricket was now twenty-six and had four younger brothers and sisters ranging from eleven to twenty-four; one was retarded and a ward of the state. His mother incurred a debilitating back injury on her factory job in '38, making it extremely difficult to manage. Cricket's logic was simple: God had put him on this earth to survive, and getting his education on the streets of Newark was a critical part. The bottom line for him was to get enough money for a better life for his family, and providing information paid a lot more than his job as warrant officer would ever generate.

His arrangement as an operative started innocently several years back as a watchdog for the Russians. In return, he received monthly payments that equaled half his army pay. He sent that money home to his mother to run things. She received the money in cash and never questioned it. If he was ever challenged, he could claim it came from his earnings. He lived frugally on base to support his cover and was true-blue American in everything else he did. In the beginning, he had only planned to do it short term, just for the money. References by his GRU handler, however, in his coded transmissions to Cricket identified too many specifics of his family situation back in Jersey that made Cricket realize there was no going back. That was eighteen months ago.

That night Cricket received a phone call from Robert. "Why don't you route me through Anchorage soon so I can stay overnight?" Robert was always direct in his need for companionship. It made Cricket uncomfortable, but it had been months since they had been together.

"Maybe in a few weeks," Cricket said. "I'm involved in something very important right now, and I need to stay focused. Don't worry, we'll do something." After a little more friendly chatter he hung up. The plan for Sirak was coming together.

The documents would be worthless without a qualified interpreter, he thought. Tecumseh would be perfect, but Oppenheimer would have to be neutralized. His international connections in the scientific community, combined with his ego, made him valuable to the Russians, yet vulnerable and therefore a poor choice for a U.S. operative. They would have to get him out of the way without sending up a red flare that something was up. In addition, any subsequent investigation by the military would need to be completely stymied. Collateral damage could not be uncovered and nonessential parties would have to be eliminated without raising suspicion. The complexity and magnitude of this undertaking left Cricket agitated and unable to sleep well into the night. He finally crafted a simple encrypted message designed to get Agent Sirak's attention and added it to the recoded communication from Tecumseh. He sent it at 0300 via RF communication.

FIRST LIGHTNING,

I FIND MYSELF UNIQUELY SITUATED IN THE MIDDLE OF THESE EVENTS AS THEY UNFOLD. ACTIONS THAT MAY AFFECT THE OUTCOME OF ALL WARS AND RUSSIA'S FUTURE RELATIONS WITH THE UNITED STATES ARE WITHIN REACH. AWAITING YOUR INSTRUCTIONS.

MIGHTY MOUSE

Twelve time zones away, Agent Andrey Sirak considered the significance of obtaining the complete documentation and operational know-how of the Manhattan Project. His meeting earlier in the day with Stalin left no doubt that getting those documents was not only to be his primary responsibility, but one in which any corroboration from Russia would be vehemently denied. The depth of involvement by the joint GRU and NKVD collaboration was so secretive, however, that the existence of traitors within their very walls would make any overt attempt reckless. Complicating matters was the military intelligence policy, which Agent Sirak followed with supreme diligence, in compartmentalizing all agents and operative activities. The German SS operated similarly. He knew that the very heart of the spy system in

Russia was dependent on the belief that all agents and operatives were being watched and reported on by another. One informed false move of betrayal or incompetence led to harsh consequences. The paranoia achieved was pervasive. Agent Sirak knew that to expect for this initiative to be accomplished by one person, however, was naïve and foolhardy, yet a group operating in a transparent fashion was unheard of and opened the door to a disastrous security breach. If it could be done, Agent Dubisskiy, Mighty Mouse, and Tecumseh could provide the core of such a group. But how could such a plan be brought together? Andrey toiled with the possibilities. He was very anxious for the likelihood of a successful outcome.

Finally, as if the solution had been sitting on the table for all to see, he replied to Mighty Mouse's communication.

JANUARY 27, 1944
MIGHTY MOUSE,

GIVE ME THE DETAILS OF YOUR PLAN.

FIRST LIGHTNING

Agent Sirak knew that the logical leader had to be an American in order to pull off the subterfuge necessary to successfully complete the assignment. Agent Dubisskiy would be invaluable, yet his very experience in the NKVD would keep him from effectively taking the lead. Tecumseh was too headstrong to lead but had the right intellect for the initiative to have long-range scientific impact. It was Mighty Mouse who had the credentials to bring the group together. In fact, that's what he did so successfully every day, the agent reasoned.

CHAPTER 35

My Dear Martha,

We just passed Mt. Martha where the Mackenzie and Laird Rivers come together. Lake Martha, the one also named after you, will be coming up on the left, but it will be hard to spot with the snow cover. Thinking a lot about you and the baby—do we need to come up with another name than George? Should get some time off in June. Probably not a good time for you to travel, but I would like for you and George to come out to Glacier after the war. I think you'll like it a lot. Red and I seem to draw a lot of flights together, which is good. I trust him as much as any friend, and he's a damn good pilot.

Yours,
Nick

"Haven't heard you talk much of Anne lately. Is everything okay, Pard?" Red had laid off any conversation about their situation for about a week, hoping that Nick would bring him up to speed on his own. Nick's silence was uncharacteristic.

"People have told me that when you lose a limb you still feel it, as if it is really there . . . but it's not. I guess that's how I feel about Anne. I don't know how I got in so deep in the few days we spent together. But now it's like one of those dreams where you wake up in a cold sweat, out of breath, and running from an unknown demon. I'll just have to stay one step ahead of my emotions until they run their course. It is getting better, though. Thanks for asking."

Nick performed a lazy turn to port for a more direct heading to Norman Wells. Their cargo of tools and equipment for the CANOL gave them a little freedom to stretch their wings, so to speak. They enjoyed the crystal clarity of the winter day with nothing but the soft gray polar twilight provided courtesy of a winter sun just hanging on the horizon.

"It seems like I owe you one hell of an apology, as well," Nick said, completing his turn and lighting a cigarette.

"Yeah, well, as my daddy used to say, 'a man's gotta do what a man's gotta do.' Truth is, you can't read my mind. If I was so set on makin' Anne a special friend, I needed to do something about it and not just hide my feelins like a schoolboy."

"Sounds like we're both moving on," Nick said, exhaling.

"Probably so. But that doesn't mean I won't look her up if I happen to be in our nation's capital."

"For me, I'm back on track with Martha and the baby."

"That's good to hear, pard. It really is."

There wasn't much on the ground in Norman Wells other than a dozen or so pipeline houses hunkered down for the winter and a small bar where one could take an edge off, or get into a fight, depending on one's mood. Nick and Red weren't due out until the following after-noon, so they invested a few bucks drinking to the remarkable effects a woman can have on a man. Red knew that Anne was yesterday's news. Nick was still sorting through the press clippings and making two scrapbooks. Martha's was thicker—Anne's was still hot off the press.

CHAPTER 36

Cricket was organizing his thoughts regarding the plan he was preparing for Agent Sirak when the flight ops phone rang. It was Robert. "I'm waiting at Dave's Pizza like you said. Are you coming?" Dave's was a favorite watering hole for soldiers from the base.

"God, I can't believe it's 1930 already. Sorry, Robert. I'll explain when I get there . . . fifteen minutes max." Cricket had told Robert 1900, but time had eluded him. This plan had become all-consuming. It wasn't just the logistics, it was also the people, the collateral damage, and, above all, the escape route. Right then he was trying to flesh out what could go wrong and the contingency plans necessary. But he had promised Robert over a week ago, and, quite frankly, he was looking forward to the break from work.

"Sorry to stand you up," Cricket said, resting his hand on Robert's shoulder in a familiar manner as the two men greeted each other. They had not been together since Robert's trip back from Manzanar and the fiasco in San Francisco. Despite their special relationship, frequency was the enemy of secrecy. It was difficult for both to continually play the traditional role of male friendship in public. They had to accept the reality that discretion and secrecy were the only way to preserve what they had. Their conversation was light while they shared a pepperoni, sausage, onion, and cheese pizza and a few beers.

"Room 324 at the Westward Hotel," Robert said, sliding a key into Cricket's hand while the two men feigned departure on the wooden walkway outside of Dave's.

"Good to see you again," Cricket said for effect. He walked away leaving Robert standing alone. For weeks Cricket was privately tortured by the decision to involve Robert in his plans to obtain the documents or not. He knew of Robert's growing involvement with Vladimir through a GRU-ciphered message, the same message in which Vladimir told Cricket to include Robert in his surveillance activities. How his GRU handlers knew of his connection with Robert was beyond his comprehension, just as how they knew the details of his family in Jersey surprised him.

Cricket knew that he was in over his head and had to cooperate. He had to instruct Ronald to plant the First Lightning message in Robert's duffle. He had to involve Robert, who took the bait and delivered the message to Vladimir. Robert would become more than just a special friend. Lack of stability would always remain an issue with him, however.

Within thirty minutes, Cricket quietly slipped the key into the lock of room 324. Being a corner room in the hotel, it had a discreet entrance. He had taken an unusually complicated route around town involving a cab and a bus in order to be certain that he wasn't being followed to the hotel. Their night together was long overdue, and he had no idea when the next opportunity would present itself. Cricket's normal dominance in their lovemaking was stepped up a notch.

"You were very aggressive tonight," Robert said exhaustedly while slightly coughing as the trail of cigarette smoke emptied from his lungs. "It's as if you are angry with me or you were purposefully trying to hurt me."

"It's just been too long, that's all. Just another frustration piled on to the load at work."

"It's not like you to be late. What's going on? I've never seen you so focused," said Robert.

"I'm involved in a top-clearance project that may keep me away for some time to come . . . maybe for several years," Cricket said, looking away from Robert. He didn't want Robert to detect any duplicity in his eyes and hoped to measure his commitment with care. He wasn't sure how to play it, but that night seemed like the right time to explore Robert's role in the project.

"I can always put in for a transfer to a base near yours. The United States isn't that big," Robert replied, openly displaying his eagerness.

"I may be transferred to a foreign base."

"They can't do this to us!"

"Don't you get it, Robert? There is no 'us' in this man's army."

Robert was always cognizant that the day might come when they would be separated, but long ago he had made up his mind to find a way of staying with Cricket. He had often thought about places where people like he and Cricket would be more accepted. They had discussed going to South America. "The war will be over one day, Cricket, what then?"

"What do you mean?"

"What I mean is where do I fit in . . . in the long term?" Robert fidgeted with an almost empty glass of scotch while hanging on to his cigarette for security. He was nervous at his own directness and wasn't sure he was ready for the answer.

"I don't know that I have the answer right now."

"What about South America? Have you forgotten about that?"

"No, I haven't. I'm just not sure about where this project is going to lead me. Maybe, if . . ."

"Go on. Finish what you were about to say," Robert said, finishing the last of the scotch and all but slamming the glass onto the nightstand.

"It's not for me to say, but if I could involve you in this project it may help our chances."

"I'd do anything, Cricket. You know I would." As if to emphasize his point, he slid his hand beneath the sheets. Cricket's penis responded in eager anticipation. Robert knew that there was nothing he could do that night other than try to make Cricket happy.

***

For the following week, Cricket continued to struggle with the finalization of his plan. Agent Sirak had become impatient with Cricket's delay. In Cricket's mind, Tecumseh was definitely in because of his ideology and an ego that would feed off the recognition from a worldwide scientific community. Vladimir was an obvious player because of his many skills, and, more importantly, his future would not be assured without his cooperation. Cricket marveled at how Agent Sirak had wrapped up the tidy trio with deadly tentacles reaching beyond any of the three men's possible escape. Cricket's dilemma was how to involve Robert effectively. The fourth person would definitely be an asset in controlling any miscues, but his Japanese sympathies could easily derail their overall plan. Yet, on the other hand, it was the very logic of these sympathies that could be counted on for Robert to support the necessity of a Russian world power to balance the tyranny of a capitalistic United States. Certainly he knew that Japan and Germany would be the two countries that would fall out of power in this war. He would have to make Robert believe that the United States would develop the super bomb first, and that their first target would be Japan. Coupled with the probability that the Germans would lose a war of attrition fighting two fronts, the U.S. would be left unchecked. The Japanese people would be dealt a crushing blow.

The final arrangement Cricket needed to make was for one million dollars to be deposited in various United States and Swiss accounts in order to preserve the financial security of his family. Activating the plan was his only trump card—he simply would not begin until the promised money was in place.

With everyone's motivation clear and their roles defined in his mind, Cricket felt confident in his ability to sell the plan to Sirak.

CHAPTER 37

"What is it with these guys," Red said while blowing the steam off his coffee. "For all their complaints on how we do things you'd think they'd find another bus to ride. Geez!" The twisted expression on Red's face would actually make one believe that this problem was serious.

Nick loved Red's demonstrations of overwrought frustration. It was always entertaining. He seemed to have the ability to strap everybody's feelings onto his back and conjure up just the right facial expression to make the drama believable. "I don't know why you let these things get to you. Didn't you ever have a teacher or boss that was a constant burr under your saddle?"

"Yeah, but these guys should know better. I understand the confidential part—it's the arrogant, 'I'm a genius, and you're a nobody,' attitude that I have problems with."

"Well, if it makes you feel better, Cricket assured me that this would be their last trip. Besides, they're only part of the general passenger list from Anchorage to Fairbanks. From there, it's just one day—maybe two if the weather doesn't cooperate—of flyovers in the Yukon Flats area. Piece of cake."

"When are they arriving?"

"Late this afternoon some time. Wheels up at 1100 tomorrow."

"You can best believe me when I say that I'll be on good behavior. But don't ask me to do anything entertaining, like rope tricks or cowboy songs. That's why you're the captain."

Nick laughed out loud. "I think we'll be okay, but just in case bring your harmonica."

Red sipped his coffee in great disgust, not acknowledging Nick's attempt at humor. "My cattle are better suited to my music than these sodbusters," he murmured.

Nick, Red, and Robert arrived at flight operations about the same time the next day. Nick needed to file the flight plans, Red needed to conduct a preliminary pre-flight check of all mechanical updates, and Robert readied the interior. The team from Los Alamos arrived at 1030 and included Major Gordon, Ronald Reisdorf, Dr. Oppenheimer, and Lt. Max O'Reilly. Twelve servicemen on their way to Minneapolis via Fairbanks for their furlough leave were already sitting in the waiting area. At the last minute, Vladimir and Cricket were added on the shuttle to Fairbanks in order to follow up on the indoctrination training of a batch of Russian P-38 pilots that had just arrived. There were eighteen passengers and three crew in all.

Nick greeted the men from New Mexico and noticed Dr. Oppenheimer was sweating and laboring for breath as he carried a courier bag that was handcuffed to his wrist. "You don't look so good, Doc," he said.

"It just started a few minutes ago," Ronald replied.

"What did he have to eat?"

"Breakfast a while ago and a cup of coffee once he got here," Ronald said. It's only since we've been here that the chest pains, sweating, and heavy breathing started."

Nick shifted his attention to the major. "Major, I'm going to have a doctor look at him before we get in the air. Can we get that bag uncuffed from his wrist, at least for now? It looks uncomfortable."

"I'm afraid we can't do that, Captain, without clearance from Los Alamos. Security issue."

Nick racked his brain for few minutes, trying to figure out what might be in the bag, but since it wasn't really his problem, he dropped the thought. This flight was ready to go except for Dr. Oppenheimer, and he was getting worse. They tried to make him comfortable by laying him down on the office couch, which allowed for the bag to rest on the floor. His face was pale and clammy, and his breathing was very shallow. The doctor arrived quickly and within minutes said, "This man's having a heart attack. Get an ambulance here immediately!"

After he attended to Dr. Oppenheimer's needs, Nick cornered the major for a private counsel. "Major, I'm not sure how you want to handle this, but it's apparent that he won't make this trip. I can hold this flight for about thirty, maybe forty-five minutes while you decide."

The major nodded, turned his attention to the Teletype area, and commandeered one of the operators. "I want your undivided attention, but first give me a minute to write out my message." It was addressed directly to Brigadier General Leslie Groves at the 509th and was marked urgent. The major explained his situation in the message with unusual efficiency and requested permission to proceed without the involvement with Dr. Oppenheimer.

"Move it, soldier," he commanded, handing his note to the Teletype operator. The scene in flight operations had now become tense. In the meantime, the ambulance had left for the hospital together with Dr. Oppenheimer on board and Lt. O'Reilly overseeing the security of the bag.

The major looked at Ronald and said, "It won't be long."

Within ten minutes the clatter of the Teletype began. The message was short, and the operator quickly tore it from the paper roll.

MAJOR GORDON,

PERMISSION GRANTED TO PROCEED AS DESCRIBED.

BRIGADIER GENERAL LESLIE GROVES

"Take me to the hospital," the major said to Nick. "We'll be ready to board your plane in fifteen minutes."

Vladimir and the servicemen were already seated on the C-47 when he saw Cricket, the crew, and the three other men board. He was at the rear of the ship as planned. Cricket found a seat near the middle, and the three men sat at the front, just behind the cockpit. Only thirty minutes had passed since Dr. Oppenheimer's heart attack, and they were ready to take off. The courier bag had been removed from Dr. Oppenheimer and was now handcuffed to the major's left wrist.

The overdose of nitroglycerine administered by Ronald in Dr. Oppenheimer's coffee had worked to perfection, Cricket thought as he glanced toward Vladimir with a confirming nod of the head. There simply would be no evidence. In fact, Dr. Oppenheimer himself would have no idea what happened. Within days he would be fine, and his medical records would show a mild heart attack followed by a positive recovery. "Might be time to cut back on your smoking," they would suggest.

Nick finished his pre-takeoff checklist with Red. All they needed was a green light from the Aldis lamp in the control tower. "We're going to run into a little muck today at about nine thousand feet. Winds are out of the northwest at thirty knots. Maybe some icing conditions—nothing we can't handle. Tell Robert to have people stay buckled up until we find some smooth air. What's the estimated time of arrival?"

"With the delay, about 1345."

"Let Robert know to pass it on, so our highness doesn't get his shorts in a knot."

"Roger that."

Within a few minutes of takeoff Nick reported his progress to Anchorage: he was over Talkeetna, an emergency landing field southeast of Mt. McKinley on the regular route. Shortly afterwards he radioed Anchorage for permission to increase his altitude to ten thousand feet due to mild icing conditions. Permission was granted, and Nick predicted they would pass over Summit, another emergency field in the river basin between Mt. McKinley and the Talkeetna Mountains, on schedule. Visibility was still marginal, so he stayed on instruments.

Two hours later, Friday, March 17, 1944, officials at Ladd Field in Fairbanks reported the plane overdue and declared a state of emergency.

CHAPTER 38

Without so much as a second look, Vladimir took the 45-caliber service revolver that Robert handed him as he moved to the front of the cabin and passed the galley area behind the cockpit. Simultaneously, Cricket drifted to the rear of the ship amid the casual chatter of the men. Robert knocked on the cockpit door for access. When Red reached back to open the door, Vladimir slipped by Robert and entered unnoticed.

"Gentlemen," Vladimir said. "Consider the fact that this flight is now under my command." The cold barrel of the revolver rested at the base of Nick's skull. At the same time the Russian's eyes were focused on Red with incredible intensity.

"What the fuck," Red said loud enough for those at the front of the plane to hear.

"What's the problem up there, Private," the major asked directly to Robert.

"No problem, sir. But I want you and the lieutenant to stay in your seat while I make an announcement. As he spoke, his heart raced with the adrenaline pumping into his system. Despite the surreal nature of the moment, Robert remained in control, fortified by the mental image of his mother and father the last day he saw them at Manzanar.

He produced another weapon that had been stashed behind his jump seat, pointed it at the major, and said, "I want both you and the lieutenant to give me your service revolvers." None of the other passengers were permitted to wear weapons, nor did they want to for that matter—they were on their way home on leave.

"For Christ's sake, what's going on, Private?"

Cricket stood up at the back of the plane with his weapon drawn, just as the attention had focused on Robert. "Give me your attention!" Cricket demanded in his loud Jersey accent.

People turned in their seat to try to find the source of the command.

In those few moments, Robert kept strict eye contact with the major—the gun pointed at his chest. Vladimir was very specific in their hijack prep runs. The major and lieutenant were trained for terrorist events and would look for even the slightest opportunity to regain control.

It was Cricket who made the announcement. "Gentlemen, this flight is now under our control. The pilot has a .45 aimed at his head, and we are well-prepared to assume command. No one needs to get hurt, if you follow my orders. Stay in your seat or you *will* be shot! The pilot will be setting a new course shortly. You will be updated, but don't plan on starting your furlough just yet."

"I demand to know what's going on," the major boomed from the front. "This is a United States military aircraft. Your acts constitute treason!"

Before either Cricket or Robert could answer, Nick's voice came over the loudspeaker. "We have been taken over by a militant group set on redirecting our flight to a foreign country. If we do as these men say, I have been assured that no one will get hurt. At this point, I do not know their politics or their purpose. Need I remind you that while on this ship you are under my command. It's my intention to get everyone of you home safely to your loved ones. Follow their orders!"

The drone of the engines filled the void in the cabin when the PA system clicked off. The soldiers looked at each other in disbelief. Robert stared at the major, barely concealing his contempt and definitely not inviting any further conversation.

"The Indians in Oklahoma used to conduct sneak attacks on neighboring villages, but they had a purpose—horses generally, sometimes women. We don't have either on board, so what's this all about?" Even under extreme pressure Red had a knack for remaining cool.

"I've watched your American movies, and we are not a bunch of Indians stealing horses," Vladimir said. "Just follow my orders." He handed Red new flight plans from his position at the rear of the cockpit, just as two P-38s pulled up alongside the C-47.

Nick could see that the planes were Russian by their markings.

The fighter on his side threw a line of machine-gun fire across the nose of his ship as a warning to cooperate and that they were armed. Both P-38s dropped below and behind the C-47, but still in view out of Nick's and Red's peripheral vision.

"They will escort us for the remainder of our time together," Vladimir said. "They will be useful in guiding us below radar making the planes disappear, once over the mountains."

"Those are our goddamn planes from our base, I'll bet," Red said rhetorically in disgust.

Vladimir's smile demonstrated a complex depth to his command experience never observed by Nick or Red in their day-to-day encounters in the past.

After a few minutes reviewing the plans, Red said, "This isn't going to be easy. We're not in a P-38, and, if you didn't notice, the weather conditions aren't the greatest. There is a high probability of icing with very limited visibility." He handed the new flight plan to Nick with undeniable disdain.

"Jesus, Vladimir. We've got people on board. Flying below radar is very risky," Nick said after a brief look. "Besides, these mountains will be treacherous. There's a reason we fly around them."

"Just do as the plan calls for. Cricket assures me you two are the best. He has mapped a route that minimizes this risk you talk about. Once you clear the uncharted mountain area to the northwest of McKinley, following the Yukon River will be a piece of cake, as you Americans like to say."

Nick reflected on the words "making the planes disappear." It was a phrase describing *nap-of-the-earth*, or NOE, low-level–type flight used to avoid detection. Geographical features, such as valleys and folds, would be exploited to stay below radar. The two P-38s would function like two field dogs flushing out the tricky spots, making up for the C-47's lack of agility. *This plan of theirs might just work*, he thought. He looked at Red with a "tell me what to do and I'll do it" expression on his face before saying, "Can we even do this?"

"The ship will handle the elevation okay if we avoid icing. The headwind and downdrafts will be a son of a bitch. Most of these mountains are uncharted—visibility will be key," Red replied with a characteristically accurate assessment.

Vladimir added, "No radio communication. Understand? If you so much as break this silence I will shoot one of your passengers at random."

"Understood." Nick paused to light a cigarette. "Shit, Vladimir, I thought we were friends. Our countries, I mean."

"This isn't about friendship, Captain."

"Then what is it about?"

"You'll find out soon enough. Now start making your new headings."

Cricket knew that the next forty minutes were critical. He looked at his watch. It was 1230. By 1310 the ship would be on the backside of the mountains headed northwest toward the valley and the Yukon River. They would follow it west, as best they could below radar, to the small outpost of Koyukuk. Once over the Norton Sound and the Bering Sea, their heading would be set directly toward Anadyr, Russia, for an airstrip specifically constructed on the Kamchatka Peninsula for this flight. The range of the C-47 was fifteen hundred miles, well within their target even with headwinds—maximum flight time of four hours. But just to compensate, Cricket made sure the tanks were full and the cargo was at a minimum. He had been over this plan a hundred times, first with his GRU handlers and Agent Sirak, and then with his "team."

From Sirak's point of view the risks were minimal. When the world found out that the Americans were building a super-bomb site within striking range of Russia, they would think it prudent that Russia act preemptively. The United States didn't run the world, and it was Sirak's job to ensure that Stalin would have equal say with Roosevelt in post-war politics. As far as the immediate plan was concerned, he knew he had the best pilot team and a route that would be hard to track. These guys were skilled at flying, and the mountains would act as a radar shield if they stayed low. The riskiest part was crossing the mountains in front of them. The crosswinds were always unpredictable and a downdraft could force a plane to drop thousands of feet. That day, they had the added threat of icing conditions.

"Put your trust in God and Pratt & Whitney today, Red," Nick said as they got one of the few clear glimpses of Mt. McKinley they would get. It was unbelievable in beauty and size. They were currently at ten thousand feet and in a gradual climb. The mountain rose to over twenty thousand feet, giving them a "King Kong and Empire State Building" experience. The wind raced over the highest bluffs, pushing trailers of snow a mile from its edge. The mountain and its own weather pattern were beginning to block the setting winter sun, which was scheduled to disappear at 1615. Nick flicked on the landing lights to assist in the transition from twilight to dark shadows, knowing it would happen soon.

As quickly as the mountain came, it was gone again with a heavy lenticular cloud cover separating it from the ship, leaving only a vague dark outline of the existing peaks. "Keep our heading due north while I try to get above this junk," Nick said.

"Roger."

"It's likely that this ride is going to get rough. Tell our passengers that we want them in their seats with their seatbelts on. That includes Robert and Cricket. I don't want someone getting shot by accident. That means you, too, Vladimir. Take the jump seat behind us."

"Roger, Captain." Red unbuckled so as to move back to the cabin to pass on the orders first-hand.

"Just do your job," Vladimir said, cautioning Red.

Robert easily maintained command while buckled up, as his jump seat was designed to give him full view of the cabin and passengers. In the rear, Cricket buckled in while sitting on a duffle bag to allow him to keep his gun trained on the passengers. Red tried to pinpoint a weakness as he surveyed the cabin. He found none.

"Get settled in, Red," Nick said upon Red's return. "The next five minutes are going to be interesting. We're icing a bit, but we should be okay. Can you see that ridge at ten o'clock, between those two peaks? I think we can use it as an alleyway through this maze."

"Whatever you say, Captain."

"Climb to 11,500 feet." Nick vividly remembered his experience with Captain Smith in the Valley of the 10,000 Smokes on the Aleutian Chain. He knew instinctively that he needed a greater clearance margin as none of these lesser peaks in the McKinley Range had recorded elevations.

Each soldier offered his own prayer of safe passage as the crosswinds hammered the ship while it cleared the first ridgeline. The visibility was approximately one mile, perhaps a little more, as they entered a huge bowl-shaped valley between peaks. Complete desolation. Nick would only have about thirty seconds before the next hurdle of peaks. "What do you think, Red?"

"About the same elevation, but I feel a little icing. Do you?"

"Roger that. Change altitude to twelve thousand." At that exact moment, and before Nick could begin his climb to the higher level, the ship was pancaked by a downdraft that pushed it almost a thousand feet below where they needed to be. Visibility went to zero as the ship lost altitude uncontrollably in the darkness of the mountain's shadows and clouds. Nick had never experienced such an extreme wind as it rolled easterly over the peak in front of them creating a crushing force and causing a virtual whiteout. Nick struggled to regain control of the ship. He fought the pressure of the downdraft, forcing the C-47 into an unintentional hard bank. He had to find an escape—the bowl had them trapped. They only had seconds—they had to get lift!

The torque from the twin Pratt & Whitney engines caused the C-47 to nearly explode with noise and vibration as he fought the effects of losing control. "It's not enough . . . It's not enough!" Nick heard himself say. Passengers on the plane were panicked, and the crew was helpless. Within seconds they cleared the cloud cover and gained visibility. The rock and snow-packed ridge leading to the unnamed peak in front of them went by like a View-Master on steroids. The final climb had to happen if any of them were going to survive. "C'mn baby! You can do it. A little bit more!"

"Keep the hammer down, pard. I can see the top." Red gripped the sides of his seat as if he were Pecos Bill manhandling a West Texas tornado.

Instantly, all control was lost as a crosswind skid the ship one hundred yards toward the unforgiving rocks, ice, and snow. They were helpless as the port wingtip clipped a mountain wall and folded the wing up and back, shearing the bolts holding it to the fuselage. The snow mushroomed from the ship's impact. The back of the fuselage broke at the loading door, tearing the landing gear assemblies loose and separating the ship into two parts. The forward velocity launched the cockpit portion forward over five hundred yards up and over the crest of the ridge with its bottom acting as a skid. The remainder of the ship rebounded from the precipitous side of the ridge, breaking the right wing loose, and plummeted fifteen hundred feet into a steep snow field high in the glacier. The soldiers were tossed upside down like surfers being pushed twenty feet deep in a wipeout without any sense of up. Nick held a brief vision of his port engine buried in an ice-encrusted vertical wall high above the glacier floor.

The force of the impact sucked the wind out of his body. As he was gasping for breath, choking, reaching for anything that would help, everyone found their expression in his uncontrollable cry for something to hang on to. "Agh, agh, agh!" Then blackness.

CHAPTER 39

Nick was unconscious from the collision of the C-47 nose section with the large boulder outcropping two hundred yards below the eleven-thousand-foot crest on the windward side of the ridge. The scraping metal sounds of the forward fuselage against the exposed rock surface of the ridge screamed for only a few moments as it was rocketed forward by the force of the crash. The sound of the metal was immediately swallowed by the buffeting winds as they continued their own assault on this raw, lesser peak in the McKinley Range. If the three men in this forward section of the crash heard the squeal and screech of metal against rock, it was lost immediately in their anguish and unconsciousness, and death. There were no trees or vegetation at that elevation, just the occasional exposure of crags and rocks showing through, where the ice and crusted snow had not taken hold. Only the raging winds driving a weather front up the mountain's face seemed to have life—a harsh existence with windchills at ten below zero.

Nick heard himself moan as he gained consciousness. He had no idea how long it had been since the crash. His pain was intense as he struggled to remember what had happened. His seat had broken loose during impact, slamming the left side of his body forward and twisting it to the left. He had multiple fractures, broken ribs, deep lacerations to his face and scalp, and, undoubtedly, internal injuries. But it was the femur penetrating through the left leg of his flight uniform that was the source of pure torture.

The cabin was filled with blood. He looked to his friend in the co-pilot seat. "Aw, no!" he cried out, seeing Red's body still strapped in and his skull crushed against the instrument panel. The loss of a good friend and the best airman he had ever flown with flooded him with emotions as he reached over and touched Red to confirm the obvious. "God dammit!" He tried to take a deep breath to get control of his emotions, but the pain was excruciating. "Nobody was like you, Red. I'm real sorry." Nick's immediate remorse for the circumstances and the outcome shrouded his thinking with guilt. *How did I allow this to happen?*

Nick tried to shift in his seat to see Vladimir. He'd rip his head off, if he could, for what he'd done to Red. The pain from the movement screamed throughout Nick's body. He was pinned down by the crushed instrument panel and flight control column; it was impossible to move other than to make a slight turn of his head. What he saw in his peripheral vision so shocked him that his initial reaction was utter disbelief. Vladimir was still strapped in his seat behind the pilot's seat. He was alive but had been impaled by a three-foot metal shaft that had once been part of the ship's structure. It was as if he had been lanced completely through the upper torso by some mysterious medieval knight. Vladimir's eyes stared in disbelief, communicating the terror of his situation. Beyond Vladimir, what was once the cabin door to the nose section, there was nothing but a gaping hole, which is where the rest of the ship used to be. The smell of burning oil and stressed metal from the crash filled the air. Shredded wiring, smashed components, and the paper from flight manuals and logs completed the collage of disaster.

"Can you speak?" Nick had heard Vladimir murmuring in Russian. It sounded like ramblings to Nick, but since he did not speak Russian, he didn't really know.

"You almost made it," Vladimir replied, regaining his English and suppressing the obvious pain. His body only allowed him very shallow breaths. He struggled to reconcile his disbelief in his wound with the reality of the crash. Cricket was so confident that this route would work that the takeover team never questioned this scenario.

"Is that all you can say? This is crazy. If any of us survive this mess there will be fuckin' hell to pay." Nick was beyond angry, but he was helpless to do anything.

"Is Robert back there? I can't see," Nick asked, instinctively checking on his traitor crew member.

"No. He moved to the main cabin before the crash. What do we do now, Captain?"

"Your guess is as good as mine. I'm completely pinned in with lots of broken body parts. Not sure I can get out. Your situation looks pretty grim, too?"

"I'm afraid to move with this metal sticking through me. There's blood everywhere."

"Anything else?" Nick's reflection on his question was *hell yes—there's a whole lot wrong! People are dead, we're all probably going to die and for what—a Russian militant plot!* But, instead, Nick knew he needed to get control of himself and focus on the situation at hand. Rescue efforts were probably being organized for when the weather broke. They needed to figure out a way to stay alive and not freeze to death.

"It's cold . . . real cold . . . feel dizzy. Not good," Vladimir replied, fading back into unconsciousness.

"Stay with me. You hear!" Nick commanded. "Can you get free of your seat belt?" Nick knew that Vladimir's chances would decline rapidly if the bleeding couldn't be stopped. "If you can help me out of the cockpit, I might be able to help you stop the bleeding, but I'm stuck."

No answer.

The added smells generated by the friction of metal on metal, the torn wiring, and leaking cockpit fluid lines filled Nick's senses. He thought about the emergency equipment that was stored in the rear of the craft—smoke bombs, a flare pistol, and the Gibson Girl, so named because of its hourglass shape. It included a radio transmitter and hand-crank generator that would be invaluable. They were all lost because of where they were stored.

The P-38 escort on the underbelly side of the C-47 lost altitude in the same downdraft that affected Nick and Red. It ran headlong into a block of ice on the mountainside's sheer wall, exploding and killing the pilot instantly. The collapsed ball of wreckage fell into the valley below and was completely buried by a trailing avalanche caused by the explosion. The second P-38 escort found a hole in the clouds and climbed to safety. After circling the crash area twice it continued back on course to Russia, careful not to attract any attention from radar.

Immediately after impact and the loss of the port wing and engine, the right wing and tail broke off and fell into the snowfield below. The starboard motor broke off separately and rolled down the steep slope, causing an additional avalanche further down the snowfield, which completely buried the motor. Because of their large airfoil surfaces, the wing and tail landed flat and virtually intact with the aileron still in place. When the remaining portion of the crash finally came to rest at nine thousand feet, two thousand feet below the cockpit, the main fuselage and the wing lay parallel to each other half buried in avalanche snow at the confluence of two large and uncharted glaciers fifteen hundred feet below the ridge where they struck. Passengers who weren't wearing their seat belts, carry-on equipment, personal items, and all the emergency communication equipment were spread over hundreds of acres of snowfield, yawning crevasses, and ice caves with deep, treacherous drop-offs. Terrific downdrafts continued to blow over the crest and mountain cornice and sweep throughout the freezing valley below. Death was everywhere.

The impact of the fifteen-hundred-foot freefall of the fuselage on the valley floor killed almost everyone on board. Those who escaped death on impact were suffocated by a small avalanche triggered by the crash. The aft end of the fuselage was packed by the snow. Major Gordon survived, the courier bag still attached to his broken body. He clutched it from instinct in his semi-unconscious state. A negro sergeant from Harlem who had an early start on his leave and was drunk with his buddies also survived. He hadn't bothered to buckle up and continued his relationship with a bottle of Jack Daniels during the flight. As luck would have it, he was thrown from the fuselage just prior to impact on the snow field floor. Ronald Reisdorf and Lt. Max O'Reilly died on impact. Cricket was thrown from the plane at the point of initial impact and fell a thousand feet into a deep mountain crevasse.

Robert survived out of habitual adherence to the procedures he was responsible for enforcing. The soldiers on his flights, however, were always careless with safety—they had either survived their duty in the Aleutians and felt invincible or were celebrating their upcoming leave and were distracted. Red's order to buckle up during turbulence wasn't followed by everyone and those men had no idea how to don their parachute. Robert always put his on. In this case it was a simple matter of pulling the rip cord after being catapulted from the ship by the centrifugal force seconds after impact.

CHAPTER 40

The sergeant from Harlem was Charles Biggs. He struggled with his orientation once on the ground due partly to his inebriation but mainly from the lack of contrast with the flat light. The snow mounds, drop-offs, and slopes were very hard to make out. He sobered quickly after sitting a few minutes, bewildered with his freak luck in surviving. He barely remembered what had happened other than the abrupt ending in a deep snow bank. *Unbelievable*, he thought. In the foreground he could see the horrific crash site several hundred yards away. Instinctively, he began the effort of crawling, stumbling, and walking toward the C-47 fuselage in anticipation of helping survivors and providing aid. The winter sun's light would be lost soon when it set behind the peaks. The elevation made it very hard to breath and progress was slow in the deep snow. In reality, he was homing in on the C-47 as a source of help more than a place to help—an undefined hope for an answer to what had happened. His inexperience in flying provided only a general knowledge of survival gear and emergency communication devices that may be on board.

"Jesus, Mary, and Joseph!" he said in utter disbelief when he arrived on the scene. From his vantage point he could see a handful of men still strapped in their seats, dead from the impact or dead from some secondary collision with flying objects throughout the fall. The smell of blood was pervasive. In one case, a soldier he had been playing cards and drinking with sat motionless, his head split wide open. With the ship's fuselage on its side, the dead soldiers were like marionettes hanging from their seatbelts—lifeless—without a puppeteer to bring them to life.

"God, what do I do now?" he exclaimed, looking for anyone alive.

"We survive. That's what we do." The weak voice was that of the major, still strapped in near the front, down-side of the tilted fuselage.

Sergeant Biggs recognized the major immediately and went to him. "I think it's just us, Major. Let me help you get loose from your harness," the sergeant said while trying to blow warmth into his hands and fingers. He removed a coat from one of the other soldiers for more protection.

"No, Sergeant. I can't move. Too busted up . . . likely a broken back. There may be no way out of this cluster fuck, but the way I see it is that we're going to freeze to death if we don't stay warm."

"How about removing that bag cuffed to your wrist first?"

"No. It's fine. Leave it."

"What do you propose, Major? My experience is limited here. By the way, my men call me Sarge."

"Alright. Sarge it is. It seems like we have a natural shelter in this broken fuselage if we can somehow find a way to close it up to protect us from the wind and drifts."

"I'd like to get the bodies out first," Sarge commented. "I'm not so sure I can be in here with them all night."

The major nodded in agreement.

Robert still had the jump seat underneath him as he was ripped from the plane seconds after impact. It wasn't thoughtfulness that caused him to pull the ripcord to his parachute, but rather an instinctive reaction to the immediate sense of falling. A cloud of snow filled the air from the ship's impact on the sheer wall, making it impossible to tell up from down. He didn't think; he just pulled, and the yank of the chute opening snapped him into the moment. The last thing he remembered was Vladimir taking over the cockpit and the blank stares of disbelief and anger from the men in the main cabin. Now, as he fell, he could feel the conflicting effects of the downdraft and crosswinds as they had their way with the chute during his descent. The artificial snow cloud vanished as quickly as it was created, and Robert actually witnessed the fall of the ship in rough parallel to his own descent. Debris followed the crash like a Macy's Day Parade. The wing and tail assembly was ripped from the housing. He was sure that he saw at least two bodies thrown from the opening in the fuselage. The sight was horrible and an intense fear choked any thoughts for his own safety. He battled the fierce winds, which made his lack of experience with the chute even more obvious. The winds blew him toward an enormous crevasse from which any escape would be unlikely. Mercifully, at the last minute a strong gust grabbed hold of the chute and carried it across the huge bottomless opening, depositing him in a heap a mere fifteen feet from the rim. Luck couldn't begin to describe his good fortune. He quickly reeled in the nylon to avoid being dragged back into the chasm by the winds. At least for the moment, he felt fortunate as he prepared for his arduous hike to the ship some distance away across the snowfield. Robert sat on a snow-covered rock pile, gazing at a most remarkable scene of destruction, questioning the probability of his survival.

As he got closer to the fuselage, he was encouraged to see movement inside the wreckage. Quickly, however, he remembered that he would be seen as the enemy. The pistol still in its holster gave him some comfort, but he would still be vulnerable when he slept, if he chose to seek the protection of the wreckage. He remembered an old-timer telling a story about being stranded for days on an ice flow and how a small igloo was able to insulate him from sub-freezing temperatures. *It's getting dark*, Robert thought. *Need to act quickly.* Nearby where he landed was a four- to five-foot mound of snow that might work. He trudged over to inspect it. He was happy when he saw that the mound was completely crusted over. *This will be perfect if I can just break through a side and hollow it out*, he thought.

He studied the mound and found a spot downwind where the side had a soft spot. Carefully, he kicked in an opening about the size of a manhole cover and started burrowing into his new home. He paced himself in his efforts, careful not to overheat, as he knew that the perspiration would accelerate hypothermia. He retrieved the jump seat and used it as a door to block him from the elements. The parachute acted as a mattress cover and kept him from getting wet from the snow melted by his body heat. *Not perfect,* he thought, *but I think it will work*. The stress of the last few hours drained from his body, and he fell sound asleep.

───────

Removing the dead bodies proved to be more of a task than anticipated. Sarge cleared a depression in the snow for a temporary gravesite near the fuselage. He struggled with each body. An hour went by before he was done. The exercise was a great antidote for the Jack Daniels and warmed him to a point where he removed his outer coat. He finished as darkness set in, yet he still needed to find a way to cover the gaping hole in the fuselage. This presented a challenge because there was no obvious material that would work.

"See if you can find a few parachutes," the major said as if reading his mind.

"Great idea," Sarge replied, relieved.

Unfortunately, most of the parachutes were gone—spread across the mountain with everything else that wasn't tied down. He did find two, though, the one the major wore and one in the clutches of a dead soldier.

"You're just going to have to improvise." The major always had a way of adding a tone of certainty to his comments, although Sarge seriously doubted he was going to make it out alive.

With some effort Sarge opened the two chutes and was able to secure them across the opening. Not ideal, but passable in order to keep the wind and snow out of their makeshift quarters. He found a way to use the pull-down seats along the starboard side of the ship as a makeshift bed for himself.

"Can I get you anything, Major?"

"A few more coats around my legs would help." His voice shook, and he was barely able to articulate the words.

While Sarge complied the major added a strange order. "Sarge, this courier bag attached to my arm contains very sensitive and confidential material that could jeopardize the security of the United States. If I don't make it, get the contents to General Leslie R. Groves of the 509th Composite Group. That's an order."

"And if I don't make it, sir?"

"Then it will be safe here for all eternity."

While the ship offered very little insulation from the cold, Sarge remained warm from the effects of his hard work. Despite their inadequate accommodations, the howls of the wind, and the constant buffeting noise of the parachutes, both were soon sound asleep. What the Sarge didn't know was that his dilated capillaries from being overheated carried the excess heat to his skin. From there his damp clothes dispelled it rapidly as the night progressed. The lack of insulating fat over his lean muscled body allowed the cold to creep that much closer to his warm blood.

The major trembled violently, as the extra coats were unsatisfactory in raising his core body temperature. He fell asleep in a stupor. By 2130 his heart became arrhythmic, its electrical impulses hampered by chilled nerve tissues, and he entered into profound hypothermia. His damaged body could not fight back. By 2250 he was dead.

CHAPTER 41

"Only an explosion and fire could have made things worse," Nick said angrily. He had been unable to dislodge himself despite his efforts. "If we weren't stranded on top of this ridge, maybe we could get help."

"I doubt if there are others alive," Vladimir replied in a voice barely above a whisper. "And we may not be either if we don't find a way to stay warm overnight." His loss of blood was great, and there was no way he could remove the steel shaft from his body as Nick had hoped. It had entered above the right breast angling down, piercing his right lung, and exited below the right shoulder blade. His breathing was extremely shallow.

"What was all this about?" Nick asked. "A lot of people are dead because of your actions."

"It's not my actions; it's your country's actions," Vladimir replied indignantly, yet barely audible because of his great pain. The steel shaft had supplied the additional cruelty of becoming a conductor for the below-freezing temperatures throughout his upper body.

"What are you talking about? I want a real answer."

"If we live, I'll show you. Look in the courier bag locked to the major's wrist. You'll see the answer. A plan to test an atom bomb here in Alaska, such a short distance from Russia, cannot be tolerated. It sets a stage for an attack by the United States. Such an aggressive act threatens our security and erodes our trust."

"So that's what all the activity in Yukon Flats was all about?"

There was no answer. Nick twisted as best he could and saw that Vladimir had passed out. He was very pale, and Nick didn't think Vladimir would make it through the night. *What if he was right?* Nick thought. An atom bomb being tested within striking distance of a foreign country would certainly be cause for alarm and escalation regardless of who's right. "God, this world's a mess!"

He didn't have much optimism for his own situation, either. The shock and cold had numbed the pain in his leg. He knew that even if he were rescued, he would probably lose it anyway. He looked at the radio in vain—in pieces with the rest of the instruments. *Wouldn't make any difference even if it did work*, he thought, as their course over the McKinley Range had taken them off the pre-established radio vectors for flight communication channels from either Fairbanks or Anchorage. Oddly enough, however, the cockpit light responded to Nick's habitual flip of the switch.

"Oh Martha . . . Martha. I don't know if I can get out of this fix," he half groaned, beginning to accept the reality of his predicament. He tried to remember the last time he wrote to her and what he had said but came up blank. In their last phone call he remembered being enthusiastic about Martha coming out west after the baby was born, but she was less sure because of the practicality of caring for an infant. He realized in that call that the business of their marriage had taken over the excitement of their relationship. It was for this reason he was having difficulty getting Anne out of his mind. There were still times when the very thought of losing her caused an involuntary primal ache in the pit of his stomach.

The cabin light helped him stay focused and find a way to get loose, but he was so jammed in that anything short of severing his leg seemed unlikely to work. He didn't know if he could actually cut off his own leg. With the compound fracture and the bone protruding, however, it would only be necessary to cut through the flesh and ligaments at the point of the break, he rationalized. Thinking that he could use Red's shirt to fasten a tourniquet just above the break to prevent excessive hemorrhaging, he began scanning the cockpit for a knife or something sharp enough to make the cut. He couldn't find anything to perform the procedure.

Time passed with little change other than the onset of the Alaskan winter darkness and the storm. His sentinel position on top of the mountain was surreal. He was in the most god-awful situation anyone could find themselves in with half an airplane as lodging and only a single light to aid him in maintaining consciousness. He thought for a while about Bud and Helen and his parents in Staples and realized up until then his life had been charmed.

He found himself dozing off, thinking about the early days in summer as a kid fishing on Cass Lake. He and Bud would grab their cane poles, get some worms, and be gone for an entire day. He laughed, remembering that they would take their shoes off on the last day of school and barely put them back on again until September. His head snapped back as he caught himself falling into sleep—warning! If he was to survive the night he would have to stay awake, as sleep always preceded death by freezing. At least for now, his winter flight gear had kept him from getting too cold.

Nick pulled a pen from his shirt pocket and began what he thought might be a final letter to Martha.

March 17, 1944
En Route to Fairbanks

My Dearest Martha,

You may not ever read this. I'm hoping to be able to give it to you and tell you my amazing story in person. But chances are such that it may never happen. In that case the letter may be just a way for me to stay awake and think about what's important.

We've crashed with little opportunity for survival. Red is dead next to me, and I am trapped somewhere in the McKinley Range with no escape. We were hijacked by a Russian militant group because of military secrets that were on board relating to the United States' intention to detonate an atom bomb in Alaska. In total there were twenty on board: fifteen U.S. military passengers, one contract worker from Los Alamos, New Mexico, Vladimir Dubisskiy (a Russian spy), and three crew. As it turned out Warrant Officer Martin Mason and PFC Robert Endo were spies for Russia, too. To my knowledge there are only two of us alive, although I don't know how long the other one will make it. I should be happy about that, as the other person was instrumental in executing the Russian hijack plan, but in reality I'm just sad. I'm sure he was acting under orders from Moscow. The details of their mission may never be known. What I do know is that too many have been lost in this war!

The worst part is that you and I may be separated forever. I love you and the thought of not sharing our dreams together breaks my heart. That beautiful baby of ours will not know its father and I don't want that to happen. By the way, if it's a boy I am partial to George . . . I've gotten used to it. If it's a girl I'm partial to Anne . . .

His thoughts trailed off.

Is it right to pass on a name of a former lover to your child? The reflection interrupted his letter and stirred up his guilt. *But Martha doesn't know and will never know*, he thought. What she does know is that Anne was a good friend. That's all she needs to know. He continued.

Whoever it becomes, I want it to know how much I was looking forward to sharing our lives. Tell the baby about the times we had and what falling in love is really like. In any event, I know you'll be a great mom and source of strength over the years.

I'd like to say a word about Red, as he lies here next to me forever protected from the pain and hardships of this life. He was a true friend, a great source of humor and companionship, and a hell of a good co-pilot. Who would have ever thought that the army would have found such an outstanding airman from the dust bowls of Oklahoma? I'm sure he would have had a special saying for the predicament we're in—just can't think of what it would be . . .

Nick heard murmuring coming from the backseat and turned the best he could in order to see Vladimir. Nick had been eating snow to stave off dehydration and knew that Vladimir's situation restricted such movement. Nick felt the tension from anger lessen and knew that if he could help Vladimir, he probably would. "Are you going to make it?"

"Beautiful jasmine . . . Okimi safety." Vladimir wasn't coherent, and his communication trailed off in Russian with what sounded like a request or a disrupted dream. Just inches away in his breast pocket was the picture of him and Okimi taken so many years ago. It flashed clearly in his mind's eye and then . . . nothing.

Nick reached behind him for a way to check Vladimir's pulse. The closest thing he could reach was Vladimir's leg, behind his knee. There was nothing; he was gone. He took a deep breath, accepting the reality that he was now on his own on this dreadful mountaintop. It didn't even have a name as far as Nick knew.

I am now the king and sole inhabitant of this mountaintop, as my Russian adversary just took his last breath. There were thoughts on his lips about someone named Okimi as he left. I hope they were pleasant enough to fill all eternity.

I'll write more later. It helps me focus and I don't want this letter to end. I'm afraid that if it comes to an end, so may I. Sweet dreams until later.

Nick flicked his Zippo and adjusted the flame to warm his hands for a few minutes. *Vladimir was right*, he thought, *I will hope for fire before the night is over.*

CHAPTER 42

When Sarge's body temperature fell below eighty-five degrees, the constricted blood vessels just under his skin suddenly dilated and produced a sensation of extreme heat. In a state of delirium, all Sarge could feel was that he was burning up, a typical symptom in extreme hypothermia. He began frantically ripping off his clothes in anguish. He was helpless, lying alone in the snow on the floor of the main cabin in the bitter cold, naked from the waist up. He fell unconscious for the last time.

———————

Robert tossed and turned in his makeshift bed of parachute nylon. The jump seat had made an effective door for his snow cave. Without the effects of the cold temperature and howling wind from the outside, the small area he had excavated for himself had actually started to get relatively warm from his body heat. He breathed deeply to calm his feelings of claustrophobia and anxiety. He was comforted, however, knowing that he would survive the night if nothing happened to the shelter. His mind drifted in and out of sleep. Thoughts of his parents provided a tranquil sense of well-being, knowing that their love for him had been unconditional. These were contrasted with the troubling belief that the United States had made a great error in treating the peace-loving Japanese-Americans so disrespectfully. For this, he could not forgive his country.

He rolled over in his makeshift bed nervously to double-check that the revolver was loaded and the safety was on. No change from the last time he checked an hour earlier. Robert was not confident about the coming day. How many people had survived? Were they armed? Would he be able to use his weapon against them? Was Cricket okay? He hadn't seen any part of the cockpit section and thought remorsefully about Nick and Red. Both of them had treated him well, and he felt somewhat guilty for his actions and possible consequences. Self-doubt flooded his mind and ate away at his convictions. His mind went back and forth, preventing an easy transition into sleep.

As night fell, the temperatures dropped even further, ushering in bitter cold winds that swept over the ridge and down the face of the sheer wall, drifting snow around Robert's igloo. Not far from the igloo, darkness outlined the ominous crevasse he narrowly escaped earlier in the day. At this elevation the crash site was literally in the clouds. And unless things changed, the lack of visibility would increase his risks the next day and limit any immediate search and rescue efforts.

Robert stirred and jumped from a convoluted dream involving a chase with himself and Cricket running through the streets of a large South American city. They were lost, trying to discover a safe escape from men with machetes. With every turn they made in the confusing, unknown city, they became more hopelessly lost. Escape seemed impossible. He gasped as he half sat up, bumping his head on the roof of his little igloo. "Whoa!" was all he said as he gasped in recognition of the morning's reality—a seventy-five cubic foot room of snow and ice.

He didn't want to urinate inside, so he nudged the jump seat to get outside. It was stuck or jammed shut. Realizing that he was shut in by a large snowdrift, he began the task of tunneling out. He paced himself to avoid overheating and finally broke through. It seemed an eternity. The dawn's light was challenging a still visible moon, which alerted him that he needed to ready himself for the day. He listened for some time for sounds of others but heard nothing. Edging outside he noticed that the wind had subsided. He peed, zipped up, and then carefully looked over the mound of snow in the direction of the crash in the light of dawn. *No movement at all, but it is still early*, he thought. He waited. Nothing.

By 0900, the sun's rays from the east had warmed the air a bit and helped with visibility by burning off some of the cloud cover still hanging onto the mountain rim. Robert could still see no sign of life at the fuselage wreck site. "Now or never," he murmured and started out through the deep snow, very careful to test anything that looked even slightly suspicious. The huge crevasse off to the right was enough warning not to trust anything. The ship was further than he estimated, and it took over an hour as he picked his way across the snowfield.

As he approached he noticed the parachute draped in an odd configuration in order to close off the gaping hole in the side of the fuselage. *There are survivors!* he thought as adrenaline pumped through his body. Regardless, he was within fifteen feet, and he still heard nothing. Approaching cautiously and with his gun drawn, he quietly pulled back the parachute and peeked in. It was like a meat locker. He scanned the plane and saw a negro lying on the snow-covered floor of the main cabin. He was stripped to his waist—dead, most likely frozen to death. When Robert saw the second body at the front of the plane, he had a sense of relief. The major was arrogant and condescending and had insulted Robert from their first meeting. Robert was thankful that he wouldn't have to deal with the major under the circumstances. Plus, the courier bag was still cuffed to his wrist. With the relief of having the major out of the way also came a sudden rush of sadness as Robert realized that Cricket was likely gone too. He quickly looked everywhere, but only found the common grave and no Cricket. He returned to the cabin and sat down. He put his hands to his face and cried. He had such hopes for the two of them. The image of a life in South America had so completely captured his imagination that it had become the one goal he had held on to for life after the war.

Robert sat for a few more minutes, considering how he would remove the courier bag from the major. Keys would make things easy, but if he couldn't find them, he had only two options: shoot the lock off the cuffs with his revolver, which might trigger another avalanche, or cut the hand off at the wrist—not something he was anxious to do. Between the rigor and the extreme temperature, the major's body was pretty stiff, so much so that he fell forward like a department store dummy with a simple push after releasing the shoulder harness. Robert struggled for a few minutes, checking each pocket on the major's uniform. They were very stiff and hard to reach into. Finally, he felt the cold steel from a set of two keys in the major's inside breast pocket. Unfortunately, neither fit the cuffs nor the courier bag lock. It actually made sense after he considered it. *Why would the major carry the keys to the very bag he was protecting? He wouldn't*, Robert thought. He would have to find something sharp, a knife or a saw, something to aid him in his grisly task.

He began to search the ship's remains when he heard the sound of twin engines in the distance. The cloud cover was breaking up, and Robert caught a fleeting glimpse of the sun's reflection off the wing of a

C-47. The search had begun. He hadn't actually considered his actions up until that point. *Do I find a way to get off this mountain myself with the classified documents?* Robert wondered. *Or do I signal the Search and Rescue planes in order to guarantee my safety?* Since the C-47 was actually some distance away, and had millions of acres to search, signaling the rescue planes wasn't a viable option yet. It may be days or even weeks before they locate the site.

CHAPTER 43

Shortly after takeoff on Friday, March 17, Nick routinely reported by radio that he was over Talkeetna, a well-known emergency landing field on the regular route to Fairbanks. Within fifteen minutes the radio operator in Anchorage received a request to increase his altitude to nine thousand feet due to extensive fog and mist.

"Permission granted. Over," Nick heard the operator reply.

"Our flight is on course to pass over Summit as scheduled. Over," Nick added as he radioed back to Anchorage, indicating that the next emergency landing field was coming up as expected.

This was the last radio message from their flight and within two hours Ladd airfield reported Nick's flight overdue.

"Give me everything you know about this flight," demanded Commanding General Dale Gaffney at the Edmonton Airfield. General Gaffney was in charge of all army air force activities that included Alaska, Western Canada, and the Northwest Territories.

"The flight was wheels up at 1145. The captain is Nick Morgan, on loan from Northwest—one of the best, sir," replied Major Dick Raegle, Commanding Officer Search and Rescue, 11th Army Air Force in Fairbanks. "Co-captain Robert 'Red' Johnson and PFC Robert Endo complete the crew. Twelve servicemen headed to Minneapolis on leave and four members of a Los Alamos research team headed by Major James Gordon and Dr. J. Robert Oppenheimer are the remaining scheduled passengers. Warrant Officer Martin Mason and Vladimir Dubisskiy, Russian liaison for P-38 pilot training, jumped on board at the last minute to be shuttled to Ladd for a training exercise. Dr. Oppenheimer was pulled off for medical reasons with a mild heart attack and was moved to the hospital on base at Elmendorf. Total on board, sir, is three crew and seventeen passengers."

"What's the status of the flight now?"

"Officially, it's still overdue, sir. But with complete loss of communication contact, we have to assume they're without instruments and lost. With the cloud cover as it is, they're also devoid of celestial navigation abilities. Unofficially, we have to assume they're down."

"Was there a Mayday issued?"

"No. That's what doesn't add up. The pilot just stopped communications. And, if it is a complete instrument failure, I believe that Captain Morgan is capable enough to establish a visual route by lowering his altitude. I know this guy, General; he's good."

"What's your next plan of action, Major?"

"The weather is closing down quickly, and we're going to lose all visuals within the hour. Our plan is to have the five C-47s we have available out at first light, flying a grid covering the eastern area where they were last heard from. All flights are canceled to free up the ships. This represents thousands of square miles, though."

"What about other planes?"

"We have a few, but they're hard to use in searches like this where they will be in the air for a long time. It could be hours and unnecessary refueling confuses the start and stop points of the search grid patterns. The small planes just don't have the range. Even with the C-47s, the fifteen hundred miles will be chewed up pretty fast. In the meantime, I've assigned our best radio operators on a round-the-clock basis to try and establish contact."

"Do you need more C-47s?"

"Three more would help. Any more and we'll be running into each other, sir."

"We'll have them to you by first light. Until then, I want to be briefed every hour. Is that clear, Major?"

"Yes, sir. One more thing, General."

"What?"

"That mountain is going to be very cold tonight. We may only have until tomorrow."

By Saturday morning, the eighteenth, Search and Rescue still had not made radio contact with the flight crew. Major Raegle had assembled his five flight crews from Ladd and Elmendorf and the three additional promised by the general in a command center for an early briefing. The room was silent, except for the major's voice retelling what Search and Rescue knew, which wasn't much other than that there were twenty men on board and where they were at their last radio contact. He asked for speculation among those who knew the route. Some suggested the best place for a forced landing would be east of the McKinley range where a half dozen rivers offered several relatively flat valleys. At least they would be somewhat accessible. The men agreed. The consensus was that support would be limited to a supply drop only in the McKinley Range itself, with the hope that survivors could find their way out on their own. Major Raegle led the discussion while sucking thoughtfully on his pipe from time to time.

Each crew was given maps of the area to mark up as they devised a grid and assigned positions. It required careful planning so that their rotation through the grid didn't cause an additional crash, but these were experienced pilots. The biggest problem was that the area west of the Summit and Talkeetna emergency landing sites, including many of the peaks in the McKinley range, was mostly uncharted. Without celestial navigation, visual flying conditions would be the only alternative.

The "search and rescue gods," as Major Raegle often referred to, were with the team as the cloud cover started to break up shortly after sunup. Each plane had a full tank of fuel and was packed with first-aid supplies to be dropped when they found the crash site. Four C-47s were to fly in formation, covering the land to the south of the Summit emergency landing site, and four others were to fly to the north.

Within hours the planes were spread across the sky, capitalizing on the good visibility, yet in reality they were covering only about three miles for each pass on the grid. They started as close to the McKinley Range as possible, at about six thousand feet, taking advantage of the relatively calm flying conditions. Major Raegle flew closest to the peaks and shuddered to think of the difficulties a pilot would encounter if somehow his ship got sucked into the range. The crews of all four ships in formation communicated easily by radio, making their turns efficiently and safely throughout the day. They listened carefully in the hopes of even the faintest radio signal while flying at a snail's pace in order to examine every suspicious configuration on the ground. "Hear anything?" "See anything?" were the calls heard all day and "Negative" became the familiar answer. Their imaginations played games with them as the snow cover made it almost impossible to distinguish the difference in shapes of the sightings on the ground. Still, they pressed forward for hours, scanning the vast area of glacial wilderness. Nothing. Desperation set in as their fuel gauges became low and the day's light began to recede.

"Let's head for the barn," Major Raegle broadcast to both crews. "We'll find them tomorrow for sure," he said with an empty heart and a lump in the pit of his stomach.

CHAPTER 44

Nick survived the night. He had managed to remove Red's coat and wool shirt. The added warmth was enough to permit a few hours of sleep. Waking up to the shock of Red's body with only long underwear from the waist up, however, ushered in the horror of the previous day's catastrophe and the grave danger of his current situation. His own body was stiff from being pinned down in such an awkward position all night. He tried rubbing some life into his good leg with his hands and succeeded, somewhat. He felt searing pain whenever he touched his bad leg, from any movement of the femur above the break. The lower part of the leg was less sensitive, almost numb, likely from extensive nerve damage and lack of blood circulation. The skin had a corpse-like appearance.

"Today's going to have to be the day," Nick said, reflecting on the need for the leg to come off. The weather had calmed, making the morning more tolerable. *Without the extra clothes*, Nick thought, *I'd have been a goner last night.* After several strikes on the Zippo, he was able to light a cigarette, which helped him focus. The first drag was reassuring. He held up a pocketknife he found in Red's flight jacket, eyeing it skeptically as if it were a sacred medieval surgical instrument.

"Something a Boy Scout would carry, not a surgeon," he uttered in disdain. Unsure of where his self-operation would take him, he decided to finish his cigarette and record what might be his last thoughts to Martha.

I'm afraid my predicament has worsened with the left leg. The good news is that if I can sever it with the knife I found in Red's jacket, I can get free of the cockpit. I'll at least have a chance at signaling for help somehow. But, if we ever are together again, you'll have to be happy with a one-legged husband. It would mean the end of my flying days and back to the "U" for more education to get a real job.

At that moment Nick heard the faint sound of two Pratt & Whitney radial piston engines unique to C-47s. It was some distance off, but the sound was an encouragement, and it bolstered his nerve.

I need to get to work. Just heard a Search and Rescue ship . . . C-47 for sure. When they come back I need to be ready for them. Maybe that's why God gave us two legs, so you could say good-bye to one of them. Wish me luck! If it doesn't turn out well, I want you to know that I love you with my whole heart. I cherish every moment we've had together and, God willing, smile in anticipation of us being together again.

Yours,
Nick

Lucky for Nick, Red kept a good edge on his pocketknife. Before beginning, Nick packed his upper leg in snow to help stop any bleeding and numb the pain. After applying Red's belt as a tourniquet, he began the grisly task. He had read stories of animals chewing their leg off to escape a trap, but the sensation he experienced was not that of panic. Nick was a precise man by nature, and he found his hand to be pretty steady, despite the occasional flashes of panic that he was cutting off his own leg. The blade traveled through the flesh with relative ease— simple if it weren't for the nerves being cut. The pain they triggered was off the chart, but he kept at it for over a half hour. With the last cut, he felt his body go free. Moving quickly, Nick loosened the tourniquet to cover the stump and jagged bone with two layers of Red's folded shirt and just as quickly retightened the belt to avoid excessive blood loss. He just stared at his work, speechless, and then passed out.

CHAPTER 45

Robert gave considerable thought as to how to remove the courier bag from the major's wrist while searching the plane for food. He hadn't eaten since the previous morning and hoped he could find the cabinet where he had stored sodas and snacks. Not much to live on, but better than nothing. The real question he kept mulling over was whether to signal the rescue ship and forgo the classified documents or to take the documents and try to make it off the mountain on his own. As he considered his options, he felt his dilemma wasn't so much the mountain, as he naïvely believed he could negotiate its descent if he were careful, it was how to use the documents to safely bargain for a secure passage to a new country—a new life. Going AWOL certainly wasn't an issue. He was way beyond that point. Finding the right contacts was everything. He found some nuts and crackers while crawling through the wreckage, which bolstered his spirits. The sodas had all exploded from pressure. He ate while sitting on a snow bank considering his next steps.

It wasn't long before Robert realized that he had already given up any allegiance to the United States. This realization encouraged him to try to make it out on his own, but he would need to verify the importance of the classified documents before he would risk his life for them. He needed to get into the courier bag.

He tried the major's pockets and flight bag one more time for keys but came up empty again. The flight bag did have a bottle of Jack Daniels that survived the crash, however. He opened it and took a few swallows to wash down the crackers. The burning sensation warmed him up and eased the soreness of his body. While considering his options, he took another pull from the bottle and wiped his lips with his sleeve. In his rummaging, he remembered seeing a twisted metal rod of sorts. *A little barbaric*, he thought, *but in all probability my best choice*. After several minutes of relentlessly hammering away at the major's wrist and hand with the crude tool, he successfully slid the cuff off. After looking around some more, he found the ship's toolbox still intact with the necessary tools to disassemble the bag's lock.

For hours he absorbed what he could from the documents. Every single item was labeled "Classified," and he struggled to understand the technical nature of most of the specifics. It was clear that the two major elements covered were the instructions for making an atom bomb, and the plans to test it in either the Yukon Flats area in Alaska or the Alamogordo area in New Mexico, or both. "Holy shit," he said, acknowledging the significance of his find. "There isn't a political power in the world that wouldn't want to get their hands on these." *These documents are a gold mine*, he thought.

Greed took over as Robert began acting on his plan to leave the mountain alone. A certain swagger brought about a more primitive side to his character. He knew he would need money off the mountain, so he rifled through the pockets of the dead soldiers for every dollar he could find. Most of them were on their way home on leave and were flush with cash, looking for a good time. Within a short time he gathered over thirty-five hundred dollars.

A grandiose sense of power consumed Robert when he was back in his snow igloo for the night. He envisioned a hacienda in South America with servants, a life of leisure, and an unidentified man with whom he could live out his days. He ate his crackers and nuts and took another long swallow of his Jack Daniels and smiled with self-satisfaction. *I'll wait until tomorrow*, he thought, *or, perhaps the next day, to make an exit.*

CHAPTER 46

When Helen answered the phone in Akron, Ohio, it was almost midnight on the seventeenth. Martha was crying and barely coherent. "They say they can't locate Nick's flight," she sobbed. "They lost track of the plane on the way to Fairbanks! I don't want this to happen, Helen. I'm afraid. I don't want this to happen."

"Oh my God, Martha. That can't be. Tell me what happened."

"They don't know what happened. The flight's been missing for over five hours!"

"Bud, wake up. It's Martha. Bud, wake up!"

"Let me get Bud on the phone. He'll know what to do," said Helen, trying to reassure her best friend.

"Who is it, honey?" Bud said, thinking that something bad may have happened to one of his parents.

"It's Martha . . . something about Nick's plane being missing."

"What!"

"Martha, walk me through what they told you."

Martha was frantic and barely understandable.

"Try to calm yourself so I can understand." Bud twisted the phone cord trying to add an element of control to the situation.

She began again. "It started with a delay being posted this afternoon. I kept calling because I wanted to pick Nick up myself. More delays came and finally I drove to the airport about eight o'clock to find out for myself. That's when they told me the flight was cancelled and to go home. They said they would call when they had more information. I just heard from the base that the flight has been lost. Please, Bud, tell me there's some sort of mistake. They can make mistakes like this, can't they?"

"I sure hope so for everyone's sake. Did they say anything about a crash?"

"No, just that the flight was lost."

"That's probably good news since it leaves open the option for an emergency landing somewhere. It's possible that the instruments just failed." Bud knew that would be highly unusual but held out hope. "Did they say when they would call back?"

"Yes, when they had more definite information. Oh, Bud, I don't like this. I just have a bad feeling that Nick's in trouble."

"We've got to hold out hope, Martha. Nick would want that. Did they say how many people are on board?"

"Twenty with the crew."

"Wow! A full-blown search is no doubt under way as we speak."

"What can we do, Bud?"

"Have you talked with anyone else, yet?"

"No."

"I'll call Mom and Dad right away. Do you want us to call your mom, too?"

"No, I'll call her." Martha voice was filled with a desperation that so many women had experienced throughout the war. It was shocking, though, when the words of hopelessness came from your own mouth.

"Helen and I will be on the first flight to Minneapolis tomorrow morning. Keep your chin up. We'll figure this out together when we get there . . . okay?"

"Okay," she said.

"We'll let you know when we're going to arrive," Bud said just before hanging up.

"I hope this isn't as bad as it sounds," Helen said, putting her arms around Bud's slumping shoulders. "These can have a happy ending, can't they?"

"This isn't good at all." Bud dropped his head into his hands as he leaned against the refrigerator to steady himself. "For a plane to be missing for this long means it has run into problems. It doesn't have enough fuel to stay up that long. Flight operations just doesn't *lose* planes, and the vagueness of information they gave her only means they don't know what happened. Or worse yet, they don't want to tell her what happened and are exercising damage control."

Bud and Helen clutched each other and wept at the prospect of what had happened. After a few minutes Bud collected himself and called his dad and mom.

———

Bud's dad was at the airport when their flight arrived in Minneapolis-St. Paul around noon the next day. They sat in a quiet corner of the terminal while Henry updated his son and daughter-in-law with the grim report he had received from the base. "The ship, its crew, and all the passengers were lost. They don't know what happened. A massive air search and rescue was delayed until today because of poor visibility, but it is now under way. All flights had been cancelled to allow for eight C-47s to comb the landscape for signs of survivors. Nothing yet." The sterile lights in the terminal added a harshness to their family tragedy.

Their words and feelings were in sharp contrast to the squeals of delight of two children near them. They watched a soldier home from the war greeting his wife and children in a warm embrace. "I want so badly for Martha to be able to share that same joy soon," Helen said, gripping Bud's hand. Their agonizing silence, however, expressed their hopelessness.

"All we can do is wait and pray right now," Henry said. He was a hardened railroad man and farmer. His German determination was visible in his set jaw. The most he could do was to put his hand on Bud's shoulder and choke back his emotions.

Back at the Morgan home Martha, Ida, Henry and Rose, and Bud and Helen were together when they received the news that Search and Rescue had come up with nothing that day. The only hope offered was that the weather would permit them to continue their efforts the next day.

Martha felt the baby kick as she sat at the kitchen table and hoped she wouldn't have to endure one of those cruel trade-offs life sometimes demanded. She was all cried out; they all were for that matter, but the worry lines on her face were the deepest.

"Get some sleep, Martha," Bud said. "We'll take shifts at the phone and let you know right away if something happens." He realized that "something happens" weren't very encouraging words, but he didn't know what else to say.

"I'll give you a hand," Helen said, standing up and putting an arm around Martha to encourage her to head to bed. "Why don't you and I spend some time together upstairs talking about our babies before turning in?"

Helen's offer of support was more helpful to Martha than even that from her mother. The bond between the sisters-in-law had been sealed forever years ago.

CHAPTER 47

When Brigadier General Leslie R. Groves was informed of the missing flight, he was immediately on the phone to General Gaffney in Edmonton. It was late Saturday afternoon. A cloud of cigar smoke hung in the office of the 509th Composite Group after a full day of meetings in preparation for the gathering on the twenty-first.

"General, I want you to know that it's imperative that we find that plane. I'm not at liberty to share details, but there are classified documents on board that represent a risk to national security."

"I understand, sir. I've been informed that Major Gordon had a courier bag handcuffed to his wrist as he boarded. It was switched from Dr. Oppenheimer after his heart attack."

"Yes, I know that, General, I authorized the switch." His tone was blunt, giving General Gaffney the definite impression that the bag and its contents were more important than the lives of the soldiers.

"Major Raegle is still out on search. We are in constant communication regarding progress, and I will emphasize the additional importance of recovering the bag when the ship is finally located. Several people witnessed the switch before Dr. Oppenheimer was taken to the hospital, so the bag itself is common knowledge."

"Very good, General. Keep me informed the minute you have any-thing new." General Groves took a long draw on the cigar as he considered the consequences of the Manhattan Project secrets getting out. If the plane crashed, the documents were likely spread across a remote mountain area and not in any condition to pose a threat. In an emergency landing situation, however, a survivor may have taken it upon himself to retrieve the bag, realizing its importance. He paused and retrieved the passenger list provided by his aide. After staring at the list for a minute, he boldly underlined Vladimir Dubisskiy's name. "What the hell was this guy doing on this flight," he said quietly to himself.

"Lieutenant," the general called out to his aide. "Get me everything you can on this man," he said, pointing to the Russian's name. "I mean everything."

"Yes, sir. I'll need a few days to make the right contacts."

"I understand. Use my office to get through any roadblocks."

Major Raegle in Fairbanks had just received the update from General Gaffney at Command Headquarters in Edmonton to emphasize their search on the courier bag handcuffed to Major Gordon's wrist. General Gaffney was imperative in his order, which referenced a very involved Brigadier General in the chain of command. Regardless, finding the plane or crash site, however, was still Major Raegle's first priority.

"I want every plane ready for wheels up at 0745," he said after assembling the men in the debriefing room. "If there are survivors out there, we need to find them tomorrow. It's going to be another very cold night. Keep the pallets of supplies ready with parachutes to drop the moment the plane is sighted. Don't wait to confirm survivors. Any questions?"

Nothing but tired faces and hungry men stared back at him in silence. He knew the crews needed rest. "I'll take that as a no," the major said. "Lastly, I want a volunteer crew to fly with me tomorrow over the first ridge line to the McKinley Range. It'll be risky. We'll go at first light to maximize visibility. It's hard to imagine, but something may have forced them to try to cut over the mountains. I pray to God we don't find them in there, but we have to look. Let me know before chow, so we can get the remainder of the crews reconfigured."

They all knew that it could be them they were looking for. Discussions were kept on the business at hand during dinner. Pilots weren't in the habit of second-guessing each other, as they knew that everything depended on the circumstances. Winds, downdrafts, icing, electrical malfunctions, navigation errors, mechanical failures, and crew and pilot judgment were all variables in a dynamic mix that was impossible to anticipate completely. On top of all that, each ship had its own personality, which was why pilots liked certain ships over others. Despite this code of respect for other pilots, there always seemed to be at least one idiot who, despite not knowing the circumstances, was willing to make a judgment about what another pilot should have done. In this case a lieutenant shot off his mouth about the incompetence of any pilot venturing off the charted course without first communicating a clear fix in their location to flight operations. He just wouldn't stop, and within minutes he was at a table by himself eating alone. "You'll see," he said while gesturing with a wave of his hand to the group before shutting up.

The others knew it was a waste to argue or reason with him. He was one of the least experienced co-pilots and had every book answer ready to defend his opinion. The only useful answer would come with time, and the seasoned pilots knew that. Each pilot hoped that the major wouldn't assign this jerk to their crew.

The major was pleased with his volunteers the next morning—all top-notch men. It was no surprise to the others that the lieutenant wasn't among them. They went through the engine, pre-taxi, and pre-takeoff checklists and brought both engines to twenty-seven hundred rpms. Once in the air, and after the heater light turned green, the major set the fuel mixture to auto-lean and adjusted the prop rpm and power for cruise. The men were quiet, knowing they would be venturing into uncharted airspace in about an hour. Exciting, but risky, as the major warned in the briefing.

"Are you okay, Matt?" The major questioned his co-pilot, not so much to second-guess his mood but to just loosen him up with casual dialogue.

"Yeah, I'm fine, Major. Just thinking what those boys must have endured the last two nights."

"Tough duty, alright," the major said as he looked intently for a "front door" to get past the initial range of peaks.

"We're going to take things pretty easy going into these mountains, but first we need to find an opening—one that would have seemed attractive to a pilot in bad weather, and maybe a little disoriented. Let's continue the heading we're on. My guess is that if they did try to fly over, they would have done so north of Mt. McKinley as the peaks become smaller. Let's see what we can find."

"I checked the wind heading on the seventeenth—45 mph out of the northwest over the range. If they chose this route they were in for some hellacious downdrafts and crosswinds. Today is as good as we could hope for—five to ten mph with the same heading."

From the major's perspective there did seem to be a sort of chute or alleyway north of McKinley headed toward an uncharted mountain that looked to be about twelve thousand feet. "Let's try this approach, Matt." The major had flown with all the men and had a great respect for Matt's skills, yet he didn't want to get into discussions with them about options. He knew each man volunteered for this flight because they had absolute confidence in his abilities. His decisions would have to be law.

They entered the range at eleven thousand feet and immediately lost five hundred feet from a downdraft. The major saw that the mountain was structured in such as way that the winds came over a triple set of peaks and were trapped in a bowl, making it very difficult to judge. Even the mild weather that day caused an unusually strong downward force. The crew could see the immenseness of the mountain and the vast wasteland below filled with crevasses, sheer cliffs, and granite rocks. They had definitely entered another dimension.

"It's hard to imagine anything surviving a crash in here," Matt said.

"Keep your eyes sharp," the major replied.

And then, there it was, just a flicker of a silver reflection from the port side. "It's there. I can feel it," the major said. The morning sun could have tricked them, but it definitely seemed manmade. The challenge was that the bowl they were in would not allow them to turn around and the angle of the sun did not create another reflection.

"Take our elevation to twelve thousand feet to clear these ridges in front of us. We'll circle out and re-enter the range."

In fifteen minutes they were ready for a second attempt. "Make sure the supplies pallet is ready to drop on my command, if this is the spot." They would keep the door closed until the last minute to avoid the sub-zero temperatures. All eyes were trained to the west to see even the slightest irregularity. The entry for the second pass was far more difficult as they came in at ten thousand feet and lost the same five hundred feet from the downdraft as before. They had about a two-mile stretch of viable surface where the lost ship could possibly be—if it was there at all. The area of focus was about seven hundred yards wide and sat beneath a peak almost two thousand feet up. On either side of the area were drop-offs of such magnitude that estimating their depth was folly. If a ship went in there, it was highly unlikely that any survivors would find a way out of the ridiculously difficult terrain.

All of the men saw the reflection again. "That's it," said Matt. "I can see the fuselage and the tail section."

"We got one shot at making a good drop. Let's make it count. Open the doors and ready the supplies. Secure the rip cord for the chute to open automatically. Take me down another two hundred feet, Matt."

Matt was sweating bullets, but he knew better than to challenge the order.

"Drop the supplies," the major ordered suddenly. There wasn't that much surface for the drop to land on. If they overshot the site, the supplies would have plunged into oblivion.

The ship roared over the crash site with the tangled wreckage in full view. The tail marking, 15738, was obscured, but that had to be it.

The major instantly put the ship into a climb that bordered on a stall. Every man on board was happy he had clean underwear back home. They barely cleared the peak and headed back.

"Did anyone see any survivors?" Major Raegle knew he hadn't and was hoping someone else had. No answer. "I'm asking again. Did anyone see any survivors?"

"That's a negative," Matt replied, answering for the team.

CHAPTER 48

Agent Andrey Sirak was furious when he was informed of the crash late Saturday night on the other side of the International Date Line. The Russian pilot flying the surviving P-38 was exhausted upon arrival at the airstrip in Anadyr. He had battled headwinds the entire trip that ate up his fuel and added an hour to the flight time. It was remarkable that he arrived at all. Regardless, Agent Sirak had left explicit instructions to be informed once the planes arrived. The pilot collapsed onto his cot once his report was written and radioed to Moscow.

Agent Sirak knew the discovery of this mission by the United States would have significant international consequences, so his deliberations needed to include a response so well designed that counterreaction would be diffused. Stalin needed to be briefed, of course, and that always contained an enormous element of risk in itself. Agent Sirak needed to consider the facts at hand. First, Russia had not been notified, as yet, of the C-47's crash and Vladimir's passage on the flight. That may take several days, even weeks, as the United States would investigate first before following protocol. Second, according to the surviving pilot, the other P-38 crashed in extremely inaccessible mountainous terrain. It was quite possible the plane would never be found.

Third, while the evidence for testing the bomb in Alaska now could not be validated with actual plans, Russia's knowledge of such plans was enough, in Agent Sirak's mind, to force a stalemate over the incident. And fourth, radio contact to Alaska would be very difficult to establish quickly now that his NKVD agent and key GRU operatives were missing and likely dead.

After considerable thought, Agent Sirak reasoned that no action was necessary until news of survivors was confirmed. The good news was that, given the circumstances, the United States would be unlikely to move ahead with using Alaska as a test site. *Success is not always neatly packaged*, he thought. In this case the progress outweighed the setback.

"Agent Sirak, please come in," the general secretary of the Communist Party said. While their loyalties to each other had survived for many years, Agent Sirak always took a deep breath before entering Stalin's office to break the news.

CHAPTER 49

The weather forecast for the mountain range on Monday, March 20 called for clear skies with winds out of the northwest at eighteen to twenty-two mph. The Search and Rescue team planned to capitalize on this window of opportunity, as the forecast for Tuesday and Wednesday warned of a storm front.

Major Raegle assembled all Search and Rescue crews in the briefing room for a run-through of what was expected. "We're going to need two flights to accomplish our objective. I'll lead the first one with the same crew. Our objective will be to make the same entry into the range as yesterday but at about ninety-two hundred feet. This will alert any survivors that we know where they are. We'll try to take close-up pictures of the wreckage, as well. The second flight will be piloted by Captain Baker, and he's looking for a volunteer crew. Their objective will be to follow our butt ten minutes later at ninety-six hundred feet and to take as many photographs as possible; hopefully we'll catch some survivors moving around. Questions?"

"What are our chances of parachuting a few men to administer first aid?"

"Unfortunately, the chances of parachuting aren't very good. The winds can be violent and would be a bitch to negotiate. Also, we just don't have a clue as to how we would get those men out. I say again: this is the roughest possible terrain you can imagine." There were several nods to the affirmative by the crew from the first flyover.

"You'll see that your target area is extremely small, as well, with major cliffs and bottomless drop-offs on either side," one of the men added.

"What's our plan if we find survivors?"

"Right now, it's to keep them alive with supplies and first aid. We're in the process of contacting a few seasoned mountain climbers to develop scenarios to get them out."

Nick had barely survived the cold weather and loss of blood on Sunday and knew he had to be ready for a possible rescue on Monday. He could tell by the red setting sunset that Monday's weather would benefit a follow-up attempt. *I need to somehow get their attention*, he thought, knowing that the main wreckage down below would occupy their efforts. He considered two options that might work. First, he needed to find something in the cockpit that could be used to reflect the sun's rays back to the aircraft's crew. It would be a long shot, as the mountain weather patterns could quickly and unpredictably produce clouds that would block the sun. His second option was to build a fire so the smoke would be visible. He needed to be ready to go to make that option work. He had an idea. If there was any fuel remaining in the heater lines, he might be able to milk it out and use it as an accelerant.

He had much work to do to make his plan work. He dragged himself about like an amputee on a roller cart gathering anything extra that would burn—remaining clothes from Vladimir and Red, seat cushions, flight manuals, maps, anything—and moved it to the top of the ridge in a pile, dragging it over the ice and rocks. At times the rocks hit his exposed femur, setting off a firestorm of pain. The jacket covering his forearms and elbows was shredded from crawling arm over arm on multiple trips to the ridge top. At the end of the day, he used his good leg like a frog's leg against the terrain as a last resort for propulsion. His crippled and tortured body fought through the circumstance. Considering the loss of blood alone, it was a miracle that Nick hung on. At 1900, exhausted and without anything to eat or drink other than snow in almost three days, his stamina left him. Barely making it back into the cockpit, Nick fell in and out of consciousness.

"Agh . . . agh!" he screamed, waking himself out of strange dreams involving ghost-like warriors stealing things from his pile of fire materials. He saw Anne's face outlined by the stars in the night sky. He remembered her for a minute or two, and then lost all recognition as he slid back into his private netherworld. At 0400 he panicked and quickly jerked upright, remembering he had not found anything to reflect the sun's rays. "They're going to be here . . . they're going to be here, and I'm not ready." He rummaged around in the freezing temperature, finding nothing. He thought of Martha and wanted to write more in his letter, but it was too cold. He had one last cigarette he was saving but decided that it would help him focus. He fumbled for the crumpled package, retrieving the last Lucky Strike in the pack. After four tries with his lighter, it finally lit. And then it dawned on him: the stainless steel Zippo would act as a good reflector.

His determination to survive up until then had occupied his focus, and he felt any prayers for his survival would have signaled defeat to some unknown scorekeeper with a clock ticking down. He wasn't quite sure how to pray for what he hoped for—getting off the mountain, Martha and the baby, Bud and Helen, Henry and Rose; it was all very confusing. He had been blessed; he realized that, but now he was trying to "pray forward," so to speak. Ultimately, he asked for God's forgiveness and to somehow find a way off the mountain, only to realize this wasn't really a prayer, but a request. He flicked an ash on the floor and recalled the early days with Martha. *God, we were in love*, he thought. His mind slowed as he exhaled a plume of smoke and recalled that flight up the St. Croix River to Grand Marais—that was the day he knew he wanted to marry her. At that moment, he knew his prayer should be one of thanks, not of requests, as the real truth of his existence pressed upon his prayer. He burned his finger slightly, getting the last hit from the cigarette, and crushed the butt into the ashtray that had somehow survived the crash. "I love you, Martha," he whispered.

Dawn brought overcast skies—not quite what he expected. Regardless, his optimism of being found was enough to motivate his efforts to milk any fuel from the heater lines. It was a good idea, he thought, but everything hurt. Unfortunately, as it turned out, he was only able to salvage a few ounces. Enough to start a fire, just not enough for the dramatic effect he had hoped for. He found a small container for the fuel and began his crawl up to the ridge through the snow and rocks. His cuts and bruises from the crash and the previous night's crawling hurt like hell, and his one kneecap was vulnerable to the granite rocks. He kept himself rolled to one side to avoid aggravating his stump, which had strangely grown almost numb and had turned gray above the tourniquet. This was different from the red, infectious pain from the previous night. By 0830 he was in place to see a few rays from the rising sun break through the clouds, which was a positive sign. He reasoned that Search and Rescue would probably come at approximately the same time as the day before—around 0915 to 0930. Good visibility was essential to his discovery.

There was nothing else to do. He sat in the bitter cold, allowing the sun's rays to warm his spirits. He scanned the wreckage some fifteen hundred feet below situated at the head of a formidable glacier. He figured that the wreckage and the bodies would be assimilated into the glacier in time, thus beginning a journey for the millennium. It was then that he noticed movement—a single man walking toward the fuselage. Nick felt like Robinson Crusoe. *A companion, another human being had made it through the crash*, he thought. He managed to stand on his remaining leg to wave his arms and call out in an attempt to be seen. "Hellooo . . . hellooo. I'm up here," he shouted. He was so far above the man he wasn't sure he could be heard, but he did see the man stop and turn around before continuing on. He continued yelling as best he could, but he was weak and finally gave up.

Nick's despondency at not attracting the man's attention below was overtaken by the distinct sound of twin Pratt & Whitney's. Panic set in, as he knew his exposure to the flyover would be brief—less than fifteen minutes. He threw his gloves to the ground and poured the heater fuel on an undergarment from one of the men, held it on the leeward side of the pile to break the wind, and struck his Zippo. Nothing! He struck it again and again with the same result. "God dammit!" Frustrated, he hit the lighter in the butt of his hand to jolt any remaining fluid toward the wick. His hands were very cold. He struck the lighter again and got the tiniest of flames for just a few seconds. Not enough time to transfer it to the fuel. He desperately pulled the bottom portion of the lighter off and blew into the cotton base to force any remaining fluid toward the wick. Once again, a flicker and then gone. He was frantic. The Zippo slipped from his hand and dropped into the snow. He felt around until he found it. It was his last lifeline!

The ship was coming in low to attract the attention of any survivors below, not considering that a survivor may be on top as well. He found it odd to be looking down a thousand feet on the C-47. He knew the crew would be focused on the wreckage. He held the Zippo in his fingertips and thrust the flat side into the sun's rays as if to physically direct the reflection straight into the cockpit. The Zippo was slick from the snow and his hands were numb from exposure. He gripped the lighter too tightly with his fingers, causing it to shoot from his hand like a watermelon seed and fall well below his position in a rock crag. Even with both legs it would take a very careful maneuver to retrieve the lighter; with one leg, it would be daunting.

Nick had flown Search and Rescue before, so he knew that procedure called for a second flight for airdrops and photographs, as needed. Absolutely sure of a second plane, Nick inched his way over the ridge and lowered himself with the strength of his arms carefully toward the Zippo. He could see it clearly. If it were a pet, he could whistle for it to come home. He lost his grip and slid a few feet, landing hard on a rock outcropping against the exposed femur. It set off such pain that he screamed. Reaching the Zippo was just not going to happen. As he lay there trapped between the rocks and gasping for breath, he heard the drone of the twin Pratt & Whitney's of the second plane. That's when he knew it was over. He knew this flight was his last chance. His body was completely ruined, probably beyond repair, his mental condition was deteriorating rapidly, and in all honesty, he wasn't sure he had the strength to get himself back to the cockpit. That's when he ironically remembered the thrill of being up on top and flying that first trip over the Aleutians and the Valley of 10,000 Smokes with Captain Marshall Smith. "Looks like I'll be on top for a while, Captain. It's a hellava view," he said in quiet resignation.

He was never able to move from that spot, not sure he really wanted to. The warm sun heated the rocks somewhat, and the perfect view of this spectacular mountain helped ease any panic over dying. He had time to make peace with his Maker and found comfort in knowing he had loved and was loved in life.

The day went fast and by 2300 that night Nick Morgan was dead from hypothermia, exposure, and a heart that just couldn't rally one more time.

CHAPTER 50

That drop of supplies on Sunday was like manna from heaven for Robert. While he had been excited at the opportunity of cashing in on the documents, he really had no idea how he was going to get off the mountain. He was physically fit and wiry, and his Alaskan experience in the military had prepared him for wilderness survival challenges, but getting off this mountain required more than just will. He needed the right tools—snowshoes, ropes, climbing gear, and the like. He was delighted when he unwrapped the airdrop.

Everything he could possible ask for was included: food, a small stove with fuel, arctic sleeping bags, kerosene lamps, a sled, and a vast array of mountaineering gear. He was impressed with Search and Rescue's forethought, as he had quickly come to the conclusion that getting airlifted out was highly unlikely. "This is perfect," he said excitedly as he started organizing what he needed. Getting the snowshoes on was the first order of business, as the effort required to move around in the deep snow was very challenging. Once he was more mobile the rest of the organizing and packing for his exit was simplified. He cautioned himself not to overpack the sled, knowing that he was sure to face narrow and steep avenues in his escape route.

Robert knew that unexpected Search and Rescue activity could get in his way. *It's best if they conclude that nobody survived,* he thought. *That way, the focus will go from rescue to recovery—a much less intense sense of urgency.* Robert's training in search and rescue had taught him that photographs were very important. They would compare photographs taken on different days to judge activity at the site. With this in mind he took only what he needed from the airdrop and returned everything to its original condition, and that meant covering his snowshoe tracks to avoid the markings of a trail. He stored the sled, packed with provisions for his departure, inside the fuselage to avoid detection. He did his cooking there, also.

He spent the rest of the day using the clear visibility to decide upon his exit path. In the back of his mind, he was still looking for the cockpit, as well. Robert's original conclusion was that it was buried in one of the avalanches triggered by the crash, but he kept looking all the same.

Throughout the day he ruled out one option after another as a safe route out. Ultimately, he went back to one of his first choices. The angle to the slope was less severe, but if he made one mistake, it was a deathtrap. After studying it from all viewpoints, he believed he could make it, but there would be no return. The only noncontrollable would be an avalanche. It was apparent that they were common to the slope by the way fifteen- to twenty-foot snowfields were visible next to absolutely barren rock slides. The avalanches were almost like calving on an iceberg wall leaving steep embankments of packed snow, just on a smaller scale. He would traverse back and forth across the most difficult portion of the incline in a switchback fashion, much the way an expert skier handles the deep powder. About a mile or so down the canyon the slope was less severe and emptied into a rock field with narrow passages—obviously the remains of previous avalanches. What came after that, he didn't know.

On Monday morning, Robert wanted to get an early start since he was quite sure the Search and Rescue C-47s would return at about the same time, weather permitting. He was almost at the wreck site when he heard something. He was so engrossed in wiping out his tracks that the sound surprised him. It was almost like a person's voice—like someone drawing out the word "hello" to create an echo. He turned around to evaluate the source, but before he could do so he heard the drone of twin Pratt & Whitney's coming up the gorge. He moved quickly into the fuselage, out of sight. After the planes passed there was silence. He concluded that the voice he thought he heard a few minutes earlier was simply his mind playing tricks on him. Stories of mirages and images of people in the desert were common. *It must have been a like an audible mirage*, he thought. And to support his conclusion he heard nothing the rest of the day.

With his cooking stove and food now located in the fuselage, the bodies of the sergeant and Major Gordon bothered him immensely. Moving them to the mass grave became a priority. They were stiff from rigor mortis and subfreezing temperatures, making them hard to manage. Once accomplished, however, the interior fuselage looked almost livable. Last on the list prior to departure was the need to consolidate the classified documents into a backpack for ease of transport. He absolutely needed two free hands to contend with his climb out. Looking at the empty courier bag triggered one last hateful reaction to his short relationship with the major. "If this bag was so dammed important to you, you can have it back," he announced in a mock sense of victory, and slid the handcuffs back on the major's wrist. "Take good care of it, asshole."

Convinced he would leave after the Search and Rescue flight the next day, Robert busied himself with securing the sled with only absolute necessities. After the sun dropped behind the mountain, he fixed a meal and trudged back to his igloo. *The added comfort of a sleeping bag will be a real luxury*, he thought.

The next day Robert wasn't able to leave, because a storm front arrived, bringing high winds and new snow. It lasted two days—the longest two days of Robert's life. The anticipation of getting off the mountain and the anxiousness of beginning a new life in South America tested his patience.

When Thursday arrived, Robert waited all morning and sure enough a Search and Rescue C-47 did a fly-by. He could see the photographer taking shots from the open door. He waited for another hour in anticipation of a second plane. None came. He wasn't waiting any longer.

The sled weighed no more than seventy pounds with all of the supplies and gear, enough to survive a week. Any longer and he figured he would be either dead or captured. His backpack weighed about twenty-five pounds with day supplies. He protected the classified documents in waterproof canvas wrap he found in the airdrop supplies.

He stood at the edge of the ridge and considered his route again. It was obvious that the sled would become a liability, so he consolidated only critical supplies into his backpack. *One chance in hell*, he thought. He carefully eased himself down to a ledge about five feet below the ridge. From there he repelled fifteen feet down to a solid landing pad beyond which would be no return. Once in position he realized that he would be protected from an avalanche and considered a possible preventative strategy. With the added weight of the new snow, he thought about firing his weapon to see if the noise would cause a slide, thus eliminating the risk of a slide while he was crossing. The disadvantage would be if the slide was big enough, it could possibly wipe out his entire escape route. He felt the risk was worth taking.

He fired two rounds and waited. He knew he did the right thing when the new snow started to move. He was scared beyond reason, however, when he realized how much snow was in play. His ledge held firm as the avalanche passed within fifty feet of his perch. Vast billows of snow and the sound of a hundred freight trains filled the air. It took almost a half hour for the air to clear. He counted his lucky stars that the gamble worked. He began traversing the new snowfield, confident that his future was secure.

CHAPTER 51

On Tuesday afternoon Major Raegle reviewed the photographs from both the Sunday and Monday flyovers with great interest. They were developed in large format to provide as much detail as possible. The three men scrutinized every detail for traces of survivors, information from the wreckage, and possible rescue routes.

"We were lucky to get two good days of visibility back to back," said Mike Norris, the lieutenant in charge of the photography. Major Raegle and Captain Baker, the two pilots of the Search and Rescue C-47s, were glued to the dozens of photographs laid out before them on the briefing room table.

"There's no sign of survivors that I can see," Captain Baker offered. "If there was anything you'd think it would be around the fuselage area."

"Maybe, but in a situation like this, personnel are sometimes flung far and wide from the actual crash and wreckage site from the centrifugal force alone. Scan the whole picture, just in case. Use these magnifying glasses if you think you see something."

For hours each man examined the photographs, independently making his own notes. It was their approach to gather their own observations first before discussing their findings as a group. This way all points of view could be explored.

"Let's take it one topic at a time," said Major Raegle. "Is there any evidence of survivors?"

"Nothing that I can see," said Captain Baker.

Lieutenant Norris was bent over the table and quietly moved back and forth between two photographs, one from each day. The cigarette in his mouth had not left but once since he'd lit it and had an ash three-quarters of an inch long. It seemed he was impervious to the pending mess it would make. The major slid an ashtray onto the table and nudged the lieutenant. "You're like a hunting dog I once owned. Once she got the scent, nothing could faze her. Best damn Brittany I ever had." The two senior officers chuckled, but the lieutenant was not deterred.

"Maybe it's because I look at these more than you do, but take a look at these identical positions on each of the days." The lieutenant laid a ruler below the area in focus on both pictures for emphasis. "Right there. That's what I'm looking at," he said slowly while finally getting rid of the ash.

"What is it?" Captain Baker said as both officers leaned in.

"That depression across the snow looks like a trail. Is it possible that someone walked about a quarter mile from this rock outcropping to the wreckage? Now, look here," he said, pointing to the second picture, "there's nothing."

"This is not good news," said Major Raegle. "It probably means that someone did survive by being thrown from the plane, landed over here, and then sought refuge in the wreckage. The fact that we see no more movement on day two likely means that the person is dead."

"Or can't move," said Captain Baker. Can you tell if the supplies have been accessed?"

"I looked, and it sure doesn't seem like they have," the lieutenant replied.

"Okay, what else?" Major Raegle went to a flipchart and wrote "possible evidence of a survivor near wreck site."

FATAL INCIDENT

"The cockpit is completely missing," Captain Baker said. "The construction of the C-47 is vulnerable to this if the collision sheered the bolts attaching the wings to the fuselage. The resulting shock would separate the back of the fuselage from the cockpit. It's a weak point in the original design."

"What do you think happened?"

"It's hard to tell exactly, Major, but my guess is that the cockpit traveled across the face of the sheer wall for a few hundred yards and fell in this snow area, causing a small avalanche of its own, and got buried. You can see the avalanche trail here if you look closely."

"And if that's not the case?"

"Hard to say, Major. It's got to be buried somewhere, but I'll say this, surviving that fall with no protection is just not realistic."

"I'm sure you're right." The men paused as if to offer tribute to the pilot and co-pilot, recognizing that every man who flies could end up this way—particularly in Alaska.

"I think we need to look at one other thing," the lieutenant said.

"What?"

"All of this debris at the base of this fall seems out of position for the rest of the crash. There wasn't a second plane, was there?"

"No. Only one plane," answered the major. It's probably the debris from the C-47 that the wind carried or maybe it ended up there from the ship's impact."

"I didn't hear of any report of another plane," Captain Baker said, confirming the major's comment.

"No. That's never been part of the scenario," the major reiterated. "Doesn't mean we can't check it out if we can get to this site."

"If it were true, it's buried for sure," the lieutenant said. Plus, it did snow pretty good the day of the crash. I couldn't find anything else to support the idea of another plane, but just to make sure, I checked every angle of these photographs."

"I think we've got a tough reality to face, gentlemen," the major said, packing his pipe bowl with tobacco. "Get some coffee if you want, but I think we should discuss our options before we break up. General Gaffney is sure to want a full report."

The men took a brief head break and stretched their legs for a few minutes before resuming their discussion. "Have the families been notified, Captain?"

"Well, that's the tough part. They have, but only to the extent that the flight has been lost."

"It's not my position to comment, sir, but that's gotta be a bitch on the other end."

The smell of Major Raegle's cherry-blend pipe tobacco filled the room. The major sat at the briefing table and motioned for the others to sit. Almost everyone on the flight crews enjoyed the aroma, as these men did today. It seemed to add a level of civility to their god-forsaken assignments on the frozen tundra.

"We have a hard decision to make, but first of all, let me thank you, Lieutenant, for the excellent photographs of the site. We'd be SOL without them."

"That's my job, Major."

The men knew what was coming and dreaded it.

"There are twenty men on that mountain, and if we're lucky one may be alive. How do we proceed? I'd like to hear each of your thoughts."

"Permission to reply first?"

"Permission granted, Lieutenant."

"I've taken a lot of photographs in my life, here and before the war. What I've learned to recognize is the beauty and sense of balance a place can bring to a picture. What I'm trying to say is that I don't think I've ever witnessed up close a place as dramatic as what we're looking at here. A man couldn't do any better in finding a final resting place.

Having said that, we owe it to the families of these soldiers to bring their sons home if possible, and, God willing, make every reasonable effort to bring one home alive."

"Well said, Lieutenant."

"Captain?"

"We have to consider the realistic aspects as we move forward, as well, notwithstanding my agreement with the lieutenant's comments. The forecast calls for a new storm front tonight that will last at least two days. It's possible that everything will be covered and chances of survival are very slim. Also, we need to deal with the matter of recovery, if rescue is beyond our reach. We're going to need experienced men, and we're going to have to assess the level of risk we are willing to ask others to take in bringing the bodies out. Getting to the crash site may be one thing. Bringing the bodies back is something entirely different."

"We're not magicians, so what I propose, and I do agree with both of your comments, is that we conduct one more rescue flyover with both C-47s as soon as the weather breaks—probably Thursday. God willing, we'll discover activity. If it's not meant to be, we'll shift our effort to recovery."

"Survival is a powerful motivator, Major," Commanding General Gaffney said after listening to Major Raegle's full report. "Let's give it one more fly-by before making the decision to shift gears. I understand you have your feelers out for men who might be capable of such an undertaking?"

"Grant Pearson and Bradford Washburn are the two most experienced men I know. Mr. Pearson is obviously available to us through the Mt. McKinley U.S. Army Recreation Camp. Mr. Washburn has been in the area with the U.S. Army Alaska Testing Expedition, although I don't know to what extent he's available to us. With your permission, sir, I would like to begin the process of involving these men. But, before I do, I'd like to go on record, General, and say that we are very likely going to lose men in the process of recovering bodies. And, it's going to be a tremendous undertaking requiring extensive resources. For those reasons I would recommend that we leave the bodies at rest where they lay."

"That decision is not in your hands, Major. I'd like you to keep that opinion to yourself, as well. From what you say, we're likely to run into several obstacles and the leader's lack of belief in the mission won't go down well. There's one other thing, Major, that I'd like you to be aware of."

"Yes, sir?"

"There are lots of people who believe that this was not an accident. There's no proof, but the circumstances are suspicious. That an excellent pilot was that far off course and risking twenty men, coupled with the coincidence that an unauthorized Russian liaison officer was on board at the same time as highly sensitive and classified documents, is too much for higher ups to accept. They make a strong case and want to get to the bottom of this. Getting that courier bag handcuffed to Major Gordon's wrist will put several men above my pay grade at ease. Do I make myself clear, Major?"

CHAPTER 52

"Has Martha heard anything?" It was after work on Friday, March 24, when Bud called. No one could stand the silence. The full week without hearing anything from Alaska was tearing the family apart. Bud had returned to work in Akron, but Helen stayed in Minneapolis to help out as best she could.

"Nothing," Helen responded. She had been taking most of Martha's calls to eliminate the repetitive telling of a story that was so hurtful. "Is it possible that they will never find the plane?"

"Anything's possible, honey. Some of these areas that Nick was flying over haven't even been charted yet. It may be that the flight made an emergency landing way off course and out of radio contact. I read that a similar C-47 crash took place north of Montreal and the St. Lawrence River in Canada. An extensive search out of Presque Isle took almost a week to locate the downed ship, and they had the advantage of making a positive radio contact. It seems that the magnetic compass was so far off because of their relative proximity to the earth's magnetic pole that the pilot was thirty degrees off his true bearings. With heavy cloud cover a celestial bearing was not possible. I know this isn't easy. We just have to hang in there."

"I know, but we're all very worried about what Nick must be going through if he's alive."

"Let me talk to Martha. Maybe I can help."

After a few minutes, Bud realized that all of his technical descriptions just made things worse. Martha ended up crying in frustration.

"Let me talk to Dad," Bud finally said.

"This isn't easy, son." His stoic monotone voice hid his emotions behind the strict German discipline. "Your mother and I don't know what to do."

"I know this isn't easy. It's strange that we haven't heard anything. One of us should try to get through to Major Raegle or General Gaffney."

"Good idea. I think it's best if you call, though, with your knowledge of aeronautics."

"Okay. It's 5:30 here. Maybe I can catch them before their day is over since it's 1:30 in Fairbanks. If that doesn't work you and I might need to make a trip to Edmonton. Might help to have a few of the other families represented, as well."

"We'll do whatever we need to. Keep us informed, son."

Within a short time, Bud had successfully connected with Major Raegle's office only to receive an official response to contact General Gaffney in Edmonton. Bud did so right away and was connected with the lieutenant handling matters.

"Look, Lieutenant, I know you have protocol to follow, but my brother's missing and we're not getting any information. The family is just sick with worry."

Bud listened to the lieutenant's red tape excuses before interrupting. "Yes, I know we have a war going on and you can't give information out on every casualty, but this crash has taken place on American soil. I don't intend to be put off, Lieutenant. I insist on talking with General Gaffney!"

"I'll see what I can do," was the lieutenant's cool response.

Several minutes went by when finally Bud heard a deep voice. "This is Commanding General Gaffney, Mr. Morgan. I understand you're calling about Captain Nick Morgan."

"Yes, General, he's my brother. We'd appreciate any information you have. He's got a pregnant wife and a mother and father who are all extremely worried."

"Technically your brother doesn't fall under our jurisdiction since he is on contract status through Northwest Airlines."

"What! He's flying under army orders for the movement of army troops for God's sake, and you're going to tell me that he doesn't fall under your jurisdiction." The silence on the other end clearly indicated that the commanding general wasn't used to this kind of retort.

"Mr. Morgan, let me tell you this. We are treating your brother's disappearance the same as the rest of the crew and passengers under his command. Just because our official communication is directed to the families of the army personnel, it doesn't mean we're not working on his behalf, too. Unofficially, I can tell you that we have discovered a C-47 wreckage in an extremely inhospitable mountain and glacier area of the McKinley Range. We have not been able to positively ID the ship, as the tail numerals aren't visible and radio contact has not been made. Regardless, we do feel that this is Captain Morgan's flight, but I regret to inform you that no survivors have been identified." The general paused respectfully.

Bud swallowed his emotions as best he could before responding. "When can a rescue team be at the site, General? It's possible that the survivors are unable to identify themselves." Bud was reacting out of his engineering mindset, knowing that anything was possible—with the right tools and plan. He certainly wasn't going to accept defeat this early.

"Yes, that's true. But, I've been informed that this wreckage site is very remote, and a rescue would be very dangerous, almost certain to cause further fatalities. We haven't given up and have successfully dropped supplies in the immediate vicinity of the wreckage. It has been a week, however, and I wouldn't hold out too much hope." The general was patient with Bud, having had the thankless experience of walking loved ones through the reality of war incidents before and knowing how helpless they can feel. The lack of a body always made it more difficult.

"When do you shift your emphasis to one of recovery?" As soon as he uttered the words, Bud felt like a traitor to the hope for his brother's survival.

"The Search and Rescue team will make that decision, Mr. Morgan."

"Please keep us informed. Thank you." Bud didn't know what else to say other than to provide a telephone number and address to speed up the flow of communications. His head dropped into his hands as a feeling of complete loss and helplessness consumed him. A misty vision of their days growing up together at Cass Lake flashed before him. Nick wasn't just his brother, he was his best friend.

Everyone in the Morgan family struggled through the following week with no new information. Under the circumstances, Bud was able to get the following Friday, March 31, off, which would allow him time to make another trip to Minneapolis.

Helen threw her arms around him when he walked into the house. Two weeks was the longest Helen had been away from Bud since they had been married. She had tried her best to keep Martha's spirits up, but it was difficult, as Martha was due at any time. Helen's emotional strength proved to be the lynchpin Martha needed in order to maintain a semblance of stability. "I'm so glad you're here," she said quietly. "Martha's resting on the couch in the living room." Helen's soft voice, willowy physique, and extremely pleasant demeanor might give someone who didn't know her the impression that she wasn't very strong. However, her character was that of a rock, but she was exhausted from too many nights crying herself to sleep.

"Martha and I are going to take a long walk downtown tomorrow. Maybe do some window-shopping and have lunch. She needs to get out. It would be best to update her on anything you have before then." She looked at Bud with her green eyes, desperately searching his face for any sign of hope. It didn't come.

After dinner the entire family sat around the living room listening to Bud's assessment of his conversation he had with General Gaffney. Martha's mother, Ida, and Helen comforted Martha as Bud disclosed the bad news. "Nick has always known what to do," Martha said in response to Bud's description of the army's inability even to land a rescue team. "It wouldn't surprise me to find out that he's leading a group off the mountain right now."

No one knew what to say or how to say it except for Helen. "There are times when you just have to let go . . . as hard as it may be. Martha, remember the time when you had to put aside your dreams of flying because you were pregnant? As much as you wanted it, you wanted the baby more, and you couldn't have both. Hanging on to the dream you and Nick had for the baby may be what God has planned for you."

"But I don't want that plan," she said tearfully.

"What would Nick want?"

"He'd tell me to make a life for myself and the baby and to remember that he loved us both."

No one needed to say anything more. Helen put her arm around

Martha's shoulder and gently rocked her. Martha's mother held her hand and told her, "We will all be here to help . . . whatever you need, just ask."

"Is there anything we can do?" Martha asked of Bud.

"I think a strong letter to the commanding general and Major Raegle may help state our demand for every effort to make a recovery. I'm sure the other families feel the same way." He looked at Henry and said, "Tomorrow, while the girls are downtown, we need to contact your senator and congressman. The story's been all over the newspapers and I'm sure they'll offer the support of their office."

CHAPTER 53

"I'm getting all kinds of pressure from the families, General, to bring those bodies back," General Gaffney said to General Groves in their phone conference. "From their point of view everything is easy—just bring my son or my husband or dad home. But I can be sure of one thing, sir: bringing bodies out of this crash site will cost us more lives in the process. Now, I've got senators and congressmen calling, as if I don't have enough on my plate." The general had tried to take the pressure off Major Raegle's shoulders so he could focus on a successful plan to reach the site.

"I've got people at the Pentagon breathing down my neck about retrieving that courier bag, General," General Groves said. The contents are classified, but I can say this, those documents could influence world politics if in the wrong hands. That's not an overstatement. Plus, there's too much that doesn't add up that warrants an on-site investigation. I understand your position on the dangers of a recovery. I've seen the photographs, but I've got orders to make this recovery mission happen. It's the only cover we have for conducting an investigation."

"I understand that Dr. Oppenheimer was to be on the flight. Did he have any ideas as to what might have gone wrong?"

"No. Nothing at all. He is the one guy in Alaska, however, feeling pretty lucky about having a heart attack. What's our next step to get some people in there?"

"I'm meeting with Grant Pearson tomorrow at Ladd. He has had a chance to view the site from the air and has considered possible entry points from the ground. We're going to discuss the feasibility of getting a team in there."

"Good. Keep me apprised." General Groves hung up, relit his cigar, and continued turning the possibilities over in his mind.

"General, sorry to interrupt, sir, but I thought you'd like to see this right away."

"What is it, Lieutenant?"

"It's the profile on Agent Vladimir Dubisskiy you asked for. It arrived on the Teletype while you were on the phone." The lieutenant laid the folder on the general's desk. "Will there be anything else?"

"No."

General Groves was anxious to explore the report but was surprised by its deficiency, considering Agent Dubisskiy's experience. On the surface the dossier appeared normal, describing his responsibilities as a pilot liaison officer for the P-38 Lend-Lease program. Then he saw an anomaly. The report indicated that Dubisskiy worked as an NKVD clerk for thirteen years. "Holy Christ! Lieutenant, get in here."

"Yes, sir. What is it?"

"It's hard to imagine that we will ever have a chance to win this war when people overlook this crap," he said, totally exasperated and pointing at the years of Vladimir's apparent service in the NKVD. "How a one-line entry showing that many years of 'administrative service' ever passed scrutiny is beyond me. This guy is a secret operative or my name isn't Leslie Groves. Dig into this. See what you can find." With more than two weeks since the crash, the general knew the chances of a survivor making it off the mountain would increase, particularly since the supply drop would give him everything he would need. Any window for capturing an experienced operative was closing fast.

"General Gaffney, this is General Groves again."

"Yes, General."

"I've got new intelligence that gives me reason to believe we had a high-level Russian operative on that flight. I'd like you to secure the perimeter of that mountain for anyone that fits the profile of a Russian in his forties who speaks English very well."

"General, you do know that we're talking about millions of square acres."

"Yes, I do. But there aren't that many passable roads out of there. The person I'm looking for should be considered very dangerous. I want you to deploy a unit on a round-the-clock patrol to look for any unusual movement. Those are my orders—check your chain of command if you need to."

───────────

The next day, General Gaffney, Major Raegle, and Grant Pearson met to discuss a possible route to the crash location. Grant had also included a local named Harry Lerdahl because of his extensive experience and knowledge of the mountain. After reviewing many photographs and citing significant safety concerns, Grant said, "With no sign of life and the fact that we'd have to excavate literally the entire slope to discover any evidence of value, I recommend that no further investigation be conducted."

"Has the major confided in you regarding his opinion, Mr. Pearson?" asked General Gaffney.

"No, sir, he has not."

"That's good," the general said, looking to the major for a vote of confidence. "Major, I thought you told me that he was the best man for this mission. Isn't that right?"

"Yes, sir, it is."

"Well then, why is he so skiddish about this challenge?"

"General, if I can speak on my own behalf I'd like to do so."

"You may not be your best advocate if you can't find a way to that site, Mr. Pearson."

"We're very likely to incur more deaths trying to bring bodies out. The evacuation of bodies would require an expedition of great magnitude. We would also need a complete team of mountain experts . . . I mean the best. I've been in the McKinley Range most of my adult life, and a land approach to this wreck site for the purpose of recovery is not advisable."

"You've not said anything, Mr. Lerdahl. What do you think?"

"Mr. Pearson is right. A land approach will involve many risks due to huge snow and ice slides that occur along that part of the mountain. Without the slides, however, there might be a possibility of reaching the wreckage by coming in from Wonder Lake with a small team of experts. The problem is that helicopter support is out of the question, because of the severe winds and downdrafts. That leaves only a ground exit route. That's where the problems will occur. Trying to bring the bodies out on the ground is most likely to cost lives."

"Show me where Wonder Lake is," the General said, pointing to the map.

Harry pointed to the Wonder Lake Weather Station thirty miles north of Mt. McKinley and about eighteen miles from the wreck over uncharted terrain.

"This kind of expedition generally takes about three months to organize," Grant said.

"You've got two weeks. Major Raegle will have access to all the supplies and mountaineering equipment you'll need. There's a depot in Adak with everything you'll need in stockpile," he said with a nod of approval to the major.

"This is not an ordinary recovery mission," Grant replied defensively and as if to imply that what he would need won't be available.

"There isn't anything in this god-forsaken land that the United States Army can't have or doesn't have, Mr. Pearson. Make your list and the major here will have it ready in a week. That gives you another week to arrange to have this road cleared out to get your equipment to Wonder Lake," General Gaffney said, pointing to the "closed for the winter" designation on the map.

───────────

Within three days the food, fuel, and equipment, as well as the logistics for its delivery, were available. Enough mountaineering equipment to outfit the entire expedition, which had grown to forty soldiers supported by aerial supply planes and a small mechanized contingent, arrived by week's end. Grant was impressed with the power of the General's star, despite his uneasiness with the mission's objective.

Grant waited before leaving Ladd, since he knew that Bradford Washburn was to fly over the crash site on his way to Ladd that morning. Bradford's participation in the recovery expedition was crucial as far as Grant was concerned, and he wanted him to get a first-hand look.

"This is far too risky," Brad said bluntly once settled on the ground in flight ops. Pearson didn't even have the chance to summarize his assessment and preparation for the task, let alone explain the general's full order.

Grant had a great deal of respect for the mountaineer and knew better than to bullshit an expert. Bradford Washburn was a world-renowned cartographer, but Alaska was his trophy portfolio, including the Yukon and Crillon Expeditions in 1935 and the Mt. McKinley Expedition in 1942. Privately, Grant doubted he could accomplish the task of getting to the crash site without Brad's help, so he carefully explained his discussion with General Gaffney before asking again from a stronger position.

"I wouldn't begin to ask for your support if this mission wasn't so damned important. Basically, there are two goals: one, get to the crash site and document what we find and two, recover bodies if possible, with an emphasis on 'possible.' If I'm accurately reading between the lines no one can second-guess our decision on what's safe or not safe when bringing the bodies out." Grant knew from their time together in the Yukon Flats that Brad liked a challenge when it came to showing off his mountaineering accomplishments. He continued his persuasion with what he felt would be the clincher for Brad. "There's another element to this mission that could be even more important. You know that that part of the range is largely uncharted. You also know that the summit of that mountain has never been climbed nor has the mountain been named. As an expert in both charting and climbing, the opportunity to greatly expand your legacy is significant. Whatta ya say, Brad?"

"It is one hellava wreck, Grant. If he had only flown a few hundred feet to the left or right he would have completely missed the mountain. This Captain Morgan was the same guy that piloted us to the Flats area, am I right?"

"Yes, he was."

"I was impressed with him. He handled his crew well and was skillful at dealing with that self-inflated major."

"He was on this flight, too—the major, that is—including several others from that Los Alamos team. There's more to this than recovering bodies, Brad."

"Well, if we do this, we'll have to climb the north side of the peak and descend about a thousand feet to the wreckage on the south side." By coincidence, Washburn's team had already planned to travel cross-country near that very location on their expedition to continue testing clothing, tents, cook stoves, and other equipment. Brad knew he could develop a feasible route to the location.

"Take a look at this," Brad said. He began hand-sketching a map of the region and charted a detailed route based solely on his memory from the flight. "What do you think?"

The men commenced to have a lively discussion, debating the size of the party they would need based on the classified pictures and report, which only Grant had access too. Even though they disagreed on many aspects of the mission's charter and feasibility, Grant knew that the dialogue was Brad's way of saying yes.

CHAPTER 54

On April 7, 1944, Martha Morgan gave birth to a perfectly healthy boy, George Henry Morgan.

On April 10, 1944, about a week after receiving Bradford Washburn's agreement to join the recovery team, Grant met the preliminary expeditionary party at the base camp at Wonder Lake. It consisted of fifteen men, a D-6 Cat, three military transport trucks, a mobile power plant, a radio truck, and three and a half tons of food and supplies. The army also seized the opportunity to test a new snow tractor called an M-7. It was set up in a rear half-track configuration with interchangeable front wheels and skis. Because of the rugged terrain, two of these would be used and critiqued during the expedition.

The logistics of moving equipment and supplies was much further under way than the plan for reaching the actual wreckage, however. Considerable confusion existed between the two senior leaders, Pearson and Washburn, as to which of the surrounding peaks in the aerial photos represented the ship's final resting place. Washburn's first-hand knowledge from his recent flyover and his detailed memory from the McKinley expedition gave him the upper hand in what oftentimes became a public test of wills, and some would say ego. Twenty-three men left the Wonder Lake camp at 0900 on the eleventh with the goal of reaching the ridge overlooking the crash site by sunset. The long trek over wind-packed snow and ice patches coupled with occasional knee-deep powder snowfields was exhausting, and by the time they reached the narrow pass to the ridge, everyone was worn out. Much of the route followed a barrier of menacing ice blocks that could wipe out several hundred yards of trail, if dislodged, in a matter of seconds. Once at the ridge they witnessed a brilliant display of winter shadows and colors on the various peaks on the horizon, which was contrasted with the scene of destruction on a lonely shelf below. The next day they would situate a new camp directly on the ridge in order to more easily negotiate their descent to the ship.

Both Grant and Brad sipped hot chocolate at camp while attempting to sort through their continuing differences over the mission.

"You're going to get someone killed if you insist on placing a large party at the wreck site, Grant." Brad had witnessed the growth in their party's size before departing Wonder Lake—over twenty men, many without the skills necessary to negotiate the thousand-foot descent down the face of the sheer wall the next day. "At best you may get one token body out, Grant, but I can virtually guarantee that coming over that shoulder and down the icefall someone is going to have an accident that you're going to have to explain to some family." Brad had worked with the army for years and knew how very stubborn they could become. In his experience it was usually the missions with the most to gain that had the greatest danger and risk. From what he could see here, the risk-reward ratio didn't fit the bill. "If you were the parents of one of these boys, would you really ask us to risk their lives to bring a body home?" he asked Grant. Brad hadn't even begun to address the likelihood of an avalanche from the slope directly above the location of the plane that could wipe out the entire party.

"My orders from General Gaffney are to get to that ship and, if possible, bring the bodies out."

"Let's find a middle ground here, Grant, before we do something we both regret."

"What do you propose?"

"Let's take our nine most experienced members of the team down tomorrow, set up camp, and assess the circumstances. For all we know, there are no bodies to bring out. In that case, there's no need to risk a descent by greenhorns."

"And if there are bodies?" Grant asked, remembering the general's challenge to Major Raegle during their meeting: "I thought you told me that he was the best man for the mission?" Grant was the acting superintendent on McKinley, and he didn't like his expertise challenged.

"Then we talk about it based on what we find." Brad had already made up his mind that the risk was too great. He felt confident that once the party reached the bottom they would agree with his recommendation.

"Okay, let's say we find bodies, but agree that the risk is too great."

"The only people who will see these bodies are the members of the team. They're not stupid. They know what's at stake. Let me put it this way, Grant. If the risk is too great we simply report that no bodies were found, which is likely to be the case since none were observed from the photographs."

Grant finished his hot chocolate and lit a cigarette. "Smoke?" he said, offering one to Brad.

"Never picked up the habit." Brad knew that Grant's change of topic meant he wasn't ready to weigh in with a final decision. It was like a game Brad used to play with his sister when they were kids, Piggy Move Up. The object wasn't to land the bean bag on the target in one throw. It was simply important to get it closer with each toss. That's the way he felt with Grant; just get him closer to the decision to leave any bodies where they lay. What he couldn't reconcile was why Grant was being pushed so hard by the chain of command.

The next day brought several inches of snow, adding to the risk of avalanches during their descent from the ridge. Grant decided that the team of nine would build a new camp about four hundred feet below the ridge in order to be in position for their descent when the weather cleared, which wouldn't be for another day.

On Thursday, April 13, Washburn, Harry Lerdahl, and Pete Wilkinson, a local trapper with respected mountain-climbing experience, reached the main fuselage after considerable effort laboriously fixing a rope for others to use while descending the thousand-foot-long face. By nightfall, Grant and the other five members of the advance party joined the three men at the crash site. Exhausted, they made a fire, cooked dinner with the provisions that had been dropped, and stayed warm in their down, mummy sleeping bags for another Alaskan winter night. The strange feeling that bodies may be present within a few yards of camp and just below the snow where the camp was set up unsettled the men.

"I'll be glad for the morning," Pete said restlessly. "It just creeps me out."

"I never knew you believed in ghosts," Harry chimed in with a hint of a chuckle. "My grandmother used to tell us when we were kids that every climber that died in an avalanche left their spirit roaming the mountain looking for their body. The spirits would blend in with the white cloud mists, which made them very hard to see."

"Why would your grandmother tell you a story like that when you were a kid?"

"I think she tried to put the fear of God in us by teaching us that if we died in the mountains we'd be there for all eternity."

"That may be what we find," Brad added. "For now, let's gets some sleep. Tomorrow's a big day."

On April 14, a full five weeks after the crash, the advance team began the difficult job of excavating snow around the wreckage to look for bodies. The common grave was found right away.

"To my way of thinking, this confirms that at least one man survived," Harry said to Pete while both were taking a break.

"Sure looks that way. But why don't we have any evidence indicating a survivor? It's just weird to me."

"Maybe he tried to get off the mountain by himself knowing that a rescue wasn't feasible," Harry concluded.

Regardless, each of the team was puzzled at the arrangement of the eleven men. All were organized with their heads in the same direction and bodies facing up. A crucial question penetrated each man's mind: *Who* did it? They continued digging around the entire wreck site. It was exhausting work and by noon they were ready for another break. No additional bodies had been found.

"Mr. Pearson," Harry finally said, "it just doesn't look as if any of these bodies could have been the lone survivor. It's not like he could bury himself. And, I sure don't see any evidence of a survivor here recently either." All eleven bodies were frozen stiff and in some cases frozen together, indicating that they probably were placed in the pile before rigor mortis had set in.

"The other thing you don't see is any sign of carnivorous activity," the same man continued.

"There are no carnivores at this altitude," Grant said. "Let's break for lunch and get our energy back. We'll set up a grid and probe with the willow wands for additional remains." The willow wands were long narrow poles and standard issue for exploring avalanche and deep snow conditions for bodies.

"You haven't said much, Brad. What do you think?" Grant was genuinely interested in Brad's experienced observations. As much as they battled each other over pre-mission strategy, this was when Brad was at his best—analyzing the possibilities.

"It's hard to understand. From what I see so far, my guess is that the negro soldier survived and worked hard to remove the bodies from the fuselage—maybe out of respect or maybe because they just freaked him out. You can see where he tried to close off the cabin area with the nylon parachute for protection, but it's also obvious that he wasn't prepared to handle the cold weather. The bare upper body is a classic symptom of hypothermia. On the other hand, the first supply drop is a few hundred yards away, and yet, there's no evidence here that he used anything from it. I'd like to check the supply drop out after lunch."

"Why don't you take Harry with you when you go. We'll start the grid," Grant replied.

"Did you get what you came for in the courier bag?" Brad's directness in the question surprised Grant. He wasn't privy to the contents, only that it was very important.

"It was empty, so I suspect there will be some disappointed generals when I return. How did you know it was part of the mission, Brad?"

"It was the first item you retrieved when you saw the bodies. An unbelievable scene of destruction, eleven dead bodies, personal effects scattered all over, and the first thing you go for is a nondescript courier bag. It looks like it was handcuffed to the major's wrist."

"Well, it once was."

"What do you mean?"

"It looks like the hand was smashed in order to slide the cuff off. There's no blood so it was done after death. I can't quite figure it out. I mean why would the person put the handcuffed bag back . . . empty?"

"Maybe Harry's grandmother was right about the spirits," Brad said, shaking his head equally as puzzled about the clues that were substantiating the existence of a survivor. He quietly finished his hot beef soup and thought hard about what kind of person could get off this mountain. The captain and co-captain were the only obvious possibilities with their experience and judgment, coupled with the fact that the cockpit hadn't been found and they were still missing. *But with no equipment and supplies, they wouldn't stand a chance*, he thought.

Despite the tedious but necessary work of systematically covering the area with the willow wands, Grant and his team produced nothing tangible from the grid, although in reality they covered just a small fraction of the mountain area.

Brad got his answer shortly after lunch when he and Harry discovered that the airdrop had been opened and supplies and equipment had been removed. Now the means and opportunity were clear, but the motive to escape the mountain remained a mystery.

"With access to all this survival gear and supplies, why would anyone leave the mountain and risk death when he could just wait it out to be rescued?" He looked at Grant more puzzled than ever before. "Did it look to you as if any of the soldiers had been killed from something other than the crash?"

"I didn't look for anything like that. Better do it now while we still have light."

The vacant expression on the face of each body made the grisly task of close inspection for foul play a macabre undertaking. For the most part, these were young men between twenty and twenty-five with nothing more on their minds than the welcome anticipation of being back with their families. It was heartbreaking. In actuality, Brad and Grant were relieved that nothing more than the major's hand was found to indicate foul play.

"For all the survivor knew, he may have felt that the bag contained money or at least something of value that would help him once off the mountain," Brad said as he and Grant sat after finishing their dinner.

"Maybe a pattern is emerging," Grant said. "Think about who is missing. First in my mind is the crew."

Grant's silence gave Brad a moment to reflect on his personal experience with the crew. He could not conjure a scenario that denigrated these men. But, Grant's comment implied a connection. "Come on, Grant. Did the captain actually crash the plane on purpose, so he and his crew could steal the contents of the bag? That would be a pretty bizarre plan, and I didn't take Captain Morgan for being bizarre. Regardless, we'll probably find all three of them when we find the cockpit."

"The other people missing are Warrant Officer Martin Mason, the Russian, and four more soldiers. That would account for the original twenty on board."

"Right, but I still can't figure it out . . . unless," he said, pausing to develop a new thought, "the contents to the bag were actually known to the survivor and valuable enough to warrant a high risk escape off the mountain." Brad's eye contact with Grant confirmed that this line of reasoning was probably as close to the motive as they would get.

"I'll take Pete with me back to the ridge camp first thing tomorrow morning. The general will definitely want this info ASAP. In the meantime, give some thought as to what route you'd take to get off this mountain if you were solo and didn't want to be observed."

"Yes, General. I already have Bradford Washburn sketching out a plausible exit route for a survivor," Grant said via radio transmission. "Right now I would have to say that any choice would be extremely difficult and hazardous." From the first-hand Herculean effort required by Pete and himself to climb the face that morning, Grant knew there wasn't a chance in hell for a single person to make it out that way on their own. There were just too many situations requiring teamwork on the ropes to get out. It also resolved the other dispute of recovering bodies—Washburn was right!

"Yes, General, I'll radio a description as best we can—probably tomorrow when we all make our way back on the ridge with the radio equipment again."

"I want you to do one more thing, Grant. Listen closely," the general said. "For reasons that I can't fully disclose to you, I want your team to not tell anyone about the discovery of any bodies." General Gaffney was very uneasy giving this order but had received it directly from Brigadier General Groves. And according to General Groves, he was only passing on the order. Because the loss of the classified documents represented a leak regarding the United States' imminent capability to deliver an atomic bomb and its impact on war strategy against Japan, the Office of Strategic Services (OSS) was now in charge. They were the two-year-old military intelligence agency formed during the war. The agency had been criticized widely for a dismal security reputation and had become paranoid, as they were rumored to be riddled with subversives and spies, especially Russian sympathizers. The decision to disavow any discovery of bodies would preserve the anonymity of all evidence. If the United States citizens knew of a Russian military espionage plot to steal plans for such a bomb, general panic and distrust would permeate national confidence. The plan, therefore, was to go silent until they could flush out the survivor.

"Since we can't get the bodies out, Grant, it's better that they don't exist at all. Do you understand me?" The general's tone left no room for disagreement.

"Yes, sir. The men are very loyal, sir, but the cover up will go down hard. They know the families are anxious for news."

"Can you get your men to agree?" The general pressed for an answer.

Grant paused, knowing his answer was the lynchpin for whatever was involved. "First off, Brad and I are absolutely okay, sir. We've already discussed it. And between us, we know the remaining seven men personally." Grant chose his words carefully as he talked. "The obvious reason not to bring the bodies out is one of safety. I know the men will wholeheartedly agree with that. As far as not acknowledging the bodies at all, we can make a strong case that with only eleven bodies discovered other family members would hold out hope. More public pressure would be placed on us and others to make an even greater effort, exposing more men to risk. We will communicate the order to cut our losses now by putting a lid on this discovery . . . besides, where could you ever find a more spectacular final resting place?"

"You're on the right track, Grant, but don't bullshit these men. Keep in mind that the most logical scenario is that the bodies were spread over the mountain," the general replied. "Go ahead and tell them that because of the classified nature of the missing contents you've been ordered to put a lid on the story because of national security. Emphasize that until we find the person who made it off the mountain, any knowledge of those men still missing will only jeopardize the investigation and possibly implicate each person not found." The general's silence that followed was compelling.

"Brad and I can make this work, sir. We know how important this is. If we're uneasy for any reason, though, can we get your involvement with the men in a follow-up meeting?"

"Absolutely. I like what you've accomplished here, Grant. I'll add my support to your name when the park superintendent position comes open. You've earned it."

Five weeks after the crash, the search of all roads between Fairbanks and Anchorage and all areas of the Mt. McKinley Park and the Mata-nuska-Susitna area east of the park began. Washburn's sketch of the only possible exit route crossed the face of a slope recently ravaged by an avalanche. Hundreds of army and OSS personnel combed hundreds of thousands of acres on foot and by air. Nothing was found, however, and the "recovery" effort was officially closed.

The flight file documenting the crash remained classified for years. Access was denied to the families of the crash victims until that changed with a Freedom of Information Act (FOIA) request. In November, 2005, the National File and Records Administration, however, reported the file as "lost." They claimed the original files could not be located when an effort was made in the mid-1980s to copy thousands of files onto microfiche film for preservation. The official statement in response to the FOIA request included one sentence:

MISSING AIR CREW REPORT 8878 NOT LOCATED AT TIME OF FILMING.

July 6, 2010

CHAPTER 55

The noise from the torque of the twin Pratt & Whitney's sent confusion through George's mind in his familiar, yet unsuccessful attempt to fight the downdrafts and control the flight. Passengers panicked with the vibration of the aggressive ascent to clear the mountain peak in front of them. The crew was helpless. He was responsible. Vast rock cliffs and cavernous crevasses waited to swallow the out-of-control ship. Instantly, all vision was lost. A mushroom cloud of snow formed from the impact of the plane, which was cartwheeling from nose to wingtip to nose. The vision of his port wing and engine buried in a ice-encrusted sheer wall sucked the wind out of his body. Gasping for breath, choking, reaching for something that would help him breath, he cried out for something to hang on to. And then, blackness, with its eerie sense of death and destruction.

"Agh . . . agh!" He struggled to release his seatbelt while thrashing about wildly. Panic took over.

"Mr. Morgan, Mr. Morgan!" The flight attendant tried urgently to wake him from his nightmare by shaking his shoulders. The passengers near him were not so much alarmed, but empathetic to the desperation of being trapped in a nightmare.

George took several gasps for air as his body shuddered in its final stages of awakening.

He jumped in anticipation of the crash before realizing that he was in the cabin of a Boeing 777 on his flight to Anchorage. He took a deep breath and shook his head before noticing the passengers around him and the flight attendant staring at him in disbelief. He couldn't help his feeling of embarrassment. The businessman in the seat next to him leaned away from him toward the aisle, as if George were mentally unbalanced and had been talking absently to an imaginary friend on an inter-city bus. *Nightmares aren't supposed to happen in public*, he thought.

"It's an old nemesis," George explained feebly to everyone, but to no one. "I'm sorry if I upset you. I should be alright now."

"Can I get you something?" Julia offered. "Some water, maybe a towel? You're soaked in sweat."

"Yes, both would be nice," George replied, as he now recognized the flight attendant in her Northwest uniform as Julia, the middle-aged attendant with short blond hair that originally greeted him on the plane. She seemed relieved that his trauma was over. After she returned with the water and towel, he checked his pulse and confirmed it was back to normal.

"Can't say that we see this very often," she offered lightheartedly to relax the moment. "Do you want to talk about it?"

"Thanks, but I'll be okay. I'll let you know if I change my mind."

In truth, he would have enjoyed talking, but what do you say about a nightmare that has plagued you for your whole life? His earliest recollection of the nightmare that reenacted his father's death was when he was in grade school. George's childhood friends at third-grade recess in the '50s were entranced with their simulations of WWII flying aces and their daring escapes, and naturally the planes that crashed in their imaginations. Unfortunately, their playtime story was all too true to George. Frequently, he would cry out for his mom after falling asleep at night. Nobody really knew what happened during that final Air Transport Command flight piloted by his father. George hadn't been born until after his dad died, and he only had the pictures taken by Bradford Washburn to tell the story.

Oddly enough, his flight to Anchorage that day was on the same airline for which his dad, Captain Nick Morgan, had worked some sixty years ago.

Everything had been fine during his dad's duty tour until March 17, 1944, when his flight departed from Elmendorf Air Field in Anchorage and disappeared during its routine flight to Ladd Airfield in Fairbanks en route to Minneapolis-St. Paul. The flight plan and weather conditions were discussed and included reports of overcast skies and twenty miles of visibility. Over the years George could never reconcile the reported events surrounding the crash of his father's plane, official or unofficial.

George took a drink of the bottled water Julia brought and reflected on this trip to the University Hospital at Fairbanks, anxious that it may finally reveal the mystery. After sixty-six years it was everyone's belief that the C-47 wreckage and several bodies entombed in glacier ice had been slowly working their way down the mountain with the glacier's perpetual movement. Early reports from the National Park Service indicated that they found the wreckage from March 17, 1944, and that it had reached a spot where they could easily gain access to it. For years they had been tracking the wreckage and had identified what was believed to be the ship's two major sections—the fuselage and cockpit. Now, they realized that what they had been tracking was a crashed Russian P-38 and the fuselage of the C-47. The C-47's cockpit was not part of the discovery. This news came as a complete shock. For George, it tied in to the fact that the classified army files regarding this flight had been "lost" by the army years ago.

Regardless of these revelations, however, it's the bodies, although mostly decomposed but with portions cryogenically preserved, that would hold incredible clues to an unimaginable story. *Is it possible that one of these bodies is my dad?* George thought. DNA tests were being conducted. George was now sixty-six and his dad was thirty when he died. The anticipation of seeing his dad for the first time, at about half his own age, was too much to comprehend.

George's thoughts turned toward the next several days and what he was about to experience. He relaxed as best he could for the remainder of the flight, but the stress over the years of waiting, coupled with the conflicting evidence to the story he'd long held as true, prevented a more restful flight. He was beginning to accept the fact that the truth may never be uncovered.

A small group of people representing the crash victims' survivors were gathered quietly, drinking coffee and waiting for the officer to begin walking them through the military's discovery. They were in a conference room at the hospital surrounded by several of the original crash-site photos taken by Bradford Washburn. George had scanned the pictures many times over the years for a survivor with the same results. Maybe today he would get his answer. He kept to himself near the back of the room to avoid discussion. He wasn't shy or uncomfortable in crowds, just uneasy. Deep down inside he felt responsible, somehow. His father was the pilot who should have done something to save these people, he thought irrationally. He wanted to hide his name tag.

An elderly lady in her eighties approached and extended her hand.

"I'd like to introduce myself. I believe you're the son of the pilot, Captain Nick Morgan?" She was smiling and not at all accusing in her tone of voice.

"Yes. My name is George Morgan."

"I have something that I think you'd like to see," she said, opening a large envelope with copies of several old letters inside. "My name is Ellie May Anderson. My maiden name was Johnson. Red Johnson was my older brother."

George's mother, Martha, had told him many stories over the years about the fun Nick would have teasing Red because of his accent and strange way of expressing himself, and how impressed and fortunate Nick felt when given the opportunity to fly with him. His name was held in very high regard in the Morgan family. George was shocked that he felt such a strong connection so quickly. He nearly buckled with emotion and simply hugged this strange woman as if she were his own mother. He tried to explain, but simply said, "This has been a long time coming." Tears streamed down his cheeks.

She knew how he felt. In fact, they all felt that way. They shared a connection that went beyond an earthly bond. Each person in the room had imagined that day of the crash and the possible days of suffering that followed, never finding the closure to a story that had become part of Alaskan history.

"My brother thought your dad was the most talented pilot he'd ever flown with, and as a friend, there was no better. Here, take these. It's all there," she said, handing him the envelope filled with postcards written by Red so many years ago.

"Thank you very much. This is overwhelming. I don't know what to say."

"Ladies and gentlemen, if I can have your attention, please, I'd like to get the program under way. My name is Lieutenant Colonel Brian Longstreet, and I'll try to be as helpful as I can. I think you've all met each other, and I know you have a lot of questions, so why don't we start with the ones most important to you at this time." The officer gestured toward a man in his eighties with his hand up in the front row.

"Why were we never told that bodies were found?"

AUTHOR'S NOTES

On occasion, many events go unexplained in times of war simply because the facts either aren't available or don't credibly tell the story. Sometimes the documented evidence isn't supported by objective witnesses necessary to narrate a full understanding of what happened. Or the events, characters, and/or circumstances are so horrific or preposterous that a judgment is made that it is better for life to "just go on." This is, of course, unfortunate, as the closure needed by most of us when confronted with a tragedy of this magnitude never happens. And a manufactured truth or a "plausible explanation" in the face of difficulty doesn't faithfully serve history nor stand the test of time. The vacuum created leaves the door gaping wide for possibilities, hypotheses, and fiction to enter. This represents the foundation of *Fatal Incident*, as it was inspired by the true story of a C-47 crash on September 18, 1944. My uncle was the pilot.

Fatal Incident is one of those stories where the fictional creation of the author challenges our acceptance of what has been presented to us over the years. At the very least, it opens a door to possibilities yet unexplored. *Fatal Incident* by no means closes any doors regarding the events of that fateful day. It simply challenges us with the possibility that we have never been presented with a complete set of facts. Consider the following documentation of evidence and events that relate to *Fatal Incident* and reflect on the possible manipulation of the facts before, during, and/or after the crash of the C-47. Clearly, the ultimate recovery of the plane and any human remains may give the investigation the jolt necessary to close the door on this unsolved mystery. After sixty-five years, the Eldridge Glacier may be ready to release these facts into evidence.

The Truth as We Know It Today

The Crash

In 1943, Northwest Airlines Pilot Captain Roy Proebstle was based in Minneapolis-St. Paul and became an ATC contract pilot. Everything had been fine during his tour of duty until September 18, 1944, when his flight routinely departed from Elmendorf Air Field in Anchorage and disappeared en route to Ladd Airfield in Fairbanks. The flight plan and weather conditions were discussed and included reports of overcast skies and twenty miles of visibility. The C-47 crew was satisfied that the flight should proceed. Fifteen military passengers on furlough to Minneapolis-St. Paul, one civilian, and two additional crew members perished in a crash in the McKinley Range that was so remote that a rescue mission was never attempted and a highly contested recovery mission didn't reach the wreckage for approximately seven weeks. All on board the plane were lost.

- Major Rudolph Bostelman
- First Lieutenant Orlando Buck
- Lieutenant Athel Gill
- Chief Warrant Officer Floyd Appleman

- Sargeant William Backas
- Technician Fourth Class Timothy Stevens
- Corporal Charles Dykema
- Technician Fifth Class Maurice Gibbs
- Technician Fifth Class Edward Stoering
- Seaman First Class Bernard Ortego
- Private First Class Alfred Madison
- Private First Class Clifford Phillips
- Private Charles Ellis
- Private James George, Jr.
- Private Anthony Kasper
- Private Howard Pevey
- Roy Proebstle, Pilot, ATC
- L. H. Bliven, Co-pilot, ATC
- Karl Harris, Civilian Engineer

Note: Other than Captain Roy Proebstle, no member of this flight, or flight crew, is represented by any characters in *Fatal Incident*.

The Report

The initial army report, based on a few known pieces of the puzzle, suggested that the probable cause of the accident was Captain Proebstle's decision to reroute the aircraft toward openings in the overcast skies at a higher elevation. As a consequence of this action the plane encountered a harsh downdraft accompanied by severe turbulence that forced Captain Proebstle to fly "off-instruments" into a cumulus-type cloud formation that resulted in his striking the unnamed mountain peak. The complete lack of communication by the pilot in this scenario would have been highly irregular. An unfounded report included claims that the captain was encouraged to fly off course in the pursuit of getting pictures of Mt. McKinley for a high-ranking soldier on board who was a camera buff. This explanation is also not very plausible considering the overcast flying conditions that day. What was certain is that they were severely off course by 40 degrees and 50 miles from their last reported position—whether by error or intent is unclear.

The Recovery

Despite the speculation, the fact remained that a rescue mission was never organized, and only after considerable pressure by Congressman Buck, whose son was on the plane, was a recovery effort made—one week short of two months after the crash! It was organized by the army and led by Grant Pearson, acting superintendent of Mt. McKinley National Park. The on-site efforts to locate bodies were supported by Bradford Washburn and a team of eleven other experienced climbers. It took place in an amazing spot, according to his field notes: "just about as inaccessible as you could possibly imagine." What is known is that the plane hit a nearly vertical sheer wall about five hundred feet below the top of an eleven-thousand-foot peak—one of its motors stuck there, and the rest of the ship fell fifteen hundred feet to its resting spot on the edge of what is known as the Eldridge Glacier. The fuselage was split open like a watermelon and the wings were broken off. All very unlucky, because if the aircraft had been a few hundred yards off—right or left of its final course—it would have missed the peak completely. What forced Captain Proebstle to attempt such a narrow escape from the mountain's grasp remains unanswered.

The Mystery

The truly remarkable part of the recovery effort was that there were no bodies discovered and, as unlikely as it may seem, there was only one small trace of blood in the plane! The recovery team reached the grim scene to find an unbelievable wreck, yet a B-4 bag belonging to L. H. Blevin contained a full bottle of whiskey, unpadded and intact. Chocolates and Doublemint chewing gum were found, as well. The plywood backrest of Captain Proebstle's seat lay next to the B-4 bag with its safety belt undone—not broken—just undone. In fact, not one safety belt was found fastened. Playing cards lay strewn about as if a card game had been hastily disbanded. After a full day of digging by the recovery team, the plane lay uncovered. The next morning the men tunneled ten feet beneath the plane and all around a fifteen-foot section of the fuselage. In frustration, they confessed, "we have dug out the main part of the airplane . . . but failed to find any bodies."

Russian Spies in Manhattan Project

- Scientific advances in nuclear chain reaction were followed nowhere more closely than in the Soviet Union—nuclear physics was an area where Russian scientists were expected to excel. Yet, their development of a "superbomb" under the code name *First Lightning* was tainted because of their reliance on stolen materials. There were signs in the fall of 1942 that the slumbering bomb program was being awakened with the appointment of director Vyacheslav Molotov. What convinced Stalin of the bomb project's importance was the growing evidence coming from field agents in foreign countries. Specific knowledge existed that the United States and Britain were advancing in their superbomb development.
- Klaus Fuchs was a German socialist sent to Canada as an enemy alien. His work in physics had attracted attention, and he began working on the atomic bomb in May, 1941, in Canada. He contacted a Communist Party member

about spying for the Soviet Union. In 1943, Klaus Fuchs was sent, along with fifteen British scientists, to help on the American bomb project. Harry Gold was his first Soviet-American contact. Fuchs and Gold traveled to Los Alamos extensively, working on various elements of the Manhattan Project.

- Other contacts at Los Alamos included David Greenglass, a machinist. In February, 1950, a deciphered Soviet cable from 1944 led the FBI to believe that a lower-level spy had been operating at Los Alamos. Harry Gold, then under arrest, provided the positive identification needed for David Greenglass's arrest. He and his wife implicated Julius and Ethel Rosenberg. Both were arrested, convicted of espionage for the Soviet Union, and executed by electric chair in 1953. Later in the same year, Robert Oppenheimer voiced strong opposition to the development of the hydrogen bomb. Interestingly, though, his name was not among the Manhattan Project co-signers of a July 17, 1945, petition to Harry S. Truman to "not resort to the use of the atomic bomb in war." At the height of U.S. anticommunist feeling later in 1953, Oppenheimer was accused of having communist sympathies, and his security clearance was revoked by the Atomic Energy Commission.

- Theodore Hall was a Harvard physics prodigy seemingly motivated by misplaced idealism. He made a near-confession in an interview for a Cold War documentary on CNN in 1998, saying, "I decided to give atomic secrets to the Russians because it seemed to me that it was important that there should be no monopoly, which could turn one nation into a menace and turn it loose on the world as . . .

as Nazi Germany developed. There seemed to be only one answer to what one should do. The right thing to do was to act to break the American monopoly."

Japanese A-bomb Design

- Former *Atlanta Constitution* reporter and army intelligence officer David Snell of the 24th Criminal Investigation Detachment in Korea authored a report in 1945 for the *International Military Tribunal of the Far East*, which stated that Hideki Tojo had planned to wage nuclear war if his scientists had been successful. Japan's atomic bomb project was started in 1938 and grew to a significant standing at Nagoya, Japan. Its removal to Konan, Korea, (now in North Korea and where Japan's uranium supply was said to exist) was necessitated when the B-29s began to lash industrial cities on the mainland of Japan. Snell alleged that the Japanese had successfully tested a nuclear weapon, called Genzai Bakudun, near Konan before being captured by the Russians. Japan's test of the atomic bomb three days prior to the end of the war matched the cataclysmic outcome of Hiroshima and Nagasaki. The Konan area was under strict Russian control after its capture and the Japanese scientists who developed the bomb were sent to Moscow and tortured for their knowledge. According to Mr. Papps, an OSS officer, the diagram of the Japanese atomic bomb was "just like ours and very workable, except for the firing mechanism." Snell claimed that he had received his information from a Japanese officer who had been in charge of counterintelligence at Konan.

Missing Air Crew Report (MACR) 8878

- The National Archives and Records Administration replied in January, 2006, that a search of army air force records for mission reports for any ATC unit came up empty. The Office of the Quartermaster General identified the MACR number matching this aircraft as 8878. The original 8878 paper files were reported as missing during a preservation effort to copy all files to microfiche. This was not considered a denial under the Freedom of Information Act because the records in their custody did not include the information requested.

As of November, 2010, the bodies and aircraft remains from the crash on September 18, 1944, still remain in the Eldridge Glacier. There is no resolution, only the tragedy shared by so many families. In ending these notes I would like to share an excerpt from a tribute written by New York Congressman Ellsworth B. Buck in 1944 in remembrance of his son, Orlando John Buck.

MOUNT MCKINLEY IS VAST. QUICK STORMS ASSAIL HER LOFTY SIDES AND SCREEN HER LESSER PEAKS THROUGH WHICH A PLANE MUST FIND ITS WAY TO REACH ITS DESTINATION. THIS ONE DID NOT. IT SETTLED TO A RESTING PLACE HIGH ON A SLOPING FIELD OF SNOW THAT GIVES BIRTH TO A GLACIER. THERE FEET OF MEN HAD NEVER TROD. THEY NEVER WILL AGAIN. IN THAT COLD UPPER WILDERNESS SNOW FALLS AND NEVER MELTS. THEY COVERED HIS BODY GENTLY, HIDING IT SECRETLY, FOREVER. HE LIKED THE COLD AND THE SNOW. UP THERE SNOW IS CLEAN, AND SO WAS HE.

AS FAR AGAIN ABOVE THAT RESTING PLACE TOWERS
THE MOUNTAIN. I MIGHT THINK OF THE MOUNTAIN AS
HIS MONUMENT WERE THERE NOT ANOTHER MONUMENT HE
BUILT HIMSELF WITHIN OUR HEARTS. THERE HE LIVES.

ELLSWORTH B. BUCK
SEPTEMBER 30, 1944

ACKNOWLEDGMENTS

As you now know, *Fatal Incident* is a fictional account of authentic Proebstle family history. Roy Proebstle and my father, Leonard Proebstle, were brothers and played their roles as Nick and Bud as I imagined them. While we may never know what happened during that flight, I was very fortunate to learn, first-hand, about the relationship between Captain Roy Proebstle and his wife, Millie (Proebstle) Onstad. It all came about in an interview with Aunt Millie several years ago in Minneapolis. My wife, Carole, and I spent a delightful afternoon learning about their life together, and the events and emotions surrounding the crash. The postcards used in the story were actual cards written in Roy's hand that she had saved. They were precious to her and were changed very little in the telling of the story. I am very grateful to Aunt Millie for her shared experiences and the connection it made for me while writing the book.

Roy and Millie had two sons. Bob Proebstle who was one-year old at the time of the crash, and Jack Proebstle, who was in the womb. The writing of this book has stimulated a renewal of our friendships, for which I am very happy. Their individual support, research, and encouragement was instrumental for making the steady journey of discovery and writing enjoyable, regardless of the complexities encountered.

At the beginning, *Fatal Incident* seemed like a fairly straightforward project. The reality, however, of not being a pilot, never having traveled to Alaska, and having no military experience overwhelmed my writing effort from the beginning. Thankfully, the availability of the online and written resources listed in the bibliography was a godsend. Through the efforts of capable writers, researchers, and enthusiasts my experiential shortcomings were made whole.

Lastly, I am learning that each project calls out the special nature and gifts of friends and relatives interested in helping. As with, *In the Absence of Honor*, I always felt that writing a novel would be an adventure—an accomplishment in which I would take great pride. The accomplishment is rightfully shared by those whose support and feedback I received throughout this process. Among those are:

- Carole Proebstle, my life's partner of forty-five years, for her gentle reminders and encouragement that I can accomplish whatever I choose
- Mike Proebstle, nephew and godson, whose skill and knowledge as a navy pilot helped demystify the language of flying and make the cockpit a friendlier place
- Mary Norris for her devotion in reading, critiquing, and offering suggestions that helped nurture the characters and develop the story
- Wonderful friends who patiently listened with interest, ever confident that *Fatal Incident* would ultimately find its way to the bookshelf
- The friendly and extremely competent staff at Greenleaf Book Group

Writing is a solitary activity, but not one ever accomplished alone.

BIBLIOGRAPHY

Alaska: The Territorial Life Magazine, Alaska Life Publishing Co.,
   January 1944 and April 1945.

Ambrose, Stephen E. *D-Day June 6, 1944: The Climatic Battle of
   World War II*. New York: Simon & Schuster, 1994.

Ambrose, Stephen E. *The Wild Blue: The Men and Boys Who Flew the
   B-24s Over Germany 1944–45*. New York: Simon & Schuster,
   2002.

Bradley, James. *Fly Boys: A True Story of Courage*. New York: Little,
   Brown and Company, 2003.

Braun, Don C., with John C. Warren. *The Arctic Fox: Bush Pilot of the
   North Country*. Bloomington: iUniverse, 2000.

Gann, Ernest K. *Fate is the Hunter*. New York: Simon & Schuster,
   1986.

Follett, Ken. *Eye of the Needle*. New York: Avon Books, 2000.

Littell, Robert. *The Company: A Novel of the CIA*. London: Penguin
   Books, 2003.

Ludlum, Robert. *The Tristan Betrayal*. New York: St. Martin's Press,
   2004.

Norris, Frank. *Crown Jewel of the North: An Administrative History of
   Denali National Park and Preserve*, vol. 1, Alaska Regional Office,
   National Park Service, U.S. Department of the Interior, 2006.

Sfraga, Michael. *Bradford Washburn: A Life of Exploration.* Corvallis: Oregon State University Press, 2004.

Web Resources

388th Engineer Battalion Engineers Plumb the NWT: Canol: www.mendonet.com/588th/canol.htm

1946 Atlanta Constitution Atom Bomb Articles: www.reformation.org/atlanta-constitution.html and /atomic-bomb.html

Army Radio Sales Co., *Spy Radios of W.W. II:* www.armyradio.co.uk

DC-3 Engine Run Checklist: www.douglasdc3.com

Education Resources: www.momomedia.com/CLPEF/camps/poster.html

Elmendorf Air Force Base: www.elmendorf.af.mil

High Gallery: www.highgallery.com

Lockheed P-38 Lightning – USA: www.aviation-history.com

Manzanar Internment Camp: www.cmdrmark.com/manzanar.html

OLIVE-DRAB: www.olive-drab.com

Russia and the Revolution: www.periclespress.com/Russia_atomic.html

Szilard Petition, July 17, 1945: www.dannen.com/decision/pet-gif.html

The History of Chalkyitsik: http://explorenorth.com/library/communities/alaska/bl-Chalkyitsik.htm

The History Place: *World War Two in Europe:* www.historyplace.com

The Japanese A-bomb: www.fortfreedom.org

The National Archives Learning Curve: www.spartacus.schoolnet.co.uk

Wikipedia, the free encyclopedia: www.wikipedia.org

World Atlas Travel: www.worldatlas.com

World Atlas – MSN Encarta: www.encarta.msn.com

World War II Memorial Newsletter: www.wwiimemorial.com/archives/newsletters/winter2000.pdf

A CONVERSATION WITH
JIM PROEBSTLE

Growing up in Massillon, Ohio, I always remembered the picture of Roy Proebstle, "Uncle Curly," on my dad's chest of drawers in the bedroom. He was a handsome man in his Captain's dress uniform, flashing a warm smile that reached out to me every time I entered the room. The story about Curly's death, however, was always buried deep in my father's heart. Occasionally, I would hear comments between him and my mom, but they were always shrouded in the sad tone invoked by the loss of a best friend. Part of my experience in writing *Fatal Incident* was the thrill of vicariously participating in that period of Curly and my dad's life, prior to World War II, when aviation shaped their future paths.

Q. **How did you link together the history and fiction components of the story?**

A. The timeline of WW II is obviously in place for all to reference. I had to make a decision, however, about just how much of the story surrounding the actual crash I was going to use. I knew that *Fatal Incident* would involve espionage and treasonous activities, and I did not want to link any of the real crew or passengers with these acts. I concluded that the best way to handle this would be to treat all parties on the plane as fictional characters. Once this was done and some alternate timeline issues were worked out, the story was easier to write.

Q. How did you approach the research effort for the book?

A. I did start with an outline, as I have on other writing projects. This helped to narrow the scope of the research required. At an early stage in the project I just started to fill my mind with everything I could get my hands on that related to pre-war Alaska. Not being a pilot or a veteran or having traveled to Alaska was the real challenge, however. These hurdles added a year to the book while I cobbled together the knowledge I needed. Capable authors, the internet, and a few subject-matter-expert friends were invaluable in filling in my experiential gaps. I found the research process very interesting and exciting as I immersed myself in the details and grew in my understanding of how this story would come together.

Q. What is your most productive time to write?

A. It really depends on my routine and my project involvement in Prodyne, Inc., a consulting firm I started in 1991. Since my office is in the home I can shift gears pretty easily. If I could write five to seven pages at a sitting I felt successful. The morning hours after working out—9 a.m. to noon—are best for me. My energy is stronger and my thinking clearer.

Q. Did you find any useful techniques in getting started with actually writing the novel?

A. Since this story is based on true events experienced by my family, I do have a lot of original pictures, letters, newspaper articles, etc. that can quickly get you into the setting of what happened. My Aunt Millie—Uncle Curly's wife at the time of the crash—is still living and had saved all of the postcards he had sent as a normal part of their correspondence. Following Uncle Curly's thoughts gave me the feeling of being there as each postcard identified the various writing locations from Bethel, Alaska, to Edmonton,

Alberta. This allowed me to construct a flight map to follow his assignments. These first-hand resources on the players involved were like listening through a wall with your ear to the glass.

Q. How did it feel to write about family members?

A. It was almost like reaching out to touch them via a medium. My father's work was classified so we never really knew what he did until after his retirement from Goodyear Aerospace. Constructing dialogue between Nick and Bud (Curly and my father) was exciting; it was like bringing them back to life. My discussion with Aunt Millie added a first-hand perspective on the dating and early married life between she and Curly. My cousins (Millie and Curly's boys), Bob and Jack Proebstle, shared my excitement and were world-class cheerleaders throughout the effort.

Q. What's your underlying motive for writing this story?

A. It was after my father's death when I started digging deeper that I realized the story we were told didn't hold water. My cousins agreed. Since no one knew what really happened I wanted to write about what could have happened. All accounts of why the crash took place in *Fatal Incident* are fictional, to be sure, but several possibilities could exist. I wanted to present one of them in order to establish a credible alternative.

Q. What were your biggest learning points is writing *Fatal Incident*?

A. First: as before with *In the Absence of Honor*, it's not only editing, but having the right editor who harmonizes with your writing style while challenging your writing. I still don't like the red lines, but the book doesn't exist without them. Jay Hodges, an editor from Greenleaf Book, walked the line between drill sergeant and cheerleader very well. Second: dialogue is as varied as the characters in the story. It's enjoyable to lock a character into a three dimensional scenario with realistic expressions unique to the character's senses, emotions, beliefs, culture, and education. I think that this is at the core of good dialogue and will be a continuing educational effort.

Q. What are you writing at present?

A. The more I write and travel, the more ideas I have for stories. Since I've not made a commitment to myself for the next project, as yet, I can only say that the choices lie between 1) two fun-filled stories revolving around very different nationally acclaimed athletic events, and 2) a story of a deeply troubled athlete whose very success becomes the devil's anvil for the athlete's failure in life. By the time you read this I hope to have made a choice.

Q. How are you staying in contact with readers interested in your work?

A. Three ways primarily: First, the website *www.jimproebstle.com* will provide updates to activities regarding the progress of the book. I'll make a commitment to respond to all questions readers may have about the book. Second, I plan to make myself available to book clubs and reading groups that choose *Fatal Incident* as their book selection. See the website for more details. Third, I find that group presentations bring the story alive to readers. To that end, I plan to make myself available for presentations wherever possible. The feedback will help me become a better writer and I look forward to bringing something new to your event.

QUESTIONS FOR BOOK CLUB DISCUSSION

Question: How did you react to the interactions in Nick and Martha's relationship? How might their relationship be different if it was taking place today instead of the 1930s?

Question: How would you deal with the ability to communicate then vs. now? Is a postcard just a slow text message?

Question: Who was your favorite character and why? Which character developed and grew substantially as the story unfolded?

Question: Did you know about the significance of Alaska's strategic positioning during World War II? Were you aware of the unique relationship between the United States and Russia?

Question: Are you more or less encouraged to learn more about the involvement of Russia's spy network in the United States during WW II?

Question: What was the emotional letdown experienced by a character that you empathized with or identified with more than any other?

Question: Did you feel like you were there—playing a part in the "big" war? Did the book provide you with a sense of Alaska that was real?

Question: What part of the story would you challenge? Did you feel like any moments were pushed past the test of believability?

Question: What other possible scenario(s) can you think of that could be behind the crash?

Question: How has the author's writing changed or evolved as compared with his first book, *In the Absence of Honor*?

There are many more questions of course, but I hope you find these interesting for your book club discussions. With that in mind I make the following offer:

I would be happy to participate in your book club, live or via conference call, to lead a discussion complete with answers to your questions about the characters, the story, or the writing experience itself. Please go to *www.jimproebstle.com* for details. I find that the more I interact with people interested in reading, the better I become as a writer—in the end we will both benefit from the exchange.

In the Absence of Honor
Emerald Book Company, 2008

In the Absence of Honor weaves together the lives of a bewildered, downsized widower; a wealthy, aging megalomaniac; two corrupt members of the local Ojibwe tribal council; and a Department of Interior agent in their battle over a valuable piece of property in northern Minnesota. Money, power, and greed are weaved together in a new story of corruption as casinos take a grip over the economic lifeblood of the reservation.

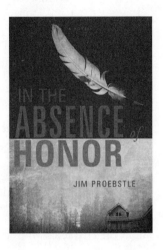

The story of murder, conspiracy, sex, fraud, and betrayal is set in northern Minnesota. It revolves around the conflict between two corrupt Ojibwe tribal council members and a wealthy brewery executive over an historically important piece of land. Ultimately, Jake, our hero, and Donna, the Department of Interior Agent, are caught up in the discovery of an Indian Mafia network skimming money from casinos throughout the United States. While corruption and greed fill the motivation for some, love and hope are the driving behavior for others. The tale whisks the reader from a small northern community and Indian reservation to powerful forces in Washington, DC.

In the Absence of Honor was honored as a finalist in the *2009 Eric Hoffer Awards* for the commercial fiction category, a nominee in the *2009 Northeastern Minnesota Book Awards* for the fiction category, and a finalist in the *2010 National Indie Excellence Awards* for the mystery/ suspense category.